Redwood Pack
Vol 2

CARRIE ANN RYAN

ISBN: 1623220068
ISBN-13: 978-1-62322-006-8

DEDICATION

This book is dedicated to my readers for pulling me through and falling in love with these Jamenson boys.

ACKNOWLEDGMENTS

Again, I find myself falling at the feet of those around me. Each book wouldn't be here without those helping me.

First, thank you to Scott Carpenter who has been on the never ending train of making my covers. You are so creative and brilliant. Thank you for making my work feel real and sparkly.

To Lia. Yes, dear, I will thank you each and every time. You have no idea how much you pull me through this.

To my Street Pack. Y'all ladies are so funny, witty, and downright amazing. Thank you for all that you do and wanting more of my books!

And again, thank you to my husband and cats. You guys are the real miracle workers here since you deal with me and my writing drama. I love y'all.

Trinity Bound

Redwood Pack Book 3

Trinity Bound

Hannah Lewis, a rare earth witch, is taken from the only life she's ever known. Held at her will by a sadistic wolf, she almost gives up hope that she'd ever see her real life again. But as her fellow captive, a werewolf named Reed, tries to calm her fears, she begins to feel a spark of something she never thought she'd feel – love. But is Reed, alone, enough to get her out of this dark basement so she can move on with her life?

Reed Jamenson, the artist of a werewolf Pack of Alpha males, knows instinctually that Hannah is his mate. Thus, despite their imprisonment, he will do all to protect her and then worry about their hearts. But is he strong enough to find a way for both of them to escape? And why does he feel as though something else is missing?

Josh Kolb, an ex-military human, stumbles upon Reed and Hannah and finds he must trust this new world of supernatural beings to survive. But that desire will lead the three to a triangle of attraction that will test the boundaries they all possess and its consequences in defeating the enemy. Can they all trust one another to save themselves and life as they know it? Even at the cost of their own hearts?

Prologue

The sweet coppery scent of freshly spilled blood tingled Corbin's nose as he inhaled deeply. His sister, Ellie, struggled against the restraints digging into her arms and legs, but she didn't make a sound.

Much to his disappointment.

He supposed he must play a bit harder to get his desired results. Yes, that would be quite nice. She was draped in his favorite sundress, bright yellow and white daisies smiling at him from a creamy ivory background. So cheerful to look at, and even better, the blood stains marked it vividly. And, of course, his Ellie needed to look pretty for her brother, even if he'd had to force her into the damn thing.

There was no use looking like a fucking Redwood without class if you were a Central.

His palm stung as he slapped her face then moved to hit her body, over and over again. The stinging increased with each brutal hit, and he sighed. Yes, this would help his headache and aid his thinking. Her skin began to redden from the contact as he beat harder. Laughter burbled from his throat as he continued. This was true contentment.

"Hit me all you want, big brother. But you won't break me. You can't break me." Ellie's voice was steady, without a hint of strain. One would think they were on a leisurely walk and not in a dungeon where he beat her. Corbin slapped her across the face, the sound of flesh against flesh echoing against the walls.

Bitch.

Fury pulsed in his blood and raced up his spine. He bit his lip and relished the tangy taste of blood. He couldn't kill her. Not yet.

It was her fault he was in this situation in the first place. If she hadn't healed that stupid woman, Willow, in the circle after he'd gutted the bitch, this never would have happened. But no, Ellie had to go and help the bitch. So Corbin was forced to save face. He'd stormed the Redwoods' den and attacked. Yes, he may have lost a few wolves to the enemy, but they were useless anyway. There were plenty of other men to die for him in any case.

"I may not break you now, little sister," Corbin snarled, "but I will eventually. Plus, the real fun comes from the play. The longer you stay your typical brazen self, the longer I can try and bleed that from you." He shrugged. "I really don't give a fuck. But you need to learn your place."

"They'll come for him, you know." A thin line of blood trickled from her mouth. He needed to stop soon so her internal bleeding could begin to heal before he started again. The next time he might take out his sharper toys. He smiled at the thought.

"Oh, they'll come. This is, after all, their weakling, their *artist.*" He spat the word. Art. This Reed was an egotistical loser without a designated title in his Pack. He was just one son of the many, nothing like Corbin, the only son and Heir to the Central Pack. He cursed under his breath as he hit Ellie again. They'd gone into the Redwood den with a purpose—to find Jasper, the Redwood's Beta, and take him. But, instead, they got Reed.

They'd kidnapped the wrong wolf, but it would be okay. If Reed's family didn't come for him, Corbin would just kill him—slowly. It was no skin off his back. He hit Ellie again, and this time a slight whimper escaped her.

Ah, progress.

Though the whole wolf debacle grated on him, what really bothered him was the witch. He needed to know more about Hannah. What made her tick? What were her powers? Why did the demon, Caym, tell him she was important? Damn it. He hit Ellie square in the face, harder than he'd planned, and she passed out cold.

Fucking temper.

He missed his other sister, Ellie's twin. But she was dead by his father's hands so they could bring Caym to this world. That sister would have at least screamed for him and moaned in pain. But no, Corbin was stuck with Ellie. Always perfect fucking Ellie, the one who wouldn't join in their father's plans.

Ah, Father.

Hector was getting on his last nerve. The old man didn't have the vision Corbin did. No, his father only saw the small picture. Ruling the wolves and killing some humans. Corbin saw it clearer, but as Heir, Corbin had to stand back and let his father have the power. That would have to change soon. He smiled at that promising thought. His jaw tightened as he clenched his teeth together and fisted his hands.

Caym prowled into his chamber and smiled at him. The demon's dark looks reminded Corbin of a fallen angel. Yet there was nothing angelic about the being in front of him. Midnight black locks of hair framed his chiseled, pale face. His black eyes had a rim of deep red around the iris, enhancing his darkness.

Simply beautiful.

"I see you've let Ellie sleep for a bit." Caym's smooth voice washed over him like liquid silk.

Corbin smiled. "Yes, I'm such a giving wolf." They both laughed.

"They have the video feed finally ready, if you'd like to join me." Caym slid his hand up Corbin's bare arm, causing shivers to race up his spine. Warmth tingled in his icy chest and his pulse raced.

"I'll just leave dear sister here. When she wakes up, she can think about what she's done."

"That sounds reasonable." Caym danced his fingers across Corbin's chin before turning to leave the room.

Intriguing.

He followed the demon out, watching him glide with each step. Caym really was a handsome man. Though Corbin liked to torture and play with women, he preferred men for his bedroom activities. And if the subtle, or rather not so subtle, touches that just occurred were any indication, Caym might prefer him as well.

Interesting.

They entered the viewing room. Two video screens hung on the wall, with buttons and knobs on a control panel beneath them. The demon sat back in a black leather chair, arms cradled behind his head. Lean muscles bunched as he stretched.

Nice.

Corbin strolled past and turned on one of the viewing screens. He walked to a chair, took a seat, and sat back as Caym rested his hand on Corbin's. The image came on the screen, bringing a smile to his lips. His two prisoners lay on the cement floor, chained to stone walls.

Very picturesque.

The male, Reed, clad only in his jeans, pulled at his chains. Silly wolf, those chains were reinforced and not easily broken. He knew from experience. Chills of need racked his body at the memories. The woman, Hannah, slept on the floor, just out of reach of Reed's hands. Perfect. Reed would try and help the girl but wouldn't be able to. It would only hurt and entice his wolf more. Corbin licked his lips in anticipation. He couldn't wait to get his hands on them both, if his father let him.

His fingers ached to see what would happen to the two in his chamber. They would give him information, no matter what it took. He hoped the process would drag on. He loved the prolonged screams of agony, the blood and pain like a cherry on his sundae. How he longed to play. And when he was through with them, he would kill them. There was no use, beyond his own pleasure, for a low-level wolf and a witch with no coven.

Caym squeezed Corbin's hand then brushed his fingers up his arm before standing and taking a step toward the screen.

"I can imagine what you and I could do with the pair of them." The demon's voice sank into his pores. His eyelids closed as his arousal peaked. "But," Caym continued, "we need to get rid of some...obstacles."

"Obstacles." Namely his father, Hector. The Alpha.

"Yes, once we achieve that, you and I could have a great partnership." He paused. "In more ways than one." He smiled, his angelic face taking on an evil light.

Corbin panted in need. "I agree."

"The two of us could strive for even greater progress together. We can call forth the whole of the demons and control them."

They both laughed with insatiable hunger. Yes, this would be a partnership made in hell. Literally.

Chapter 1

Cold spread from a pinprick of sensation as a droplet of water hit Hannah Lewis's cheek. It trailed down to her eye, forcing her to open them to blink it away. Stone walls surrounded her, and the frayed edges on the cement floor dug into her skin. The only means of escape seemed to be a lone rusty metal door in the stone wall. No windows illuminated the room. Cut off from the outside world, she couldn't feel the earth.

As an earth witch, she needed the sensation of soil beneath her feet, the air dancing across her face and through her hair. But cut off, she drifted without an anchor. Hannah slowly sat up, and her muscles ached from her stay.

She snorted. *Stay*. Right.

That sounded like she was happy to be here. No, the bruises and cuts from her *captivity* hurt. But she thanked the goddess she wasn't hurt any more than she was.

The man sharing her room moaned in his sleep. No, not a man, a *werewolf*. By the shouts of their captors, she knew him to be Reed, a wolf of the Redwood Pack, son of the Alpha. They'd brought him in three nights before. At least she thought it was three nights. She couldn't be sure anymore. He seemed to hurt more than she. They had chained him to the wall, same as her, but far enough apart they couldn't touch. And if they were to speak to each other, the guards came in and beat Reed. Never her though. It was almost like a cruel joke to have someone share her burden but be allowed no contact. Her gut twisted, and bile filled her mouth.

Her fingers ached to touch his smooth skin and heal his pains as the healer she was. But she couldn't get close enough to him to do so. Another cruelty. She couldn't bear to see him hurt.

Reed shifted, then snapped open his eyes. She gave him an encouraging smile, the best she could come up with under these conditions. He smiled back, that small gesture almost lighting up his face. Maybe in another time, another place, when they weren't being held in the Central's basement, with no clue whether they would live or die, they would have met and gone on a date. She smiled again at the thought. Yes, that would have been nice. Her smiled faded. But that was not the case. And by the looks of this place, it would never be. Sadness filled her at the loss of something she didn't know she wanted.

Reed reached out and spread his fingers toward her, careful of the cameras watching their every move. Hannah did the same, longing to feel contact. To remember who she was.

The metal door scraped open, the screeching sound echoing in the dank room. They both pulled their arms back as she began to shake in fear. She cursed herself for her cowardliness. But it had been too long since she held hope. She didn't want to die. Not here. Not now.

The Central Alpha's son, Corbin, walked into the room with his smooth glide and a snarl on his lips. Hannah hid the shudders fighting to rack her body at the sight of him. His eyes were dark orbs with no light of goodness hiding within. Whatever was on his mind reeked of evil, an evil she wanted no part of, but it looked as though she had no choice.

The man strode to her, nodding to his two accompanying guards. The guards walked toward her and unshackled her arms and legs. Pain tingled in her fingers and toes as the blood rushed through them from being cut off from good circulation for so long. *Oh goddess. What is he going to do with me?* The guards lifted her to her feet, their grips digging into her arms, hurting her further.

"Let go of her. Take me," Reed's growled from his place on the floor, his voice gravelly.

Oh, how she wished she could just be with this stranger and not go where Corbin wanted. But she couldn't let him be hurt either. She didn't know why, other than the fact she hated to see anyone harmed. It pained her to think about him in her position. He might be a werewolf and be able to heal at a faster rate, but she could take what Corbin brought. She had to.

Corbin laughed at Reed and took a previously unseen whip to her companion's back. Reed groaned in pain at the contact of the whip flaying his flesh. Hannah whimpered at the sight of his blood leaking to the floor. The guards pulled her toward Corbin, her feet trailing the ground as she fought their hold. They merely shook her violently for her to comply. The Alpha's son grabbed her from them and forced her against him. Bile rose in her throat at the oily feel of his skin, his aura.

She looked back over her shoulder at Reed. He lay bleeding, glaring at the guards and Corbin, still struggling against his chains to reach her. Why did she feel such a connection to a man she'd never met outside these stone walls? And, by the look on Reed's face, he might feel the same. Corbin dug his fingers into her arm and shook her, forcing her back to her cold reality.

As the man pulled her to the door, she fought against his hold. His hand came across her face, the sting radiating in her cheek, bringing tears to her eyes. Reed's shouts and pleas followed her out the door until the men closed it with a slam, along with the hope she would get out of this alive. A sinking feeling bottomed out in her stomach. This might be the end.

Corbin dragged her down the hall, and she pulled against at his grip, struggling to get free. She screamed at the guards for help. Surely, there was at least one person out there who could help her. *Dear goddess*. Her captor's hand, again, contacted her face, bringing stars to her eyes and a thin warm trickle of what must be blood down her chin.

At the end of the hall, a door with natural light spilling out along the cracks on the side and bottom, tingled that last spark of hope. Could she escape? She fought to release herself from Corbin's hold. If she got out, she could get help and come back for Reed. She didn't know when she'd started to think of not only herself, but Reed, but she didn't care. Her foot came down on Corbin's instep. She used the surprise to kick him in the groin and twisted free. The evil man yelled, as she ran toward the light. She panted and prayed she could make it. Corbin's hand shot out and grabbed her again. The spark of hope dulled to a slight numbing light. He took her arm in an unforgiving grip and threw her against the wall. Her head cracked against the stone, but she was thankful he hadn't used the whole of his strength.

"Don't you fucking try that again, girl. Or I won't kill you when I'm done with you," he snarled. His torment promised pain and suffering if the reward was death. She held onto the whimper that threatened to escape her throat. She refused to give him the satisfaction.

Corbin lifted her up and carried her to another room off the hall. Before she could pull her mind out of the fuzziness caused by his strikes, he had her strapped down onto a cool metal table, the leather straps digging into her arms and legs and around her stomach. He tightened the straps with a bruising force. The one on her stomach cut into her skin, a thin line of blood forming.

Oh goddess.

Fear crawled on her skin like thousands of tiny bugs searching for a home.

What was he going to do?

Hannah took deep breaths, trying to calm herself. If she panicked and lost her focus, she might lose a chance of escape. She almost laughed at that. Escape? She wasn't some alpha heroine in a romance novel. No, she was just a witch who needed her earth and missed a guy who shared a cell with her. She must be crazy.

The strong scent of lemony citrus invaded her nose when she inhaled again. She almost coughed at the pungent aroma. She looked around at the sickly sterile environment and shivered at the cold practicality of Corbin's torture chamber. The scent was harsh to her senses. Though not as strong as a werewolf's, her sense of smell was more attentive than a normal human's.

Corbin moved above her, blocking her view of the room, a gleeful look in his eyes. Like a kid on Christmas morning waiting to open his enormous amounts of presents and stocking stuffers. She swallowed down the vomit threatening to rise. This was going to hurt. Badly.

The evil wolf carried a cat-o'-nine tails in one hand and a whip in another.

He never stopped smiling as he hit her five times with the tails then five times with the whip. She cried out with each hit, each stroke. She might have been strong in some respects, but the blinding pain racking her body and her blood soaking the floor was too much for her to handle. Tears leaked from her eyes as he hit and hit.

"Tell me, Hannah, what is your power? Why are you so damn important?" Corbin sneered the words, looking engrossed in his flaying.

Powers? That was what this was all about? She was just an earth witch, a rare one due to her healing. But that couldn't be what he wanted. Right?

Corbin hit her again, her vision going black, as the door opened. Hector, the Alpha, Corbin's father, walked in.

"Enough, Corbin." Hector's voice radiated power and demanded respect.

Corbin stopped but looked like he was about to revolt. He took a deep breath, glared at Hannah, and then painstakingly placed the tools of his trade on their bench. With one last smirk in her direction, he stomped away like an insolent puppy.

Hector stepped purposely toward her.

She braced for his fist or hand, too pained to do anything but take it.

But the strike never came.

"Hannah, why won't you use your powers?"

She couldn't, not without the earth. But she wouldn't tell them that. No, she couldn't tell them anything. Once she did, they wouldn't need her anymore. Then they would kill her. And maybe Reed.

Chapter 2

Reed Jamenson watched as Corbin dragged Reed's mate out of the dungeon against her will. He growled and pulled at his chains again as fury boiled in his veins. Hannah, sweet Hannah, with her curly brown hair and plump lips, dragged like a marionette doll whose strings were pulled too tight. Her screams seeped through the metal door, and he pulled at his chains, willing all of the strength a werewolf like him could possess. Blood seeped beneath the manacles as he struggled to no avail.

Typical. He wasn't strong enough to protect a mate he'd just met. Wasn't even strong enough to protect himself. Shame dimmed his fury. That's how he'd ended up in the Central's clutches to begin with. Too weak to escape capture. He might have sacrificed himself to save his brother's mate, but he could have done more. The Centrals had come to their den and attacked, killing countless Pack members. His brothers had fought valiantly, purposely. Yet, Reed, only an artist who thought he could fight, had lost.

They'd knocked him unconscious, thrown him in their truck, and taken him away. Three nights or so had passed, yet his family hadn't come. Did they want to? When the Centrals had taken Willow, his sister-in-law, she'd been gone for only a day at most. Their family had chased after Anna, his other sister-in-law, but they were too late for her. Grief warred with his other emotions. What group would he land in? Or would they come for him at all? He was the fourth of six sons and one daughter. He held no power in the Pack, no purpose. He was just a man who liked to paint and fancied himself an artist. A nobody. Yeah, he was a werewolf and could kill a man with his bare hands, but he still felt inadequate sometimes.

His arms and legs were a mottled collection of bruises and cuts spliced together in a macabre pattern that almost appealed to his artist senses. Almost. Every time they came in and he tried to help Hannah in any way, they beat him. His back and side were sore to the touch. No doubt he had bruised, if not broken, rib or two. They kept away from his face oddly enough. But Corbin and his cronies didn't stray from Hannah's. And Reed couldn't protect her. Rage bubbled up from deep inside him.

Reed shook his head to rid himself of those melancholy thoughts and took deep calming breaths. Acting irrational wouldn't help; it could only harm in this situation. And frankly, he needed to get out of here and save Hannah. Even if he had to do it himself. They'd dragged her out of here and he could do nothing but watch and pull at his chains.

The thought of her honey and bitter apple scent made his mouth salivate. Her corkscrew curls lay flat against her face when they let her walk or when she shook her head. His fingers ached to pull at one gently and see if it would spring back. He wanted to paint her angelic face, her chestnut hair. That's what he did when he found a subject he found desirable. But Hannah was no normal subject. Her wide gray eyes stared at him with a glimmer of hope, and he prayed he could deliver. Though he was in a dark, gloomy dungeon, his cock still hardened at the thought of what she would taste like when he licked her skin. Or lower.

"I'm sure you can find out hot stuff, once you actually get our mate out of here."

Reed's wolf practically snickered at him. But that was par for the course. Fucking wolf never took anything too seriously, but still wanted to protect in his own way.

"We'll save her. We have to."

Reed could only agree.

The metal door creaked open, and the demon walked in, a limp form in his arms. Reed bit back a moan. *Hannah.*

The smell of blood, her blood, reached his nostrils before he saw the thin trails on her stomach, arms, and legs. He was going to fucking kill whoever had touched her. Corbin, the demon, the random guard who looked at her wrong, he didn't care. They would die. Painfully.

Her spilled blood enraged him. Muscles bulging, he pulled at his chains and tried to take a swipe at the demon. His hand turned to a claw as his wolf tried to take control, which was a departure from his wolf's usual jovial self.

The demon merely laughed at his attempt and stood back. With a nod to the camera, the chains attached to the collar around his neck tightened and pulled, blocking his oxygen. He still fought his chains, not caring if he passed out. The demon gave another nod. The two goons who'd taken Hannah out the door before came back and locked her to the wall again. She slumped to the floor unconscious, and he growled in pain for her.

The demon smirked and walked out of the room, the goons on his heels like strays begging for scraps. Reed's collar loosened, and he gasped for breath. As his body absorbed sweet oxygen, he took a closer look at Hannah. For some, most likely sadistic, reason, they'd placed her closer to him. He didn't care to think of the whys yet, but now he could touch her, hold her, care for her. Though he wasn't like North, his brother the doctor, he would do his best to heal her as well.

He scooted on the stone floor, flicking pebbles of the broken wall away from her so she could be comfortable. Well, at least as comfortable as possible. She looked like a broken doll with her eyes closed and chocolate curls surrounding her pale face. He brushed a curl away, the soft hair like silk on his cut-up skin, and saw a large bruise forming on her face. A slight nick on her lip had already begun clotting, and Reed had to hold back a growl of anger. He didn't want to scare her. Only kill that slimy fuck, Corbin.

Long gashes ran up her torso, arms, and legs. The thought of the whip or whatever the fucker had used made him want to vomit then go back and use the damn weapon on Corbin. Yeah, that sounded nice. Maybe he'd give it to Hannah when she woke up so she could have a go and take vengeance on the man. That thought was almost enough to perk him up.

Reed leaned over her, careful of her injuries and whispered her name.

"Hannah," he whispered again, caressing the unbruised side of her face. Despite the coldness of the room and the loss of blood, warmth radiated from her skin. He inhaled her honey and bitter apple scent again, this time detecting a faint earthy scent.

Interesting.

His mate was a witch. He liked the idea she already knew of the supernatural. Once they got out of this, he wouldn't have to explain everything to her like Jasper had with Willow and Kade had with Melanie. It was nice at least something was going his way.

"Hannah."

She mumbled something incoherent and turned into his palm, nuzzling him. His heart swelled at the unfamiliar touch of a mate leaning closer. Was this what his brothers felt every time their mates walked into the room? He liked it already.

Even bruised, bleeding, and beaten, his mate was cute.

Her lips parted and Reed felt the very inappropriate urge to kiss her. He shook his head. *Seriously man, not the right time.* And frankly his mind was too befuddled to think about any aspects of mating besides the big picture.

Reed looked around for something to clean Hannah with, but in the moldy dungeon, not much was available. Desperate to at least clean up the dried blood, he tore strips off his shirt that lay on the ground next to where he was chained, the sounds of ripping fabric echoing off the stone walls. He took the strips of cotton and placed them against the wall, collecting the droplets and small streams of water along the stone. Now damp with whatever moisture he could get, he took the strips and carefully cleaned around her wounds. Only small gashes rose along her skin, thankfully. For the most part, there only seemed to be bruising and angry red lash marks. The bastard had only cut her skin in some places.

His scent mingled with hers, crisp apples and wolf. He liked it. And by the growling contentment he heard from his wolf, he did too. He could get used to this. But something still nagged at him. Something was missing. Was it because of where they were? Because they hadn't completed the mating? This was his first time meeting a potential mate. He didn't know quite what to feel—what was right. Not all things could come back to instinct.

That missing feeling crept up on him. Was this how Kade felt with Tracy? He had met another potential before he met Melanie, and it hadn't worked out. Did Kade also feel this missing element? Something lacking? Was Hannah really the right one for him?

Reed shook it off. This was not the time to think about such things. He needed to heal Hannah.

He traced her face again with the tips of his fingers, reveling in her beauty even with the swelling around her bruises.

Hannah opened her eyes and screamed.

"Hannah, shh," Reed gently whispered. "It's okay. It's me, Reed. I won't let him hurt you again. I promise."

Reed stared into her dove gray eyes, pleading for her to believe him, even though he knew some things might be out of his control.

Hannah took a deep breath and then sank into his arms. Her warm weight felt like heaven. Like home. He held her to his chest, careful of her hurts, and whispered reassurances in her ear.

"Hannah, don't panic, baby. We have to be quiet. The cameras are still on, and they can hear us." He kissed her temple, too weak not to relish her sweet taste. "I don't know why they put us so close together this time, but we can use it to our advantage. We can try to formulate a plan and get out of here. I'll protect you. I promise."

"I'm not incapable." Hannah's soft voice reached his ears. "I can help to."

Reed let out a dry chuckle. "Good, because we may need it."

She let out a surprised laugh then cringed in pain. Reed stiffened and his heart sped up.

"What hurts, Hannah? Tell me and I can help. I don't know much, but I'll do what I can."

He couldn't let go of her completely, but he did survey her body to check her cuts. Okay, he also looked because her curves were damned delicious. Bitable for sure.

He tore more off his shirt, noticing the way Hannah's gaze never strayed far from his naked chest. Reed almost preened for her but caught himself, finding that slightly inappropriate. As he cleaned up the rest of the dried blood, she cuddled into him, and he bit his lip not to groan at the contact. Definitely not the time to be thinking about pounding into her soft curves.

He stroked her face again, staring into her eyes. He could get lost in those eyes.

"Really, Reed? How cliché can you get?"

Reed held in a laugh at his wolf. Yeah, that pretty much summed up his thoughts for the moment.

"Dammit, I hate my powers sometimes," Hannah grumbled.

Startled at the curse coming out of her seemingly sweet mouth, it Reed took a moment to comprehend what she'd said.

"Huh?" *Smooth.*

"My powers. I'm a healer. But I can only heal others. Not myself." She bit her lip in what he thought was annoyance and looked damn cute.

"You're a healer?"

"Uh huh. So I can heal you, if you don't mind me touching you." Again, her teeth bit into her plump lip.

His eyes widened, and he told himself to remember the thing about touching for later. Their Pack was missing a true Healer. One who could heal by the touch of their hand and would strengthen the Pack. North, his brother, was their doctor. But it wasn't the same. Could this be fate giving him a nudge?

"Um, you can heal me. I don't mind." He felt his ears warm, and he knew he must be blushing like a school boy. *Oh, yes, that would show her how perfect I am for her. Act like a virgin in the back of my mom's Buick.*

"Okay, this won't hurt. But it might tingle."

She placed her warm hands on his chest and ribs. They both gasped at the contact. Did she feel something too? He didn't think witches had clear mates like werewolves did, but he couldn't be sure. His body tingled where her skin touched his. He felt the muscles and ribs knitting together, blood pulsating in his veins.

Who knew healing could be so erotic? He growled at the thought of her hands on another male while she healed them. Did they feel this good too?

Hannah quickly lifted her hands. Reed felt lost at the loss of her touch.

"I'm sorry. Did I hurt you?" she said, panting a bit, but still sounding worried.

"What? No. It felt good actually." Again, he felt his face heat up.

"Oh, but you growled." She scrunched her brows, utterly confused and very cute.

"No, I was just thinking about something else. I didn't mean to scare you."

"Oh you didn't scare me. I don't think you could ever scare me." She ducked her head, but not before Reed caught a shy smile on her face.

He didn't know what to feel about that. Did that mean she didn't think he could protect her? Or did she feel safe around him? He hoped it was the latter.

She smiled then settled into his arms, careful of her wounds. Hannah felt incredible next to him. Right. But still, something was missing. Something important. He just didn't know what. And even though they fit together quite perfectly, he didn't tell her they were mates. This wasn't the right time, and frankly, he had no idea how to bring it up. They needed to get out of the basement first. Then he needed to kill some sadistic ass.

Chapter 3

Josh Kolb rubbed the back of his neck, the tension of the day ebbing through his nerve endings, screeching at him to take a break. Right, like that would happen. Weary exhaustion crept through his body. He was getting too damn old for this shit. He'd been working for his buddy's security company for five long years since he'd got out of the SEALs.

He'd just got off a job he was sure was slowly sucking the life out of him. Mrs. Carnoski, an elderly woman who in no way resembled a nice grandmother type, was an ice queen with a stick up her ass. No matter how many times he showed the woman how to set the alarm and work the system, she still needed his "help." And by help, he meant she needed to press her Botox body against him and flirt endlessly with innuendos no one could mistake. Josh cringed at the thought of her touching him. Not even on his weakest days would he ever want that bag of bones.

Still fuming and a little uncomfortable, he walked to the hot dog stand and ordered a reindeer dog. He loved Jim's. Homemade sausage from reindeer, boar, elk, or anything the man could hunt for himself. Jim would grill it once it was ordered then add caramelized onions and cream cheese. Add a bag of chips and a Coke and Josh had himself a delicious meal for five bucks. Not too shabby.

Josh strode to the nearest bench and relaxed against the cool metal backing. He took a deep breath of the crisp mountain air. Snow was on its way. In the mountainous outskirts of Seattle, most were used to seeing rain, but the winter months were finally leading to snowfall. Josh shrugged. It didn't really matter what the weather was, nothing about his daily routine would change. He'd eat, sleep, watch TV, and work out—alone. Then he'd go to work and wish he were alone. What was a little snow?

He was off the job for the day but didn't know what he was going to do. He could go home, but why? Nothing was waiting for him there. Just a shabby apartment with bare walls devoid of personal touches. Josh swallowed the last of his dog, licking the cream cheese off his fingers before washing it down with the rest of his Coke. Fuck, he was lonely. And not happy about the fact he cared that he was lonely. He was a SEAL, for fuck's sake. He shouldn't care one way or the other. But here he was, at the onset of winter, sitting on a park bench, alone and pissy, and apparently a pussy about it as well. Josh shook his head.

Letting out a deep breath, Josh closed his eyes, and opened up his senses to his surroundings. The wind brushed his face, cooling the melancholy temper heating his cheeks. Murmurs of conversations from passersby, customers and townspeople quickly shopping and mingling before the coming storm drifted through on the wind. He turned his head toward voices, most likely two teens, both low, almost a whisper but with such a hint of excitement and dread, it carried to his ears on the wind.

"Did you hear?" one of the boys asked, fear on his tongue. "One of the Jamenson sons was taken after the fight. Reed, I think."

"Reed? Which one was he?" the other boy asked.

"The artist. No real title, but still the Alpha's son."

"Crap, what are they doing about it?"

"I don't know. But you know the Centrals are about to get their asses kicked. You can't just steal the son of an Alpha and think it's okay. No matter how crazy you are."

"No shit."

"I just hope they find him."

"Yeah. But it's weird, ya know."

"What?"

"Reed being taken so soon after that witch was. Remember that?"

"Huh?"

"That witch who owned the herbal shop in Callensbury. Some guys came in, roughed up the shop, killed her mom, and then took her."

"Really?"

"Yeah. I wonder if it's connected somehow."

"Well, if it is, I'm sure the Jamensons will find out. That's what they do."

"But they can't find them. It's been what...three days or so?"

"They will. They have to. The Jamensons are like gods. They'll do it."

"Sure."

Both boys walked off, leaving Josh to ponder their words.

Someone had kidnapped the Alpha's son? Interesting. As a human, he shouldn't know about werewolves, witches, and whatever else went bump in the night. But being on some of those more risky missions put him right in the path of nightmares better left unknown.

Not to mention Josh was a Finder.

One look at the person's face and he could close his eyes, open his senses, and Find them anywhere in the world. Not a bad talent to have in the SEALs. But he didn't want to use it in his new life. Too many memories. Too many people lost and never Found. Because no matter how hard he tried, he couldn't Find someone across the veil of death.

Flashes of chestnut hair and gray eyes merged with sandy blond hair and forest green eyes. What the hell? He'd never laid eyes on these two souls, but he could see every definition of them clear as day. Memories of their daily lives passed too quickly for him to discern any real significance other than the fact he felt as though he knew these people. Or needed to know them down to the very essence of his heart.

The images molded into fights, shouts, and scrapes. Men came for each of them, stealing them from their homes. Their lives. In that moment, he knew who he was looking at.

Reed and the witch.

How could he see their pasts? That wasn't something he normally did. No, he could only Find their present.

Josh closed his eyes, ignoring the first fall of snowflakes brushing his cheeks and eyelashes. He opened his senses the way his grandmother had taught him before she passed long ago. Tunneling through the webs of souls he'd met, through the threads of destiny and paths less taken, he searched for the two he'd never met. He needed to Find them.

There.

The sandy-haired wolf, Reed, sat next to the curly-haired beauty, the witch. He wished he knew her name. Darkness surrounded them, creating an almost hazy interpretation of what he should be seeing, as though something was trying to block him. But he could still pull on that thin, but strong thread of connection between the three of them. Yes, for whatever reason, there was a connection, clear as day. What to do with that would have to be shelved for now and dealt with at a later date.

Josh concentrated harder, grasping at their location. *Ahh.* Reed and the witch were in a basement of some sort, deep in the forest. He looked harder and around the dilapidated building, searching for landmarks so he could get to them.

Wait. Go to them? Since when was he mounting a rescue mission for two people he hadn't met? He wasn't in the SEALs anymore. His internal military objective slapped him upside the head. *Once a SEAL always a SEAL.* That wasn't just for those pesky Marines. He would try to rescue them for the clear reason that it was his duty, not only because he felt that tenuous connection between the three of them.

No, definitely not.

Josh opened his eyes, looking at the slight accumulation of snowfall that promised to be a monster of a storm in the coming day. Fewer people lingered on the streets, and the temperature had slowly dropped. But Josh wasn't thinking about the people in his line of vision. No, the owners of those green eyes and then those gray eyes firmly held his attention.

No matter how hard he tried to deny it, it was there. But what was so special about this duo? Why did he have to be on this bench at this time to hear about the kidnapping from those two kids? Fucking fate and all that shit.

Josh closed his eyes again, remembering the looks on their faces in their captivity. Pain radiated in his head at the thought. Why was he so close to this? Why did it hurt *him* so much that they were out of his reach and in dire need of help?

What was Josh going to do? Could he talk to someone and let them handle it so he could run away? No, not run away; let someone closer to the situation and the captives deal with it.

Josh snorted. *Yeah, just throw away the responsibility. That sounds like a plan.*

He was ex-military. A human. He wasn't supposed to even know about the existence of another world. The supernatural. If he went to the Redwoods and asked them for help or gave them the information he knew, would they believe him? Or laugh at his face and tell him to go away? Or worse, would they believe him and kill him if they thought he was part of the plot of involving the loss of their loved ones?

Too complicated and strenuous by far. Fuck. He'd have to go in alone and get evidence. More evidence than just the fact he'd seen them in his head. Yeah, because that didn't sound crazy. His parents and other kids sure had thought so. But this wasn't about him. Two people who, for some reason he could Find in a way he could with no one else, were in trouble. They needed his help.

That settled it. Josh would go to them, to that old building with its dark basement and hazy surroundings, most likely due to some highly dangerous magic he had no defense for. He would get them out right then if he could, see what he was able to do. But if that didn't work, he'd get evidence of where they were and find a way to get it to the Redwoods. They were strong werewolves after all. Some of the strongest. Surely they could rescue Reed and the witch if they had help.

Yes, that sounded like a reasonable plan.

Josh stood up and stretched his aching back. *Fuck.* He rubbed the back of his neck in frustration. He was most likely running to his death. But he couldn't leave them out there, alone but for each other. No, not when he was an able body who could maybe help. And frankly, it wasn't like he had anything else to go back to if he didn't make it. These two were important to him for some reason; he just had to save them and find out why.

Chapter 4

Hannah shivered in Reed's arms and he held tighter, trying to keep her warm. The temperature outside had dropped dramatically and slowly seeped into the small room. Her little body refused to stay heated in the dank basement. Her cold curves snuggled up to him, as he tried to infuse his warmth into her. His body temperature might be higher than a normal human's, but no matter what he did, she just couldn't stay warm.

Hannah sneezed in her sleep, jerking herself awake. Reed laughed at how damn cute she was. Seriously, who sneezed themself awake?

"That wasn't funny, jerk." Her small smile and delicate blush belied any harshness in her tone. "Reed, don't laugh at me. This isn't any time to laugh." Her mouth curved a bit more, and she gave him a look like she was trying to hold back her own laughter. Reed wanted to lick the curve of her lips, taste them to see if she carried that honey and bitter apple scent in her pores.

"I'm sorry, dear Hannah." He tried to put on his best solemn face but barely refrained from laughing. Even though they were stuffed and locked in a basement, he couldn't help but relish the fact he held her in his arms. The only thing to make it better would be getting out of there. Oh, and if they were naked. But that was just a given.

"You better be. It's not nice to make fun of a sleeping person." She sobered. "But thank you for making me want to laugh, even though there really isn't anything to laugh about here."

Oh how he wanted to make everything better with a flick of his wrist, to be able to save and protect her. But he couldn't; there was nothing for him to do. The walls were too enforced, too many of the guards held strength that rivaled his own. Plus, Corbin held weapons no honorable werewolf should hold. If he didn't have to protect and shield Hannah, he might have been able to do it. But with his mind distracted by the fact he'd found his mate and still felt as though he was missing something, he didn't feel comfortable risking her life. Reed shook his head. He needed to find a new topic, something that would get their minds off their captivity. The only thing that came to mind and piqued his interest was sitting in his lap, rubbing her bitable bottom on his erection every time she moved, whether she knew it or not.

"Tell me about yourself, Hannah." If he hadn't been holding her, he wouldn't have noticed the almost indecipherable stiffness in her body, but he continued. He needed to hear more about her, and if her reaction was any indication, she needed to let out her tension and share. "What are you like outside of these four walls?"

Hannah took a deep breath, her breasts rubbing against his arm as she did so. Reed held back a groan. This wasn't the time to bend her over and mount her.

"I disagree on that."

Reed ignored his wolf. He was pretty sure the animal thought about sex more than he did. And that was saying something since he'd been pretty deprived recently.

"I shouldn't be telling you anything about me." Hannah's face scrunched up in confusion.

Reed felt a pang of hurt at her words, but reminded himself she didn't know they were mates. His fault, he knew, but it was still the right choice, for now.

"I won't share what you say here. But I want to know more about you. Who are you, Hannah?"

Hannah let out a deep breath and bit her lip.

31

"I'm an earth witch. I control the soils and can call on other parts of nature if I need to. But I'm only moderately functional with that stuff. My real talents are in the healing."

Reed nodded, urging her to continue.

Hannah held out her hand, absentmindedly playing with the hair on his arms. Goosebumps raised on his flesh at her soft touch.

"I owned a potions and herb shop with my mother." Her voice broke at that last part. Tears fell down her cheeks.

"Hannah, baby, I'm sorry. I didn't mean to upset you. We don't have to talk about this anymore."

She bit her lip in her delectable way and shook her head.

"No, I need to tell you. I want to tell you." She stared off into space, her mind on whatever memory haunted her dreams. "When Corbin's men took me, they destroyed the shop. My mom and I were working that day. It wasn't too busy so she told me to go in the back and mix up some more lotion for dry skin. She said she'd take care of the register and customers. If it got busier, or if someone needed me, she'd get me. I didn't hear the door open from where I sat. I was too engrossed in what I was doing. It takes a lot of concentration to make a good potion and herb remedy. So I didn't hear anything until I heard her scream."

Reed held her closer, her heartbeat fast against his as tears ran faster down her face.

"I ran to the front, not thinking of something that could hurt me. I just had to get to my mom. You know?"

Reed knew. That's how he'd gotten here too.

"And then..." Her voice broke again, and Reed rubbed small circles on her back, trying to offer soothing comfort where there was none to give. "I didn't see her, only a shadow, and a puddle of blood. But I knew. She was gone. And I had been in the back, not paying attention to what was going on."

"Hannah, it wasn't your fault."

"But I could have helped her."

"Hannah, they went there for a purpose." Shit, wrong thing to say.

"Yeah, to find me. And they killed my mom for it." Anger and despair swirled in her eyes.

Reed was at a loss of what to say—an uncommon occurrence for him. Usually, he was the one people came to for cheering up. He was the one with the words and pleasantries. Yet with his mate in his arms, he felt inadequate.

"It's not your fault. It's Corbin's and Hector's fault. They were the one who had those men come for you. They were the ones who took your mom away from you. There was nothing you could do." She must have felt a hundred times more helpless than he felt at the moment.

"I know that. But it still doesn't make it right. When I came out of the back room, I saw her and screamed. I didn't use my powers. Shock, I guess. But I should have. Maybe then I would have gotten out of there. But no. They came for me and knocked me out. I don't remember what happened after that. I woke up here, and then a couple of weeks or so later, you came too."

Reed held her to his chest, trying to give her the strength she needed, knowing he was lacking. She stopped crying, exhausted emotionally as well as physically. A salty trail of tears remained on her cheeks. Reed wiped away their evidence with the pad of his thumb, taking in the softness of her skin.

"No matter what happens, I will find a way to kill him." Reed's voice deepened with a promise of vengeance. He sounded cold and calculating, unlike his normal self. But maybe like he was worth something.

"You'll have to take a number and stand behind me. Because I plan on killing those bastards and dancing on their graves."

His Hannah was a force to be reckoned with. Sexy. He nuzzled her hair, inhaling her honey and crisp apple scent.

"Reed?" Her soft voice tickled the faint hairs on his chest.

"Yes, baby?"

"Why do they want us?"

That was the question, wasn't it? One he'd been contemplating since he woke here next to, but not touching, the sweet witch in his arms.

"I think they took you because you are a rare healing earth witch. You might be able to aid them somehow."

"That's what I thought. Odd to think a man so bent on pain would want a healer."

"I'd try not to think about that too much," Reed whispered as shivers racked Hannah's body.

"But what about you?"

"I'm not really worth anything. I'm just a plain werewolf. It must just be for ransom. They could have taken any of my brothers and had their powers on hand. But no, they took me." A nobody artist with no title. Just the blood of the Alpha running in his veins.

"Hey, that's not true. You are worth something. You are powerful. I've seen you. Don't count yourself short." Her indignation at his self-deprecation was nothing short of cute. Wrong, but cute.

"I'm only an artist, Hannah. I'm the son of the Alpha, but I don't have a title. I'm not really Alpha enough to be useful to the Centrals or even part of the Jamensons frankly. My brothers are so much more."

"Reed Jamenson, this isn't the time for a pity party." She scowled at him, her bottom lip puffing out.

He looked at the stone walls with their chains and lack of light.

"Hannah, baby? This is the *perfect* time for a pity party."

Their laughter mingled, boarding close to hysterical. Shit, they really needed to get out of here. Fast.

The metal door screeched open, bringing their laughter to a frightening halt. Without a word, Hector strode in, lifted his arm, and shot at the two of them.

A slight trickle of light bounced off the barrel of the gun a split second before Reed threw himself over Hannah. The deafening sound of a bullet leaving the chamber echoed off the walls. Reed flinched as the lead bullet tore through his flesh. He grunted but didn't scream. No, Hannah was doing enough of that for both of them.

Hector shot again, the burning smell of acrid flesh as another bullet penetrated his skin stung his nostrils. Hannah called his name, but he bit his lip, holding back a groan of pain. He mustn't show weakness. The bitter taste of blood filled his mouth as he bit his tongue to stop from reacting.

Two more shots. Two more ringing after effects that made him want to vomit. Two more lead bullets mutilating his back. If it were Hannah in his place, she'd surely be dead. But he was a werewolf; he could withstand this. Hopefully.

Hector laughed, and Reed forced himself to turn to the evil sound.

The man lifted the gun and blew at the tip, as if smoke would resonate from it like in the olden days.

Sick bastard.

Blood trailed down his back and seeped into his jeans and onto Hannah's peasant skirt. He looked at his mate below him, wide-eyed but silent. She bit her lip but remained calm in his hold, giving him the strength to persevere and take whatever punishment Hector dealt from his whim of fancy.

"That was just a warning. I grew tired of the two of you mooning over each other. Fools. You really think you will live past this to quench those desires. No, you will not fuck each other like the crude instruments of fate you are. This is not a vacation or a honeymoon. You are my captives. I will cut you and beat you as I wish. And if I feel like it, I will rape the witch and make you watch."

Hannah shuddered in his hold, and despite the blood loss, he did not relent his grip. That fucker wasn't going to lay a paw on her.

"Your family will come for you, young Reed. They always come for those we take from them. Funny how they think they are the strongest and the best of the wolves. Arrogant pricks. They haven't stopped us yet. They are too cowardly to truly embrace their power, and now they grow weak from it. Gluttoned and bloated on their own self-worth, they will die by my hand."

Reed bit off a growl. He would enjoy slicing that vile tongue out of the bastard's mouth.

"We may have gotten the wrong brother, but you will prove your worth to me. Or if not, it's no worry. You will still be some form of entertainment. I will rape and then kill the witch in front of you. Then I will kill you. Slowly. It's no matter."

Hector pulled the gun up and shot Reed in the back once more. This time Hannah and he both let out a whimper. *Fuck that hurt.*

"Just for good measure. You know the drill."

With a nod at the guards, the bastard walked out of the room, head held high.

As soon as the door slammed shut, Hannah pushed him off her. Reed groaned in pain at the contact.

Hannah knelt over him, pale and wide-eyed. Crimson blood painted her hands in a cruel landscape, and Reed felt horrible she had to witness and touch his weakness.

Her chestnut corkscrew hair cascaded around her face, her dove gray eyes imploring. She'd be a treasure to paint. A blank canvas promising a beauty of strokes and colors.

Okay, I might be reacting to the blood loss. Just saying.

He was getting a little loopy. But she was just so pretty. He could stare at her forever.

Hannah smiled down at him and caressed his cheek.

"You're quite handsome yourself."

Shit, he hadn't realized he'd spoken out loud. Oh well, she was beautiful, no use in keeping in those thoughts.

Hannah bit her lip then turned him over to his stomach. He sucked in a breath, but held back a wince. He didn't want to show any more weakness than he already had in front of his mate. The cool cement floor felt nice on his heated skin.

She took a shaky breath and placed her palms over the wounds on his back and chanted a calming melody. His skin stretched, and his wounds knitted together.

Warmth seeped through the pain, a tingling sensation more pronounced than when she'd healed his ribs before.

After a few minutes, she sighed, and Reed stole a look at her. Exhaustion crept over her features and her eyes drooped.

"Hannah, you need to stop. You're hurting yourself."

"I'm sorry, Reed. I'm just too far from the earth. You'll need to heal the rest of it yourself." She stroked his cheek. "Change."

"You shouldn't have shown the fullness of your powers. They'll know now." He nodded to the cameras.

Hannah lowered her head, and whispered, "You're worth it."

Humbled. Yes, that was the feeling warming his soul at the moment.

She laughed a sad laugh, then continued, "Plus, you lost so much blood, and if you died, the smell would've gotten to me eventually."

He laughed then grunted in pain at the sickly holes in his flesh.

Hannah pulled him to a sitting position then went to the clasp of his jeans to help.

His cock hardened at her touch, and they both blushed. Well, as much as he could blush with the amount of blood he'd lost.

Neither of them said a word at his reaction, but he did smell a faint hint of her arousal.

Interesting.

Together, they stripped him of his jeans and boxer briefs. Though he could tell she tried not to, her gaze dropped to his cock.

Her cheeks reddened. She was embarrassed, aroused, and fucking sexy.

He crouched and looked into her gray eyes and changed.

Muscles tearing and forming, bones breaking and rearranging. He wanted to grunt in pain. Because of his numerous wounds, this was not the usual peaceful change. No, this was excruciating. At least the chains attached to his limbs and neck magically enhanced, to shrink and stretch, accommodating his new form.

As fur sprouted from his skin, covering his body, he also felt the wounds knit together, healing. And yes, that hurt just as well.

Once he became his wolf, he sat on his haunches, panting from exertion. Hannah scooted toward him, a calm expression on her face. *Thank God, she isn't scared.* He wasn't sure he could take his mate's fear of him on top of everything else. Hesitantly, she brought her hand to his head, petting his fur. If he were a cat, he surely would be purring in contentment right about now. She moved her hand in gentle circles, and he leaned into her touch. She quirked up a lip in a half smile, and he licked her palm, mostly because he wanted to see her smile more, but also because now, as a wolf, that honey and crisp apple smell was damn enticing.

Hannah giggled at the feel of his tongue, and she batted him on the nose.

"Bad, Reed."

He tilted his head in innocence.

She just laughed again and petted him some more.

Eventually, they both grew tired, and Reed lay down on his stomach. Gently, he used his teeth to pull her sleeve toward him. Thankfully, she got the hint and used his warm body as a pillow. Her delicious curves wiggled into his side while she got comfortable. Oh yes, when he became a man again, they would have to do something about their budding sexual tension. Naked.

"Goodnight, Reed."

He shifted his head in a nod. Her breaths soon deepened and steadied in a peaceful sleep.

"I could get used to this."

Reed agreed with his wolf. But could this intelligent, witty, and beautiful woman really want an artist and not an Alpha?

That was something to deal with later. They just needed to get out of here. Preferably alive.

Chapter 5

Snowflakes stuck to Josh's eyelashes, and he batted them away. A strong gust blew past him, the cold chilling his bones. He surveyed his surroundings, taking a silent step through the undergrowth. Tall trees reached to the sky, blocking whatever sunlight filtered through the dreary storm clouds. Their limbs, heavy with leaves and the extra weight of collecting snow, drooped down. Snow bundles dropped on his shoulder and, in one unfortunate incident, his face. If only he could have Found these two in the nice spring or cool fall months. No, he had to search for them at the onset of winter and the beginning of what looked to be a deadly snowstorm. Lucky guy.

When he left his bench on Main Street, he had quickly gone home to fetch some of his equipment. He dressed to stay warm, grabbed a pack with extra clothes for Reed and the witch, some food and water, and weapons. Lots of weapons. Knives and blades of various shapes and sizes adorned his body. He had his SIG strapped to his side, with extra ammo in his belt. Sadly, he didn't have any silver, but lead would at least slow the beasts down if they came after him.

And they would. He knew it because, as he'd followed the trail in his mind to this remote bunker, his sense of unease swelled to a staggering sensation. *Shit, I might not make it this time.* He was but one man, one human at that. But looking down at the lair that held two people he *needed* to Find, he set aside those worries and the creeps it gave off. And if anyone truly knew him, they would know that it was fucking hard to give Josh the creeps.

They were more important—for some unknown reason.

Those two boys in the alley had mentioned they thought the two disappearances were connected. Well, Josh knew for sure they were. He was also damn sure it was the Centrals too. If his memory served, Josh now stood on Central Pack land. Not a good thing for a human—especially one who despised the rumored brutality of this particular Pack.

These guys were werewolves and could kill him in a blink of an eye with their bare hands. Josh might be strong, pretty damn strong for a human if he had to brag, but not strong enough for the supernaturals. Hence, the overabundance of blades attached to various places on his body. He could reach them all in a split second. That might not be quick enough, but they were a security blanket for him nonetheless.

If there was any doubt the man in his visions was Reed, he'd had an eyeful when he tried to Find them again, because he found himself watching a naked man, an injured naked man, twisting and curving into a werewolf. He'd heard them speaking in hushed tones to each other when he focused. Reed said the woman, Hannah, had healed him before he changed, so she must be the witch.

Hannah. Reed. He liked those names.

What he didn't like was the reaction to Reed's nude body. Josh's cock had filled and his body had hummed. But that wasn't something he wanted to dwell on.

Josh adjusted the erection that hadn't subsided since seeing Hannah and Reed's faces the first time. Damn inconvenient.

What made them so special? Why could he Find them yet had never met them? He had to know. The slow desire welling up inside of him at the thought of the two had nothing to do with his decisions. Nothing.

Right.

Sure, they were attractive. Hannah was a curvy, sexy goddess, and he was man enough to admit Reed was damn sexy. That, though, didn't seem like a good enough reason to risk his life. But he'd do it. He couldn't let them die.

Josh crouched down below a copse of trees, searching for movement from the enemy. He might not know the Centrals personally, but their cruel and sadist ways made them that nonetheless. He closed his eyes, opened his senses and used his Finding. In his mind's eye, both of them sat huddled together. In human form, Reed held Hannah close to his chest, an overwhelming sign of protection. Josh didn't know why both a surge of disappointment and hope flooded his system in a wave of emotion. It made no sense.

The stone dwelling had no discernible features but a few doors guarded by cameras and a few electronics and a couple of closed windows, high above the ground.

Ah ha.

There.

He saw small window too high from the ground for anyone to care about. But it was far enough from the cameras that Josh could use his jammer on the electronics to cut the feed and show only static, scale the wall, and squeeze through the window undetected. Hopefully.

With one last survey of the grounds, he made it to the building, jammed the signal, scaled up the wall, and crawled through the window in under thirty seconds. Nice display of talent, if he didn't say so himself. Of course, he didn't say so, as that would be bragging. And SEALs, even ex-SEALs, never did that. Much.

Thankfully, or perhaps stupidly on the Central's part, no guards stood in the hall where Josh dropped to his feet. Still, he hid in the shadows, taking in his location. A long hallway stretched to the end of the building, doors branching off the corridor in a nonsymmetrical pattern. Dim lights hung overhead, illuminating the hall in an eerie glow.

Again, Josh used his Finding to follow the path to the two people crowding his mind in an unrelenting fashion. As he walked quietly towards the pair, no guards stood by or stopped him. That creepy feeling came back, making the hairs on the back of his neck bristle, but he shook it off. He couldn't think about what wasn't there, only what he needed to do to get out of there.

Just as he thought that, footsteps echoed. *Fuck.* Josh slid into a corner, fading beneath the shadows—something he was quite good at. He could hide from anything if he felt the desire. No one expected him to be there so who could possibly find him?

The guard in a black uniform and combat boots walked past Josh's corner and had no idea it would be his last patrol. Too bad for him. With a swift flick of his wrists around the guard's neck, the guard fell, and Josh pulled him into the shadows. Josh didn't want to leave the evidence, but he needed the key haphazardly dangling on a chain around the dead man's neck. It was a risk, but by the time someone found him there, Reed, Hannah, and he would be long gone. Safe from the oily clutches of the Centrals. At least he hoped so.

He slipped the key off the guard's neck, and walked towards the metal door from his vision. With a look over both shoulders to make sure he was still alone, he slipped the key into the lock. It clicked open as he turned the key, mercifully quiet and Josh let out a breath of relief.

When he opened the door, it made a loud screech, forcing a curse under his breath. So much for being quiet and stealthy. Fucking door hinges. How much did it cost for fucking oil? Then again, this wasn't the *Wizard of Oz*, and the door wasn't the Tin Man. They probably loved making that creepy sound every time they opened the door. Added to the spine-chilling torture feel of the room.

At the sound of the door, both heads turned toward him. Hannah, with her luscious brown curls and dove gray eyes. Reed, with his sandy blond hair and jade green eyes. Even bruised and bloody, they made quite a pair.

Reed let out a gasp when he looked Josh in the eyes.

But not a surprised one. No. This one held hope and awe. What the fuck?

Josh put a finger to his lips, urging them to be quiet. The jammer might block the camera signal for a bit, putting it on an automatic loop, but Josh couldn't be too sure with magic and werewolves in the mix. They both gave him a nod, Hannah wide-eyed but silent, Reed more curious than anything. Could the wolf smell Josh was different? Shit. Not something he should be thinking about. He needed to get them out of here.

Josh hurried over to them and checked for serious injuries. Reed seemed to be mostly healed, if not just a bit scraped up. Hannah had numerous lacerations and bruises, more than Reed, but looked okay. She was only a witch, not a wolf, so it made sense she would heal slower. How quickly a day could change things. He was human for fuck's sake, and now he was thinking about the healing times for different species. Talk about a game changer.

The locks on their chains and collars, luckily enough looked like the one on the metal door. How cocky were these bastards? He slid the key in, and with a snap, the locks opened, and the chains fell to the floor. Both rubbed their wrists as Josh moved quickly and efficiently to the collars at their neck. Fucking animals. Who the hell *collared* people?

Hannah put her hand on his arm, a jolt of electricity flashing between the two. She gasped, and he held back the urge to do so. She gave him a smile, and he desperately wanted to brush the curls from her face, soothing the bruises that couldn't hide her radiant beauty. Reed crouched behind her, still protective. He too was beautiful; with his chiseled cheekbones pronounced against the shadowed, healing bruises.

Dear God. He could understand thinking sexy thoughts about Hannah, but since when did he think males were attractive in any way? Either that weird connection confused him, or he really was falling for Reed. He didn't know which one, if either, he wanted to be true.

Reed bent over Hannah to whisper to them both. "Camera."

"Don't worry about them now. We have about ten more minutes and then we'd have to worry."

They both looked curious with a similar tilt of their heads but didn't say anything, merely nodding.

"Who are you?" Reed whispered, leaning closer.

"Josh." Why the hell had he said his name? He was never a name, just a presence, on any other mission. Why did he want them to know his name? Know him? "I'm no one. Just a friend."

"You're human." Hannah's surprised gasp was still whispered.

Exhaustion overwhelmed her features, and Josh couldn't take it anymore. He picked her up and cradled her to his chest when he stood. She felt warm in his hold. Right. An instant heat flooded his system as desire rocked him. That annoying connection flared, but he tamped it down. So not the time.

Reed let out a soft growl, pulling Josh to a stop.

Shit, she's his mate. And here he was holding her to his chest and liking it.

Josh cleared his throat. "Sorry, man, I'll let go of her soon. But we need to leave, and since you're stronger than me, I thought you'd be better at the front, protecting her." And he really liked the feel of her curves, even if this was the first and last time.

Reed look perplexed. Huh?

Josh didn't know what to think, but he still felt that connection to both of them. What the hell? He nodded at the other man, and they both left the room cautiously, Hannah still barefoot in Josh's arms. They hurried down the empty hall, past the shadowed corner where the unlucky guard lay dead, and to the window without a hitch. Reed pulled himself up and out of the small gap in the cement walls, and Josh lifted Hannah through. She looked back with a small smile, and his cock hardened again. Fuck, he was going to need therapy once he left these two. Hannah jumped into Reed's arms as Josh pulled himself through right behind them. With a possessive nod, Reed handed her back to Josh, and they all started walking quickly to the surrounding forest.

The hair on the back of Josh's neck rose at how easy it all had been. Something wasn't right, but he couldn't worry about everything all at once. He needed to get the two lovebirds out of here and away from him. That way he didn't have to think about the two ever again.

Right.

Josh could practically taste their nervousness as they reached the tree line. Barefoot and shirtless, Reed had to be cold as hell, but they didn't have time to get him properly dressed. They needed to get the fuck out of here.

A howl spilt the night, freezing them in place.

Oh hell.

Reed looked around, his nose on the wind.

"Josh, take care of Hannah; I'll watch our backs." Reed's deep voice resonated calmness. Not what Josh thought he'd hear from the man.

Hannah cleared her throat and elbowed Josh in the gut. Ouch.

"I can take care of myself. I'm a witch, you know. An earth witch at that. I'm in my element."

Josh let her slide down his body to the ground.

"I hope so," Reed said unenthusiastically. "Because we're surrounded."

Chapter 6

Hannah could feel the vibrations from the earth beneath her bare feet. The soil tickled the skin between her toes. She inhaled the woodsy scent, relishing the fact she was now connected to nature, not the stone walls holding her in. Relief spread through her at being part of the earth again. She'd spent too much time behind walls in chains. Her body was weakened, but soon, after time and fuel, she'd be at her peak. A true witch. She could smell the wolf scent of Reed, the human male scent of Josh. Wetness seeped from her core at the thought of both.

Hannah shook her head. Not quite the time to be drooling over two prime specimens of man. Well, wolf and "special" man. But whatever.

She took a deep breath and struggled to find her strength. They might die here, fighting together. But for some reason she had never felt as safe as she did right now, surrounded by these two men. Reed, who'd protected her with his body against the onslaught of lead bullets and held her through the night for warmth. Josh, the stranger who'd risked his life for two prisoners. He wasn't completely human; he held something else along the ridges of his aura, but she couldn't discern what.

But it wasn't just that they both protected her. No, usually she could accomplish that herself because she hated feeling weak. No, for some reason, an unknown force pulled her toward the two men, who at the moment stood on either side of her, blocking her from an outside enemy. There was a tingling sensation, a connection between her and each of the men.

Oh goddess.

What kind of person wanted two men at the same time? Two strangers at that. Not to mention the fact that who knew how many dangerous werewolves were about to attack them? Not the greatest of timing.

Reed let out a growl. "They're coming. Try to get away and be safe." He looked into her eyes, pleading, before doing the same to Josh.

Reed planted his feet, his fists clenched. Josh did the same on the other side of her, yet with a gun in one hand and a blade in another. As a human, he would need all the protection he could get. A gun wouldn't necessarily kill the beasts, but it would slow them down. And frankly, he looked damn sexy all armored up. Reed looked sexy, too, with his natural charisma and powerful werewolf body.

And, this was totally not the time again to let her thoughts wander.

But what a place they would go.

Hannah gave a nod and closed her eyes, calling to the earth. She might be a healer, but she could still go on the offensive with the earth and kick ass if she had too. Well, at least she hoped he could. She'd trained with her mother—Hannah held back the sharp pain of loss at the thought—but she really hadn't used it. Plus the last few days and her tiredness caused her bones to ache.

Another wolf's howl echoed in the not-too-far-distance. Hannah concentrated and moved her arms like an orchestra conductor to take a large pile of soil, rocks, and roots in her hold. The resulting mass looked like a crested wave and slammed into the wolves trying to come from behind in a sneak attack.

Power surged through her as she lifted up the dirt and felt the connection to the earth deep in her tissues and tendons. When she used this power she always felt like she was on top of the world and could stop anything. The rough wave looked like a cresting peak of control that she alone had the knowledge and capability of. It smelled of earth, nature, and home—everything she held dear. As wave hit the wolves, her power fluctuated back and shocked her body. Hurting any living thing forced her to pay a price, but in this case it was worth it.

Stupid wolves. Didn't they know she could feel them when they trampled too heavy-footed on her earth?

Josh and Reed each granted her a look of pleasant surprise then a sexy smile.

They'd underestimated her. They wouldn't do it again.

But she was glad they approved of her. She wasn't some weakling needing help, however soft she might be inside and out. And she certainly didn't need a strong man to hold on to, though it couldn't hurt. And if there were *two* strong men...

And going away from that subject.

Josh fired into the mass of fur and flesh coming down on him. A sharp cry followed. Good, he'd hit one. The smell of seared flesh hit her nose, and she was grateful for Josh's weaponry.

Reed stood by her side, apparently determined not to leave her. Rather than changing into a wolf, he fought as a man, hand to paw. An ugly gray wolf jumped toward his face, and he crushed its skull. With his bare hands. *Geez.* She figured he was fighting as a man because the lack of food had cost him some energy. But apparently he wasn't lacking in strength. And Reed thought he wasn't Alpha enough. He was plenty for her. And then some.

His slender, lithe body packed heat and strength. Lickable.

And enough of that.

She sent another wave of earth towards a group of wolves. With a flick of her wrist, she buried another wolf and it yelped in pain. She balled her hand into a fist and grabbed a large rock with her powers and hurled it at another wolf, leaving it in a furry mass on the dirt floor. With another movement of her arms, a mound of soil fell on two more wolves. They yelped a bit louder than before. Apparently the sexual tension from her and the men increased the force of her magic. Interesting.

More wolves came from every direction. She concentrated and used the roots of the trees around her to trip them up by reaching out and grabbing their paws and tails. But she could only use a few trees. She wasn't strong enough to do more than that. Out of the corner of her eye, she saw Josh throw his empty gun to the ground as a wolf jumped on him. He pivoted, took out another blade and stabbed his opponent in the flank.

She pulled deep within for more power, knowing she would need rest and food once they made it out of here. If they made it out of here.

Over her other shoulder, she saw that Reed continued to fight, though blood seeped out of various nicks and claw marks. He growled before pulling the fur of another wolf to use for leverage as he broke its neck. The crack barely made a sound over the loud, vicious sounds of the battle at hand. Blood and fur littered the ground in an abstract pattern, mingling with the soils and snow.

Both men's backs were turned from her, and her attention lay on the two wolves coming for her. She braced herself for their attack, arms ready to pull at her magic to bury them in earth. Her concentration was focused on them so intensely she didn't hear the footsteps behind her until it was too late.

A hand gripped her hair and pulled her backwards. The wolves that crouched in front of her turned their backs, shielding her from Josh and Reed. The man that held her turned her toward him.

Caym.

The demon.

He fisted one hand in her curls, and the other came to stroke her face.

Shudders racked her body, and fear took hold. This was it. She'd die by his hand. If she were lucky. Bile rose in her throat at the thought of what else he could do.

"Hannah!" Reed shouted behind her, trying to reach her. But then he grunted, and she could only guess something had stopped him.

She looked into the demon's dark, fathomless eyes.

Pure evil. But not callous like Corbin. Who was the true master? And why did she care?

"Get your hands off of her." Josh's fist connected with the demon's face, forcing Caym's head to snap back.

The demon laughed.

He laughed. What kind of evil was he?

Caym stopped stroking her face then shot out his arm in a blink of an eye to grab Josh's.

No.

Josh struggled to get free, but the demon smiled and bit into the meaty part of Josh's forearm.

Dear goddess.

Hannah screamed, but Josh didn't. He looked at the demon then punched him square in the face, before ripping his arm from the demon's sharpened teeth. Caym gave an odd smile then, after, letting Hannah drop to the ground, walked away.

They reached for each other, and Josh helped Hannah to her feet. She bent down, tearing a piece of fabric off her skirt to try and stop the bleeding. Jagged tears surrounded the bite. Blood flowed freely down his arm, and tears filled Hannah's eyes. The wound looked horrible. And what did a demon bite do? Did it turn him into one? Would it infect him and make him sick? Or kill him? Shudders slid down her spine.

Oh goddess.

Hannah looked up into Josh's face. He'd gone pale, with a sickly green hue. She needed to clean the wound then try and heal him. But she didn't know the consequences of that. And there were always consequences working with something a witch didn't know. Not to mention they were in the middle of a fight.

Though she suddenly realized it'd gone quiet. Hannah looked over her shoulder, surprised to see Reed killing the last wolf. A mound of dead fur and flesh surrounded him, but he didn't seem to care. Bloodied and sweaty, he walked towards them, determination on his face.

Everyone who didn't lie in the pile of death seemed to have vanished. What on earth? Was this all a joke to them? Why had the others left? And why had the demon bitten Josh?

Something didn't add up, but pinged on her memory. She buried it back though; she had to think about Josh and Reed. And herself.

Reed finally made it to them and placed one hand on her cheek and the other on Josh's shoulder. With her hand still on Josh's arm, the three of them gasped. A spark of electricity, magic, or just a simple connection flowed through them. Josh grunted and swayed against her body. Reed widened his eyes and gave a small smile, while she bit her lip in confusion. The three of them glanced at each other but didn't speak.

Reed lowered his hands while they all looked at each other for answers. *What was that? Are we going to talk about it?*

"We need to find some place to go," Josh whispered as he looked up toward the sky.

Apparently they were going to ignore the spark. Hannah grumbled inwardly.

She followed Josh's gaze. *Oh crap.* A blizzard. Just what they needed. Dark clouds moved in overhead and the wind picked up, howling through the trees. Fat snowflakes began to fall from the sky, quickly accumulating on the forest floor. With each gust of wind, the temperature dropped another couple of degrees, chilling her to the bone.

Reed went to Josh's side and put the other man's arm around his shoulders. Then he, because Reed was smaller than Josh, leaned in and wrapped his arm around Josh's waist to lift him slightly off the ground.

"I can walk myself," was Josh's disgruntled response.

"I'm sure you can. But we need to get out of here quickly. Let us help you." Reed's smooth voice held a hint of nervousness but a calming undertone.

They ran together through the forest. Well, they ran as best as they could with two barefoot people half-carrying an injured human. The snow began to fall around them about twenty minutes into their escape. Hannah panted heavy breaths, praying they would find somewhere to ride out the storm soon. From the looks on both men's faces, their thoughts ran along the same paths.

But other thoughts threatening to edge out the panic and hope for shelter worried her. What would they do when they got there?

And what would they do about each other? Was she really thinking about a ménage with these two men just because they panted for each other in a few brief moments? How will each of them react? How should she react?

Even as the cold surrounded her, her body warmed to the thought of being loved and touched by these two men. Tingles shot up her body and she didn't bother to suppress them. They kept the cold from seeping into her bones more than it already had and made her think of a future that she didn't have before. A future with two men. Could it really work? Did she want it to?

Chapter 7

Jesus, his chest hurt. Reed shook off the burning pain of newly healed tissues and even newer slices and bruises and heaved Josh a bit farther into the forest. He didn't know why the surviving wolves had left, but Reed thanked whatever the reason. Though he might have been stronger than the wolves that leapt at him with their gleaming teeth and sharp claws, he couldn't have lasted much longer.

Hannah's breath came out in fast pants on the other side of Josh. They needed to get to shelter soon. But Reed couldn't help but remember the way she'd stood and fought by their sides. *Dear Lord, she was amazing.* He'd never seen magic like that, hadn't even known earth witches possessed that type of power. Add into the fact she was a rare healer and his Hannah was a force to be reckoned with. And damn sexy when she did it.

And Josh. For a human, his fighting and perseverance rivaled most Alpha's. When he'd run out of ammunition, he'd gone for his blades and hand to hand without even looking like he was thinking. Thank God for his training, whatever that was. The human that didn't smell quite human was a mystery to him.

A damn sexy mystery.

Reed lifted Josh a bit more, trailing the human's feet in the snow. Whatever the demon had done to him, it didn't look good. Josh leaned heavily against Reed and groaned with each stumble and time they had to climb over a large hill or rock. His skin had paled enough that Reed didn't even think he had any blood at all. And scariest of all, though it was freezing, Josh's body warmed Reed's side like a furnace.

Snow fell in earnest around them, beauty in an evil nightmare. The trees parted farther up their makeshift path, revealing a hopeful shadow.

Please don't let me be hallucinating like a man dying of thirst in a desert.

"I think I see a cabin up ahead. The lights are out so I don't think anyone's home. But at least it has a roof." Relief spread through him as he told the others.

"Where? I don't see it." Hannah couldn't hold back her hope; it reflected in her voice.

"Me neither." Josh's voice was weak, filled with pain.

"It's there; I can just see farther than you. But it's there. Believe me."

They both nodded. Again, relief filled his chest at the thought of their trust.

They walked a bit farther until the cabin came into view for everyone. With a grunt of relief, they reached the door. Reed let Josh sway on his own two feet, leaning against Hannah, as he went to the door. Locked. Reed took about two seconds to search for the key before shouldering the door open. The lock busted with an audible snap, and he ushered them both in.

Hannah flicked the light switch to find no electricity. Josh looked lost on his feet, so Reed moved to help him stand, while Hannah found a lantern and matches. The soft glow illuminated what appeared to be a hunting cabin. The floor plan was larger than most hunting cabins he'd seen. A small living room with a hallway off to the side led to most likely a bedroom. A table and chairs stood off to the side in a makeshift dining room and there was a doorway to what must be the kitchen. Fur skins littered the wooden floors, insulating whatever heat it could. Stuffed dear, bear, and wolf heads adorned the walls.

Reed gulped. He *really* hoped those were all normal animals and not werewolves. Not something to think about.

Luckily, during their trek to this abandoned cabin, they'd left Central land and now stood on neutral land. No Pack held deed so Reed was safe from meeting another Pack and be called out for trespassing. But they weren't on Redwood land either. No, they were further away then when they started. They'd had to go in the opposite direction of his Pack because they wouldn't be able to reach the Redwood land without crossing the Central land unless they made a wide circle. It sucked but couldn't have been avoided. They were sheltered, maybe would even be fed soon. And they were away from the Centrals, at least for the time being. Things could be worse.

The feel of Josh's weight against him reminded Reed of where he was. *Oh yeah, things were worse.* They needed to take a look at that bite.

Reed shifted slightly and inhaled Josh's scent. He smelled of ponderosa pine, a sweet wood. Odd, since that tree was typically found in the southwest, but that really wasn't the point.

Reed cursed under his breath, startling Josh. He shouldn't be sniffing this man, no. He had Hannah. And Josh was most likely a narrowly straight man.

But hell. Reed's wolf knew.

"He's our mate, too."

Shit.

When Josh had first walked through that metal door to rescue him and Hannah, Reed had gasped. The human had stood tall, with a powerful body that demanded attention—and maybe Reed's tongue. He had brown hair that stood up in long spikes that begged for Reed's hands and blue eyes that saw into Reed's soul. When the connection set in and his wolf growled in contentment,

Reed knew he was done for. His cock, already hard from Hannah's presence, had throbbed and ached for release.

How fucked up was fate anyway?

How could he have *two* mates at the *same time*? Was he supposed to choose? Could he have them both?

What if they both walked away?

Holy shit.

This was why he didn't really want a mate to begin with. All decisions went out the door and choices right along with them, and the world revolved around another person who may or may not even return their love. And if they weren't a werewolf, they couldn't feel the mating heat. It was just a simple attraction to them.

Fuck.

Again, Reed shook out his thoughts. He didn't have time to worry about the inevitable. No, he needed to get Josh resting and try to figure out what to do with a fucking demon bite. Not to mention, he still had the overwhelming need to protect Hannah, to protect them both, because, even if they both walked away from him once he told them they were his mates, they were still his mates. He protected what was his.

Huh. Who knew he had such Alpha tendencies?

"Reed, get Josh to the couch," Hannah ordered in a soft voice. "I'll set the wards."

Reed merely lifted a brow at her stern, yet, sexy tone while Josh whistled in appreciation.

Their mate was full of surprises.

Wait, their?

So, not going there. He couldn't. It was taboo. But he still smiled at the thought. Could it work?

Reed walked Josh to one of the plush brown couches and set him down carefully.

Josh winced in pain.

"Shit, did I hurt you? How can I help?" Because at this moment, he'd do just about anything to save him. Anything.

"No, you didn't do anything." Josh heaved a breath as Reed pushed him onto his back and covered him with the blanket from the back of the couch. "My arm just hurts like hell. What was that thing, and why did it bite me?"

Reed let out a breath. He could almost forget Josh was human until he'd ask a question like that.

"It was a demon."

Josh's eyebrows rose. "That's a new one."

Reed would've asked what he meant by that, but then he got a good look at the wound on Josh's forearm.

It looked as if a ravaging beast had taken hold of the flesh and tugged and torn until a mess of ligaments, muscles, and flesh swam in a pool of blood. He was pretty sure he could see bone fragments floating in the open wound, as well one of the bones in the forearm, though he didn't know if it was the radius or ulna.

The man must have been in an incredible amount of pain. Yet, except for the green hue of his skin and occasional moan or grunt, Josh struggled through it like a pro. What atrocities had the man seen if he was able to withstand this with only minor complaint and remain conscious?

Reed went to the kitchen, and thankfully, the water still worked. He filled a bowl and found some towels. On the way back, he noticed food stores and thanked whatever hunter had left there them for a rainy day because the three of them sure needed it.

Carefully, Reed cleaned the drying blood around the wound, doing his best not to aggravate it further. Josh sucked in a breath through his teeth when Reed got too close to the edges.

"Sorry, man."

"It's okay. It needs to be done. It just hurts like a bitch, you know?" Josh smiled at him, and Reed could feel his face heat to the tips of his ears.

Damn, the man was sexy.

Dark brown hair, cut close in the back, but slightly longer in the front, so it spiked up just a bit. Pale, scarred skin on a slightly bulkier and taller body than his own. Ocean blue eyes that seemed to change to a foamy blue in the light.

Like before with Hannah, Reed felt the urge to pick up a brush and paint.

Trying to get a closer look at the wound, Reed placed his arm on Josh's bare skin. The man gasped at his touch.

Reed pulled back, but not before he saw a wave of desire flash across Josh's face. The other man's pupils dilated and his lips parted, a flush rising to his pale skin.

Interesting.

Was Josh gay? No, bi maybe, like him. He'd seen the way Josh looked at Hannah. The expression was probably a mirror image of his own face, but for some reason, he didn't feel a twinge of jealousy, only a feeling of rightness. In fact, the idea of the three of them felt even more right than the idea of just him and Hannah alone. Weird.

"The wards are set; we're as safe as we can be, considering. How's our patient?" Hannah's brisk steps broke whatever heat had passed between the two men, but Reed didn't care too much. He was too busy looking at the rosy-cheeked beauty walking towards them.

Still barefoot, she'd wrapped herself in one of the furs on the mantel and looked like a sexy cavewoman with her curly hair going every which way.

Reed rubbed the back of his neck, trying to release some of the sexual tension piling onto the tension from their imprisonment. His cock rubbed against the zipper of his jeans, threatening to leave a permanent scar. Tingles shot up his arms as her bitter apple and honey scent floated on the air to him, mixing with Josh's ponderosa pine and he held back a groan. These two would be the death of him.

"I cleaned his wound, but I didn't try and bandage it. I thought you'd look at it first."

She blushed. "Okay."

Reed moved back but didn't get out of her way completely. He wanted to see her work, to smell her honey and crisp apple scent. She put her small hands around the wound, her teeth biting her bottom lip and tears forming in her eyes. They both gasped as Reed felt the energy in the room shift. The sexual tension calmed as the energy swayed and ebbed before funneling through Hannah and into Josh. He watched as parts of Josh's arm knitted back together, ligaments winding against the muscle and tissue and his skin fusing together.

Really cool, but still kind of gross. He could totally do a project with some acrylics on canvas.

"Oh, darn it," Hannah cursed under her breath.

Reed gave a look to Josh. *Yeah, she was really cute when she tried to curse.*

"What is it?" Josh sounded worried.

Not surprising because Reed was worried too.

"It won't close all the way. I was worried to even attempt this in the first place since I've never healed a demon bite before, but it looked so bad I couldn't *not* do it. You know?" She bit into her lip. She was gonna draw blood soon if she didn't quit doing that.

"It's okay, Hannah. You tried. Thank you." Josh placed his hand on hers and gave it a squeeze.

Reed had the sudden urge to join them but held back.

The wound indeed looked better but was not healed per se. It still looked red and angry around the bite mark, and he was sure that, unless Hannah could use some herbs, it would be infected soon. Plus, they still had to contend with the whole bitten-by-a-demon thing and its repercussions.

All three looked at each other. The underlying current of unease at the unknown infection and the connections between them lay heavy.

"Reed, let me heal those bites from the wolves; that way you are at full strength."

Though he really wanted her hands on him, he shook his head. "I don't want you to use up all your energy; I'll heal."

"No, really, it's okay. As long as I can go outside at some point and recharge and get some food and sleep, I'll be fine. Please, let me help you."

He gave Josh a look, who smiled back at him. "Okay."

She placed her cool hands on his overheated chest, and he felt the warmth and tingles that came from her healing. He could only imagine those precious hands on other parts of his anatomy. Coincidently, said part started to rise in attention at her touch.

This is looking to be a hard night. Hard being the operative word.

When she finished, Reed cleared his throat again. *I really need to stop doing that.* "Let's get Josh to one of the beds and light a fire in there and out here. The couch can't be comfortable."

"It's okay." Josh gave a pained laugh.

"That settles it then. We'll light the fires, try to get something to eat and maybe some sleep. I can hear anything coming at us for a mile or so since we're so isolated. What about your wards?"

"I set them about that far, as well, so I'll know. We'll be prepared, but I don't want to stay here too long."

"I agree," Josh mumbled, fading into sleep. "Just don't leave me alone too long and don't go too far. I like you guys close." Josh fell asleep as soon as they laid him in the large queen-sized bed in the room with the other fireplace.

Wow, the guy must really be out of it if he was spouting his thoughts like that. Reed kind of liked it.

Reed smiled down at the human. "Don't worry, I'll protect you."

Josh smiled in his sleep, and Reed let him be, walking out of the room towards his other mate. He took her hand, leading her to the couch. She sat with a vacant expression on her face.

"Hannah, what can I do for you? I'm going look around the cabin and get you some shoes, but what else?"

She smiled at him and shook her head. "I don't know; everything's different. What they did back there..." Her voice broke, cutting off her sentence.

Reed placed an arm around her shoulders, pulling her into his side. He didn't want to think about what had gone on in that stone basement. The blood, the pain, the loss. It was too much.

"Shh, it'll be okay. You're tough. I've seen you. We'll figure it out. Together." At least he hoped.

"I'm just so tired, but I don't want to sleep." Her eyes held horrors he knew would take time to get over, if she ever did.

"Okay, just lie down on the couch and rest. You don't need to sleep. I'm going to go in Josh's room, get the fire set, and do the same in here. We need to find a way to contact someone. If we can't then we'll get out of here soon and get help. I'll look for some clothes for us, then some food. How does that sound?" Telling her his plans made him feel better, like he might actually accomplish something. If she knew he wanted to care for her and Josh, maybe she'd relax enough to sleep.

"Let me help." She made motions of getting up, but Reed stopped her.

"No, not now. Let me get everything but the food. I think you may need to help me with that part." He blushed a bit. "I'm not a great cook, so that might be your job. But you rest."

"I'm better with potions than food, but I can do my best."

"That's all I ask." He gave her a smile, fought the urge to kiss her goodnight, and went to do his chores. At least doing something productive would help his rising fears—and rising erection.

"Once Josh sleeps a bit," Hannah said when Reed came back from Josh's room, "he'll hopefully be able to move. I don't like staying here. Away from everyone." That haunted look came back in her eyes.

Reed would have done anything to sweep that look away.

He looked around the cabin, noting the lack of phones or radios. Well crap. It looked as though they'd have to wait out their growing strength before they made it home. Wherever home was for his two mates. Reed couldn't be so lucky to think their home would be his.

"There are no phones, are there?" Hannah whispered.

Reed shook his head. "No, but when we get rested, we can go to my Pack, the Redwoods. They'll take care of us. Protect us." He held his breath, waiting for her response.

Hannah nodded. "Okay." A sad look came into her eyes. "I don't have anywhere else to go."

Reed felt for her. How horrible would it be to be Packless? Have no connections? No family?

"I'll take care of you," he promised.

She batted his arm. "I said I can take care of myself."

Reed smiled. "Then you can take care of me, too."

She smiled back. "Sounds like a plan."

They paused as the heat grew between them. Reed shifted, his arousal increasing as he inhaled her luscious scent.

Hannah's breaths came in shallow pants. Her cheeks reddened as she lowered her eyes, her eyelashes dusting the tops of those rosy cheeks.

"I think I'll try and get some sleep in the room across from Josh's, the heat reaches there."

She stood up quickly, and practically ran to the room like a frightened rabbit.

Too bad Reed was a wolf and liked to chase.

"Sounds good to me. Let's go."

Reed ignored his wolf. He looked down the hall where his two potential mates lay across the expanse of the hallway from each other. No, this wouldn't be complicated at all. *Right.*

Chapter 8

Josh cracked open his eyes, straining at the glow of the roaring fire by his bedside. He quickly shut them again against the raging headache currently doing an Irish jig on his temples. Crap, where was he? Images of wolves and sharp teeth, curly brown hair, then green eyes flooded his mind. Oh yeah, Reed and Hannah.

He'd saved them. Well, he got them out; they seemed fit enough to save themselves. Another image, this time of the man— no demon—with deep black eyes and sharp teeth impaling his flesh. He flinched at the memory, causing pain to lash up his arm.

Fuck.

When he opened his eyes again, he surveyed his surroundings. The large wooden sleigh bed he slept in took up most of the room. Dark, musty drapes covered the windows so he couldn't tell if it was day or night. But cold seemed to slip through the slits, letting him know the storm was either just starting fully or in the middle of its downpour.

On the side wall, a large brick fireplace stood out, heating the room. Josh guessed that either Reed or Hannah had lit it for him, not wanting him to be cold. For some reason that warmed him from the inside out.

Josh tried to swallow, but it caught on his tongue. It felt as though he'd eaten dried rags and then chased them down with cotton. He needed water or something to sooth his aching throat, but couldn't call out for help or find the energy to get out of bed and get to Hannah and Reed. How was he supposed to leave the cabin and go for help if he couldn't even get out of bed?

He shook his head, trying to clear it of sleep as flashes of his dreams came back. Memories of demons with forked tongues, fire burning flesh, and screams made him want to shudder in fear. But he didn't. He couldn't be weak. Not when others needed him.

But those weren't the only dreams bugging his subconscious. No, they mingled with images of a gray-eyed beauty and her green-eyed companion. Reed and Hannah had loved and kissed and sexed him throughout his fantasy. Panting, moaning, and thrusting interplayed with chanting and proclamations of forever and love.

Josh didn't know which of the two dreams frightened him more. Painful death by fire and demons or the love of two supernaturals.

Not to mention the fact he'd never known he was attracted to men. But, damn, Reed was sexy as hell. And by the gasps and heated looks on the other man's face, Reed thought the same of Josh. What was he going to do with that?

And hell, Reed and Hannah were mates. They might not have fully connected, or whatever the hell werewolves did in a mating, but they were for each other. Josh was the odd man out. Again.

Some part of him, though, couldn't forget the energy that shot through them when they all touched at the same time. There was a link there, better left ignored in his opinion. He'd wanted to make sure they were alive, not impede on their ogling love and some shit.

Josh let out a sigh. *Keep telling yourself that, man.*

Straining almost every muscle he had, Josh slid himself out of bed, his feet flinching at the feel of the cool wood beneath him. Sometime during his sleep, someone had taken off his shirt, boots, and socks.

Josh felts his skin heat at the thought of Reed or Hannah—or both—touching his bare skin.

Enough of that.

He pulled himself to a standing position, releasing a groan.

Dear God, every joint in his body hurt like that of an elderly man.

Josh looked toward the end of the bed to find his shirt laid out. It was still dirty, with soil and bloodstains, but didn't smell that bad, so he shrugged it on, exhaling an oath when he did. *Yeah, this is going to be a long day.*

The cotton slipped over his arm, and he gasped out in pain.

The demon bite.

If only he could forget.

Josh looked down at the offending wound. Though Hannah had helped it along some in the healing process, it was nowhere near where it needed to be. Red, angry lashes spread out from the bite like a sadistic web. He hated to think it, but it looked like an infection that was spreading. But he didn't want to think about that. Apparently he didn't want to think about a lot of things lately.

He pulled his socks and boots on, grateful to whoever had put them near the fireplace. They were nice and toasty on his cold feet. Sucking in a deep breath and gathering his strength, he left the warmth of the bedroom and ventured out to the living room. The resulting image made him smile and his cock harden.

Hannah sat before the fireplace, legs crossed in a position that promised more aerobic activities in his mind.

Her corkscrew curls circled her face, making it look like she'd just rolled out of bed after a long night of passion. Damn, had she and Reed done anything when he'd been asleep? So not his business, but the image that ran across his mind made him want to groan with need.

Hannah bit her lip in concentration, a delectable habit of hers, while chanting something he couldn't quite make out. From the looks of it, she was meditating and doing a damn sexy job of it.

The front door opened, letting in the chill from the outside. Josh immediately pivoted towards the intruder, blocking Hannah from their path. He cringed at the sharp pain digging into his side from his fast movement but ignored it.

Reed stood in the doorway, red-cheeked and wide-eyed. He gave Josh a worried look then quickly covered it up with a smile.

Damn that smile could stop a train in its tracks.

Reed shut the door behind him, shook off the snow that had collected on his hair and shoulders, and came farther into the room.

"Good to see you up, Josh." Reed looked him over, his gaze leaving scorch marks as it passed.

"Yes, Josh, how are you feeling?"

Josh spun around to Hannah, who'd opened her eyes and smiled warmly at both of them.

Reed and he both started toward her to help her to a standing position, but she waved them off, gracefully straightening her legs and stretching her back like a cat.

Like a fucking sexy ballerina. Damn.

Josh coughed to cover his staring. "I'm feeling a bit groggy and could use some water. But the sleep helped."

"Oh, I'll go get you some." Hannah stretched one last time and ran to get him a glass before Josh could even open his mouth to say he could do it.

"Let her help you; you scared her. Me too." Reed smiled again and led him to the couch where they both sat.

Hannah hurried back in as they were getting comfortable.

"Here you go; I hope this helps." She smiled again and Josh almost fell in love right there.

Not something he should be doing.

Reed and Josh left enough space on the couch for her to sit in the middle. She snuggled up between them, reminding him of a very vivid dream with the three of them. Josh shifted a bit to relieve the pressure against his zipper.

His thought from before repeated like a loop in his brain. *Gonna be a long day.*

"We need to get out of here. I don't feel comfortable staying in a cabin we don't know, stealing from them, hiding from someone—or something—trying to kill us." Josh was adamant on this. Fear crawled up his spine at the thought of what hunted them.

"We know," Reed said. "The snow's getting pretty bad out there though. I don't know if we can hoof our way out of here. Plus, we needed to make sure we were all ready for the journey."

Reed paused, and Josh felt his stomach fall. They'd waited because of him. He hated being the weak one—the human.

"I can't get a hold of the Pack at the moment," Reed continued. "We're essentially cut off, but at least we have each other."

Josh liked the sound of that.

"Okay, I understand. What about our defenses?" Something he was good at.

Hannah spoke up. "Well, between my wards and Reed's senses, we should be able to get fair warning. It's the best we can hope for the time being."

Josh was at a loss. Did they even need him? He didn't know how he felt about that.

"Josh, I need to know something." Reed looked serious, almost as if he didn't want to know the answer.

"Okay."

"How did you find us? Why did you help us?"

Josh looked at both of them sitting stock still on the couch, as if waiting for him to tell them he was in on the Central's deal. He couldn't blame them for their worry, but it still stung just a bit.

"I'm a Finder."

Silence.

Okay, apparently I need to explain exactly what that is.

Josh rubbed the back of his neck, suddenly nervous about what they would think of him.

Hannah's soft voice urged him to continue. "What's a Finder, Josh?"

"I can Find anyone I've met before. Anywhere and anytime. I just need to see their face personally, and then I can concentrate on the memory and Find them."

"That's remarkable," Hannah whispered.

"I agree, but you've never met me. I'd remember." Reed quirked a brow.

Did they not believe him?

"I know. I've never seen either of you before. But when some kids mentioned you, flashes of your lives and who you were came to me. I had to Find you."

Hannah brought her hand to her mouth, trembling. "Thank you."

Josh held her other hand. "You're welcome. I don't know why the two of you are so special, and why things worked the way they did. But I'm not unhappy about it. I'm glad I Found you."

Reed nodded and something flashed across his green eyes.

Huh?

Relief spread through him at their acceptances, but he didn't know why he'd told them exactly. He'd never told another soul outside his family about his gift—if it could be called that. But it felt good—complete even—to do so with them.

"I knew I smelled something different about you," Reed murmured.

"Are you saying I smell?" Josh fought the urge to sniff his dirty shirt and sat back slightly offended.

"No, no." Reed waved his hands. "I'm a wolf, remember? I have a better sense of smell, and while your scent was definitely human, it held a trace of something different. Now I know why."

"Oh." Josh shrugged, feeling slightly better.

"Were you always this way?" Hannah wondered aloud.

Josh nodded. "I don't remember *not* having this ability, so yes. And no, it wasn't some military experiment or anything."

All three laughed, the tension of their conversation dissolving away.

On an offhand thought, Josh closed his eyes and tried to Find Corbin, just to see if the bastard was close. But his vision grew hazy, almost at a disconnect.

What the hell?

He rubbed his temples as a headache set in.

"What's wrong, Josh?" Hannah asked.

"I just tried to Find Corbin. But I think the wards or something is messing it up. Don't worry; I'm sure it's nothing." The bite mark on his arm tingled, but Josh tried not to connect the two incidents. No, it was just the wards. It had to be. His Finding would come back, and everything would be normal. He'd go home. Alone.

"You know, Josh, that's a very useful talent," Reed commented.

Ice settled in Josh's chest. "I won't be used by anyone for anything."

Hurt crossed Reed's face and Josh backed down. "That wasn't what I meant. I'm sorry. I was just complimenting your gift. Not everyone can say they are useful in the world. I would never use you for myself or my Pack. And if they go against their nature and even think about using you, then they'd have to deal with me." His eyes grew hard, threatening.

"Me too," Hannah added in, a fierce expression on her face.

Warmth filled his chest at their promise of protection and acceptance. He'd never thought he'd ever tell anyone what he was, let alone feel as though they understood and wanted to know more. It was interesting to say the least.

Josh let out a breath. "It's okay. I'm sorry for overreacting. It's just odd to have others know what I am, ya know?"

Reed and Hannah looked at each other before smiling at him.

Yeah, the wolf and the witch would know for sure.

Hannah reached out and grabbed both of their hands, warmth infusing into his bones.

He shouldn't get used to this. He *couldn't* get used to this.

The windows rattled as the wind howled outside. Cold seeped underneath the panes and doorways, cooling the room considerably, despite the roaring fire. His arm rocked with pain, but he didn't flinch because he didn't want to worry the others.

Reed went to the door, making sure it was secured. Hannah put another log on the fire, to keep the warmth from leeching to the outside. Josh looked through the windows to see the blizzard had come down on them. Fat snowflakes fell to the ground in a blur. The wind picked up, carrying snow-drifts and slamming them into the surrounding trees and walls of the cabin. The snow had already accumulated to what Josh estimated to be at least three feet—and counting.

Shit, it looked as though they'd be stuck here for a lot longer than they wanted.

Josh tried not to feel excited about sharing a small cabin with two people who drove up his sex drive faster than anything he'd ever felt, but he couldn't do it.

If he was going to be stuck with them indefinitely, he'd use it to his advantage. Even if it was going to kill him that much more to say goodbye when the time came.

Hannah came up from behind him, putting her hand in his. "Thank you again, Josh." He turned toward her. Tears filled her eyes, but they didn't fall. "I don't know what we would have done. The things they did to me were horrible. But I couldn't watch them hurt Reed anymore." A single tear fell, leaving a thin trail down her face.

Josh wiped the tear from her cheek, hating to see her in pain. "I'm so sorry you had to go through that. But I'd Find you again if I had to."

Hannah looked down at the bite mark on his arm that throbbed with his heartbeat.

"Yes, Hannah, I'd do *everything* again," Josh stressed.

"Thank you, Josh. For everything." Reed came up behind Hannah holding her shoulder.

Josh's stomach grumbled, and he blushed. *Well, that broke the moment.*

"Oh, you must be starving." Hannah bit her lip. Damn she was cute, but why was she nervous? "Reed and I ate some canned green beans and carrots, but we aren't really good cooks. There is a gas stove so we don't have to worry about electricity. Oh, and plenty of frozen meat, starches, and canned goods. We just can't put a meal together and not risk poisoning ourselves."

Reed shook his head, looking unrepentant. "What can I say? I'm good at bachelor food or going to one of my brothers' houses. Plus my brother Jasper just mated Willow, who's a baker. I'm in love with her cooking." A light went on in his eyes, like he was remembering good food and fond memories.

What would it be like to have a family that would feed you and give you such good memories? Josh just couldn't comprehend that.

"Well then, today's your lucky day. I'm a pretty decent cook. I'm not gourmet or anything, but I'll feed you."

Reed's face brightened. "Thank God. I may be a wolf, but there is only so much meat I can eat without missing side dishes."

Hannah smiled then bit her lip. "I know. I'm not a wolf, so anything you can make would put me in your debt forever."

Josh liked the sound of that.

"Oh," Hannah continued. "if you ever need a potion or herb concoction, then I'm your girl."

"I'll keep that in mind," Josh said.

"I can paint you a picture of our meal if you want, or something to add ambiance, but that's about it," Reed added in.

Josh quirked a brow as he went to the pantry to find some potatoes. "You paint?" He went to the ice box and got lucky and found some frozen vegetables.

Reed smiled. "I'm an artist."

"By that smile, I'd say you love it." Hannah sat on the counter, watching Josh cut potatoes into cubes.

Reed shrugged. "It's my life. I've been doing it awhile; I love it."

Josh turned toward him while he browned some stew meat in a large skillet on the gas stove. "How long is awhile?"

"About a century or so."

Hannah looked Reed up and down. "And you don't look a day over ninety."

They broke out into laughter, not at all ill at ease with Reed's age. What would it be like to be so long-lived?

Josh shook his head to clear his thoughts. "So, Reed, tell me about your family. I heard you mention some of them, but I don't remember them all."

"Oh, I have tons of family to go around." Reed explained. "I have five brothers and one sister."

Hannah and Josh stood wide-eyed.

"There are *seven* of you?" Josh asked.

"Yep, my poor mother."

They chuckled at Reed's answer.

"Kade is the eldest," Reed explained. "Then Jasper, Adam, me, the twins, Maddox and North, then our baby sister, Cailin."

"So many boys. How did your mom manage?" Hannah asked.

"I don't think the six of us were too bad. Cailin though is a trouble-maker. She's just hitting her stride at twenty-three. I'm afraid to see what will happen when she gets older."

"Wait," Josh interrupted. "Cailin is the *baby* at twenty-three?"

"I told you I'm almost a century—ninety-eight actually. Cailin's still our baby sister. And with six older brothers she doesn't forget it." Reed gave a smile only a big brother bent on terrorizing his younger sister could give.

Or at least that's what Josh thought a look of terrorizing one's little sister would look like. He didn't have any siblings to really know.

"Wow, I'm only twenty-five. You must think I'm a toddler." Hannah looked troubled at this thought, but didn't bite her lip.

Reed reached out and held her hand. "It's not the same thing at all. Cailin and you are both adults. It's just Cailin's my sister, while you are definitely not." Reed smiled, and Josh felt as though he was intruding.

"And you're pretty close to my age—twenty-nine." Josh pointed to himself with a ladle.

"Well thank the goddess for that." Hannah said. "I guess we'll just have to be careful with the old man over here."

Reed looked on in mock-outrage. "Hey, you two whipper-snappers. When I was young we respected our elders. And I can always get us the senior discounts." Reed wiggled his eyebrows and Josh threw a dish towel at him.

It was nice to laugh and play around about something, and just for a moment, forget the dangers lurking outside.

Reed smiled. "So tell me about you, Josh. Any family?"

Hannah and Josh sobered. "No. I have no one."

"Since I lost my mom, I'm alone now too."

The kitchen fell silent except for the sound of the boiling stew on the stove.

"I'm sorry. I didn't mean to bring it up. But you aren't alone if you don't want to be." Reed spoke softly. "You can always go home with me to the Redwood Pack."

As good as that sounded to Josh, he didn't think he could think about the future. Not one that didn't include the two people in the kitchen with him.

Josh looked around the cabin, trying to break the sudden tension in the room. "I don't think we should use the bedroom tonight and waste the wood. It's gonna get real cold, real quick. So I think it'd be best if we all pile up in the living room in front of the fire and close to the nearest exits in case we are attacked. We may have to cuddle."

The tip of Reed's ears reddened and Hannah blushed. *Damn these two were cute as all hell.*

"Okay, but we'll take turns keeping watch," Reed agreed.

Josh and Hannah nodded, and he went back to the stove to check their meal. "Stew's ready. It won't be too bad, though it didn't have all day to simmer and we don't have bread, but it'll do."

"I don't care how it tastes. It smells divine." Hannah closed her eyes and inhaled. The look of pure ecstasy on her face made Josh want to bend her over the dining room table and fuck her until they both dropped to the floor in a sweaty pile.

He looked over to Reed and knew the man's thoughts were on the same page.

Fuck.

Reed checked the fire and Hannah set the table while Josh ladled stew in to the bowls. They sat down together, talking and eating a surprisingly decent meal. It almost felt like they were a family. It was nice. A little too nice. Because Josh couldn't allow himself to get used to this.

They'd leave him like everyone else always did.

A crimson hue flashed across his eyes. Blood and dark evil attacked his thoughts, and Josh held his forehead. Weariness spread over him.

What the hell was going on? He'd never had an attack like this before. This wasn't part of his Finding. No, this was something different. Was it because of the bite? It felt like something else was trying to take over his body and cloud his emotions.

Irrational anger seeped through his pores, anger at those that had left him. Anger at the two strangers sitting across from him who would fuck tonight and leave him alone and needing. He didn't want to feel needy. He wanted to be alone.

"Josh?" Hannah's soft voice intruded his increasingly violent thoughts.

"I'm getting a bit tired. You mind if I just crash on the couch? You can wake me when you're ready to go to sleep and I'll take the floor. Okay?"

Both of his dinner mates looked at him with worried expressions.

"Okay, try and get some rest. We'll do the dishes and try to be quiet," Reed answered.

Josh nodded, too afraid of what would come out of his mouth if he spoke. He left the two lovebirds at the table to talk about him behind his back. Yeah, fuck them.

He slung himself onto the couch, head aching. His arm pulsated to a staccato tempo, pissing him off. He glanced down and paled. His wound looked even redder than before but for some reason he didn't want to tell the others. What was going on with him? He needed to leave here soon, before he did something he might regret.

Chapter 9

Hannah watched Josh walk out of the room, a painful expression on his face. She hated to see him in pain. The feeling was much like what she'd felt when Reed was hurt.

"He looks tired." Too tired for someone who'd just slept eight hours.

"I know," Reed agreed. "I don't like it. But when we get to the Pack, we'll try and figure it out. I think it may be the bite, but I don't want to say anything just yet."

"I know. I'm scared. I've never seen anything like that before."

"It's okay, Hannah. We will figure it out." Reed reached out and held her hand.

He was always doing things like that. Touching her hand, arms, kissing her forehead or cheeks. She loved it every time he did so and didn't want him to stop. She felt as though she'd known him for so much longer than just a handful of stolen days. How would she say goodbye? Did she have to?

Reed stood and cleared the table. Hannah grabbed what she could and followed him into the kitchen that stood off the living room. They started doing the dishes, and the cold water bit into her hands, stinging.

"Hey, why don't you do the drying? I don't want you to freeze your hands off since we don't have heated water at the moment. Should make showering interesting." Reed quirked a lip, and Hannah blushed.

Goddess, the image of him in the shower, water sliding down his naked skin.

Hannah gulped, knowing she was blushing like a school girl.

She dried the bowls using a towel she found in one of the drawers. That reminded her.

"How are we going to replace anything we use?"

Reed kept rinsing the bowls and gave her a smile. "I've thought about that. We'll leave a note."

Hannah exhaled in relief. "A note? That'll be enough?"

Reed nodded and bumped her with his hip. "We'll leave our information and pay them back. Don't worry; I'll take care of it. And you."

"I'd like that. But don't think I won't reciprocate." She smiled then froze. Had she really just said that aloud?

From the pleased look on his face, she thought she had.

What did that mean?

They finished the dishes, their arms and legs brushing and bumping together as they worked as a unit. She didn't know quite what was going on, but parts of her liked it. Parts of her *really* liked it. But then those same parts reacted whenever Josh touched her or looked into her eyes.

Her heart hurt at the choices she might have to make if what she saw in their eyes was true. She wanted both men. And if she was honest with herself—she was falling for them, too.

Did that make her a slut?

Because the fantasies rolling through her mind made her think of even sluttier thoughts. Really dirty, slutty thoughts.

They both went into the living room and sat on the love seat across the room from where Josh lay sleeping. He had his arm over his eyes, blocking out soft glow of the candles, so she couldn't see the bite. But she knew it was there. To her dismay, even though it was cold in the cabin and he needed the warmth, he'd kept his shirt on this time.

She remembered what it had felt like to strip that off and look at his lean muscles as he slept. She'd only done it to make him more comfortable. At least that's what she told herself. Sure.

Reed wrapped a blanket around them both as they snuggled to keep warm in the dropping temperatures. But she still felt on edge, because even though they felt safe in their forest oasis, werewolves lurked and hunted them.

Hannah shivered at the memory of that basement, and Reed held her closer then took her hand in his.

Tingles raced up her arms as he rubbed small circles in her palm with his thumb.

Dear goddess, the man is smooth.

And apparently none of them were going to talk about what was going on. Fine with her for now, but once they left the cabin, they would have to break the barrier. She didn't know what would come of their talk and it scared her.

"You two look comfy." Josh's voice sounded rough with sleep.

"Hey, do you feel better?" She refused to take her hand away from Reed's. Had she just make a choice?

"A little. I just can't sleep with those fuckers out there, ya know?"

"I know what you mean. But as soon as this storm lets up, we'll get out of here. We'll get somewhere safe." Reed smiled, but a cold gleam entered his eyes. "Then we'll make sure the Centrals know not to fuck with us."

The men looked at each other and seemed to come to an understanding.

They were so strong, just in different ways sometimes. But in this one case, she knew they would be on the same page.

Josh sat up and patted the seat next to him. "Come sit by me. The fire helps, but it's getting cold in here."

Reed shuffled to the couch, pulling her with him, and they sat down. Josh pulled the blankets around the three of them, cuddling close into her side. Her womb clenched at the feel of both men on either side of her, warming her from the inside out.

Dammit. Things couldn't go on like this.

Finding the shred of courage she possessed, she blurted, "What's going on? With us?"

Both men stopped the subtle stroking on her arms and froze. Their faces looked guilty, but slightly intrigued. That was a good sign. Right?

They removed their hands, and she immediately felt cold at the loss of contact.

Josh furrowed his brows and tilted his head. Reed took a deep breath.

What was going on? Hannah feared their answers.

"You are my mate," Reed finally answered, a look of pure joy and anticipation on his face. He smiled and looked into her eyes.

Happiness, unprecedented happiness, filled her. She knew about werewolves' mates. She was his fated destiny. His other half. Together they would live in love and faith because it was fate.

She'd known there was a connection, but she'd never thought to even hope for this outcome.

A link. Between the two of them.

"Oh." She uttered that single word with a mix of joy and pain.

What about Josh? There would be no Josh. She was Reed's, as he was hers.

And Josh would be alone, without them.

Josh grunted, a hollow sound full of pain. Then his expression blanked and he stood. "I'm happy for the two of you, though I'd suspected it since we met in the basement. I'm going to leave the two of you alone for a bit to talk. I'm going to go back to the bedroom for a bit."

Reed's hand shot out, catching Josh by his uninjured forearm before he could leave the room.

"Don't go."

"Yes," Hannah added, "stay. Please don't go."

She looked into his ocean blue eyes full of pain.

Wait. Why did she feel such desire, desire that matched what she felt for Reed, if she was Reed's mate? Wasn't there like a wolf law against that or something?

"No, I need to go. You two are mates. I can't be here right now. Don't you understand?" Josh's eyes were hard. What could he be feeling?

Hannah's chest hurt. *Oh goddess.* Apparently her heart wanted two men, but why? Why did this have to happen now? Why did Reed have to say anything and make Josh go away? Why did Josh have to feel anything for her anyway? Even though she felt the same way. Damn it. He must hurt. It wasn't fair.

But life wasn't fair. Her mother's short life and her own captivity were proof positive of that.

Reed's voice broke into her thoughts. "Josh, you're my mate too. Our mate."

Wait. What did he say?

"Oh." What else could she say? What did this mean?

Josh's eyes widened and his face paled. "No way."

"Yes, way," Reed replied. "I feel it here." Reed put his hand over his heart. "My wolf also knows it. I know it's not what you expected, but it's true. You're both my mates." He looked between them, pleading in his eyes but strength in his features, as if preparing for rejection.

Josh shook his head. "Don't get me wrong. I find you both attractive, which by itself is odd. Not that you aren't hot, but the fact that I'm looking at a *man* that way..." Josh blushed. "But I'm straight, Reed. I've never wanted another man. I just don't know."

Reed gave a hollow laugh. "I've always been happy with men or women."

Hannah didn't like the sound of that. Why was he bringing up past relationships at a time like this? She didn't want to feel jealous, but seriously.

"Don't look like that, either of you," Reed interjected. "You two are the first two I've ever felt the mating heat with. Ever." Reed looked at them through smoldering eyes. "You're both my mates. Believe me."

Hannah took a deep breath. Two mates? Was that possible? She knew that wolves had potential mates, others out there that could be their other half. But some never found even one, let alone two in a long life time. Did this mean Reed would have to choose? Did he want Josh and not her? This was just too confusing and made her heart hurt.

Reed cleared his throat and rubbed his hands on his thighs. "I've never heard of this happening before. I mean, one of my brothers has had two potential mates. Kade met Tracy first, but that didn't work out." He let out a hollow laugh. "Thankfully, he met Melanie soon after and now they are mated. But it wasn't at the same time, and once he met Melanie, he wanted nothing to do with Tracy."

She didn't know exactly who these people were, but she needed to discuss the three of them in this room, not others.

"But," Reed continued, "this is about us. Not them. I don't want to make a callous decision. I don't think I *can* make a decision. I don't want to choose." Reed looked at them both, his heart in his eyes.

"This is a lot to take in, Reed," Hannah whispered.

"Don't worry. I don't want in." Josh's voice was cold, emotionless.

A part of her heart broke off, shattering into a thousand pieces.

She'd been wrong. She never had a choice. She never did. Josh didn't want her...them.

Her arms tingled as a hollow feeling spread through her. He'd walk away. Alone.

Hannah looked away from Josh. She couldn't bear to see the man she'd almost fallen for anymore if he didn't reciprocate those feelings. Her gaze landed on Reed. She saw a mirror of her emotions on his face before they faded away into resignation.

"I didn't mention all of this to let you walk away, Josh. Don't go. Let's just sit on this for a bit and talk it out. See where things go." Reed took a deep breath. "Please."

Hannah jumped in. "That sounds very reasonable. Please, Josh. Let's just wait a bit." Tears filled her eyes, but she blinked them away and forced a smile on her face. "I mean, we just escaped from a lunatic's prison and everything. Let's take a day or two to settle."

Josh clenched his jaw. "So let me get this straight. We just parade around here like Goldilocks in a fucking cabin we don't own, waiting for Reed to get off his ass and choose between us? That's rich. And how about the fact that I want you, Hannah? That I keep dreaming about you and me and forever? Reed is dreaming those same dreams. I already know whom he'd choose. Why should I just sit here and watch him choose you and not me?"

Embarrassment covered his features and he quickly shut his mouth.

Hannah was speechless.

Josh wanted Reed and her. All three of them wanted each other? And to think, the week before she'd had no one. Now she had two of the sexiest men on Earth wanting her. Nice.

Reed stood and paced through the room.

"I don't know what's going on," Reed finally said. "I need to go home to my family. To the Pack. But I also don't want to leave you. I know I *can't* leave the two of you. Let's honestly see where this goes, with the three of us."

Wait. What?

"The three of us?" Hannah squeaked.

Josh cleared his throat, looking slightly embarrassed. Not at all like the tough military man he normally did. "You mean like the three of us together—at the same time?"

Reed gave a startled laugh. "The looks on your faces are priceless. Yes, I mean the three of us at the same time. But I don't mean like an orgy on the floor at this exact moment or anything."

They all paused for a moment. She pictured the sweaty, naked goodness that would come from an orgy on the floor, and by the looks on the men's faces, they were picturing the scene too.

"Okay, enough of that." Reed laughed again. "I mean we should at least acknowledge that there is an attraction between the *three* of us. Then we can work on it and getting home safe."

Josh scowled but nodded.

Hannah didn't say anything. A werewolf and a gifted human? Is this what her mom would have wanted for her? What would the other witches say? Did she even care?

What did *she* want? Did she want two men? Could she handle it? Well, it wasn't as if this one moment would decide her fate. Things could always change in the future. Right?

Taking a deep breath, Hannah nodded.

She'd already known her decision before Reed asked. Why did she even hesitate?

All three of them exhaled at her nod.

"Good," Josh interjected after a moment of silence. "Now what?"

Reed rubbed the back of his neck. "Well, I'd say we should shake on it, but I'll do one better. Let's kiss on it."

Josh let out a rusty laugh. "Okay, what the hell. It's been a day of revelations that's for sure."

Hannah nodded. Then bit her lip, not trusting her voice.

Both men took a step toward her.

What had she gotten herself into?

Chapter 10

Reed's pulse raced at the thought of the Hannah and Josh. This was it. Everything he'd wanted and more.

Hannah stood in front of him, her teeth biting into her plump lip, like she did when she was nervous. Her chestnut hair curled in disarray around her face, emphasizing her curious, yet heated, slate eyes.

Josh stood on her other side, clenching his fists. Whether in frustration from this situation or from the sexual variety, Reed didn't know. But he hoped it was the latter. His normally spiky brown hair lay down on one side, looking like he'd just got out of bed. His blue eyes stared into Reed's soul.

Shit, Reed knew he had to be the luckiest guy on earth.

He couldn't believe they actually said they'd think about a threesome in real life—and not just in the bedroom. Happiness practically burst from every pore. Even though the situation they were in—kidnapping, bullets, basements, and borrowed cabins— made it seem inappropriate, he couldn't quite gather up the nerve to feel bad about it.

Reed watched Hannah bounce on the balls of her feet then lick her lips, anxiousness mixing with her nervousness for what was to come. He looked over at Josh's forearms, the veins popping out of the muscles. Damn that human was strong. Reed could imagine Hannah using her tongue and teeth and Josh using that strength in other areas—particularly on Reed.

Hell, yeah.

Josh coughed. "Um, so how should we go about doing this?"

All three of them laughed.

"Oh, I can tell this is going to be fun." Reed smiled then walked to Hannah and framed her face in his hands.

Her pupils dilated, and her breath quickened.

He heard the rustle of clothing as Josh moved behind him. Reed's cock hardened almost to the point of pain at the thought of Josh and Hannah together, then both of them with him.

His gaze lowered to her lips as her tongue darted out and licked them. He inhaled her honey and crisp apple scent, the aroma rocking him to the bone.

"Kiss her then kiss him. This is it."

He couldn't agree more with his wolf. Reed bent and touched his lips to hers. A shock rushed through his system. Her taste. Dear God, her taste. She tasted just like her scent but more potent. Her soft lips slid against his, and he groaned. Her lips parted, and his wolf growled. Her hands roamed his back, hesitantly at first, then firmer as she got into the kiss more. He tilted his head, deepening the kiss, sucking on her tongue and drowning in her taste.

Knowing he only meant this to be an initial kiss, and not wanting to leave Josh out, he forced himself to lift his lips from hers. He panted and looked down at her pouty, swollen lips as her eyes slowly opened.

"Oh my." Her voice had deepened with sexual energy.

Sexy as hell.

He held her in his arms, watching her breathe rapidly. Josh came to their side and brushed a lock of hair out of Hannah's face.

Hannah moved her gaze from him to Josh, her body pulsating in Reed's arms.

Surprisingly, Reed felt no jealousy watching Hannah's eyelids lower with desire as she looked at Josh. Reed himself wanted to groan at the look of pure promise and ecstasy on the man's face. With only a slight reluctance, in that he wanted to hold the both of them forever, he loosened his grip on Hannah as she pivoted fully into Josh's arms.

Hannah tilted her head up, and Reed watched as Josh lowered his face and kissed her. Both of his mates, together. Perfection. Josh bit her lip and growled.

Fuck, the human was damn sexy.

Josh kissed harder than he had. He seemed to put his whole body into the action, grinding against her and sucking her lips, then nibbling to take his fill. Hannah moaned and squirmed against him, much like she had with Reed.

Reed had to adjust himself as his erection pushed painfully into his zipper. This was going to be amazing—the three of them. An unknown feeling swept over him...completion? Suddenly, Reed knew he wanted this more than anything he'd ever known or seen. He'd never heard of threesomes as a fixture in daily life and not just in the bedroom in the Pack. Would they accept them? Did he care? This was fate. He couldn't argue with fate, nor could he argue with how he felt and how the three of them acted around one another. No, this was for real. The Pack would have to learn to adjust.

"Stop over thinking everything. It will work out. These two are keepers. Now, shut up and watch them go at it. Nice, isn't it?"

Reed smiled at his wolf. Yeah, they were keepers for sure.

Hannah gasped into Josh's mouth, and Reed groaned. *Fuck yeah.* They pulled apart, breathing heavily.

"I think I need to sit down." Hannah backed herself to the couch and sat down, out of breath.

He and Josh reached for her at the same time and the other man's hand ended up in his. Josh tried to pull away, but Reed wouldn't let him. The other man tensed, his hand freezing in his, but relaxed after a moment.

Hannah looked at them both then smiled. "I'm fine, really. I just had the two best kisses of my life." She let out a giggle. "They were different but so amazing. So perfect." Her gaze traveled down their bodies, leaving a trail of heat and desire, before landing on their joined hands. Her tongue reached out and licked her lips.

Reed looked at Josh, studying his strong features. His lips weren't as full as Hannah's or his, but still looked edible. He reached up with his other hand and brushed an unruly lock of hair from Josh's forehead. Why did he have such long hair up top if he was a military man? He'd have to ask that sometime.

"Kiss him," his wolf growled.

"Have you ever kissed a man before?" Reed needed to know. Josh said he'd never found another man attractive so Reed guessed the answer. He just needed to hear it.

Josh let out a surprised laugh. "Can't say that I have."

Reed nodded, squeezing his hand. "I'm going to kiss you now."

Josh looked toward Hannah and gave her a small, sexy smile.

Hannah laughed. "If you two kiss each other the way you just kissed me, I may just die watching."

Josh knelt beside Hannah and in front of Reed. Josh smiled again. "I have a better idea. Why don't I kiss you?"

Reed widened his eyes as Josh pulled him by the back of his neck over Hannah's legs and crushed his mouth to his.

Sweet ponderosa pine burst on his tongue. Teeth clashed against teeth, as Josh thrust his tongue in and out of his mouth. Reed groaned as an overwhelming sexual fog took over, weakening his already weak resolve.

Dear God, I could live on Josh's and Hannah's taste alone.

He held onto Josh like a drowning man, playing an intricate game of war with their tongues and lips. Reed pulled back then bit into the fleshy part of Josh's lip. Hard. Then he soothed the sting as Josh's eyes widened.

Oh, they would have to see which of the two of them would be dominant. If either. It would be arousing as hell to take turns and then both take Hannah—together. He almost came in his jeans at the thought.

They pulled apart again, breathing heavily, much like they had with their kisses with Hannah. His wolf howled in utter bliss and contentment, and Reed wanted to join in.

All three of them looked at each other then burst out laughing, the tension from the unknown dissolving away. Tears leaked from their eyes as their laughter grew.

"I'm sorry," Hannah gasped through her laughter. "I don't want to laugh. But I was afraid it'd be awkward."

"It's not awkward. I thought it would be, but it was damn good," Josh added in.

"Hell, yeah. We should do it again," Reed agreed.

"Hey, it was totally worth it." Josh smiled, then got a wicked gleam in his eye. "Best guy kiss ever."

Reed punched him in the arm. Josh's eyes widened, as he rubbed the spot.

"You sure do pack a punch for a little guy," Josh practically leered.

"Uh, dude, I'm a werewolf. And only like an inch shorter than you."

Hannah giggled. "Yeah, this won't be complicated at all."

"Hey," Reed interjected, "we can do it. Fate's cool like that."

"Reed, man, you sound like an old man trying to use slang." Josh laughed.

"Hey, I *am* an old man."

All three dissolved into laughter.

This felt good. Like family. His family.

A soft crunching, like snow under a paw, reached Reed's ears, interrupting his peace. Hannah froze, her eyes wide.

"The wards. Someone's breached the wards."

Josh grunted, closing his eyes in pain, and grabbed his arm.

"Fuck, my Finding's back—I think."

All three jumped to their feet, ready to fight.

Their time in their forest oasis faded away. Back to reality and the dangers that hunted them.

Chapter 11

A howl broke through their uncomfortable silence. Shit, Josh didn't think their interlude from danger would end this fast. But he should have been expecting it, been prepared. Now instead of thinking about the aftereffects of kissing the two most important people in his life—and likening it—he had to fight. Maybe to the death.

He wanted—no, needed—to protect Hannah and Reed, no matter what. Though how he'd accomplish that, he didn't know. He was the weakest of the three of them by far. An uncomfortable and unfamiliar feeling settled in the pit of his stomach. He'd have to get used to it if they stayed in this odd three-way relationship.

Did they really need him for anything? Would they just walk away when they realized he had nothing really to give? And what would happen when Reed, and maybe even Hannah for all he knew of witches, stayed young forever, and Josh grew old? He knew humans could be turned into werewolves but he'd heard the horror stories of the change. Would he have to turn into a wolf?

Another howl, this time closer. Thoughts warred in his mind, but he shook them off. Not the time to be thinking about relationships. He had to bear down and go back to his training. It was what he was good at.

Hannah stood beside him, with her palms held outward and fingers spread.

"Do you have enough, you know, juice, or whatever?" Wow, he really needed to brush up on his magical knowledge.

Hannah smiled, nervous tension evident in her eyes. "Yes, I have enough. I'm near the earth, and that's why I meditated before. Plus the kiss helped." She blushed and lowered her eyes.

Reed exhaled. "I'd heard that sex increases some witches' powers. Good to know."

Is that right? If so, we'll have to work on that.

Reed planted his feet, ready for battle. "Something just brushed along a tree outside."

"Shit," Josh cursed. "I don't want to be surrounded in this cabin; I think we need to go outside."

Reed nodded. "I agree. Let's go outside and take the fight to them."

Josh tilted his head, his focus on the two who called themselves his mates. "And if it's too much..." He let his voice fade, unable to voice the all-too-real possibility they would die once they crossed the threshold.

Reed met his gaze but didn't say anything. He didn't need to. Understanding lit his eyes. They'd run if there were too many, if there were no other options. At least they'd try to run through the snow drifts. They had too much to lose now.

Reed would protect him and Hannah at all costs. Josh didn't know why he was aware of these unexplored feelings at the moment, or why there was even a l, but there was something here worth swallowing some pride. They'd run and trek through the snow to save their lives and save each other. That was how it had to be. Though Reed might not need it, Josh would be by the wolf's side through thick and thin, protecting his ass as well.

Josh walked out the door first and onto the patio, crouched low to duck for cover if needed. Shit, with all the snow, they couldn't see anything. Hannah mumbled something under her breath and the snow moved in drifts and made pathways. Hannah fell in behind, sandwiched between him and Reed. He was a fucking idiot. Reed had wanted to go first, but Josh ignored all of his previous internal ramblings and went through the door first anyway. Stupid. What role did a mere human play in a war of supernaturals other than for cannon fodder and playing the role of the redshirt?

Cold wind lashed against his skin. Though it was daytime, the sun didn't peak through the clouds. It was light out, but still pretty dark. The blizzard warred in full force, causing limited visibility in the falling snow. Shit, if only he possessed Reed's eyes. Another reason he shouldn't have been a prideful prick and let him go first. *Dammit.*

Josh heard the growl a split second before Hannah pivoted and used her amazing powers to send a dirt-filled snow-drift smack into two wolves. They yelped and tried to dig themselves out. She buried them deeper.

That's my girl.

Josh looked behind him, squinting through the snow. Reed glanced around then cursed under his breath. The sexy man quickly rid himself of his clothes and stood naked in the middle of a fucking blizzard.

"I need to change; too many wolves." Reed shook his head but didn't blush, apparently either too cold or comfortable with his nudity.

And the man didn't have anything to be ashamed of. Lean, like a swimmer, and yet still muscular, Reed's golden skin formed a stark contrast to the white snow. Josh risked a glance and saw his dick.

Fuck.

Yep, no need to be ashamed there. Long and thick, maybe not as thick as his own, but they'd compare later. What would

Reed do with that thing? There was no way it would fit. Okay, he really needed to get his mind out of the gutter.

Reed cleared his throat, and Josh looked up, feeling only slightly guilty. Out of the corner of his eye, he saw Hannah's with a guilty expression on her face. They were all goners.

Reed crouched down low and, before Josh's eyes, changed to a sandy-colored wolf with rust-colored streaks woven into his fur. The wolf opened his mouth in almost a yawn, showing off some long and dangerous looking teeth.

And all Josh had was an aluminum bat, since he was out of ammo and his knives were back at the compound. He'd lost most of them during the fight and after the demon had bitten him, he hadn't been in the right mind to remember to pick them up. Something he'd never do with a clear head.

In a tangle of fur and limbs, Reed jumped into the fray, taking down two opponents. Vicious growls erupted as blood seeped from wounds on both sides. Snow continued to fall, making it hard for Josh to see exactly what was going on and if Reed was okay.

Josh stood by Hannah's side, protecting her from wolves getting too close. She might be amazing with her magic, but if she missed just one wolf, she'd get hurt just as badly as a human. Josh couldn't take that. A muddy brown wolf leaped from the bushes toward Hannah, and Josh swung with the bat. The metal clanged against the side of its head, the sound of its skull crushing echoing in his ears. The vibrations from the connection of aluminum to flesh and fur ran up his arm, jarring the bite. Josh cursed under his breath at the pain.

"Josh, behind you!" Hannah yelled over the growls and wind.

He pivoted, hitting the gray wolf in the flank as Hannah used her power to bury another wolf. Shit, the wolves kept coming, with no end in sight. What should they do? Was it time to run?

Out of the corner of his eye, he checked on Reed. The sandy-haired wolf fought off two of the mangier wolves, growling and biting. Josh wanted to help, to see if he could hit the other wolves away, but he couldn't leave Hannah's side. Was this what it meant to be in a group of three? To constantly be in the middle, trying to choose between mates?

Reed twisted his head towards Josh, caught Josh checking on him and glared, before turning back to his fight. Okay, apparently Reed could handle himself.

A chocolate brown wolf with black ears and the left side of its face black, stared at him. His green eyes looked familiar to Josh, but he couldn't quite place why. Startled, Josh raised the bat, ready to swing at the wolf, but something tugged at his sleeve. He looked down at Reed's pleading eyes, as Reed shook his head.

What the fuck?

Wolf-Reed yelped at Josh then barked at the other wolf. They really needed to find a system to talk when Reed was in his wolf form. The other wolf gave a nod then turned his back to Josh, blocking him from the fight.

This stranger was going to protect them? How did Reed know him? Was he part of his Pack?

Josh looked toward Hannah, but she shared his confused look. Josh shrugged, no time to deal with it. He'd take any help he could get.

A growl sounded behind him. Josh turned quickly to see a wolf coming at his face, teeth bared. He slammed his bat into the wolf's side, and it let out a yelp. He pivoted, hitting it again with all his strength. The wolf went down and Hannah buried it in dirt and snow. Teamwork at its best.

Wolves came from all directions. Josh worked with Hannah in tandem, fighting them off, killing those who dared too close. Despite the freezing temperatures, sweat rolled down his back. His vision darkened as his arm throbbed. A wolf came from behind a bush and bared its teeth at Hannah, ready to pounce. Before he knew it, he was at her side, beating the fucking thing to a bloody pulp.

Josh looked around and exhaled. They seemed to be winning—for now. He took what he could get and grabbed Hannah's hand.

"We need to run. Now."

Hannah nodded, gripping him tightly. The other wolf, Reed's friend, stopped in front of them and beckoned them with a nod. Apparently they were following this stranger to a safer place. Anything sounded better than the debris of dead wolves and enemies they were currently facing.

They trailed the dark brown wolf as Josh looked for Reed, the man he'd kissed like his life was on the line less than an hour ago, followed with a slight limp and blood on his paws and flank.

Some fucker hurt Reed. Made him bleed.

Oh, Josh was gonna kick some ass. That was for sure.

Thank God, Hannah looked unharmed, though she was quiet and out of breath. It could have gone worse, and they weren't out of danger yet.

He pulled Hannah through the trenches, the snow up to his knees. A wolf howled over the blowing wind, and she tightened her hand around his. Reed and the other wolf had almost no problem navigating through the snow, and Josh was glad he only had to pull one person. Off in the distance, a tan SUV came into view. A godsend in the middle of an icy hell.

Cold had leached through his jeans, numbing his legs, but he held on, praying he'd make it before Hannah froze or the other wolves came back. Once they made it to the car, Josh wrenched opened the door, thanking God the other wolf had left it unlocked. Using whatever strength he had left, he set Hannah into the back seat and tossed the bat in behind her, careful not to hit her.

He looked at the two wolves at his feet and, after nod from Reed, got into the back, holding Hannah close to his side for whatever warmth they could find. Josh watched as both Reed and the other wolf change back into human forms. The other man looked a lot like Reed. Too cold and full of painful adrenaline to stare at any naked bodies now, he handed Reed the clothes that he had carried for him. Josh looked in the back of the SUV and found another set. He gave them to the stranger who helped save their lives.

"Josh, Hannah, this is my brother, Adam." Reed motioned to the stranger. Taller than Reed, and a bit bulkier, he had the same green eyes but had dark cropped hair. They could have been twins.

Adam pulled his brother into a deep embrace.

"It's good to see you, Reed, but let's get the fuck out of here before someone comes back for us," Adam grunted.

"Sounds good to me, this is Josh and Hannah." Reed nodded towards them sitting in the back seat.

Hannah squeezed his hands, tense like he was, waiting for Adam's reaction.

Before Reed could think or feel bad, Josh spoke up. "We're his mates. No need to be embarrassed. But it's fucking cold out there, and I'd like to get away from those maniacs out there and get somewhere warm."

Adam stood there a moment longer as a pained look flashed across his face. But as quickly as it came, he brushed it away, putting on a blank mask.

"Get in the car; we need to get moving." Adam grunted again and went around to the driver's side, keys in hand.

Reed leaned into the back seat and kissed Josh then Hannah, surprising them both—and Adam. He gave an apologetic look when he backed away and jumped into the passenger seat.

"It will be okay," Hannah whispered in his ear, even though the wolves would hear them. She took his face in her hands and kissed him softly.

Josh smiled and watched as they passed the trees outside of the Jeep's window as Adam hightailed it out of the forest. Away from their cabin and captivity.

And to think, only yesterday he'd been enjoying a reindeer hotdog with caramelized onions and cream cheese. He'd closed his eyes on a bench and heard two kids talking about people he didn't even know.

Now he had two people that might be his mates, one a beautiful woman with soft curves and the other a man who made him hard like no one before. A crazy Pack of werewolves were after him, bent on killing him and the two people he was falling for. He'd met a member of Reed's family with a pained look and was now on the way to meet another Pack to explain one of their sons might be in a three-way relationship with a man and a woman.

It was odd how things could take a turn so quickly. For the better or worse, Josh didn't know. But it didn't seem too complicated, right? *Fuck.*

Chapter 12

Tall trees blurred as they passed them as Hannah sagged against Josh's side. No one spoke, either too tired or finding it too awkward to deal with the emotions running through the air, which became so thick it lay heavy on her tongue.

Her body ached from all the magic she'd poured from her system, protecting herself and the men in her life.

The way Josh had introduced them to Adam as Reed's mates made her feel warm and soft inside. Whatever doubts he might have, he believed in at least something concerning them. Reed had said their names with such caring and affection, Adam would have known exactly who they were from his voice alone.

And Adam. Poor Adam. The look of pain in his eyes when Josh spoke had hurt her heart. Something bad had happened to Reed's brother, something no one should go through. What it was she could only guess, but she didn't know for sure. Hannah knew there would always be a barrier between them and Adam for that reason alone. And she didn't know if she could blame him for it.

"How did you find us, Adam?" Reed asked.

"I didn't really." Adam answered. "I sort of stumbled across you. I'd been looking since they took you, but I couldn't get onto the Central's land and find you. Then after I drove around to the other side of the territory to find another way in, I came across your scent." He took a deep breath and his hands tightened on the wheel. "I'd never been so relieved."

Reed squeezed his brother's shoulder, but didn't say anything.

Josh rubbed circles into her wrist, infusing warmth from just his touch. She leaned into him once more and kissed his stubbled cheek. With a deep breath, she leaned forward and placed her free hand on Reed's shoulder.

He gasped at the touch and looked over at her, warmth in his eyes.

"You're hurt," she said, her voice barely above a whisper. "Let me help."

Reed smiled. God how she loved that smile. "Okay."

She used most of the power she had left and healed the wounds on Reed's side and hands. It took more because she couldn't put her hands directly over the wounds. But she didn't want to wait any longer, not when she could still heal him.

Adam inhaled loudly beside her.

"You're a healer," Adam murmured, an odd mix of awe and resignation in his tone.

Confused, she glanced at Reed. But he only mouthed "later" and shook his head.

Okay, she could wait, but something was off.

But Hannah nodded and leaned back into Josh's arms, sighing when he held her close, kissing her forehead and temples.

Goddess, he felt like heaven.

As the drive continued on, no one spoke, all too tired to expend the energy. Hours passed, and Hannah reflected on the kiss the three of them had shared in the cabin before their time was cut short by the angry mob of wolves.

The kiss felt right. Good. But could she live in a threesome? Ignoring the fact that people would scoff and call them names better left unsaid, could she deal with the emotional aspect?

Having one man seemed too much for some women. The attachment, the overwhelming intensity, the sex... Everything added up to an emotional toll. But multiply that times two and it seemed astronomical.

But the benefits and feelings of two men with her made Hannah want to ignore her misgivings and jump in head first.

The car slowed down as they passed an ivy covered stone archway guarded by two people she could only assume were wolves by their energies. The two guards nodded at the Jeep, and Adam continued up the drive.

Magnificent large trees covered the land. Between the trees, dark green grass was interspersed with a covering snow. She hoped the empty spaces of land would be filled with beautiful flowers come spring time. She was immediately sucked into the Redwood den. She loved it. The energy surrounding her pulsated and tugged on her, calling her home.

This was it. The missing piece clicked into place, and she knew it. She'd never want to leave. She'd stay here with Josh and Reed forever if they'd let her.

The Redwoods called to her.

Adam wound along the road, passing homes hidden among the brush. Frankly, it was a beautiful den. They pulled up to a home, nestled beneath a canopy of two large trees with branches reaching up to the sky. It was a two-story, older looking home with fresh paint and shutters.

"This is my home," Reed said simply.

Reed's home. Could it be hers and Josh's too?

Hannah shook her head. This was too much too soon. She tucked away those promising and somewhat nerve-wracking thoughts for later.

The front door to Reed's home opened and people filed out.

"Oh Reed! The sentries called to tell us you were coming." A short light brown haired woman with warm eyes ran to Reed and held him close.

"Hi, Mom. I've missed you," Reed choked out, holding his mom and rubbing his cheek on her hair.

Brothers, sisters, or sisters-in law, and his parents came at him, hugging, patting, and crying, reassuring themselves Reed was actually with them. That he was home.

With such an out pouring of love, Hannah felt out of place.

Goddess, she missed her Mother.

How would it feel to be part of such a family, to never be alone? It was what she thought she wanted with Josh and Reed. But could they achieve it?

Josh came from behind and held her hand. The feelings of reassurance and hope slid through her as he squeezed it. He understood. He was alone, just as she was. But it seemed like he had been alone longer. Would he want to give that freedom up and be a family? Their connection and the pulsating thread knitted between their three souls flared.

Please, let this work. Please, let us be a family.

"Come on, everyone. Get inside and get warm. I'll introduce everyone once we do." Reed ushered his family in, then stood back to take Hannah's hand and nod at Josh.

They walked into his home and found themselves in a cozy living room with a large L-shaped couch. She wanted to sink into the comfy cushions. Art covered the walls and framed pictures of family members dotted shelves layered with books. It looked like an artist's home.

Hannah fell a little bit more in love with him right then.

Reed's family talked above each other, eager to hear about his captivity. But they didn't outright ask who Hannah and Josh were, though she could tell by their not-so-casual looks they wanted to.

"Hannah, Josh, this is my family." Reed laughed under his breath. "From the top, this is my father, my Alpha, Edward. And my mother, Patricia." Reed pointed to a couple holding hands but looked to be Reed's age. Edward had darker hair, almost black, but still looked like Reed enough there was no mistaking the family resemblance.

Hannah waved.

What was she supposed to do in this situation? Talk about awkward.

"Over there is my eldest brother, Kade, and his wife, Melanie. She's holding their son, Finn." Kade looked a lot like Edward, only about an inch shorter and a soft blend of their mother's features mixed in. Melanie was a short blond beauty, smiling and rocking baby Finn to sleep.

"Next to them on the couch are Jasper and his wife, Willow." Jasper had even darker hair than Kade and seemed taller, about six and a half feet. Willow had light brown hair and had pixie features. She was slender except for one noticeable thing.

"And our soon-to-be baby." Willow gave a radiant smile and held her protruding belly.

A tug of maternal instincts Hannah didn't know she possessed startled her.

"I don't think we can forget that, Willow. You're a little hard to miss." Reed laughed.

Jasper growled. "Watch what you say about my mate, dear brother." But his eyes were filled with laughter when he said it.

Their family dynamics made her smile.

"You've already met Adam. So here are the twins, North and Maddox." The twins looked like wiry versions of Jamensons but with dark blond hair that obviously had come from their mother. They were practically identical but for the large scar running down the side of Maddox's face.

"And last, but not least, Cailin." Reed gestured toward the most beautiful woman Hannah had ever seen. She had long indigo-black hair with blunt bangs, big, green Jamenson eyes and full lips.

These brothers had a hell of a thing on their hands if they were typical big brothers and wanted to protect her from men and the outside world. And from the Alpha energy she felt swirling around the room, she would place money on it.

"Hi, it's nice to meet everyone." Hannah's voice was small. She didn't know what else to say.

"Yes, nice to meet you. Reed, can we get someone to look at Hannah? We haven't seen a doctor yet." Josh asked.

"Of course, sorry, I'm being an idiot. North? Can you help?" Reed asked the twin who must have been the doctor.

"Sure, let me take a look. I'm not a healer, but still a doctor." North stood and walked over to her, placing his hand on her arm in a comforting gesture.

Reed and Josh growled behind her at the touch. Talk about territorial, but she liked it. Who knew? Hannah noticed the looks passing between the family members but fought down the apology in her throat.

Were they judging her? She didn't want to be a burden to this family and she honestly didn't want to hurt Reed.

North walked back to the couch and opened his medical kit that he must have brought over when he heard Reed was home, and cleaned her visible scrapes and bruises. The lash marks on her stomach had healed overnight through the use of earth magic, thankfully.

"Son," Edward interrupted, "why are you two undamaged, but not Hannah? Why would you allow her to be hurt in your place? Or is there something else going on I need to know about?" He quirked a brow, waiting for his answer.

Hannah felt a wash of an age-old power. Alpha. Edward apparently wanted answers. Now.

Reed looked at Hannah with a question in his eyes. She nodded.

"Hannah's a healer. A witch."

The people in the room fell into silence. Even baby Finn seemed to know this meant something. What, she wasn't sure of. Yet. But Reed owed her answers. Both times he told someone she was a healer, they reacted strangely. Why?

Reed's mother put her hands over her mouth, and then smiled a watery smile. "We've been waiting for you."

Edward looked her up and down, assessing her with those beyond his years, wisdom-filled, green eyes. "Yes, Hannah, we have."

Hannah looked around the room; eyes filled with awe stared back at her.

"What are you talking about? What do you mean you were waiting for me'?" Hannah asked, her voice rising in a squeak. *What is going on?*

"You're our Healer." Edwards placed emphases on the word, as if it meant more than her normal abilities.

"What is that?"

"Hannah, I was going to explain. Take a seat, baby." Reed looked at her and she knew something big was happening, but she still trusted him.

"Reed?"

"Every Pack has certain titles associated with the Alpha's family. Dad is the Alpha, the one in charge. Kade is the Heir, the first son. So he's in line to take over. Jasper is the Beta, meaning he deals with Pack business and takes care of us. Adam is the Enforcer; his job is to protect the Pack from outside forces. Maddox is the Omega; it's his job to protect and soothe the emotions of the Pack. And lastly, there is the Healer, the one who Heals the Pack physically. We've been without one since the last war with the Centrals a century ago. But Hannah, with you here, we aren't looking anymore. You're our Healer, Hannah." Reed held her hands, his eyes imploring her to believe. To accept.

"I don't know, Reed. This is a lot to take in. I can't think about this right now." Hannah shook her head. It was all too much.

"It's okay, don't worry. We can talk about it later. God knows we need rest." Reed leaned forward and kissed her forehead while Josh rubbed her back.

Reed told the story of his ordeal. Of Caym capturing him and putting him in the dungeon. Of meeting Hannah and not being able to help her. He didn't share everything, like her torture. That was something that she had the right to choose to share. He told of the demon's plans as he knew of, though that wasn't much. He spoke about the compound and wards and everything they could possibly think of to help his Pack. Then he spoke of Josh and how he rescued them, but Reed didn't mention Josh's special abilities. That was Josh's secret.

Josh.

"Crap. I almost forgot. My head's too crazy. We need to have someone look at Josh's arm." Hannah turned towards him and reached for his arm.

"What happened to your arm, son?" Edward asked.

"The damn demon bit me. Pardon my language." Josh rolled up his sleeve to show the still-healing bite.

Kade and Jasper growled and moved to stand in front of their wives.

"Hey, back off." Reed growled. "Josh is hurt. We don't know why the demon bit him, but he needs our help. Now."

His family's eyes grew wide, as if they were surprised at the aggressiveness in Reed's demand. Why would they be surprised that Reed had a backbone? Maybe that was why Reed felt inferior to his brothers' power and strength. She held back the urge to say something rude to them or kick their ass. Reed was protecting what he deemed his. Plus, Reed looked damn sexy when he acted all Alpha. She liked it.

"Reed, I don't want to cause a rift between you and your family," Josh whispered, his voice sad.

Hannah gasped and looked into Josh's eyes. Would any of them be okay if Josh walked away and out of their lives?

Reed fisted his hands, his eyes darkening like the coming of a deadly storm. "No, you can't leave. We need you here. And don't forget the Centrals are after you too. You risked your life for two strangers, and I won't let you risk it again because some *people* don't feel comfortable."

Kade growled and Melanie rubbed his arms.

"It's not that we're uncomfortable," Jasper reasoned, ever the Beta. "But we need to know more about what happened."

Adam narrowed his eyes. "Yes, Josh, tell us. How did you find them?"

Josh opened his mouth to reply, his eyes narrowed into slits.

Damn it, they are going to fight. This isn't going to end well.

"Adam, it's none of your fucking business." If looks could beat the crap out of someone, Reed's would have. "Josh found us. He's a good guy. And he's my mate. Hannah too. So back the fuck off."

The room went silent again.

"A trinity bond." Patricia whispered.

A trinity bond? What is that?

She didn't realize she'd spoken aloud until Patricia tried to answer. But Edward cleared his throat.

"It means," Edward said, "that there are three people in a mate bond. It was written long ago that a bond of such nature would come into our lives and into our Pack. But I'd thought it forgotten. I see I was mistaken." He raised an eyebrow, but didn't continue.

Hannah knew he was hiding something. She didn't know why, but Reed's father obviously refused to reveal everything he knew about this bond and what it would entail. Why wouldn't he tell them? It was between the three of them—Reed, Josh and her. Was it because she and Josh were strangers? Though it stung, she understood. They were new, and this was a time of a coming war.

Why would they unveil all of their secrets to two people they'd just met? Maybe Edward would tell Reed; after all, he was his son.

Reed squeezed her hand. "I see. I'm sure there's more that you aren't saying, as always. But we need to rest and heal."

"While you do that, we'll regroup and talk about what we will do with the Centrals." Kade interjected. "This can't go on."

"Agreed," Edward said. "Come to our place and we will discuss this. The three of you can stay here and get some sleep. Talk. Get to know one another."

Pure anger passed over Reed's face. How could they just shut out their son like that? Hannah felt rage for him, and by the tension on Josh's face, he did too. Why didn't the Jamensons know Reed needed to be there?

"Fine." One word. One word filled with so much anger that Hannah thought she would have to hold Reed back.

"If it's all right," Adam interrupted, "I need to sit this one out. I need to leave for a while. I don't know when I'll be back."

The room fell silent—again.

"Adam, why? What's wrong?" Patricia asked.

"I just need some time away to think. I can't do it here."

Edward looked on his son, the Enforcer, then nodded. "I understand. We can handle well enough. But we will *always* be here for you."

Tears filled Hannah's eyes, but she refused to let them fall. Even with the tension and worries, they were still a supportive and loving family. And if it worked out, they could be hers if she mated Reed.

Adam walked toward his mother and kissed her wet cheek. "I love you, Mom."

His family went to him one by one, patting him on the back, and hugging him. Josh and Hannah stood back. She felt too much like an outsider to intrude on a clearly private and painful moment.

He kissed Finn's head and traced a finger down his cheek. Whatever else happened to Adam, Hannah knew at that moment Adam had lost a child and his mate. It was the only answer. Her heart hurt for them all.

On the way out the door, he paused and looked back toward where Josh and Hannah stood. "Take good care of him." His deep voice resonated in the room as he cast a dark look at the three of them. For some reason he was angry as all hell at whatever was happening between her, Reed, and Josh. Then he walked out of the house without another word, leaving a grieving family behind him.

Reed cleared his throat and went to stand between Hannah and Josh, showing a clear sign of the solidarity of their bond.

"Thank you for taking care of us, but we need to get some sleep now."

The Jamenson men exchanged glances and nodded. Apparently they weren't going to talk about the fact that they had been thinking about kicking Josh out of the house. Well, then.

"Of course, we'll just get going." Patricia started forward and hugged and kissed them goodbye, the rest of the family following suit.

They soon found themselves alone in a large and cozy home, knowing they were part of a trinity bond. Reed turned a heated gaze on the two of them, leaving goose bumps in its trail along her too sensitive skin.

Oh crap.

Chapter 13

Reed watched the chicken sizzle in the pan as Josh added more oil to the beginnings of chicken cacciatori. He added olive oil to the boiling water plus linguini pasta. Though Josh was doing most of the cooking tonight, Reed wanted to feel useful.

After his family had left, the three of them had stood in the living room high on tension and low on energy. Josh suggested dinner, and Hannah quickly agreed. Reed could have gone for food, sleep, or frankly sex at this point but didn't argue. They took turns taking showers and getting dressed while dinner cooked. Pat had come back to the house soon after she left with a pile of clothes for them. Josh fit in some of Kade's borrowed clothes and Hannah in some of Melanie's.

Hannah walked into the kitchen. "I feel so clean now. I hadn't realized how much I wanted a shower until I felt the hot water on my skin." Both he and Josh groaned.

In borrowed clothes, she looked amazingly fresh, clean, and sexy. That shower had done her well. Her skin looked soft and begged to be nibbled by his teeth.

Damn.

"You look good; the shower helped me as well." Josh's voice grew deeper when he spoke, and Reed's cock hardened. Again.

"It smells good in here. I wish I could cook like you, Josh." Hannah grinned, and Reed felt just a bit more in love with her.

"I'll teach you." Josh went back to his cooking, unaware of the looks between Reed and Hannah.

Josh wanted to stay for at least a cooking lesson? What did that mean? Reed couldn't get his hopes up, but he wanted to anyway.

"Josh, do you think Reed can brave the stove long enough for me to clean your arm again?" Hannah asked.

Josh laughed. "I sure hope so, since at this point, he only needs to stir."

Reed held a clean wooden spoon across his chest and nodded solemnly. "I will do my best."

They all laughed as Hannah led Josh out to the living room to clean his wound. Reed's fear that something was wrong with the bite never quite left his system, though there were no outward appearances of a curse or such. Well, at least that's what he thought. He didn't know much about curses, but Josh could walk and act on his own free will and he wasn't violent. That had to count for something.

The two of them came back into the kitchen soon after, Josh sporting a new white bandage, and thankfully, Reed hadn't burned their dinner. The pasta decided to boil over at that thought, causing Reed to blush.

"Shit, sorry, guys." Reed moved quickly to the pasta, bumping into Josh on the way. A zing of pleasure and warmth traveled up his arm as Josh placed his hand on him to steady to them.

"It's okay, Reed," Josh said, desire evident in his eyes. "I left the lid on when I left. You didn't burn down the house. Yet."

Reed smiled, and they finished making dinner then plated up the cacciatori. Hannah had buttered the bread and placed it on the table.

"See? I helped." Hannah winked.

"Yes, babe, you did great." Josh leaned over and kissed her softly before sitting down.

"Better than I did." Reed kissed her as well then kissed Josh before finding his seat.

"Thank you for making dinner, Josh." Hannah beamed, before taking a bite and moaning.

Fuck, she's the hottest thing I've ever seen. Through the gleam in Josh's eyes just about tied Hannah for that honor.

They ate with little conversation, a sexual undercurrent dancing along the edges.

"We need them, Reed. Now."

Reed couldn't have agreed more with his wolf. Tonight the three of them would spend the night in the same house. He just hoped they were together in the same bed when they did it. Preferably naked and sweaty with lots of intimate touching.

After they put the dishes in the dishwasher, Reed felt at a loss as to what to do now.

"So, are you two tired?" Reed asked. "I know we've had a trying couple of days."

"Not really. I know I should be, but I'm kind of wired," Hannah answered.

"I agree. I have some pent-up energy." Josh's voice deepened, and Reed moaned.

"I know a way we can use that," Reed teased.

"Oh really? How, pray tell?" Hannah asked.

Reed didn't answer, but prowled toward her and pulled her into his arms, crushing his mouth to hers. The sweet taste of honey and bitter apples burst on his tongue. He licked the seam of her lips, begging her to open. When she did, Reed danced his tongue along hers, both of them gasping for breaths. He held her face in his hands, as hers roamed his back under his shirt. Her soft skin felt like smooth silk against his.

Josh came up behind Hannah and moved her thick, curly hair out of the way as he trailed kisses along her neck. She moaned in Reed's mouth, alternatively grinding between the two of them. Josh's hand brushed Reed's, and both men gasped at the fire burning at the touch.

Hannah pulled away, gasping for breath. "What's going on here?"

As if she didn't know.

Reed looked toward Josh, not surprised to see the heated desire there. But it was the slight alarm and worry mixing in that made Reed pause.

Do they not want this? Not want me?

An ache went through Reed's heart, but he held back the fear. They needed to talk, not make assumptions. That's what had gotten in the way of Jasper and Willow's mating for so long. He had sworn that would never happen to him.

"Hannah," Reed soothed, "I want to make love with you. Tonight."

Hannah stiffened, but he could smell her arousal. "What about Josh?"

"Josh does too." Josh nodded, and Hannah relaxed.

"But what about *Josh?*" Hannah asked again.

Reed looked at the man in question. "I want to make love to Josh as well, but I don't know if we are all ready for that. I want you first. You will always be first and center for me."

Josh rubbed small circles in both of their backs. "It's the same for me. You're the center. Always." He let out a rugged laugh. "Plus, I'm still a little too new to the whole guy-on-guy thing. I may need to take it slow there."

"I'll help you," Reed promised. "Don't worry."

Hannah let out a breath. "Okay, I understand. I want the both of you too. But we will have to promise always to talk, be open. Voice our concerns. I don't want to offend anyone. This will be complicated enough without hurt feelings."

"Agreed," both men said that the same time.

"Though tonight, I think we're done with talking." Reed took Hannah's hand, walking her to his bedroom.

Josh followed behind, turning off the lights as he went.

They walked into his bedroom and surveyed the large, dark cherry sleigh bed with cream and green linens. His room felt masculine and right for him, but Hannah might want to change something later. The thought of her—and Josh—adding personal touches made Reed grin.

"I want you both, I do." Hannah bit her lip, nervous about something.

"Okay." Reed was slightly scared about what else she may say.

"I'm not ready to complete the mating," Hannah whispered. At Reed's widened eyes, she explained. "I'm a witch remember, I know some things about werewolves—like mating. I think we need to get to know one another first before we connect our souls that way."

"Wait? What is she talking about?" Josh asked. "I thought we were already mates. What is completing the mating? And what do our souls have to do with it."

Reed ignored the light sting in his heart that she didn't want to mate yet, though he shouldn't have been surprised. After all, they'd just met.

"Okay, take a seat, both of you." Reed led them to the bed, and they each sat on the edge.

"There are two parts to mating. Seed and marking. When I bite your fleshy part where your shoulders meet your neck, we will be bound through our wolves." Reed held up a hand when Josh wanted to interrupt. "I'll explain, don't worry. My wolf can be bound to you, even if you aren't a wolf yourself."

"But will we have to become wolves?" Josh asked.

Reed sighed, "I don't think Hannah will. I'll have to ask my mom. But once we are fully mated, the fact that she is a witch should tie her to my lifespan. Witches are paranormal just like werewolves. They live longer than humans as it is—but not as long as my family. When a witch is paired by fate to a werewolf, their life binds to the wolf in order to prolong their time together. But when I die—hopefully in the distance future—she will as well." Reed shrugged. "It's harsh, but most of us live well into our thousands. But you, Josh, would have to turn into a wolf if you decide to be immortal, or long lived, like us." Reed looked into the other man's eyes but couldn't see any emotion there. "I can't turn you into a witch, and since vampires—even the sparkly ones—don't exist, there is only that option. Or we'd have to watch you grow old and die. I don't think I could do that."

Josh nodded. "What's the other part of mating?" He didn't say anything about becoming a wolf, but Reed let it slide. The man would have to think for himself.

"The other is through sex." Reed laughed at the expression on Josh's face. "If I spill my seed in both of you, then our human souls will join, and we will be fully mated. I know when humans have sex their souls don't join, but since we're not human, we work differently. We may call them our human halves, but in reality, we aren't human at all. We will be able to feel each other at long distances. We don't get any cool powers like telepathy, but it's still pretty cool, so I hear."

Josh stared wide-eyed, but thankfully no disgust crossed his features. "This is more in depth than I thought."

Hannah reached for his hand, and Reed did the same.

"It's okay; we don't need to make any promises like that tonight. We can go to sleep and talk about it later, or I have another option." Reed stood and walked to his nightstand and pulled out an unopened package of condoms.

Hannah gave a squeak and Josh grunted. Reed didn't know what to think. He wanted them both but he didn't want to push them.

"I want us to be safe," Reed whispered. "But make no mistake—I do want you. Both of you."

He watched both of their faces as they panted with arousal. Nice.

"As long as I don't actually come inside you both, there will be no mating. That means we can still have sex; we just have to be sure that we're always careful."

Both nodded, and Reed relaxed.

Hannah bit her lip and looked upset.

"What's wrong, Hannah?" Josh asked, rubbing her shoulders.

"I know it's stupid, but I don't like the fact that he already had condoms here, even though he just met us." Hannah lowered her head, embarrassed.

"It's okay, Hannah. I'd be jealous, too." Reed went back to the bed and sat next to her, pulling her in his arms. "I haven't been with anyone in years, actually." At their outrageous looks, Reed laughed. "I just couldn't find anyone, and I really didn't care too much. I only have these because North always hands them out in case we find a human we like. We can't get diseases, and we can only impregnate our mates, but it's good to have them for the humans anyway. Try not to think of our pasts right now. We have plenty of time to talk about all of that. I know you won't stop thinking about it just because I ask, but at least try just for now. Only think about the future, because the two of you are it for me. Forever."

Hannah nodded, and Reed kissed her again, inhaling her sweet scent.

Josh cleared his throat, pulling the two of them out of their haze.

"Before we go too far and can't think, I thought I'd say something. Reed, I don't know how far I can go with you. I'm sorry, I'm just not ready." Josh lowered his gaze, as if he was afraid he'd hurt Reed.

But Reed understood. "I know, Josh. It's okay. If we go through with the mating, and I hope to God we do, then we have lifetimes to be together sexually."

Josh's eyes widened at that, and he was just too cute to resist, so Reed leaned over Hannah to kiss him. That sweet woodsy taste danced on his tongue, mingling with Hannah's to form a perfect symphony of pleasure. He pulled back then kissed Hannah again. Josh tugged off her skirt and top, leaving her clad in only her panties and bra. Reed growled at the sight of her pale flesh against her white lacy underthings.

Hannah sighed into his mouth and gripped his shoulders, grinding against his leg. *My little witch is eager. Good.*

Josh trailed his fingers up her sides and pulled her away from Reed. With a groan, Reed watched his two mates kiss and moan. He rubbed his erection, turned on as hell. He stood and quickly divested himself of his clothing, leaving him naked but for his boxer briefs. The two in front of him writhed against each other, clearly into what they were doing. Reed pulled off Hannah's bra, brushing the undersides of her breasts while he did so. Hannah gasped, and Josh looked on in appreciation.

"Dear God, baby, you're magnificent," Josh rasped.

Oh, and how she was. Reed had known she was curvy in all the right places, but damn. Her breasts were full and heavy—more than an overfilled handful, and he had large hands—with dark rosy nipples, already two little hard points of desire.

Dear God, he wanted her more than anything.

Josh lowered Hannah to the bed so they were both sitting and kissed her again. Reed slid back onto the bed to sit on the other side of his witch and lowered his head to pull Hannah's nipple through his teeth.

"Oh, goddess, Reed." The rest of what she would have said was swallowed by Josh's mouth as he kissed her harder.

Reed bit and suckled her nipple, twisting and pinching the other in his hand. Hannah leaned into his touch, begging for more. Reed could only oblige.

Josh pulled away to disrobe fully and sat back on the bed. Reed and Hannah paused to take in Josh's long and thick cock, fully erect with its mushroom head pulsating and a little bead of pre-cum at the tip.

Fuck.

Both men shifted so they sat facing Hannah and her eyes widened. Reed went back to her breasts, indulging in her firm mounds and sweet taste.

Josh massaged her arms, legs, and stomach, rubbing small circles, kissing and licking as he went along.

"Guys," Hannah gasped. "It's too much, and you're barely touching me. So many emotions and sensations. So many hands."

Both men gave hearty chuckles and continued their slow torture.

Reed leapt off the bed and took off his underwear, then slid Hannah's down. He stood back and took in his fill.

Dear God, she's beautiful.

Kneeling beside her, he reached down and traced her brown curly hair to her wet nether lips. He gulped and struggled for control, and then he gently separated her folds with two fingers. Her pink center pulsated and swelled with desire as she gasped at his touch.

Reed looked up at Josh who sat on the other side of their witch, his pupils dilating wide with a rim of ocean blue around them.

"Taste her, Reed," Josh rasped. "Tell me how good she is. I need to taste these rosy nipples; they're begging for my mouth."

The other man leaned over their mate and took her nipple into his mouth. Reed groaned when Hannah rocked her hips against his hand at Josh's touch.

He leaned over and ran his finger around her opening, skirting the edge of her clit, careful only to tease.

"Reed. Please. Touch me. Let me come. I can't take it!" Hannah screamed.

"Is that what you want? You want me to touch you? Here?" He kissed the inside of her thigh.

"No. I mean, yes, that's good, but please. Josh, that feels so good." Hannah arched into Josh when he pulled her nipple into his mouth.

"Please what, Hannah? Tell me," Reed demanded his voice husky.

"Reed. Please touch my clit. Please!"

"Well, since you asked."

Josh laughed. "I think I'm going to like playing with Hannah and you, Reed."

Reed smiled then lowered his mouth to her clit, her honey and bitter apple taste decadent on his taste buds. He flicked it with his tongue at the same time he shoved two fingers into her.

She bucked, and Josh held her down.

"How does she taste, Reed?" Josh asked.

"Let me show you."

Josh bent down as if to lick Hannah, but Reed caught his lips instead. Josh gasped into his mouth then kissed him back. Hard.

"Fuck," Reed muttered when they pulled back.

"Fuck is about right. She tastes fucking amazing on your tongue, but I want to taste from the source. Soon." Josh knelt, wide-eyed, near Hannah, who moaned at the two of them.

Reed sucked and licked, while curving his fingers just right to rub her g-spot.

"Reed...Josh..." Hannah breathed.

Reed groaned and bit down on her clit. She rocked against his face, her pussy closing on his fingers as she came, their names ripping from her throat.

"Jesus, Reed. Did you see how magnificent our girl looks when she comes?" Josh asked in wonder.

"The way her ivory skin blushes with arousal and how her nipples reddened to little pluckable cherries after our mouths feasted on them? Oh, I noticed."

Hannah opened her mouth to speak but only let out a soft moan.

Reed chuckled. "I suppose that means you liked it?"

Hannah nodded.

"Baby," Josh whispered, rubbing her ass as Reed sheathed himself in a condom. "Have you ever had a cock in your ass?"

She bit her lip and shook her head.

"Do you want to?" Reed asked, holding himself still while he waited for a response.

"I think so. I want to do everything with you both." Fear lurked in her eyes, but it was obvious she was also overcome by desire.

"We won't do it tonight, baby," Josh said. "But we will prepare you just a bit. I don't want to hurt you. So we will make sure you are loose and ready for us when one of us sinks our cock into your ass. And then, when you are fully there, I can be in your ass and Reed in your pussy. What do you think about that?"

Hannah nodded, needy. "Okay."

"I'd say fuck yes to that," Reed answered and laughed.

"What's next?" Hannah asked then giggled.

"Oh, I have an idea." Reed slid her to the end of the bed where he could stand and still reach her. "Josh, stand on the side where she can reach you."

Josh smiled with understanding, and Reed leaned over Hannah to take her lips again.

"You taste delicious, baby," Reed whispered.

"You're not so bad yourself."

Reed stood back and watched as Josh took Hannah's head and pulled her to his engorged cock.

"Swallow me, Hannah," Josh groaned.

Hannah opened her mouth wide, the cap of Josh's dick making a slight popping sound as he slid into her mouth. Josh held her in his hands, keeping her head still, and slowly worked his way in and out of her mouth. Reed almost came on the spot watching Hannah's throat work as she tried to take more of him with each stroke.

Reed rubbed her clit, watching her gasp around Josh's cock. She was already wet and flush, waiting for him to fill her. Reed didn't wait any longer. With his gaze on hers, he hooked a knee over his elbow and slowly entered her.

He paused, loving the feel of her around him and then he pounded into her, relishing in the sounds of flesh against sweaty flesh and the moans of all three when they hit the right spots. Josh grabbed his hand, and the three of them came together in a rush of pleasure and intensity.

"Dear Lord. How can you still be hard, Reed?" Hannah panted, heaving for breath.

"I'm a werewolf," Reed answered simply. "I have all sorts of talents."

Josh laughed. "And we're two of the luckiest people out there, right, Hannah?"

Reed skimmed his hands up both of their sides, and they shuddered. He lowered his hand and took Josh's cock, which hardened at the touch.

"Damn, I'm the lucky one. You have a quick recovery time for a human."

"All the better to please you with, my dear." Josh laughed.

"Hey, I thought I was the big bad wolf here." Reed pulled Josh by the cock and kissed him on the lips.

"Well, that was a new touch for me," Josh said.

"Good," Reed and Hannah agreed.

"Now, it seems to me that Reed has been monopolizing that pussy of yours. I think it's my turn." Josh smiled then moved to the edge of the bed before flipping Hannah to her hands and knees.

"Here" Reed handed him a condom then moved around to the other side of the bed to kneel in front of her. He shuddered when Hannah licked the bulging vein under his cock.

She licked up the side then put her mouth around him. He felt her throat muscles relax and she swallowed him whole.

"Jesus, she's tight." Josh groaned as he pushed inside her.

"I know. She's perfect," Reed agreed.

Hannah sucked and swallowed. Reed fucked her mouth while Josh fucked her pussy. Reed reached over and pulled out lube from his nightstand and coated his fingers. Bending over her with his cock still in her mouth, he slowly traced her puckered hole. Hannah stiffened but relaxed, waiting for his next move. He slowly worked one finger in, listening to her moan as he moved past the thin ring of muscles. Josh pulled her cheeks apart, aiding him. He worked his finger in and out until he felt comfortable adding a second, then a third.

When Hannah lifted a hand to cup and fondle his balls, he stiffened then his hot seed poured down her throat as he roared in approval. Josh groaned and followed soon behind. He couldn't wait fill her womb with his seed, completing the mating then, one day, watch her grow heavy and ripe with their young.

Both men pulled out slowly, careful not to hurt her. Josh set Hannah down on her side as she lay there boneless. Reed ran to the bathroom to grab a wet cloth. He cleaned them all up then got into bed, under the covers, holding Hannah against his chest, Josh nestled against her back.

"I'm falling in love with both of you," Hannah whispered. "But I don't understand it. I've only just met you; I don't even know you." She fell asleep snuggled between the two of them, all sweaty and glowing.

Reed looked over her head to Josh, who nodded.

"I'm feeling the same way, but I don't know what to think about it," Josh whispered.

Reed reached for Josh's hand, clasping it tightly. "We will work it out. Get some sleep. We need it."

They slept in a sweaty pile, limbs linked and tangled, and all Reed could think about was that this was the best time of his life.

Chapter 14

Josh woke to a plump, curvy butt rubbing against his crotch. His dick woke up and pressed against the seam of her ass, probing for an entry. Her tousled curls lay haphazardly around her as she pillowed her head on his arm. His other arm wrapped around her, resting on Reed's side. This could be happiness. The happily-ever-after-hot-regular-sex-three-kids-cozy-fireplace kind of happiness.

But that wasn't for him.

This was just a phase. It had to be. They would grow tired of him, and then he'd leave. He'd be left with nothing, something he was used to. But this time it'd be harder. Much harder.

Reed shifted in his sleep, rubbing against the bite mark. A low tremor of pain radiated up his arm.

Damn.

Throughout the night, even through the amazing sex, his arm had throbbed. He'd tried to ignore it, but he knew something was wrong. Was he dying? Could someone turn into a demon from a bite? No one really had any answers for him.

Hannah's butt wiggled again, and Josh let out a long, guttural moan.

Reed's narrow fingers ran up along Josh's side in a smooth motion. He smiled at the sleepy man.

"Did you sleep okay?" Reed asked.

"Never better actually. The two of you feel amazing to sleep next to."

Reed practically beamed at him. "Good."

Shit, this was getting to feel too normal. Too perfect.

"I need to piss." His words rushed out.

He mentally slapped himself. *Great job, dude. Tough Navy SEAL can't just be content in bed. Has to ruin it by opening his big mouth.*

The bed shook slightly with Reed's laughter, then the other man bit his lip, presumably to try and not wake up Hannah.

"Go, you know where it is. I'll be up in a minute."

Naked, Josh slid out of bed while Reed hugged Hannah closer to his side when she whimpered at the loss of contact.

"Look in the top drawer for some pajama bottoms," Reed said. "They should fit you since we're about the same size except through the shoulders and torso. We can worry about getting you both some clothes and everything else you'll need from your places or the stores later." Josh stiffened and Reed sobered. "Even if you don't live here permanently, you can't go home yet. It's not safe. Let me at least make you comfortable. Please."

Josh nodded. "Okay, we can talk about it."

Hannah snuggled into Reed's side and touched his sandy-blond hair. The two of them molded together perfectly, as if they were made for each other. Josh snorted. Considering they were mates, that was likely the case. Josh yearned to jump back in bed and hold them close, but he didn't. He couldn't. He had to wean himself off the two of them.

Josh also couldn't rely on the Pack. He didn't want to be a burden. And at this point, as a mere human, that's exactly how he felt. He quickly took care of his business in the bathroom and looked at the bite mark. Still bruised and red in some places, the web of red marks didn't seem to have changed. They still stretched from his wrist to almost his elbow.

At least that was something.

With Reed and Hannah still in bed, he took the time to look around the house. It looked like an affluent bachelor pad decorated with an artist's flair. Comfy furniture with a large screen TV and entertainment system appealed to the man in him. Reed's kitchen however left something to be desired. If Josh moved in, they'd have to change a few things to utilize the space better. And he was sure Hannah would want to add some feminine touches and colors. Not to mention the fact that they would need to add space somehow once they had kids.

Josh pulled himself up short.

What the fuck was he thinking about the future for? They didn't have one. Why was he going about trying to pick out fucking china patterns and thinking about green-eyed babies with curly brown hair? There wasn't a place for him here. He couldn't contribute. He was just a human in a paranormal world. And even though Reed said they were mates and Josh was honest enough to say he felt the connection between the three of them, a permanent threesome, or triad, would never work. It couldn't work. There would always be jealousy and hurt feelings. Especially since there was sexual tension between Reed and him.

Josh left the kitchen and went through a door he hadn't seen before. Art covered the walls. Canvas and paint supplies filled every surface. Reed's studio. Josh had known he was an artist, but they'd been so busy with fighting he hadn't really thought about the talent that lay in those narrow fingers. He groaned remembering how talented they were with that oh-so-soft touch last night. His dick hardened, tenting out his pajama bottoms, first at the thought of Reed and then remembering the feeling of being inside Hannah. Her soft warmth milking his shaft last night, even through a condom, was the most earth-shattering experience of his life.

"Hey, you found my room." Reed walked into the studio wearing only pajama bottoms, looking tousled but relatively awake.

Not to mention fucking sexy.

Reed padded over and kissed him gently, his sandalwood taste on his tongue. Josh wasn't sure if he'd ever get used to kissing a man and feeling the difference from when he kissed Hannah. But he liked both. A lot. He ran a hand down the other man's arm, noticing the goose bumps left in its wake. He'd never thought he'd like touching a man, but it didn't feel wrong. It felt right. And with the addition of Hannah, it felt more so.

Could he go further with Reed? Let them go down on each other? Then submit to him and let him take him? Or could he take Reed? He shuddered at the thought. He wasn't ready by any stretch for that, but he still got turned on. That was a good sign. Right?

Reed kissed him again, this time letting his tongue slide along the seam of his lips. Josh opened for him, allowing the man entry. They each fought for control, the kiss intensifying with each passing second.

Reed pulled back first, breathing heavily, as Josh shook his muddled brain.

"Good morning." Reed laughed.

"Yes, it is," Josh agreed.

Reed took his hand and Josh let him. *Huh, not too bad.*

"I have something I'm working on I want to show you."

"Okay, lead the way."

Reed went to the back corner and let go of Josh's hand long enough to pull the fabric off an easel.

Josh gasped.

A naked Willow knelt in a grassy grove, the angles and her hair covering the most essential parts. She looked towards the observer, her warm brown eyes glowing with hope and promise. Her hands rested on her protruding belly, cradling her and Jasper's child.

She looked magnificent. And Reed was beyond brilliant.

"Wow, Reed. This is remarkable."

Reed took a deep breath. "Thank God. I was worried. I loved it, but I wasn't sure. No one else has seen it."

Josh looked at him in surprise.

"It's a secret for Jasper. I didn't even let Willow sneak a peek. She only posed when I did the prelim sketches. I'm going to give it to them both after the baby shower. I just don't want Jasper to kick my ass for seeing his wife naked."

"I'll protect you." He grinned. "Plus she looks like an angel, and this will be something they will treasure always. She doesn't look nude. Honestly, she looks like a mother. It isn't pornographic; it's something for their family."

Reed hugged him hard, kissing his temple. "Thank you. That was the perfect thing to say."

Josh shrugged. "It's the truth."

"Well, thank you anyway."

"If it's a secret, why is it not hidden more?"

Reed laughed. "Well, since nobody is allowed in my studio without permission, and even that is rare, they don't have a chance to see it."

Josh blushed in embarrassment. "Shit, I'm sorry, man. I just barged right in and didn't even think about your privacy."

Reed touched his cheek. "It's okay, Josh. Really. You didn't know. And I didn't mean it that way. I'm sorry. Honestly, I'm not even too concerned by it. I want you to see everything I have, everything I am. Hannah too. And if I do need to paint something I don't feel is ready for others' eyes yet, I will let you know and do more to prevent accidental sharing. Don't worry."

Josh exhaled. "Okay, but let me know if I'm intruding. You've already done so much."

"Josh," Reed said, shaking his head, "I've done nothing. You saved me and Hannah. I want you here with me. Let me take care of you how I can."

Though it wasn't easy to do so, Josh nodded. If it made Reed feel better, he'd give in, but he knew this wouldn't last. Something would happen.

Was he ready for forever?

"Reed, I don't know about our future. I need time."

"Okay."

"But what we can do is talk about the Centrals. Do you have any idea of your father's plans?"

Reed sighed. "I'm not part of Dad's enforcers. And I'm not *the* Enforcer."

"What does that mean?"

"Adam is the Enforcer. Capital E. He is the one in charge of taking care of forces that want to hurt us, though he answers to

Dad. And now that he's gone, even for a little while, I think that will go to Kade, since he's next in line for the throne. Dad also has men outside our family that act like guards. Neil, the husband of Melanie's friend Larissa, is one of them. They help Adam and Dad. Kade and Jasper do a lot as well. I'm stuck in the middle. Not really useful."

"Reed, you're everything." Without thinking, he rubbed Reed's chin, liking the stubble across the pad of his thumb. "Look at the work you do here. You help out the Pack with their archives and paint their history. And you teach the children at school. I mean, that counts for something. You can do what others can't. I don't know why you feel inferior to your family. You shouldn't. Plus, you are a fighter. No matter what you think, I know this. I've seen you. You fought off twenty wolves single handedly, and only ended up with a few scratches. You are a strong wolf, believe in that."

Reed shook his head. "You understand so much, after such little time."

Josh smiled, not liking the sad look on Reed's face. "It's not that hard to take in, Reed. And when we finish getting ready, we can go over to your Dad's house and see what's going on. They can't just leave us out."

Reed laughed. "Yeah, they can. He's Alpha. He can pretty much do whatever he wants."

"Well, then we'll ask." *Forcefully.*

"Okay. It can't hurt."

"Reed, how did all of this happen?"

"What?" A cute, confused look appeared on his face.

"How could the Centrals take you? How could the Redwoods let this happen?" Josh winced at the way that had come out. Shit, he didn't want to offend anyone. He just needed to know how the Centrals got so powerful.

Reed sucked in a breath and clenched his fists, anger radiating off of him.

"Reed, I didn't mean…"

"No, Josh. It's okay. I'm not mad at you. It's just a fucked-up situation. You see, evil doesn't follow the same kind of rules we do. They don't have to worry about killing people with their powers. They relish it. They don't have to worry about crossing the lines of demonic nature and fucking with fate. They do what they want. And no matter what we do, the Centrals have the upper hand because we can't cross those boundaries. We fight back, and we do our best to keep the damage to a minimum, but until we can find a way to use magic and energy that doesn't cross into evil, we're always going to be behind."

Well, fuck.

"Reed, some things aren't black and white. There has to be a way."

"Sometimes even the gray isn't strong enough."

Reed closed his eyes, lines of tension on his face. Josh couldn't resist and brushed the lock of hair that fell across his brows away.

Damn, he wanted him.

Josh lowered his face and brushed his lips against Reed's. The other man pulled him closer, their rigid cocks sliding against one another, creating heated friction.

A polite cough made them pull apart, slowly.

Hannah stood in a pair of borrowed boxers and Josh's shirt, looking like a damned fuckable pixie.

"Good morning, boys. You look like you've been busy." She gave them an impish smile.

"A little," Josh rumbled.

She prowled over to them both, kissing Reed, then Josh, giving him the best good morning he'd ever had.

With Hannah in his arms, and Reed by his side, he could almost see a future. Pain pierced his temple as a sudden headache came on.

"Josh, what is it?" Hannah asked.

"Just a headache. I need some water." He strode away without a look back.

There was no future with them. He needed to stop thinking about shit like that. It led to nowhere. He was a loner. That was all he was.

Pain lanced up his arm, pulsating around the wound.

Great, that was all he needed.

Chapter 15

"Are you ready to go?" Reed came up behind Hannah and held her close.

Hannah buttoned up the last button on her borrowed blouse and took a look in the mirror. She finally felt clean after four showers. The dirt and grime from the basement hell wasn't seeping into her pores anymore. Though she wasn't wearing her own skirt and top, it still fit well enough that she didn't look too bad.

Hannah shrugged. "Sure."

"You look beautiful."

A laugh escaped her. "You have to say that; you're sleeping with me."

"True." Reed grunted when her elbow came in contact with his stomach. "But you are beautiful. I'd say it anyway."

"He's telling the truth." Josh came in the room, freshly showered and looking quite edible. "Just saying."

"Okay, boys. Now that my ego is restored, I guess we can go."

"As long as you're happy, milady." Reed bowed extravagantly.

"Really, man? Milady? Did you say that back when you were a young man?" Josh laughed.

"Ha ha. Let's make fun of the old man. But remember, I can keep both of you busy and satisfied with my old man cock. So what do you say now?" Reed raised a brow.

"I'll take it for a ride?" Hannah asked, smiling.

Both men burst out laughing, and she joined them.

"Sounds good, babe." Josh held her close, brushing his lips against hers. "Let's go to the Alpha's. This should be fun."

"Don't worry. I'll protect you from the big bad Alpha." Hannah laughed.

Josh's eyes darkened. "I don't need you to protect me."

Okay. Touchy subject.

"I was just kidding. I'm sorry."

Josh shook his head. "Sorry, I knew you were. Apparently my headache is making me act like an ass."

Reed cupped Josh's cheek. "Do you need something for that? Can I help?"

Hannah cupped his other cheek. "I'm a witch, after all. I can make you something."

Josh quirked a lip. "I'm okay for now. If it gets any worse, I'll take you up on it. Thank you."

"Okay, then. I guess we're ready." Reed sighed.

He looked so nervous, but Hannah didn't really understand why. This was his family. But then again, they'd cut him out during the decisions last night. Reed said it was because he was just an artist. But she'd seen him fight to protect her and Josh. He was fierce and strong, despite what he thought of himself. He'd been kidnapped, tortured, and shot; yet his first thought was always her. Why couldn't his parents see that? Was it because he had two mates? Would that lower his status because he wasn't normal?

Since all of the Jamensons lived relatively close to one another in the den, it was just a quick walk to Edward and Pat's house. Along the way Hannah looked at the tall trees with snow on their branches and the snow covering the forest floor. Though winter was just starting, up in the mountains, it got colder quicker.

She inhaled the crisp mountain air. Even with the natural setting, the den felt like a home. Welcoming and warm despite the cooling temperatures, not to mention loving. Could it be her home? Could she get used to this?

Hannah sighed. Everything had changed so fast. But she didn't know if she resented it exactly. Last night had been amazing. She blushed just thinking about the movement of three bodies and their sweat while making love. She'd only been with a couple of men before Reed and Josh, and never in her lifetime would she have thought she'd be the girl sleeping with two men at once.

And liking it.

Okay, if she were honest with herself, *loving* it.

Geez. What must Reed's family think of her? She was a slut with even sluttier thoughts. She'd had the most amazing sex of her life with two men and didn't feel bad about it. Oh, she worried all right, but she'd do it again. Planned on it. She'd let them do things to her she'd never let another do, and she wanted more of it. When Reed had played with her bottom, she'd thought she'd come right on the spot. She held back a moan at the thought of Josh buried there, with Reed in her pussy.

Goddess. If his parents knew what had gone on in that bedroom with their son, Hannah and Josh would surely be on the next ride out of the den. She bit her lip and groaned in frustration.

Josh squeezed her hand. "It'll be all right."

At least she wasn't alone in this. Josh must be feeling the same as she was. More so. He was looking at his sexuality in a whole new light, crossing taboo boundaries and enjoying it. Thank the goddess they had each other, especially since they were about to go talk to the "in-laws" and she had to keep from blushing and bursting into flames on the spot.

They walked up to the large open house and Pat opened the door before they knocked. It must be nice to have werewolf senses sometimes.

"Oh, good. I'm so happy you're here. And you look so well rested." She winked and looked at the two men.

Oh. My. Goddess.

Mortified, and knowing she was as red as a tomato, she allowed herself to be hugged by Pat, while Reed and Josh barely held in their laughter.

"Now, you boys stop it with that look. I didn't mean anything by it. Get your minds out of the gutter." Pat fisted her hands on her hips with a not-so-serious scowl on her face.

It was such a mom pose that tears sprung in Hannah's eyes.

Oh my. I miss you, Mom.

It's had only been three weeks. Three little weeks since she'd heard her mom laugh, telling her to keep her head out of her potions and to find a nice young witch to settle down and make babies with. Three weeks since her mom had hugged her and told her she loved her. She'd known Reed even less since he'd come to the basement after her.

Sorrow crept over the ache in her heart, gripping and not letting go.

"Oh, baby." Pat pulled her into the foyer, out of the cold, and enveloped her in her arms.

Hannah sniffed. "I'm sorry. I'm just a mess right now."

"It's all right. That whole Centrals ordeal, meeting both of your mates, and losing your mom in such a short period of time would be too much for anyone. You just cry it out and let the Jamensons—and Josh—take care of you."

"Thank you, Pat."

"Oh, baby. When you're ready, you can call me Mom. But not before that. Your mother was such a nice woman. I'll miss her."

Hannah leaned back, startled at the news.

"You knew my mother?"

Pat smiled. "Yes dear. It was long ago, when you were just a baby. I held you in my arms and knew I wanted a girl. So I went back to Edward and said, after six boys, I wanted a baby. So two years later, after some wrangling with that Alpha, I got my baby girl, Cailin. And Edward is wrapped around that girl's finger like no other. If you hear him tell the story, it was his idea."

"I never knew that," Reed said, wide-eyed.

"You never asked." Pat shrugged. "But what a world we live in with fate as our guide. I got to see this baby again." She squeezed Hannah closer. "You look so much like your mother."

At that point, whatever resistance to sobbing Hannah had left, fell out the window.

Tears flowed down her cheeks. Josh pulled her from Pat's arms and kissed the top of her head.

"I'm so sorry, my Hannah," Josh whispered.

"Oh, Hannah. I'm sorry; I didn't mean to make you cry." Tears fell from the woman's eyes, and Reed held his mother close.

"It's okay, Pat. It's just hard to hear. But so, so nice. Thank you for that story."

Both women sniffed and pulled out of the men's arms, trying to compose themselves.

"It's just so good, seeing you three together," Pat said.

All three of them gave her awkward looks. What else could she do when the mother of one of the men she's sleeping with says the three of them look good together?

"I'm so happy another one of my babies found their mate. Well, mates in this case. After Adam..." Pat shuddered.

"Mom," Reed interjected.

"No, your mates need to know why Adam left. I saw the look he gave the three of you, and you need to know it's nothing you've done."

Josh held Hannah closer while Reed sidled up to them.

"Adam's mate, Anna, was taken by the Centrals. But unlike with you, we didn't get to her in time. They'd beaten, raped, and killed her. And the child she carried. Adam never recovered, and Maddox, who felt every emotion she felt, never did either. Our family was now just starting to heal, and then the Centrals came back."

Hannah's tears fell harder, leaving a salty trail of lost dreams in their wake.

"I think with Kade, then Jasper, and now you getting mated so soon after one another, Adam's feeling lonely. I just hope he finds what he needs. Because I don't know if he'll find what he needs here if, no, when, he comes back."

Pat let out a breath, visibly shaken and sad. "Okay, that's enough of that. Let's go into the living room." Pat led them though the hallway into the homey living room where Edward sat alone, reading something on his iPad.

Who knew older werewolves were so tech savvy?

"Ah, you're here." Edward set down the tablet and stood, walking to Hannah and giving her a hug.

Surprised, she hugged him back.

Edward let out a huge, booming laugh. "Sorry, we're wolves. Very affectionate. And you're family now. Get used to hugging."

As if to prove his point, he hugged Josh.

Josh just laughed faintly and did the whole man hug, pat on the back thing.

When Edward moved back from hugging Reed, they all sat down on the couch and waited for Edward to begin.

"Dad, are we early? Where is everyone?" Reed asked.

Edward sighed. "They've already left. We've had the meeting, son."

Reed lowered his brows and scowled. She held his hand, barely able to control her own fury. Josh reached over her and rubbed Reed's shoulder, tension rippling in both men.

How could they have decided everything without their participation? Weren't they the ones who had just been held prisoner?

Slowly, very softly, Reed spoke. "Why were we not involved?"

Edward raised a brow then glanced at her and Josh.

Oh. He doesn't trust us.

Hurt, Hannah bit her lip.

Reed growled. "My mates are trustworthy. You never had a problem with Willow or Melanie."

"And yet our Pack has been weakened by the traitors in our midst. I need more time before I share all of our secrets. I'm sorry Josh and Hannah, but more lives are involved than just those of us in this room. I need to be cautious."

She understood where he was coming from. As Alpha, he had more than his share of responsibility, but that didn't mean it didn't hurt to hear. Especially since he was the father of one of them men she was falling in love with.

Reed growled again.

Edward growled back, a magic she didn't understand washing over them. "Watch your tone, boy. I am still Alpha of this Pack. I don't know them, and frankly, I'm interested in just how Josh found the two of you. It's too coincidental for me."

Josh took a deep breath, rubbing his hand on her leg.

Hannah stayed silent, as if waiting for a fuse to be lit, for the bomb to explode.

"I'm a Finder," Josh explained.

Edward's eyes widened. "I see."

Josh cocked his head. "Do you?'

The Alpha sat back in his chair, rubbing his chin. "You are not the first I've met, but the first I've met in a long while." He nodded again, a thoughtful look on his face. "Good to know."

"He will not be used," Reed growled.

Edward actually laughed. "It's good to see you standing up for your mate. But I didn't say I would, did I? You are blessed in your mates. I will not use him. I only find it interesting."

Reed moved to stand. *This can't be good.*

Hannah jumped in. "Let's move on. Okay?"

Edward laughed again. "I like you, Hannah."

Hannah smiled while she squeezed Reed's hand.

The Alpha cleared his throat. "We tried to find you, Reed." Pain shot across his eyes. "But the Centrals used dark magic to cloud your presence. It was luck that Adam even found you."

The room sat in silence at the mention of Adam.

"We can fight," Edward continued. "Go to their territory, attack, and try and find retribution. But with the Central's dark magic, that dammed demon, and their witches..."

Hannah gasped.

The witches were working for their enemies?

Reed brushed her cheek with his finger. "Some are working for the Centrals. We've tasted their magic. But we don't know who. I'm sorry, Hannah."

She could only nod. What coven would align with that type of evil? Witches were white magic, though they didn't call it that. Goodness. The sort of thing Centrals did would only taint the inherent nature of witches.

"We will retaliate." Edward promised. "Mark my words. But we need to be strong. Find a way to use magic that doesn't cross our lines, one that is good. We need to know who exactly is there and how to fight the unknown."

Josh cleared his throat. "When I was in the SEALs, we came upon their den before." He paused, glancing at Reed and her. "I can give you the precise layout of what I know and any other info I may have."

"Impressive," Edward said.

Hannah smiled at Reed and Josh. Both of her men had such talents and hidden depths.

Wait. My men?

Huh.

She kind of liked that.

"Dad, you need to keep us in the loop. We will fight," Reed said.

"Yes," Hannah added. "All of us."

She looked at both her men, daring them to say anything against her.

Josh gazed into her eyes while Reed squeezed her hand, then they nodded as one. "Yes, all of us," they said together.

Edward nodded. "Okay then." Then he turned to her. "You are our Healer, Hannah."

"Oh, I don't know. I'm just a healer; I don't know if I'm *your* Healer."

"Hannah, I feel it. We all do."

Pat and Reed nodded in agreement.

"But..." She trailed off as a warm feeling of belonging settled over her.

She looked into Edward's eyes, and he smiled.

She *was* their Healer. She wasn't alone anymore.

Reed kissed her softly, then Josh did the same. She blushed in embarrassment.

"You feel okay?" Reed asked.

"I feel like I can Heal anything. You know?"

"Hannah," Edward interrupted, "once you are mated fully and become part of the Pack, you will feel every Pack member. If they are hurt, you will know. Maddox will help you in your training so you won't be overwhelmed."

She was overwhelmed as it was. How could she deal with all of these people? How many were there? The enormity of the situation hit her. She'd made her choice. She was Reed's mate. Part of the Redwoods now.

If she were already feeling like this now, how would she be when she felt the rest of the Pack? She needed to talk to Maddox. If he felt all the emotions, he'd be a total help.

"You will be an asset to the Pack; I can tell," Edward added. "I mean, look at what you've done to my son. Josh too. I've never seen Reed so happy and relaxed." He wiggled his eyebrows.

Again, Hannah blushed scarlet.

Do all werewolves talk about their kids' sex lives? Geesh.

"You are important. But remember, Hannah," Edward added, "you are not above others in the Pack. You are not more worthy than they are."

Reed let out a strangled cough.

"Is there something you'd like to add, son?" Edward asked.

"No, I'm fine."

"No, you aren't. Tell me."

Reed sighed. "Fine. I just don't believe you. You can't tell me that Kade or Jasper or anyone else in our family isn't more important the others. Yes, all Pack members are valued. But they are critical to our survival."

Edward looked at him with confusion.

"Reed, you are just as important."

Reed gave a hollow laugh.

"You are the one who paints our culture, our history. Since you were a pup, you've been keeping records and remembering those who would've been forgotten. Without you, our Pack would not have that backbone. Our future pups would not know their history by art. You are just as important as all my children."

Reed stayed silent, and Hannah eyes filled with tears at the pain and sense of loss on his face.

"Reed, we were coming for you. Never doubt that. No matter what, we would have found you. I felt you here." He placed his hand over his heart. "But we couldn't find you."

Then the tough Alpha of the fiercest Pack of werewolves in the nation, grabbed his son in a backbreaking hug with tears in his eyes.

Pat stood up and joined her family, crying with them. Then she stood back and pulled Josh and Hannah in the hug.

This was her new family if fate allowed it. Warmth infused her bones.

Pat patted both her and Josh's cheeks. "You may not have completed the mating, but you are our family now. We don't let go of what is ours. So you're stuck with us regardless."

Neither she nor Josh said anything, merely nodding.

Edward pulled back first, clearing his throat and unsuccessfully trying to put on his stern Alpha-mask.

"Go home. Get to know one another. When I know more, I will tell you."

"Thank you, Dad." Reed nodded.

They all hugged goodbye, then the three of them walked out of the house, hand in hand. They had accepted her into Reed's family. Just like that. Warmth spread through her. Things were happening so fast, but she could wait to see what would happen next.

Chapter 16

After lunch the next day, Reed stood in his old storage room, staring at the skylights and hoping it would allow enough light in to room for Hannah. He bent and lifted a few old paintings he'd finished but never quite liked and just stuck in this room, forgotten.

"Reed, don't do this. I don't want to take up your space," Hannah argued.

"Baby, I've been wanting to put these in an actual storage unit for years. I want you to feel comfortable here. This way you can do your potions and grow an herb garden. I know you've been itching to do it. Don't lie. Let me do this for you." He needed to do something to show he wanted her here permanently. And if giving her this room was only a small token, he'd do it without regret.

"But what if you need more studio space?" Hannah bit her lip in that sexy way of hers.

"Then I'll build on," Reed said simply. He had the money he'd accumulated from his paintings over his long life, and the space on the land around his home. Plus, Kade was an amazing architect and Jasper an equally amazing contractor who could whip something up for Reed in a heartbeat. It paid to have talent like that in the family.

"That does make it sound permanent," Josh said quietly, an odd look on his face.

"I hope so," Reed whispered. He didn't dare say anything else.

He thought he saw something dark flash across Josh's eyes, but it went away as fast as it appeared. Maybe a trick of the light? He shrugged it off. He was probably just seeing things.

Together, the three of them cleared away the rest of the canvases and paints, leaving a room with benches and pretty good natural light. They'd only need to add some paint to the walls, sand down the wooden benches and tables, and then add in whatever garden supplies Hannah needed to start up her workspace. Once the spring came, she'd be able to start one outside too. Maybe he'd talk to Kade about building a greenhouse.

"Where do you want these?" Josh asked.

He held a bag of soil over one shoulder and some cuttings from Reed's mother in his other hand. They'd gone to the town center in the den earlier and bought at least the beginnings of what Hannah would need. Plus they'd visited Willow's bakery and eaten some of her cinnamon rolls. *Yum.*

"Here, let me help." Reed walked toward him, but Josh shook his head.

"No, I got it, just tell me where."

Hannah pointed, and Reed watched the man's muscles bunch and flex under the weight of the bag with every step.

Dear God, that man is fucking sexy as hell.

Reed bit back a grown and went back to sanding the benches and tables.

"We should just mate them already. They are perfect for us. They want us. Why are we waiting?"

Reed could only agree with his wolf, but he still had to wait for the two of them to actually say they wanted forever. He was damned sure, but he saw the hesitancy on both their faces.

Reed shook his head and walked over to Hannah, who stood frozen looking at her new room.

"What do you need? What can I get you?"

She looked up at him, tears in her eyes. "Nothing." She paused. "Everything."

Her head came up, and Reed saw fear underlying the weariness.

What could be so wrong to make her look like that?

She let out a breath. "I'm afraid if I give in and hope for more, it'll crush me once everything falls to pieces and I lose everything."

Josh came up behind her and pulled her in his arms. "Don't think about that; it will only make your head hurt. I know because mine already does."

Reed kissed her softly. "Live for now. Find your way. We can still be together. Forever. Don't think about the unknown and what could happen when we don't even know what *is* happening."

Hannah nodded and wiped away the tears before they fell. "I've been such a cry baby lately. I hate it." She sniffed, and they laughed.

"What do you need?" Reed asked again.

She gave a half smile. "I want to feel the soil."

"Sounds reasonable. Go for it. I'm going to paint this wall, if that's okay. You said you wanted a landscape, right?" At her nod, he smiled.

Just as her fingers itched to plant and feel the earth, his did to paint and share his talent with his mates.

"Let me help, Hannah." Josh went and opened the bags for her, listening as she explained exactly what she was doing.

Reed's heart warmed at the thought of the three of them sharing the same space, working together as one. It was just a small step, but it meant so much.

Josh let out a big laugh. "I have a black thumb. I'll let you get to the planting. But I can sand these shelves and get these benches and tables ready."

Josh got busy, and all three of them worked silently on their goals to make Hannah's room hers.

Hannah moaned, and Reed looked over to see her arms above her head and her body stretched like a cat.

Fuck me.

He went on alert, hard as a rock, and out of the corner of his eye, he saw Josh do the same.

"What?" She batted her eyes playfully, knowing damn well what she was doing. "It's been two hours. I need a break. Any ideas how to work the kinks out of my back?"

"Two hours?" Reed groaned. "I'm sure I can help you with your back. Come here."

She shook her head, smiling.

"Okay, then. Why don't you come here?" Josh teased.

She bit her lip and shook her head again. "Nuh uh. You come to me." Then she darted out of the room, leaving Josh and him looking on in astonishment.

"First one who catchers her gets to taste her?" Josh asked.

"Deal."

They both made it to the couch in the living room at the same time and stopped dead in their tracks.

Hannah lay on her back on the white couch, which was big enough for three to lie down. Naked. Her hand circled her nipple, and the other trailed down to her damp curls.

"Dear God," Josh rasped.

Reed growled, too turned on to speak.

Both men stripped quickly, and Reed pounced on her.

Sometimes it's nice to have werewolf speed.

Hannah gasped and smiled. "Caught me."

"Oh, I'll catch you again. And again," Reed growled. Then he crushed his mouth to hers, drowning in her honey and bitter apple taste. He fisted his hand in her hair, pulling her head to the side so he could go deeper with his tongue. His cock lay in the valley between her thighs, sliding in her juices, teasing.

Then Josh surprised the hell out of him by wrapping his strong arms around Reed's waist, kissing a trail up his spine. Reed pulled is mouth off Hannah, letting out a gut-wrenching moan. Josh continued until he gently nibbled his neck then leaned over and kissed Hannah, forcing a startled groan out of her. He could feel Josh's erect cock sliding against the crease of his ass, and he growled in need.

"Josh, damn, that feels good," Reed grunted.

"Well, you did reach Hannah first so you get a taste. But I never said anything about not tasting your skin." Josh bit his neck then licked the mark. Reed shuddered.

Hannah laughed. "Hey, don't I get a say in this?" She wiggled beneath him, her slick folds rubbing along Reed's cock.

"Well, I was going to lick up that sweet cream of yours, but I think it's Josh's turn. But I will let you swallow my cock. What do you say?" Reed licked her neck and plucked her nipples as he asked.

Hannah shivered and moaned. "Anything. Just touch me. Someone. Both of you. I don't care. Please."

Josh pulled Reed off Hannah, kissed him fully on the mouth, and grabbed his cock. Reed moaned and rocked into the man's firm hand.

Damn, this man turned him on like no other. Being near Josh and Hannah gave Reed a perceptual hard-on and was starting to give him a permanent limp.

Josh released him and nudged him towards Hannah's pouty mouth. Well, if he couldn't have Josh's hand, he'd be happy for that warm mouth of hers.

He was one lucky wolf.

Josh knelt between her legs and feasted like a starving man. Hannah buckled and moaned, fisting her hand in the man's dark mane.

Reed ran his hand up and down his dick, rubbing in the bead of pre-cum at the tip. He could come just watching the two of them.

"Reed, get here. Now."

He loved when his Hannah got demanding.

He moved so he stood in front of her and tapped her plump lips with his erection. She opened, and he slid into her, pumping in and out of her mouth while she licked, sucked, and used her teeth on the way out.

"Geez." He groaned when she swallowed him and he hit the back of her throat. She hollowed her mouth then screamed as she came against Josh's face, Reed following right afterward.

"Damn, hold on. I'll be right back." Josh lifted himself from the couch and ran naked to the back of the house. He returned quickly with a wicked smile on his face and condoms in his hand.

Though it hurt to think about the fact they didn't want a true mating yet, he ignored it. They were getting closer, moving in together, at least for the time being. He'd take what he could get.

Josh pulled Hannah in his arms and kissed her. "Reed," he said between breaths, "Lie down on your back."

Intrigued, Reed lay down, still hard, and watched the two he loved kiss and fondle each other. Josh lifted his head then turned Hannah around so she stood bent over Reed's cock, her ass against Josh's groin.

"Suck him off again," Josh demanded. "Make him want your pussy."

"Oh, I already want her, but I won't say no." Reed laughed then almost choked on his tongue when Hannah took his balls in her mouth.

Well then.

She sucked them and then licked his cock like an ice cream cone. Reed wanted to close his eyes in bliss but held himself still, fighting for control.

Josh pounded into Hannah from behind, gripping her hips. His knuckles were white against her skin, and his veins popped out along his forearms as he rammed into her.

Fuck, they were both so sexy.

Hannah's nose brushed his pubic hair as she took him down the back of her throat, and he couldn't take it anymore.

He came in a rush, holding her hair as she swallowed every drop.

She lifted her head and screamed both of their names as she came, Josh following them both with a roar.

He loved his two mates.

Now he just had to get them to stay for good.

Josh lifted Hannah up and onto Reed's lap.

"Still hard?" Josh asked.

"Fuck yes, give me that pussy, baby," Reed rasped.

"I don't know if I can take another one," Hannah whimpered.

Both men froze.

"Are you hurting? What can we do?" Reed tried to get up, but she clamped her thighs around him.

"I'm not sore; I just feel so good. But I want you. Please."

Josh handed her a condom, and she wrapped it around his length. Slowly. Then she slid down him, equally as slow.

Hannah used her abs muscles and moved herself up and down his cock, milking him. Her pussy fluttered around him, and he gripped her hips, slamming upwards into her core, rubbing against her g-spot.

"Did you forget about me?" Josh asked, running his hand along his freshly hardened length.

Hannah continued to ride him like a gorgeous buckle-bunny, and Reed turned his head.

"Come here."

Josh took a deep breath and shifted to face them both.

"Will you let me touch you?" Reed asked.

Please God, I need to taste this man.

"Just tell me what to do," Josh said, looking lost.

"You've done this before. I'm no different from Hannah."

Hannah laughed. "Well, maybe a little different, but let him lick you, Josh. His tongue is so talented."

Her breasts bounced as the rode him, and he tilted his hips to go deeper. She moaned and picked up the pace.

Josh moved closer, and Reed released one hand from Hannah's hip to grab the other man's dick and lick the tip.

Josh groaned. "Do that again."

Reed complied then took it one step further and put the whole thing in his mouth.

"Fuck."

Josh rubbed Hannah's clit while she worked Reed's cock. Reed swallowed Josh and fondled his balls. The three of them worked together in a frenzied pace, panting, sweating, and moaning. Reed's balls drew up tight, and he exploded in the condom. His only regret was that he couldn't spill his seed in her womb. But that would come. It had to.

Josh shouted then released down Reed's throat. Reed swallowed every drop, loving the heady taste.

Hannah collapsed, utterly spent, across Reed's chest. She laughed and squirmed at their joining. He had no energy to move, he figured he'd slip out eventually.

Josh's body shook, but he kissed them both then took the condom off Reed.

Damn, even that was sexy.

"I'll take care of this but make room for me." Josh ran out. Well, more like stumbled quickly.

He came back soon after and cuddled into Reed's side after throwing an afghan on top of them.

Sighing, Reed held them close.

"I could get used to more afternoons like this one." Hannah nibbled on Reed's ear, and he squeezed them both.

Yeah, so could he.

Chapter 17

"So, you're sure it's okay if we come with you?" Hannah asked Reed, looking quite delectable in her leggings and knit dress.

Reed looked down at her and smiled.

He loved this woman.

In the prior two weeks, they'd gone back to both Josh's and Hannah's homes and retrieved what they could. The Centrals had destroyed Hannah and her mother's place. She could only save a few keepsakes and her photo albums. But most of it was a lost cause. They'd shopped for clothes for her and anything else she might need. But Reed could tell she was still hurting over the additional loss of things that reminded her of where she'd come from. Josh's apartment startled Reed in its starkness. The ex-SEAL had no connections to the outside world, no family. He could just disappear, and prior to meeting Reed and Hannah, no one would know he was gone or even miss him.

Well, that would change now. Josh was his. He'd make sure the man knew it.

When they weren't getting to know one another, they'd been looking into Josh's bite. They'd scoured the old texts and literature to see what they could find, but so far had come up short. Reed wouldn't give up though, he couldn't give up.

"Yes, you can come. I want you there," Reed finally answered.

"Are you sure?"

Reed pulled her into his arms and kissed her. She looked so damn cute bundled up. Though winter had taken over the den, it hadn't snowed since that horrible blizzard. No, the weather was oddly dry, too dry in Reed's opinion. Something felt off, but he couldn't place it.

"Yes, I'm sure. Why not? It's a hunt. I'm going to be a wolf, and you two can hang out with me. It's not like I go out and chase a deer or anything. I mean, some of the younger wolves like to get in touch with their wolf sides to enhance their tracking and hunting skills, but I don't like to do it. I train with my brothers, but I don't need to kill a deer to be strong." Reed smiled, and Hannah wiggled in his arms.

"Don't I know it."

"I want you both there, please?" Reed asked.

Josh came into the living room and hugged them both. "I want to see what happens, so I'm in."

Ever since Josh had let Reed touch him, Josh had been doing that more often. Slight touches and caresses. But they still hadn't had sex fully. Reed was okay with that. He knew Josh was new to the whole thing, and he'd give him time. That didn't mean he couldn't appreciate the military man package though.

"Then it's settled. I will go wolf, and you two can hang out with me. Sounds like a date."

"A hairy one," Hannah added.

Reed put his hands over his heart. "Ouch."

"Well, it's true," Josh said. "Before we go though, can you tell me about wolves?"

"What do you mean?" Reed asked.

"Where do werewolves come from?"

Reed sighed. "It's only a legend, but it's said werewolves were formed from the Moon Goddess. I don't know what exact mythology she comes from, or even if she exists, but I feel her here." Reed put his hand over his heart. "She was saddened by the atrocities of man and the weakening of their souls, and the Moon Goddess stepped down from her ivory crescent throne and walked among the dense forests and rivers."

Hannah nodded. "I remember this story. My mom told it to me."

"There she found a hunter deep in the brush, searching for his next kill. The Goddess knew this man must eat and provide for his family, but she was disheartened at the depravity of the souls she watched over. The act of free will was not unknown to her so she stood back and waited for the decisions the hunter made."

"Sounds kind of creepy," Josh teased.

Hannah hit him in the stomach. "Shut up. Sorry, Reed, go on."

"So the hunter found his prey and wounded a wolf, not killing it. The Moon Goddess walked toward the hunter and asked what the hunter wanted to do. Startled by the Goddess presence, the hunter bowed yet stood protective over his kill. The Goddess told him man needed to understand the connection between earth and man. The man, confused and shocked, wasn't prepared for the magic pulsating through his system when the Goddess bent and touched her palms to his heart and the wolf's.

"That night she created the first werewolf. Not man, nor beast, but a medley of the two. Man would dominate and walk the world, yet the wolf would be internal always—challenging man's wants and desires. During times of the full moon, the Moon Goddess's pull is immense, a tactile entity and man will change into the beast he hunted and killed, running through the forest of earth on four paws rather than two feet. Though in times of great stress and need, man can choose to be wolf."

Reed blushed. "That's the legend, not my words."

"No, it sounded amazing. I wish I had a history like that," Josh said wistfully.

"You could, you know." Reed snapped his mouth closed and his body tensed.

Dammit, he didn't want to pressure him. Josh needed to take his time and decide if he wanted to be mates and become a werewolf. The other man didn't need Reed breathing down his neck.

"I know," Josh whispered. "Just give me more time."

Hannah patted both of their hands. "Come on, no sadness. This will be fun. We're going to see another side of Reed. That's the whole point of us staying here. To get to know one another before we decide if we want to commit to eternity. Oh, and the sex. I'm staying for that too."

Both men burst out laughing.

They needed each other more than he thought. They balanced one another, kept them on their toes. They were perfect.

They walked out to the backyard, and Reed inhaled the crisp cool air. The moon pulled at him. As werewolves, they hunted at night. He didn't want to endanger his mates by going outside in the dark, but he couldn't leave them alone and unprotected either. The full moon lit up the forest so even a human could see their way. Though it was cold and should probably be snowing, the air felt dry, very odd for northern Washington. A tingling feeling went up his arms. Maybe it was because he needed to shift.

"So we're going to hunt together. My family will most likely be hunting with the rest of the Pack or not at all. We don't have to change at the full moon if we don't want to."

"Is Willow going to change?" Hannah asked.

"She can, changing into a wolf doesn't hurt the baby, but she won't most likely," Reed said. "Melanie wants to go out tonight with Kade, so Finn will be hanging out with Jasper and Wil."

"Are they okay with you not joining them?" Josh asked.

Reed shrugged. "We don't have to go out as a Pack. It's nice, but since you two aren't wolves, it might be dangerous."

"Would they hurt us? I thought wolves retained their humanity, even after the change." Josh sounded worried.

Reed shook his head. "You have to remember, at three years old, pups can start to change. So there are toddlers and adolescents out there who are still learning their control. They are never alone, which makes it safer, but I don't want there to be an accident."

Hannah wrapped her arms around him and kissed under his chin. "Okay. Now get naked."

A discreet cough over Reed's shoulder stopped him from laughing. Damned wolf was too good at hiding and he hadn't sensed him until now.

"Hello, Maddox," Reed grunted.

"Don't sound so happy to see me or anything, big brother." Maddox casually strolled into the backyard and said hello to Hannah and Josh, but there was nothing casual about his little brother. Energy and tension rolled off him, something Reed was used to. The power that Maddox held would kill a smaller man. Since he could feel every emotion in the Pack, Maddox always had to have a higher control than anyone else.

"Sorry, Maddox, I was just surprised to see you here."

Maddox shrugged. "I thought I'd hang out with you guys for a while then go off on my own."

Something the Omega does well.

"Plus, I thought if Hannah had any questions about being part of the Pack in a position as the Healer, she could ask me. Or at least know I'm here if she needs me."

"Oh." Hannah bit her lip. "I don't have any right now. I don't feel any different. I guess it's because I'm not part of the Pack yet."

Maddox shrugged again, looking out in the forest at something Reed couldn't see. If there was even anything there. "Okay. Just let me know." He turned to Reed. "Is it okay if I join you then?"

"That's fine with me as long as it doesn't bother Hannah or Josh."

Hannah nodded.

"Sure, man," Josh put in. "I don't see why not. Plus, I'd like to see another wolf change, if that's okay."

Maddox nodded but didn't smile. His brother never seemed to smile these days.

"Fine, but don't be showing off your junk to my mates," Reed joked.

Well, it wasn't that much of a joke.

Maddox raised a brow. "Worried?"

Reed's only response was a growl.

Hannah laughed then looked Maddox over. "He is kind of cute."

She squealed when Reed threw her over his shoulder and carried her to the other side of the lawn.

"And you?" Maddox asked Josh. Reed could hear the humor in his tone.

Josh just laughed and held out his hands. "Not interested, man. Sorry."

Maddox just stared. "Didn't think you were."

The skin on Reed's arm rippled.

Damn, he needed to change. Soon.

"Reed, are you okay?" Hannah whispered.

Reed looked down at her wide-eyed face. "Yeah, I just need to change soon. But it doesn't hurt; don't worry. The moon's pulling at my wolf. I haven't changed in the two weeks you've been here. Not since the cabin."

"You shouldn't hide your wolf." Maddox stared at him.

Reed looked at Maddox and swore. He could never hide anything from the dammed wolf.

"I've been preoccupied. But I haven't hid anything. My wolf understands," Reed said quickly.

His wolf didn't respond. Shit.

"You shouldn't deny your nature," Maddox argued.

Hannah jumped in. "Hey, don't fight. Reed's doing great. He doesn't deny anything. He's never hidden that he's a werewolf or anything like that from us." She paused and turned toward him. "Right? Have you?"

"I hope you haven't," Josh added. "Not because of us."

"I'm fine. Don't worry. I've just been doing other things," Reed sputtered. "I'm going to change now."

Hannah poked him in the chest. "You better. Because I love that you're a werewolf. I think you're cute."

Maddox coughed.

Bastard.

"And," Josh continued, "I like you as a wolf. You need to show me this side of you. Plus eventually I might turn. If you don't show me how it is, how am I ever going to know if this is right? I need to know everything and you can't deny who you are any more than Hannah can deny that she's a witch. Change," Josh ordered.

Happiness filled Reed. Josh was thinking about the future and was actually considering becoming a wolf. *Thank God.* Why the hell was he hiding from them? He hadn't changed over the past two weeks because he hadn't wanted to scare them. Hadn't wanted to remind them of the inherent danger that came with being mated to a werewolf. But why?

Reed shook his head. He was an idiot.

"Okay," Reed replied. "I'll show you."

"Touching," Maddox deadpanned.

For a guy so in tune with everyone else's emotions, he sure was an ass.

Josh pulled Hannah into his arms and smiled. "Go for it."

Reed kissed them both then stripped down. Hannah whistled and he shook his ass.

"Dude. Never. Do. That. Again." Maddox rubbed his eyes. "I think I'm blind."

Whoops, forgot he was there. Whatever.

Maddox took off his shirt, and Reed growled. "Hey, what did I say about your junk?"

"You just whipped yours around. I'm going to bend so they can't see. Geez. Get over it. If they want to live with the Pack and go on hunts, they better get used to nudity."

Hannah laughed. "Oh, I'm fine with it. Continue, Maddox." She yelped when Josh bit her neck.

"I will deal with you later," Reed growled playfully.

"I'll count on it," Hannah purred.

That's great. Get an erection right when you have to change in front of your brother. Not awkward at all.

Thankfully Maddox was already in the throes of his change so he couldn't remark about Reed sporting wood. Reed bent down and pulled on his magic. His skin rippled again, fur sprouting. His muscles and bones stretched, broke, and rearranged.

Soon he sat on his haunches as a wolf, breathing in the mountain air that seemed crisper to his new scenes. Hannah walked toward him and kneeled by his side. She kissed his muzzle then petted his flank and rubbed behind his ears. He leaned into her touch. If he were a cat, he'd be purring by now.

Josh slowly stepped forward and crouched near Hannah.

"You okay?" he asked.

Reed gave a slight nod, and Josh rubbed his back. He sighed inwardly. Both his mates felt so good and understood who he was. This was perfect.

Maddox grunted behind him and nipped at his heels. Reed turned and looked at the gray and tan wolf with green eyes. So, he wanted to play? He loved fighting with his brothers, but Maddox usually stayed away. This should be fun.

Reed let out a short bark and tilted his head at Josh and Hannah.

"Go," Josh said. "I can track you. We'll find you. Have fun with your brother."

"But be safe," Hannah added.

Maddox and Reed took off into the forest. His paws beat down on the dirt floor, and the wind rustled his fur. Why did he deny himself this? This was part of him. He was a werewolf.

"It's about time. I've missed this too, you know."

Reed sighed at his wolf. Yeah, he'd fucked up.

"It's okay. I understand why you did it. But we need to mate with Josh and Hannah already, then everything can go forward."

Reed wanted to laugh. If only it were that easy.

A gray ball of fur slammed into his side as Maddox came out of nowhere.

Shit, he really needed to pay attention.

Both of them yipped and growled, biting but not using too much force. They fought and rolled through the brush until finally Maddox pinned him.

He always won. Stupid brother.

Maddox bit into Reed's scruff, growled, then released him. Sometimes Reed could best one of his brothers, but Maddox always knew what Reed's next move was. Eerie.

His brother inclined his head then shot off into the distance, most likely going home. Maddox always stayed alone unless someone needed him. He might be an ass, but if someone

176

needed him for something, he'd be there in a moment's notice. Being the Pack's Omega wasn't a job for him but a duty. A calling.

He heard footsteps on the dead leaves behind him. Hannah and Josh.

"Found you." Hannah laughed.

Reed batted her hand with his head so she would pet him. He leaned into her side when she gave in.

"Needy, aren't you?"

Reed merely looked up at her and blinked.

See how cute I am? Pet me.

Both his mates let out a laugh.

Josh picked up a stick and waved it at him. "Want to play fetch?"

Reed lifted a lip to show off his elongated canine.

Seriously?

Josh threw the stick, and Reed refused to follow its trail. He wasn't a dog for fuck's sake.

"I don't know, man. What do wolves do? Do you want to go find a rabbit or something?" Josh asked.

"No. Not Thumper," Hannah said.

Josh boomed out a laugh. "Not every bunny is Thumper, babe. But seriously, Reed, what do you want to do?"

"Well, not play fetch. I was surprised Reed didn't bite you. How about a game of chase?" Hannah asked.

Reed perked up. Hell yeah. With Hannah as the prize, he'd totally hunt and chase for her.

Hannah smiled and grabbed Josh. With a look over her shoulder she laughed. "Come and get us."

Reed let them get a head start. He could scent them and would find them easily, but it was more about the chase. And odd feeling crept up his spine, tangling his fur. He inhaled, trying to figure out what it was but could only scent Josh, Hannah, and the land. What was it? He listened for what it could be and only heard a deer run away in the distance.

Odd. He shook it off. He needed to get to his mates and that would make him feel better. That must be it.

Reed ran on all fours through the undergrowth and found Josh first. The human wasn't trying to hide but stood near a tree, looking the other way, shaking his head. Reed made no noise as he crept up behind him. Josh, the SEAL that he was, turned quickly and tackled him. Reed rolled with him until Josh lay pinned beneath. He licked the other man's face.

"Hey, not nice." Josh laughed.

Reed quirked his head.

"Hannah? This is so odd, by the way. She went off that way." He lifted his head. "She didn't go too far; she just wanted to give you more of a chase."

Reed let Josh stand then bumped his hand. Josh scratched behind his ears, stroking his fur. He could get used to this.

They followed her honey and bitter apple trail until the scent of sulfur hit his nose.

Shit.

Smoke filled the trees, and Josh coughed.

Fire.

A scream sounded in the distance.

Hannah.

Chapter 18

Hannah coughed and sputtered as the smoke burned her nose and throat, filling her lungs.

Dammit, why did she leave Josh and Reed to play? It wasn't safe. Yet she'd forgotten that in the heat of the moment and run off alone.

The fire grew closer, and Hannah didn't know where to go. A rock face was the only thing she could see that wasn't burning around her. The fire had come up so fast; she didn't even see where it started.

The air grew thick, dry. She'd known it felt drier than normal all day, and that fact scared her. Between the lack of moisture in the air and the decade's worth of undergrowth, the fire would spread fast, not only potentially killing her but endangering the entire Redwood den. With most of the Pack on the hunt, this would be the perfect time for the enemy to attack them. It only made sense that this was at the hands of the Centrals or another enemy, and not something natural.

The earth screamed in pain around her. Her magic wanted to heal, to save the dying plants and animals. But she couldn't. She only healed humans. And she couldn't even save herself, let alone something else.

The fire urged its way closer, dancing in the moonlight. Hannah ran to the rock face and looked up to the cliff. There was no way she could climb it. She coughed again. All other paths were blocked by the fire or debris. She was trapped. What would she do?

"Reed! Josh!" she screamed, but she didn't think they'd hear her. Dammit. She felt more alone now than she ever had before. She'd had but a taste of what life could offer, and now it would be wrenched away from her.

She used her powers to pull the dirt and soil on top of the fire, trying to bat them down. But every time she did, the flames came back harsher, higher. She couldn't manipulate fire or even water. She could only heal and play with dirt. Her powers were to heal and aid, not destroy. What use was that now?

A wolf howled in the distance.

Reed.

At least she prayed it was.

"Reed!" she called again but choked on smoke.

Reed jumped through the flames but didn't make it to her side of the flaming wall as he hit an unknown barrier. She could smell burning fur in the air, and she bit back a sob. What was he doing? He was going to kill himself. There was no way out. He needed to leave, save himself.

"Reed, you need to go you can't save me. Go, run fast. It's too late for me."

He growled, jumped again through the flames, this time making it passed that unknown barrier and threw himself over her as the flames licked higher, hotter. It raged out of control, faster and louder than she thought possible without any aid. This wasn't normal fire. Reed licked her face and covered her with his body when the flames reached them.

Her brain grew dizzy. So much smoke.

Reed growled again and licked her face, covering her body more when she pulled her legs up.

"We need to get out of here. Please. We need to get to Josh." Hannah coughed, and he licked her chin.

She shifted from under his body and stood up. They began to move, but the fire grew. Fire shaped like arms reached for them. No, this was demon fire aided by witches, magic so dark and evil she didn't even know if there was a counter spell against it. They weren't going to make it.

Reed used his teeth and pulled on the sleeve of her burned dress, careful not to touch the slight burns on her arms. She stood on shaky legs, followed him to the rocks, and found a small alcove.

"We'll still burn here."

He growled, pushed her to the ground and covered her body with his. The flames licked around him, hunting them, and Reed groaned in pain.

She screamed. He was dying in her arms, and there wasn't a thing she could do about it.

He howled in pain again and shifted to human.

"No! What are you doing?" Hannah screamed.

"I can't shift. No magic," Reed rasped. Burns marked his skin and his flesh boiled in some spots.

Tears ran down both of their faces as she coughed.

Why hadn't she mated with him fully before? What was holding her back? She'd been ready. *Dear goddess, please let us live. Spare us.*

She framed his face with her hands. "I love you."

Reed closed his eyes, strained agony on his face. "I love you, too."

He held her closer as she sobbed.

A figure in the flames caught her eye, and she froze. Was it the demon? Only they could walk through demon fire. Was he here to kill them or prolong their torture?

The man walked out of the flames into her field of vision, and she gasped.

Josh.

The bite mark. The demon had bitten him, and now he could walk through flames. Oh goddess. What did this mean?

"Hannah! Reed!" he called. "I'm coming. Hold on."

Despite the oncoming fire, he ran to them and picked Hannah up, cradling her to his body. "Let's move."

Reed stood, naked, on shaky legs, and coughed. "You carry Hannah; I'll be by your side. She can Heal me, but no one can heal her."

Josh kissed him. "Stay close."

Hannah looked into Josh's eyes and saw darkness. Despite the flames, a chill raced down her spine. His pupils had dilated three times their normal size and his body rippled with unspent energy. What did this mean? What did the demon do to him?

"Aren't you hurt?" Hannah rasped.

Josh shook his head and started walking into the fire. "No, the fire doesn't hurt me. It feels warm. Good. I can't explain it, but I don't want to think about it right now. I just want to get the two of you out of here. Come on."

The fire screamed in fury as they ran through it. Reed buried himself against Josh's side, though he was about the same height. They ran and because she was in Josh's arms, the fire didn't hurt. What on earth?

They ran and ran until they made it out of the ring of fire. They coughed and gasped, as Josh dropped to his knees still holding her to his chest. Reed lay on the ground, bleeding, with third degree burns covering his body. His arms and legs were covered in burns that made her want to cry just looking at them. Angry welts dotted his chest and groin.

Dear goddess.

She sobbed and pulled every last ounce of energy she possessed and poured it into Reed, Healing his wounds. Warmth and connection filled her, different from her usual Healing. Her palms glowed as she watched Reed's flesh knit together in front her. Reed moaned and relaxed on the dirty leaf-covered ground.

"Pack magic," she breathed.

That had to be it. Her powers were so much stronger now than they had been before. There was only one explanation. She had accepted Reed and told him she loved him. Though they hadn't fully mated, she was Pack. She knew it. Taking a deep breath, she pulled more, liking the new warm sensation that came with this form of Healing. Her old healing had a slight tingling, but nothing like this. Finally, all the wounds had been healed and closed and Reed only had freshly healed, pink skin.

Before Reed could say anything, she turned to Josh and placed her palms on his chest. He gasped as she Healed his lungs from the smoke, though his body had no burns.

Thank the goddess.

She leaned back and fell on her bottom, tears running down her cheeks.

"That was close," Reed rasped.

"Too close," Josh added.

Hannah couldn't hold back anymore and sobbed, for the dying earth at their feet, for Reed's pain, and for whatever Josh might become. She hated crying. She wasn't a weak person, yet with every battle and every painful incident, she seemed to fold into herself and cry. She could fight her way out of most things and use her magic, but in the end, her emotions would be too much and the tears would fall. She wouldn't give up, but she'd still cry. It was too much, but unlike before she knew now what she wanted.

Josh and Reed. Together. In their trinity bond. Forever. She wanted the whole package. The marriage, the kisses, the children, the late night-feedings. Everything.

The fire died down around them, leaving only ash and smoke in its wake. Their enemies had lost this round, but she knew it wouldn't be their last attempt.

Reed coughed. "You used Pack magic, Hannah."

She gave a small smile. "I know."

"Thank God, you have that power," Josh whispered. "I know your usual healing is amazing, but I don't think it would have been enough this time. I don't know what we would have done. I know Reed heals fast, but without you, it might not have been enough."

Her heart lurched. "I'm Pack. I'm yours. I'm Reed's too." Hannah whispered.

Josh's black eyes didn't blink. He shook his head. "No, I can't be. Didn't you see what I just did? I walked through *fire* and I don't have a mark on me. There's something wrong with me. Don't you get that? I need to go. I don't know what is happening, but I can't stay here. I can't put you two or the rest of the Pack in danger."

Reed shook his head and coughed again. "No, you need to stay here. You can't go. We'll figure it out. We've already been researching, we won't give up. I won't let you hurt anyone." The men stared at each other, and Hannah knew Reed wouldn't let Josh leave no matter what.

Finally, Josh nodded. "I need your word, Reed. Kill me if you have to, but don't let me hurt anyone."

Hannah gasped and her heart ached. No.

Reed's eyes filled. "I promise."

Josh was too much a man to let himself become a danger. But she'd be dammed if she allowed Reed to put him down. No, she'd find a way to save him. Josh was her mate after all.

Hannah shook her head. "All I could think about when the fire came at us was that I should have made love to you both and mated you fully. I'm ready."

Reed inhaled. "Really?"

Josh gave a hollow laugh. "That's all I could think about too. Well, other than the ability to walk around in fire and not get burned, but we can talk about that later."

Hannah laughed. "All I can think about is the two of you. I love you, Josh."

His eyes widened, and he smiled. Really smiled. "I love you too, Hannah."

Reed coughed and sat up, healed. "I love you, Josh. I know you aren't ready to hear it yet, but I don't want to go further in this war and in our lives without saying it."

Josh traced Reed's brow. "I love you, too."

Hannah laughed. "Apparently all it took was a fire and a few new abilities for us to come clean about our feelings, huh?"

Josh laughed. "So how exactly does the full mating thing work?"

Reed smiled. "It's fate. You and I will make love to Hannah and not use condoms. Our seed will make the mating happen. As for you and me, it's the same way, but we don't have to do it all at once. I guess it's a little different for a trinity bond than others, since there are three of us. But as long as I do the *mounting*," they all laughed, "then we will be mated. Make sense?"

"Wait," Josh interjected. "Why is it only you? Why does it have to be your *seed*?"

"Because I'm the werewolf and the one whose species needs the mating this way. We can always have you *mount* me just in case we want to make sure the mating sticks." Reed smiled.

Josh laughed. "In other words, we need to have sex in as many ways and as many times as possible."

Reed joined in his laughter. "Not a bad deal." Reed sobered. "There is also the marking. That will bind my wolf to you, not just my human half. But I want to do that later, once we know what going on with you. I don't want it to hurt you."

Josh nodded. "I understand."

"Okay," Hannah cut in. "Let's get to it then."

Both men looked at her.

"What? Come on, Reed's already naked. Strip, Josh."

"Here?" Josh asked.

"Now?" Reed asked.

"Yes, here. Now. We need to reaffirm our existence and love. Plus, we are outdoors; I can feel the earth calling to me. Make love to me. Make me yours."

Chapter 19

Hannah watched as both men shifted to rest on their knees. Reed, freshly healed and looking almost pain-free, kneeled, naked, watching her. His sandy blond hair, slightly crispy on the ends, stood in a disarrayed halo around his beautiful artistic face. Josh knelt by him, strong and not quite as beautiful, but equally as handsome.

Josh took a deep breath and lifted the shirt above his head. Hannah caught her breath as she watched his biceps and abs flex with the movement. She swallowed and tried not to gasp.

Damn, they were both specimens of male perfection. Washboard abs, long, lean muscles. She ached to trace her fingers along every inch of them. They had that pretty little line at their hips that made such lickable trails to their, ahem, groins.

Hannah bit her lip and looked down. Reed, already naked, was hard and ready, his balls low and filled. His cock was long, longer than Josh's, and wide. Josh shucked his shoes and pants. The military man was commando. Hannah grew achy and wet. She quickly rid herself of her clothes as she stared at Josh's cock, long, and wide, wider than Reed's. Together they would fill her and hit every right spot. They were just different enough that she'd known who was in her in the throes of passion and she loved them both.

Hannah got on her hands and knees and crawled to Josh. She knew she looked like a desperate woman, but she didn't care. These two were hers. And after they made love, they'd be hers forever. She batted her eyes at Josh then wrapped her lips around the head of his penis. His sweet, woodsy taste seeped on her tongue just like when she tasted Reed's sandalwood flavor. She swallowed, forcing his cock farther down her throat. Josh tugged at her hair.

"God, I love your mouth," he grunted.

Reed went behind her and danced his fingers down her spine. She shivered in need. He traced his fingers over her sex and through her folds, until he slid one finger in to the knuckle.

"You're wet," Reed rasped.

She let go of Josh's cock with a pop. "Always. Just for you two." She licked up Josh's balls then took him in her mouth again.

Reed pinched her clit, and she jumped.

Oh. My. Goddess.

He scraped her clit with his fingernail, and her pussy fluttered.

Stop teasing.

But she couldn't say it because Josh was fucking her mouth. Hard. And she loved it.

Who knew she could be such a naughty girl? Maybe Reed and Josh just brought it out of her.

Josh played with her nipples while Reed entered another finger, then another, until she was filled with four of them as he worked her channel. She was about to come, just riding that crescent where she begged for stars, but both men backed off.

She lifted her head from Josh, her lips swollen. "Don't stop, please."

Reed chuckled and teased her folds with the tip of his cock, and she wiggled back, begging. "Oh, I like to hear you say please. But I don't want you to come until I'm in you. I want to feel your pussy clench around me, milking me."

She shuddered, almost coming at his words alone.

"Dammit, Reed, fuck her," Josh grunted. "Shove that fat cock into her, because I'm about to go just listening to you."

"Yes, what he said." Hannah agreed. Goddess, she wanted them both. Loved them both.

Reed slowly entered her, inch by agonizing inch.

Oh. My.

"That's it, baby, take me." Reed groaned. "Do you know how good you feel around me, bare? I never want to be in you again with a condom. I want to feel you. I want to fill you. Fill you with my seed and watch it take root. I want to you grow round and ripe with our child. With Josh's child. A child belonging to the three of us."

With each promise he reamed her. Goddess, she wanted everything he said and more. She wanted them. And she had them.

"I can't wait to feel what you feel, Reed," Josh breathed as he plucked her nipples and fucked her mouth.

Reed pounded into her, Josh too, until she found the crest of that wave again and fell. Stars shattered behind her eyelids, and her body rocked with emotions, feelings, connections. Everything. She could feel Reed's soul intertwine with hers. She could feel his every desire, want, hope. All centered around her and Josh. As she felt his warm seed pulsate in her womb, she bonded. She was Reed's, as he was hers. Forever.

"Oh my God," Reed whispered. "I didn't know. They said...but I didn't know."

Oh, she knew.

She lay on the ground, in Reed's arms, and felt his being.

"Josh, I want you." She needed him. Needed this feeling. She didn't want to lose him. She needed this last part of the puzzle to be whole. Josh.

"I want to come in you," Josh said. "I want you to look at me like you're looking at Reed. I see it. The link. Like a physical entity that I can feel, taste. I want it with both of you. Please don't deny me." Lines of strained tension covered his face, and she reached out to him.

"Please."

Reed rolled over, leaving Hannah on the grassy floor. Through the canopy, sunlight peaked through the trees, and a burned amber scent drifted along the air. Josh lay between her legs and positioned himself. He twined his fingers with hers, looked directly into her eyes, then slowly, oh so slowly, entered her, filled her.

"Mine," Josh murmured.

"Yours," Hannah agreed.

"Ours," Reed added.

"Ours," Josh and Hannah whispered.

"Josh, please. Harder." She ached. She angled her pelvis, inviting him deeper. Josh was always the harder of the two, more demanding. She loved it, craved it.

"As you wish." Josh smiled a truly feral smile then slammed into her, pushing against her womb.

He did it again and again, crashing into her. Loving her.

****

With Hannah wrapped around him, Josh knew he was in heaven. Nothing could change it, not any amount of demons, torrents of fire, or whatever the fuck he was turning into.

Reed knelt behind them and reached over Josh to skim his hand between Hannah and him.

"Reed, touch her." Josh groaned.

"Oh, I will, then I'll touch you," Reed promised.

Oh shit.

He knew Reed would be topping first. That was the way it would be done. He trusted Reed and knew he could do it. He wanted to feel that long cock in his ass. It didn't scare him anymore. The connection between Reed and Hannah didn't scare him anymore either. He wanted that too, with both of them. And he wanted to feel Reed around his cock in the future.

Fuck. He almost came on the spot just thinking about it. But he had to maintain control. He didn't want to come in Hannah until Reed did what he wanted to do. He had only a few good shots in him since he was human. He envied the hell out his Energizer Bunny of a mate. Reed could stay hard for hours, days even. Josh might have a quick turn around, but Reed was fucking amazing.

Speaking of fucking...

Hannah reached up and cupped his face.

Tears in her eyes, gasps on her breath, she mouthed, "I love you." And he almost lost it again.

Like a curvy goddess, his mate lay below him, her heavy breasts bouncing with every thrust.

"I love you, too," he rasped, and she smiled.

God, that smile.

Hannah closed her eyes and moaned. Josh looked over his shoulder and saw Reed playing with her hole, and she bit her lip.

"Like that, do you?" Reed asked.

"Yes. You know I do," she answered.

"Oh, we'll both fill you at the same time. Just not tonight. Tonight, I'm going to fill our mate. What do you think about that?" Reed asked.

Both Josh and Hannah groaned.

Yes, please.

Reed took Hannah's juices and covered Josh's puckered hole.

He froze mid-thrust.

He'd never let Reed play back there before, but oh, how he wanted that.

"Lube," he forced out.

Reed licked his neck. "I don't have any. I wasn't planning on this. But I do have Hannah and me. It will be enough. I won't hurt you."

Josh shook his head. "No."

Reed stood back. "Oh."

"No, that's not what I mean. Lube," he rasped and had to pull out of Hannah to think. She whimpered and he leaned over to kiss her. "I have lube in my jeans pocket."

Hannah laughed.

Reed lifted a brow. "Boy Scout, are you? Always prepared?"

Josh blushed then grunted and slid his dick through Hannah's folds and back out again. "Actually, yes, but that's not why I brought it. I was planning on seducing Hannah in the woods before the fire." Josh shrugged and rocked against Hannah, loving the way she moaned.

Reed smiled full out, white teeth and everything. "Thank God."

The sexy man scooted to Josh's jeans and pullout out a fresh bottle of Liquid Silk.

"Nice." Reed laughed. "Now where was I?"

Josh wiggled his butt, and Hannah laughed. "I think you were right about here." He wiggled again.

"Sounds good to me," Reed grunted.

Reed bent and licked between Josh's cheeks and he squirmed with the new and not-unpleasant sensation. In fact, it was a fucking fantastic sensation.

Reed worked the lube, coating him, then slowly entered a finger. Josh froze. The tight, filled feeling sent shivers down his spine.

Jesus.

Reed rubbed the finger on a sensitive bundle of nerves, and Josh almost came again.

"How does it feel?" Hannah asked, a knowing smile on her face.

He leaned down and kissed her, loving the mix of her sweet taste and the sensation of Reed adding another finger.

"Like manna."

Hannah laughed, her pussy clenching around his shaft.

"Don't laugh; I'm fighting for control as it is," he groaned.

She pouted. "Oh poor baby. Is it too hard for you to be in me and Reed to play with you at the same time?" She gasped and shut her eyes when he slammed into her.

"If you're coherent enough to be teasing me, I'm not doing my job right."

"And," Reed added, "if you're coherent enough to be teasing her, I can add another finger."

Josh buckled when Reed added a third lube-coated finger, then a fourth.

Oh, sweet Jesus.

"That's more like it." Reed laughed. "I think you're ready for me."

Josh tensed.

"Hey." He slapped Josh's ass in one quick motion, and Josh moaned at the sting. "Don't tense up on me. I like you nice and loose."

"Okay, I trust you," he breathed.

Josh felt the touch of the head of Reed's penis at his entrance, and he forced himself to relax. He looked down at Hannah and saw the love in her eyes. He smiled. He could do this. He wanted this.

Reed pushed past the tight ring of muscles, and Josh stiffened at the invasion, but forced himself to relax. He felt overfull and loved, deep inside Hannah and Reed deep inside him. It was the three of them. It was always about the three of them. Forever.

Reed slid in inch by agonizing inch, pulled back, then slid in again until Josh felt the other man's balls against his ass.

Oh God, he felt so full. So wanted.

"Oh, fuck me. You feel so good. So tight," Reed said, straining. Then he worked back out then in again.

Again and again. With each motion, Josh mimicked it in Hannah, the three of them working up a rhythm of flesh, sweat, and heat. Josh felt his balls tighten, then he screamed their names and emptied himself into her. He felt Hannah tighten around him, and Reed fill his ass. Together they rose up then crashed down.

He felt Hannah's and Reed's souls intertwine with his, and he knew he'd never be alone again. Wherever he went, they'd always be with him.

Their trinity bond, and all that came with it, settled in, previously unknown but freshly hatched, waiting for its discoveries to be revealed.

Chapter 20

They walked through the forest, past the trees that should have been burned to a crisp, but stood proud and strong. Reed shook his head. What the hell had happened? It was so weird. The fire had come, burned, and almost killed them. Yet no sign of it remained, no trace but a faint whiff of burned amber on the air.

The hunt had taken them farther than they'd thought, driven by fire. They finally trekked back to his home, no, *their* home and Reed smiled. He could feel Hannah's and Josh's souls tangling with his. Kade and Jasper had told him the connection was deeper than the bond with the Pack. More tactile, leaving one feeling naked. But he hadn't truly understood until he bonded himself to his mates. No wonder looks of joy that passed over his brothers' faces whenever their mates walked toward them. Kade said he felt it with Finn, too, to a lesser degree, and that their children would also be bound to them like a web. And as their children aged and moved apart, developing their own lives, the connection would fade.

He could only feel sorrow for Adam. When Adam had lost Anna and their baby, Reed grieved with him and had helped pick up the pieces and glue them together in an oddly connected jumble that was their brother. But the loss also scarred Adam more than the scar that ran along Maddox's face from a fight. Reed still didn't know the story behind it.

"Come on," Reed said when he spotted the house. "Let's get inside and get dressed." Still naked, the cold was starting to tingle certain bits better left unexposed.

They got inside and immediately Reed warmed.

"I'm going to jump in the shower. Is that okay?" Hannah asked.

Images of droplets of water running between her breasts, dusting her nipples, then carving a trail down to her sex filled his brain.

Josh let out a booming laugh. "Go for it, baby. Reed needs to get his mind out of the gutter." He gave a pointed look at Reed's crotch.

Reed blushed. Yeah, thinking about his woman nude and in the shower, while he himself was naked and couldn't hide his growing erection, might not be such a great idea. *Whoops*. Well, who could blame him?

He walked to their room and took out a new set of clothes. He pulled them on then shook out the kinks in his back. His newly healed flesh felt a bit tight. Watching Hannah using her Healing powers on him had been a revelation. She was the true Healer and part of his Pack. Incredible.

Josh laughed. "You're thinking about her again."

Reed joined in his laughter and shrugged, not ashamed in the least. "She's hot. And she's ours. At least I'm wearing pants this time. And as much as I'd like to make love to both of you again, I need to call my father."

The phone rang, and both men burst out laughing again.

"Do you hear the music to the *Twilight Zone*?" Josh asked.

"No, just my nosy Alpha of a Father who knows everything," Reed answered then walked to the phone and picked it up.

"Son." His father's voice sounded relieved and edgy all at once.

"Speak of the devil," Reed joked.

Something dark came and went in Josh's eyes, worrying him. The other man's pupil's dilated then went back to normal. A chill raced up Reed's arms and his heart sped up. He took a shuddering breath and held it in. *Please, don't let anything bad happen to Josh, not when I just found him.*

"It's good to hear your voice, son," his father quietly said.

"It's good to hear you too, Dad," Reed choked out. Okay, stop being a sissy.

"I felt you, your connection to the Pack," his father added. "So I knew you weren't gone. But that fire out there scared the crap out of us. We didn't know exactly what was going on. And when Maddox came to us screaming that the place he'd left you was now consumed in fire, I about died. Reed, I almost had to knock Maddox unconscious to keep him from going back for you. He would have and would have died."

Neither spoke. He knew his brother loved him, but he hadn't realized it was that deep. Damn, his family humbled him.

"Did it come at you, too?" Reed finally asked.

"No, we were safe. The den is protected by more magic than that fire could hope to destroy. But the land you were on, though it might be Redwood land, isn't protected by the same wards. I'm going to try and fix that, but it takes too much power. Your little Hannah may be of assistance there." His father made it sound more like a quiet order than a question. But he knew Hannah would do all in her power to protect her new Pack, her family.

"I'll let her know."

"Good."

"It scared the hell out of us, Dad."

"No kidding. How did you get out?"

"Josh."

Should he tell him anymore? He couldn't keep secrets from his Alpha. But what would happen if he revealed the source of Josh's new power? Would they lock him up and throw away the key? Or worse?

Josh came up from behind and held him. "Tell him. He needs to know," he whispered.

"Josh saved us," he repeated to his father. "Hannah and I were trapped, the fire coming at us, and Josh walked through the flames to get us. Dad, the fire didn't touch him."

He heard an intake of breath and a quiet curse.

"We will find the source of this. Josh is my son now. I know he can hear me, so Josh, you are mine. Mine to protect. You are a Redwood and a Jamenson, even if you don't take the name. I won't let what that bastard did to you taint you. You got that?"

Josh stood rod straight and nodded.

"He says yes, Dad." Jesus, his dad was a great man, a noble man. A man who didn't care that his son was bisexual and loved both a man and a woman. Not many men, especially the Alpha of a werewolf pack, would be as accepting.

"Reed, I won't let you lose your mate. Not like Adam."

Reed released a shuddering breath. "I know, Dad. I know. We'll figure this out."

"Damn straight."

They all let out a ragged, tension-filled laugh.

If only it were that easy. But nothing seemed easy anymore, if it ever had been.

"Get dressed and come over. I felt it when Hannah and Josh came into the Pack. I'm sure the others with the power have too." Meaning Kade, Jasper, Maddox, and Adam. "Your Mother wants you here. She's already cooking up a storm and invited the rest of the family. Consider it a pre-wedding and thank-God-you're-alive party."

Reed laughed. "Great! I'm starving. I'm sure Josh and Hannah would love it."

Josh nodded, a smile on his lips.

"Good. See you soon. I love you, son. All three of you," his father gruffly let out, then hung up before Reed could speak.

"I love you, too," Reed answered to the dial tone.

Hannah came out of the bathroom, looking fresh and damned cute.

"I heard the last part. So we're going to dinner? Good, I'm starved."

"Yep, I'm going to go jump in the shower and wash off the smoke," Reed answered.

"I'll go jump in the other shower and meet you here in ten." Josh raised a brow. "Separate showers. We need to meet your parents."

Yep, loved them.

****

They walked into his parents' home to the sound of a large family gathering. Finn screamed in glee as North took him around the house, playing airplane. Reed smiled, thinking of the children they'd soon have if he had anything to say about it, of all the children that would fill the house. Willow was due any day now, and Kade made whisperings of wanting another soon. They were growing up. Even though they'd long since reached adulthood, they were now moving on. It seemed like yesterday they themselves were six rowdy pups making too much noise and stress for their mother. He'd been close to eighty when Cailin was born. She hadn't grown up with them in the same fashion, but she was still his baby sister.

"Oh, my, Reed. It's so good to see you here." His mom came at him with her arms outstretched but bee-lined to Hannah, enveloping his bonded mate—that was great to say—in her arms. Well, he knew where he stood now.

"Hi, Pat. We're happy to be here as well." Hannah hugged his mother back, and just for one moment, he could forget all their troubles and tribulations.

His mom kissed all three of them and ushered them into the living room. There, the rest of the family hugged and kissed them. Tears fell on the women's cheeks. Damn, he hated he had scared his family so much. But thank God they were okay. He only prayed that, wherever the hell Adam was, he was the same.

Maddox was the last to join them and stood still, watching. He walked slowly toward them, and everyone quieted down.

"I never should have left you there." Maddox whispered.

"Bullshit," Hannah said.

Maddox laughed. Laughed. The room stood stunned. When was the last time they'd heard his brother laugh? Before the loss of Anna that had hardened him as much as Adam? Before the scar?

His little brother wiped the tears from his eyes. "That word coming out of that little mouth just sounds wrong."

Hannah didn't laugh. She stood with her fists on her hips and scowled. "If you were out there, you could be dead. I'm glad you were away. I don't know what we would have done if we'd have lost you. You're part of this family just as much as anyone else in this room. So swallow that pride of yours and that self-pity. We are fine. We all are." She lifted her chin, daring them to say anything.

Reed loved this feisty side of her.

"Now," she continued, "I think your mom has made us an amazing dinner. Let's go and eat it. Shall we?"

The toughest male werewolves in the country, maybe even the world, scurried to the table in the dining room and sat.

His mother wrapped an arm around Hannah and laughed. Willow and Mel joined in.

"Well, my dear you are officially a Jamenson. As you can tell, it's the women who control the family. They just need to remember that every once in a while."

"Darn straight," Mel added, Finn now in her arms.

"Oh, this is going to be fun." Willow laughed.

The women joined them at the table, and Reed spoke up. "The fire came out of nowhere. Literally. It hunted, tried to kill us. It didn't react like a normal fire and then disappeared as quickly as it came."

"It was demon fire," Hannah whispered.

His dad cursed again, muttering an apology to Finn.

"Demon fire. Darn Centrals. They think it's okay to come onto our land and use demon fire?" Edward rumbled.

"What is demon fire?" Willow asked, her arm wrapped protectively around her swollen belly.

"May I?" Hannah asked. With a nod from his dad, she continued. "Demon fire is just what it sounds like. Fire made from the depths of hell and summoned by a demon. It also takes a witch with immense power and an affinity toward fire to control it. I don't know of a way to counter it. I don't even know if there is a way." She shuddered, and Reed held her close.

"We can't allow this to happen," Cailin said.

"I agree," his father said.

His mom uncovered the dishes on the table and was about to serve when North interrupted. "Josh, before we actually eat, I want to look at that bite mark."

Everyone at the table froze.

"You told them," Reed said to his father.

"Yes, it needed to be done. For his safety, not only ours."

Josh rubbed his shoulder. "It's okay. I want them to know. Secrets only hurt people. Plus they only want to help." He stood up and walked with North to the back room.

Reed wanted to get up and join them, to scream and curse God, or at least ask how this could have happened. But he didn't. Josh needed to feel normal, and that couldn't happen with Reed hovering over him.

"We'll find out what happened. It'll be fine." His mother's voice was cool.

His mom might love to knit and cook, and she cried at the drop of a hat, but if someone endangered her pups, she'd kill them without breaking a nail or a smile. Bloodthirsty, thy name is Momma Wolf.

"Reed," Jasper cut in, "you said the fire disappeared. Are there any remnants?"

He shook his head. "No, just the smell. That acrid, smoky flavor that settles on your tongue. No damage."

"Yes," Hannah added, "but it felt like fire, and it damaged anything it touched at the time. The earth screamed in pain. I felt it."

She shuddered, and Reed wrapped an arm around her shoulders. The smell of fear and pain wafted off her skin. He couldn't imagine what it felt like to have his soul so irrevocably entwined with nature to feel it breathe and gasp. His Hannah was such a caring person to begin with, but add in the fact that she needed to Heal in order to feel calm, and it was all too much. Reed shook his head.

"We can't get into the Centrals' den," Kade said. "It's cloaked with some kind of magic. The stuff they're using to do it isn't anything we've seen before. They're touching dark magic. We don't have anything to fight against that—yet."

Reed nodded. They'd already discussed the magic the Centrals possessed. That didn't make it any fucking less futile.

"We'll have to go on lock-down," Jasper added. "No outside visitors, and people can only leave if they're in pairs, and even then, only if they truly need it." He rubbed the bridge of his nose. "I know it sucks and sounds like we're a cult or something, but I can't think of another way of keeping our people safe."

Reed nodded. "Okay, we'll go on the defense. Like we have been, but more alert. And we'll look for the magic that can be our offense."

"There has to be a balance," Hannah added. "That type of dark can't exist without some type of light to balance it. That's the way of magic. We just need to find it."

"Easier said than done," Maddox grumbled.

Cailin sighed. "It'd be easier if we just went dark."

The room went silent. Reed swore he could have heard a pin drop.

"No," his father said coolly.

One word, spoken as the Alpha, and that was it. No discussion. But they really wouldn't have discussed it anyway. No matter what, the Jamensons wouldn't go evil. That wasn't their way, their nature.

Cailin's eyes flashed, her back as stiff as a board. She turned to their father and lifted her chin. "I would *never* do that. You above all should know that. I was just saying it would be easier, not right."

"Then don't say it," Edward chided. "You are the daughter of the Alpha. You need to set an example and spouting off without thinking doesn't show that."

Cailin glared but didn't answer.

Reed had no idea what it meant to be in her position, the daughter of the Pack. He'd never really thought about it. Maybe he should have noticed her anger before. He took a deep breath. Complicated didn't even begin to describe his family.

His mother spoke up, breaking into the silence. "Enough you two. Come on, I don't want to let the food go cold. Eat."

He was so grateful for his mother. Something was going on with his little sister, but he didn't know what.

Willow rubbed her tiny hand on her heavily protruding stomach. "I'm so happy the three of you are mated."

Hannah blushed, her ears red. As a werewolf, Willow could smell the three of them all over each other and feel the bond slowly settling into place. Reed kissed Hannah's forehead and held her closer. "Thank you, Wil."

Mel leaned over beside Wil and rubbed the pregnant woman's stomach with one hand, holding Finn in the other. Mel was really becoming her own wolf in their Pack, someone they could look up to when she became the Alpha's wife, and not just the Heir's.

She laughed. "Yes, we needed more women. So welcome, Hannah."

"Hell, yeah," Cailin yelled, and pumped her fist.

Kade threw a roll her on the head. "Language."

"Kade," his mother scolded. "Don't throw food."

They broke out into laughter. This was his family. Dysfunction and all. Not too shabby.

"What's so funny?" Josh asked as he walked into the room, North on his heels.

They quieted again, but Reed just smiled, though his heart beat in his ears. "Cailin's potty mouth attacks again and Kade is the equivalent of a twelve-year-old in a cafeteria. Come on and sit; we're just about to eat."

Josh smiled. Man, how he loved that smile. He sat on the other side of Hannah and grabbed Reed's hand and squeezed. Hard. His mate might be putting on a brave face and masking his fear well for others, but he couldn't hide if from him. And by the way Hannah leaned over into him, Josh couldn't hide it from her either.

Josh kissed her temple, then leaned over and did the same to Reed. With a shake of his head, Reed leaned back into his chair.

North didn't know what to do with the demon bite. Damn it.

His father cleared his throat. "Since we are all here now, I'd like to formally welcome Josh and Hannah to our Pack."

His family smiled at his two mates.

"For most of my life, our Pack has been without a Healer. But now, in Hannah, we have one. A talented one by the way her power resonates off her." His dad smiled. His Alpha's strength washed over them, welcoming them into their fold. "And, we have a new enforcer to join our ranks."

Reed started. "What? Who?"

His dad threw back his head and laughed. "I mean your other new mate...Josh."

Reed looked over at Josh and saw a similar confused expression.

"Um...sir...I'm...I'm not sure I understand you," Josh stuttered.

His father lifted a brow. "Oh, I think you do, son. I need another guard. Someone to protect the Pack. And with your background and desire to help, I think you fit the bill. I know you've been looking for how to fit in and contribute, so here you go."

Josh furrowed his brows. Reed wondered what he was thinking.

"Don't look at me like that." His dad scowled. "I didn't make this job up for you. We really need you, and you'll be an asset. Don't let your fears of rejection and loss, cloud your judgment."

Josh gulped.

"But he's human," Hannah blurted out as a heavy blush filled her cheeks.

Josh laughed, Reed joining him.

"About that..." Edward interrupted. "Without the bite, you'd be human, and eventually, if you wanted to stay with Hannah and Reed for eternity, we would change you into a wolf. But with the bite, you may be turning into something else."

Hannah and Josh blanched while Reed's pulse quickened. Oh, Jesus, what had his dad found out? He couldn't lose Josh. Not now.

"I've talked to the elders." His father cursed, then shot an apologetic look to Finn. "They never like talking to anyone, and always talk in riddles, but that's their prerogative. They said that Josh might be stronger than humans now, long lived as well."

Hannah gasped, but the others in the room remained silent. Reed wouldn't lose Josh to old age?

"We'll have to wait and see," his father continued. "I can tell something is different, the way his power resonates. He may not need to change to a wolf to live in the bond the three of you hold."

The three of them relaxed somewhat.

Josh nodded. "Okay. I can do that. I'll be honored."

"Good." His dad smiled. "We need some new blood with good ideas to help protect the Pack. Kade's taking over Adam's job for as long it is needed, but I want you to help him."

"Okay," Josh answered.

Reed gripped Josh's hand harder and leaned into Hannah. His family trusted his mates. It was a far cry from when they weren't even allowed in the room during certain discussions. Things were coming together.

Chapter 21

Blurry images filled with grays and blacks mingled with reds and crimsons flashed across Josh's vision. He squinted, focusing on the forms, trying to make sense of them. People milled around, moving past him. Josh tilted his head. Where was he?

He kept walking, past the stares of the people that had said they embraced him, sending flames into his back. The mummers of curiosity at his presence in their den stung like little pin pricks dancing along his skin. Why did he care what these strangers thought? He had nothing. No ties. Nothing to show for his efforts.

Deep, throaty laughter echoed along the forest's edge, calling him. He followed, the sound pulling him like a bull on a chain. A giggle broke through the masculine laughter, causing him to stumble.

His witch.

Hannah.

He changed directions, trailing after the voice that called to him.

The trees blurred, a smoky haze dulling his vision. He shook his head and stopped.

His Hannah stood in front of him naked, bare to the elements.

"Josh, I've missed you," his vixen whispered.

He strode towards her, intent solely on tasting her lips. She looked up, utter trust and pleasure in her gaze. Her skin felt soft under his trailing fingers as he led them to her neck.

And squeezed.

Her eyes bulged, a plea on her lips.

And he smiled.

****

Josh shot up out of his dreams, panting heavily. He glanced down at his hands, thankfully they were not around his mate's neck. Swallowing hard, he looked down at Reed and Hannah, sleeping peacefully, curled into one another.

Dear God, what the hell had happened?

What kind of sick fuck would dream about squeezing the life out of the woman he loved? Shaken, he gulped and tried to calm his rapid heartbeat. The dream had started off peacefully as he walked through the den, but shadows cast doubt upon him, threatening to drown him in their forsaken promises.

Josh slid out of bed, careful not to wake his slumbering bedmates, and locked himself in the bathroom. He turned on the faucet and splashed his face with ice-cold water. He gripped the sink, swallowing the bile rising in his throat and looked at his reflection.

A flash of red passed over his eyes, and he bit back a scream.

Jesus, what was happening to him?

Was he in control?

He couldn't hurt Reed or Hannah. No. That would kill him quicker than a bullet searing his flesh. But what could he do about it? Leave?

"Josh?" Reed called quietly from their room.

"I'm okay. Go back to sleep; I'll be there in a minute," Josh promised.

"Are you sure?"

Josh shook his head again and walked back into the bedroom. He strode to the bed and kissed Reed softly on the lips. Oh, how he loved that now familiar sandalwood taste.

"I'm fine, just a nightmare." Just a horrific nightmare that threatened everything he had but didn't deserve.

Reed scrunched his brows. "Okay, get back in where it's warm." He lifted up the blanket, inviting him in.

Josh smiled then slid into bed, curling his body around Reed's naked form. He reached around and caressed Hannah, who lay sleeping in Reed's arms. He brushed a kiss on Reed's temple and settled in.

"Good night," he whispered.

"Dream well," Reed answered, half asleep.

Oh, if only he could.

****

Later that day, Hannah and Josh were in her workshop getting a few things done. Water splashed on the sideboard, and Josh cursed. Dammit, his mind just wasn't on his actions today.

"Are you okay?" Hannah asked.

"Just clumsy." He smiled.

"Really, Mr. SEAL? Now why don't I believe that?"

He sighed. There was no hiding from this woman sometimes. Well, with most things. "I didn't sleep well, I guess." He shrugged and kissed her frown. "I'm fine. I got up in the middle of the night and splashed water on my face, and when I came back, I held the both of you. It helped."

Her smile could have melted glaciers. "I'm happy we could help, but I don't like that you can't sleep. Do you want me to make you something?"

Josh shook his head. He never did drugs—illegal or the herbal variety—they messed up his Finding, and he told her so.

"Maybe I can work with something. I mean, you have a psychic talent that must be related to magic in a way. If I dig deep enough, maybe I can find a way to help."

God, he loved this woman and her caring nature.

"Don't trouble yourself. I can work through it. I've been through worse." He shuddered, thinking back to his times on deployment when it was worse.

Hannah gripped his hands and ran her thumbs in soothing circles on his pulse. "I hate when I see that shadow in your eyes. I feel like I know you so well, but I hardly know anything about your past. Tell me, please?"

He looked down into her dove gray eyes and could have drowned in the warmth and worry. He'd never spoken about his family or where he'd come from before. Not to anyone, not even his buddies on his team. And those guys were the ones who he'd die for—and almost had. But he'd held himself back because there was a part of himself that he couldn't share. And now, in this weird three-way relationship, he was doing it again.

Josh sighed. He hated sharing his feelings, his thoughts. It wasn't something he did, something he could do. He was a SEAL, dammit. He'd die strong and in honor, and not by opening himself up.

"What do you want to know?" he asked after the silence stretched too long for him to get out of it.

"Anything, Josh." Hannah bit her lip, taking a steadying breath. "I'm not asking you to tell me all of your secrets. But frankly I don't know why you think you need to have any. We're bonded. Mates. I can feel you in my soul." She held her palm to her heart, fire in her eyes. "And even if we didn't have the paranormal connections we do, we're sleeping together and, in every way but on paper, married. I know *nothing* about you. How do you think that makes me feel, Josh? Like I'm not worthy. Like you don't care enough about me *or* Reed to share yourself with us. I know you are a SEAL. I know you are tough, and can protect us. But you're shielding yourself from us, Josh. It's like you take one step forward with our mating then take two steps back when you realize it's too much." She took a deep breath.

Dammit. His heart ached. He hated seeing what his inability to give a piece himself did to his mates. "Hannah—"

Hannah held up a hand, effectively shutting him up. "Wait. I know you're scared of what's going on with that bite and the Centrals. I get that. I'm scared out of my mind too. But we need to be able to get on with our lives while all this is going on. Because if we don't, then I don't know what to do. I don't know if I can take it anymore." Tears filled her eyes, threatening to spill over.

"Hannah." Josh pulled her into his arms, her shuddering body warm against his. "I'm so sorry, baby. I'm just not good at this. But I promise I'll do better."

She lifted her head, her gaze steady on his. "Tell me about your family."

Josh froze. Of all the things she could have asked, she'd gone there.

Hannah closed her eyes and exhaled, struggling to release herself from his grasp. He held her harder.

"I lived in Montana with my parents," Josh began.

Hannah quit moving; as if afraid he'd spook and quit speaking. Well, she wasn't too far off there. He'd better just get it all out now in one fell swoop to get it over with.

"We had a small ranch where we raised horses. It'd been in our family for generations. My father was good at his job, my mother great at being a homemaker. They had everything they wanted. A perfect normal life. Then I turned five and the little boy on a neighboring ranch wandered away from home."

Josh took a breath, bracing for the memories. The pain.

Hannah wrapped her arms around his waist, comforting him.

"I'd seen the kid before because our mothers had forced us to hang out together. So when my mom came in and told me the boy was lost, I closed my eyes and thought of him. It was a reflex. These images came at me of the boy walking out in the pasture after a stray cat and falling. I could see him clear as day, sitting beneath a tree with a bump on his head and tears down his cheeks. I thought the tree looked familiar, so I told my mom." Josh shrugged like it was no big deal

But it had been.

"Her eyes had widened, and she slapped me."

Hannah gasped, and he kissed the top of her head.

"Yeah, I know. It was like she knew what I was talking about, but didn't want it to be true. Took me years to figure that out. But anyway, my mom told me never to talk about that again, but I didn't understand. I just wanted to help the boy. So I told my dad. I don't remember exactly what happened after that, it's been awhile, but they found the boy eventually, exactly where I'd seen him."

"Was he okay?" She asked.

"Yeah, a gash on his head and sprained ankle, but he was okay. And so was the dammed cat he found." Josh let out a dry chuckle.

"The next day my mom took me to a shrink," he continued, trying to suppress the urge to vomit or flee. "Apparently this *affliction* wasn't a new thing for my mom. Her father had it and killed himself."

"Dear goddess, why?" Hannah's jaw dropped.

"I'm not sure, but my parents were religious fanatics, and apparently my grandfather was too. So maybe he thought it was cleansing. I just don't know. They put me in therapy and gave me a drug cocktail that fucked up my system. When that didn't work and I could still Find, they shaved my head and used shock therapy."

His body flinched at the thought of those electrodes and their pain.

"Oh, baby, I'm so sorry. What kind of evil human being does that to a child?" Hannah lifted to her tip-toes and kissed the bottom of his chin.

"They did that until I was ten, and then I guess they just gave up. Or maybe they couldn't hide the burn marks anymore. I don't really know, but I was fucking grateful."

"Me too. But what happened next? That couldn't be the end of it. And what about your dad?"

"My mom tried her own therapy while my dad looked the other way. She beat the shit out of me with the slightest indication I wasn't normal. She called me the devil's child, believing the only reason I was like this was because the devil put me in her womb. Doesn't make sense since it was her blood that made me the way I was in the first place, but that's how she rationalized it."

"Goddess. I really want to kill your mother, Josh."

"So did I. I stayed there until I was eighteen, and then I joined the military. I never looked back. I got some papers in the mail a couple years ago saying my dad had died from a heart attack and my mom had killed herself in grief. They gave the ranch to an uncle and left me out of the will. But I'm okay with that, honestly."

"I wish you would have been able to resolve some of the differences, but frankly, I don't know if you could have done that in this case."

Josh laughed. "Not so much. But I found another form of family in the SEALs. I used my Finding sparingly, only when I truly needed it. But I didn't tell anyone about it. I didn't trust anyone enough."

"Well, I'm glad you trust us enough."

Warmth spread over him at her words. They loved him. Truly. He wasn't alone. Didn't have to hide. He'd told Hannah his past, and she hadn't run away. Jesus, that felt good.

He looked down at her face, her big gray eyes, her pouty lips, and fell just that much more in love. He brushed a speck of dirt off her cheek then framed her face with his hands. This was it. His perfection. His future. Those dove gray eyes looked up at him with the unending love and support. Mix in the jade green from the man he loved and shared and Josh felt complete. He sighed. It was everything.

He leaned down and kissed her, the taste of bitter apples and honey melting on his tongue. He could drown in her taste and never get enough.

His body shuddered, and a graying darkness crept behind his eyes, pulling him deep, tearing at their bond. The bond trembled but stayed true. Josh lifted his head, curled his lip, and grabbed Hannah's ass, lifting her to the bench.

"Josh," she gasped.

He lowered his head and took her lips, shutting her up as he tore off their clothes. Lowering his mouth, he nibbled her jaw, her neck, then down her breastbone to her nipples. He bit down. Hard.

She buckled off the bench, lifting herself toward his face. He grabbed her and lifted, and she wrapped her legs around his waist, her core wet and hot against his dick. Josh kicked the clothes out of the way so he wouldn't trip and slammed her against the wall, not caring if he hurt her. Somewhere deep inside, he knew this was too hard, too brutal, but he didn't care. He only needed more of her. He took her bottom lip between his teeth and closed his eyes, too afraid they'd glow red like before and scare the shit out of her. Or worse, show her his secrets.

He positioned himself at her opening, her wetness telling him she was ready. In one thrust, he was inside, her pussy clenching around him.

"Josh," she screamed.

He reared back and slammed home again. And again. Her breasts bounced, and his balls clenched. He moved one hand up and brushed her clit. She came in a rush, her heat pulsating around his cock.

Josh lifted her, still deep inside, and pivoted, laying her on the table, knocking pots and dirt on the floor. He grunted, gripped her hips, and thrust. His body shook, his balls rising, ready for him to come. Hannah lay below him, eyes wide with passion, a rosy glow from her climax covering her skin, herbs and soil spreading on that milky flesh. He pistoned, grappling for that last shred of control before he lost it. She came again, a scream on her lips, and he followed right behind her.

He stood over her boneless form and took a deep breath.

What the hell had just happened?

Josh pulled out, his seed still spilling. Shaken, he reached for some towels and cleaned her. He didn't want to taint her with whatever he was. What if they made a child? Would it be like him? Maybe his mom had been right. Maybe he really was Satan's child.

He wiped her hips and cursed when he saw bruises clear as day in the shape of his hands. He was a monster, a fucking lowlife who didn't deserve the pixie in front of him.

Hannah looked up at him, her smile fading. "Josh? What's wrong?" She looked down and furrowed her brows. "It's okay. It's only a little bruise. I'll heal in a couple of hours. I liked it, really. I never knew you could be so powerful. You didn't hurt me."

Josh shook he head. "But I did."

"But I wanted it. Don't worry, Josh. I like how every time we make love it's new and different."

Happiness exuded from her, but he couldn't trust it. This time she'd been lucky he hadn't broken her. But what about the next time? What about when he couldn't control the beast inside of him?

Chapter 22

The sun shone through the windows, warming Hannah's bare shoulders, her bruises long gone in the days since their love-making. But she still remembered them, felt them. She sat in Reed's studio, wearing only a sundress though it was winter, letting Reed sketch her. Her curly hair framed her face and tickled her back and shoulders.

She'd lied. Josh had scared her. Not the rough sex. No, that she'd liked. What had scared her was the way he'd turned into himself, like he wasn't really present. So internal, her Josh. He was doing his best not to be, but he still kept parts hidden, parts she feared would break out and destroy something she held dear. Not only their bond, but Josh himself.

Reed was so different from Josh. More open, more emotional. Yet he, too, hid a part of himself. This mate always had to be the smiling one—the happy one in his family. But he felt emotions so deep that it scared her and she was so happy he had her and Josh to lean on. With the amount of turmoil surrounding the Jamensons, Reed needed them because, if he leaned too far, he'd break. And she couldn't deal with that either.

"Hey, what do you guys want for dinner?" Josh asked, pulling her out of her increasingly depressing thoughts.

Reed smiled and laughed.

"What? Am I missing something?" Hannah asked. How on earth had that been funny?

"No, it's not funny; it's just that I'm happy." Reed shrugged, laughter still dancing in his eyes. "I love the fact the three of us are doing this. You know, the whole domestic bliss thing."

Josh shook his head, the edge of his mouth turned up in a slight smile. Hannah wanted to hold them both close to her and never let go.

"Well," Josh grumbled, "someone needs to cook. I'll die if I'm forced to live on a diet of cheese quesadillas and yogurt. I have no idea how the two of you have made it as long as you have. Reed especially."

Hannah rubbed her stomach. "Greek yogurt is manna. Yum."

"Sure," Josh answered. "I'll make rosemary pork chops then."

"Uh, Josh, what does that have to do with yogurt?" she asked.

"You could dip it in the yogurt," Reed answered, a pleased grin on his face.

Josh smacked him upside the head, a fake scowl on his face.

"No, that's gross. I want rosemary pork chops and the two of you aren't any help. No yogurt." Josh said.

"Hey, but what if I wanted yogurt?" Hannah whined, just to see the look on Josh's face.

He sighed and kissed her lips, lingering. "Fine, you can have it on the side. The things I do for love. Okay, I'll go take out the meat, then I need to head out to Kade's. He's going to train me on enforcer duties. I shouldn't be home too late. Kade said he wanted to be with Finn and Mel early."

He kissed them both and left.

"Okay, now quit moving," Reed said, and went back to his sketch.

Hannah watched, the graceful way his hands flew over the page. His talent amazed her. The utter beauty of his project and the way he immersed himself in every work he did just showed the breadth of his passion.

A passion that he'd used on both her and Josh last night.

"I don't know what I'm doing," she blurted out.

Reed paused. "With what?"

"With two men. This whole thing. I mean, this is so unlike me."

Her heart thudded in her chest, and her mouth went dry. But she couldn't take those words back, though she desperately wanted to. The thoughts and worries churning in her mind since she'd met the two of them struggled to get out. It wasn't that she didn't love them—she did. She couldn't, however, move on without talking about the fact they were a freaking threesome, something so taboo that only people in romance novels ever made it work. But this wasn't one of those—this was real life.

Reed set down his pad and pencil and walked toward her and cupped her face.

"We aren't just two men. We're your mates."

"I know, but it's so weird. I mean, not what we're feeling because that's incredible. But the idea of it just seems wrong. Everything's happened so fast."

Reed laughed. Okay. Not the ideal reaction. She bit her lip and fought the urge to hit him. How could he laugh at her feelings?

"You aren't the only one who's thought it, baby," Reed finally answered.

Wait. Was he regretting everything? Her heart pounded, and her eyes widened.

Reed held her close and shook his head against hers. "That isn't what I meant. It's just with the fire, the war, Adam, you, Josh, the demon..." Reed pulled back and shrugged. "Everything."

Reed leaned down, and she rested her forehead on his. "I know, I'm happy. Really." Wow, she seemed to be clarifying that a lot recently. "Any doubts I may have, I'm overcoming them. And I feel as though I know both of you so much better. But, Reed, you have so much history. I need to know more. You know?" Geez, first Josh, now Reed. She kept pulling and prying. Pretty soon she'd poke where she shouldn't, and she just might lose them. But she needed to know.

Hannah put her fingers on his lips when he tried to speak. She needed to get this out before she lost her nerve. "Not now. The three of us will get it over time. But I was a shop owner and a potion maker with my mom." Her voice caught, but she pushed down her pain. "I lived with my mom for most of my life. That's what I thought I would do. I would live a normal life span and maybe find a witch husband and grow old. I'm not sorry I didn't get that—I'm blessed. But I need to be more independent of the two of you and still be intertwined."

Reed kissed her softly. Heat pooled in her womb, but her mind whirled. "That's what a relationship is. Independence and connection. We will find the balance. Our bond is different because there are three of us and also because we aren't human. We are putting in three different types of people and melding them. Everything will calm down, at least with the three of us."

"And what about the outside world?" she asked.

Reed sighed. "Well, that's usually Adam's responsibility. But he's not here. Dad and the others say they can still feel him, so we know he's alive. But he's hurting. I hate that he's in this position, in so much pain."

"But there's nothing we can do about it," Hannah said softly. "We can only care for him when he gets back."

Reed choked, "I don't know how Adam can do it. I don't know what I'd do if I lost the two of you."

"I guess the best we can do is don't think about it. Submerse ourselves in the time we have and protect the Pack from what could come; it's all we can do."

"I love how wise my mate is."

"Well, it's true. I pretty much rock."

"That you do." He leaned down, kissed her nose, then trailed his lips on her cheek and found her mouth.

He tasted of sandalwood, wolf, and that special something she couldn't describe but was all Reed. She melted into his arms, worries and stresses of their conversation fluttering away as their kiss intensified.

Reed pulled back, his pupils dilated with passion. Goddess, she loved that smile. In it she could see their future, their love, and his nature, everything she never thought she'd wanted but everything she so desperately needed.

"Stay right there," Reed whispered. "I have plans for you."

Intrigued, she followed his path with her gaze as he carefully laid out a large drop cloth on the floor then went to a drawer and pulled out paint.

What was he doing? Weren't they going to make love? Why was he going to paint her? *Now?*

"Hey," he said, then kissed her softly. "Don't look like that. I told you I had plans for you." He picked her up and set her down on the cloth, then stripped her of her clothes, his fingertips tracing warm circles on her flesh as he did so.

Okay, this could be interesting.

He stood there, fully dressed, looking sexy as sin and undeniably hers.

"I love you, Hannah."

She didn't get a chance to respond because he crushed his mouth to hers, her nipples rubbing against the soft cotton of his shirt, sending tingles down her spine. He gripped her sides, rocking against her, then lowered them both to the ground. Kneeling, he stripped off his clothes quickly, then bent over to get a paintbrush.

Her breath quickened at the look on his face. His eyes had lowered and looked of molten heat.

"I've always wanted to paint you," he whispered.

"I thought that's why you sketched me."

"Oh, I'm going to paint your portrait, no doubt. But right now, I'm going to use these edible paints I bought and stroke you until you come. What do you say to that?"

She moaned. "Yes, please."

Reed smiled and picked up a brush and dipped into the blue. Her pulse raced as he slowly teased her stomach with the tip, and she shivered.

"It's cold."

"Let me warm you up then," he purred.

That was the response she was hoping for.

He leaned over and kissed her stomach, licking around the paint, nibbling her flesh. He raised his gaze, his long lashes utterly erotic surrounding his jade green eyes. Then he took one long lick in the paint, spreading it over her stomach.

Dear goddess.

"Tastes like sugar." He dipped the brush again, painting swirls and leaves along her torso, arms, and legs. Every time she wanted to move because he teased her so well, he tapped her with the end of the brush.

"Stop moving," he scolded. "I'm concentrating."

"But I want you. Please."

"You'll have me soon, I promise."

He changed brushes, this time using the silver paint. She bucked off the cloth when he bent and took her nipple in his mouth. He suckled and bit down, sending shockwaves of heat down to her core. When he released her, he trailed the tip of the brush around her areola, and she gasped.

She'd die if he did any more foreplay. She was burning up from the inside out, basking in her need of him.

But he didn't relent; he merely painted her other breast until she squirmed with need.

"There. My masterpiece is complete." Reed sat back on his haunches, looking like a cat with a big bowl of cream.

"Are you just going to look at me? Touch me. Please." Who was this girl begging for attention?

"Oh, I'll touch you. I'm going to lick every inch of you, then I'm going to take you," he promised.

"Can we skip the licking part? Not that that doesn't sound amazing, but I want you. Now." She moaned.

Reed gave a throaty chuckle, and she wanted to hit him. "Patience."

"Screw patience. Screw me."

He lifted a brow. "I like that mouth on you. I'd like it better on me. But that'll be later." Then he proceeded to lick every square inch of paint off her body like a starving man. She moaned and ached at every touch, every nibble, his touch sliding in every crevasse.

When he sucked her nipples into his mouth, she grabbed his hair to keep him there. Tendrils of heat curled around her body, soaking into her skin, bringing her closer and closer to climax. But every time she reached the edge, he pulled her back.

Damn frustrating man.

She closed her eyes, climbing to reach her peak, until she felt something blunt circle her lower lips and flick against her clit. She opened her eyes, wondering what it could be, and froze. Reed kneeled between her legs, a clean paintbrush in his hands and the rounded end without the brush playing with her pussy.

"These are clean, ready for you. I wanted to paint you, and I will," Reed growled.

She smiled and shook, then he dipped the end all the way in. The brush wasn't as wide as Reed or Josh, but felt so wonderful and smooth in her swollen channel. He slowly moved his wrist in a small circle, the edge of the brush rubbing against her g-spot. She almost came right there, but he pulled back, teasing.

"Please, Reed."

"Soon."

The brush rubbed again, but this time, he used another brush and painted her clit. She came hard against both, a scream ripping out of her throat. That had to be one of the hardest orgasms she'd ever had, and he hadn't even touched her with his hands—just his brushes. Talk about a new appreciation for art.

"Jesus, Hannah. The way you blush when you come, you're gorgeous." Reed leaned down and took her lips with his.

Her tongue danced against his, and she pulled him closer, wanting him inside. He cradled her face then moved his hands down to spread her thighs and slowly entered her.

Oh. My. Goddess.

How she loved this man.

She looked into his eyes, never breaking contact when he sank deep inside then pulled out and repeated it in a never-ending rhythm. With each pulse, she rose higher and higher, until she crashed down, falling into an abyss of pleasure, Reed following soon behind.

Breathing heavily, her mate collapsed on top of her, paint spilling around them. She held him close, soaking in his heat and scent.

"I love you," she said. "I never thought of playing with paint that way."

Reed growled in what could only be pure satisfaction. "I'm an artist; what can I say?"

Chapter 23

Reed sighed. Dammit, that still wasn't the right color gray. No matter the blacks, whites, and silvers, nothing could blend together correctly. It looked drab. Boring. Not at all like the eyes of his mate that stared up at him with love and adoration. He growled in frustration, the sound echoing off the walls. No one was home to hear his annoyance, but it still felt good to release it.

It'd been a couple of days since their painting pleasure. Josh was out with Maddox, learning more about the Pack and what it meant to be an enforcer since Adam wasn't around. Josh had been gone most of the day, and Reed missed him. How silly was that? Like he was a teenage girl waiting by the phone for the quarterback of the football team to call. Josh worked hard at what he did, and according to his brothers was frankly a natural at it. He fit in to the Pack like he was born for it.

Hannah wasn't even here to watch him work or do her thing around the house. After their talk the other day, they'd decided she needed to do something on her own to feel like she was contributing to the Pack. Not to mention the fact that she needed to learn how to use her elevated Healing abilities. A friend of the family, Larissa's little girl, Gina, had a terrible cold that wouldn't go away, and Hannah had gone to help.

He shook his head. Since when did he need people in his house to keep him company? He'd spent nearly a century alone and lived just fine. Well, he had the numerous members of his family, but that wasn't the same. Despite himself, he missed that growly ex-SEAL and the curly haired gray-eyed beauty. They completed him.

Reed gagged.

He had *not* just quoted *Jerry Maguire.*

Okay, he needed to get back to painting.

Hannah's face stared at him from his canvas. Well, most of her face. He still couldn't get the gray right. The others hadn't seen it yet, and they wouldn't, not while it was still in the beginning stages. It felt too personal when it wasn't finished. Like he was a piece of a puzzle not fully formed, one that wouldn't match up with the others yet.

He added more silver to his mixture. At this point, it felt like a pointless waste. Could he even capture her spirit with a paintbrush? The way she laughed with a stroke of paint? The way she cried with a flick of the brush? The blush on her face with the blending of colors?

He'd painted others in his family, yet this was by far the hardest, the most personal. And Josh was next. Reed didn't even know where to begin with that one.

Reed shook his head. How on earth had he wound up with two mates?

He sat back on his stool and remembered another time he'd done the same thing, talking with Willow about her insecurities in mating Jasper. He'd told her he'd be happy with a man or a woman in his mating. Or even both. But he'd honestly never thought he'd actually be in a relationship with two other people.

The dynamics of the three of them were scary as hell. Not to mention the fact that his two mates had somehow secured jobs and positions in the Pack. But he hadn't.

He shook off his own insecurities.

What the hell? Talk about being a mess. He'd always felt a bit off kilter in his family, like he was lacking somehow. But it shouldn't make him feel like shit that his mates had found the place in the Pack when he couldn't.

How was this going to work?

God, how melodramatic could he get?

He was in a committed relationship with two people he loved. They were planning a future. Yet why did he feel so unraveled? So weird?

Maybe because Josh was acting weird. Those dark moments that Josh thought he hid so well were coming closer together now. The whole demon bite thing scared the shit out of Reed. He'd seen the bruises on Hannah's hips when he came home one day. She'd said she was okay with it, that the sex was consensual. But it scared him. And even though she denied it, he knew it had scared her too.

There were times during the day Reed found Josh standing in the middle of the room, clenching his fists, a hazy look in his eyes. Then the man would shake it off and smile like nothing happened. It chilled Reed to the bone.

He cursed. He'd kill the Centrals when he had a chance. Every last fucking one of them. They were only playing with his family because they could. He wasn't one of the violent ones in the family—no—that honor went to Adam and Kade. But he'd protect what was his.

****

Hannah rubbed her hands together, warming them. Was she ready for this? Cailin wiped Willow's brow as she squirmed.

She'd only been the Healer for a few short weeks; now here she was, helping deliver a baby. Her skin grew cold and clammy, despite attempts at creating friction.

Okay, it wasn't a big deal. Just delivering a baby. Women did it every day. Not a big deal. Then why was she feeling light headed?

"Hannah, dear, do you need to sit?" Pat asked. "You're looking a bit pale."

"Here, let me help you." Mel came around the table and led Hannah to a chair.

She shook her head, clearing her thoughts. "No, no, I'm fine, really. I'm just new at this."

"Tell me about it." Willow laughed from her perch on the medical bed, her belly protruding and rippling in a contraction.

"Look at me, acting like an idiot, while you're over there taking this like a champ." Hannah mentally slapped herself. Talk about being selfish.

"I don't know about that." Worry flashed over her face, and Hannah ran to her side and gripped her hand.

"Hey, you're doing great."

"I'm so scared. I thought I'd be ready for this."

Pat and Mel laughed softly.

"Not so much, dear," Pat said. "I don't think I was ready for any of my boys. And I certainly wasn't ready for Cailin."

"You never are," Cailin said with a smirk.

"True, but you made it to adulthood. That's quite a feat."

Willow grunted and crunched up her face as another contraction hit her. "How did you go through this seven times, Mom? I mean, I don't think I can do it this once."

"Willow, it's a bit late for that now. Don't you think?" Hannah teased. She rubbed small circles on Willow's stomach, warming mom and the baby. Another contraction came, and she closed her eyes, concentrating on the pain wafting from Willow and syphoned it. This was her gift. She only hoped she did some good with it.

The door opened, and North walked in. Thank the goddess she wasn't alone in this.

"How are you doing, Wil? I hope these ladies are taking care of you. Everyone outside is thinking of you, hoping you're doing well." North smiled.

"That's our cue. Come on, Cailin, we'll go sit with the men. Now, Willow, baby, don't worry. North's delivered hundreds of babies, including his dear sister. He'll take care of you and my grandbaby." Pat kissed Willow and walked out the room with Cailin on her tail.

The Jamensons surprised Hannah with every turn. They were so close and at times were too much, but she loved them anyway. She had closed her eyes again and was concentrating on keeping Willow's pain down when Jasper walked through the door.

Okay, the amount of people coming and going was getting a bit distracting.

"I know, I know," Jasper said. "You said it might be too much for me to be here. But this isn't the eighteen hundreds. I need to be in here. I'll be good. I promise. I can take it"

North threw his head back and laughed. "Sure."

"What?" Hannah asked.

Mel shook her head, a smile on her lips as she held Willow's hand. "We kicked Kade out during Finn's birth. He growled a bit too much at every contraction. It's hard pushing a baby out while coddling a mate at the same time."

The room broke out in laughter, and Jasper hurried over to hold Willow's hand and give her a soft kiss.

Her eyes closed again, she pulled on her magic, infusing it into her patient with all her strength. Willow immediately stopped squirming and calmed.

"You're a marvel, Hannah. I wish you would've been here for Finn," Mel whispered in awe.

"I'll be here for the next baby."

"Uh, yeah. Give me a bit of time for that, okay?" Mel laughed.

"Hannah, you look like you have this under control," North said. "Do you want to do the actual delivery?"

Her eyes widened, and that faint feeling came back.

"I've never delivered a baby before, and I don't want to mess up. How about I just watch and help with the pain." *See, that didn't sound like a cop-out. I'm helping, right?*

"I trust you both." Willow gave a pained chuckle, and Hannah put more magic into her Healing. "Both of you just help me, okay?"

Jasper kissed her again, a pained smile on his face. "North knows what he's doing. He's an expert. Plus Hannah's our Healer; she'll help and learn"

Willow nodded. "Yes, for our next baby."

Her mate cringed. "Let's just get through this birth first, okay?"

Hannah smiled and leaned back during a pause in the contractions. She loved this family. Her hand came up on its own accord and rested on her flat stomach. She wasn't pregnant; she took herbs to make sure she wasn't. The three of them weren't ready yet. But they'd have babies in the future.

Her heart clenched. She'd have babies with two men. Two fathers. Totally remarkable and scary as hell.

Willow whimpered, and Hannah got back to her work. Peace flowed through her, magic filling the room and her patient. With one last cry from Willow, Hannah felt that little tendril of new life. A baby.

"It's a girl," North said, holding a bloody, wiggling infant. "Come and cut the cord, Jasper."

"She's okay? All ten toes and ten fingers?" Jasper asked.

"Count them yourself. Come and meet your daughter."

Tears filled her eyes as she massaged Willow's stomach to help with the healing.

"Brie," the new mom whispered in awe.

"Brie, baby. We have a daughter." Jasper cradled the little form and stared down.

"Jasper, let me clean her up and make sure she's okay," Hannah said. She wanted to make sure everything was perfect with baby Brie. After all, this was her first birth.

The new father nodded quickly and placed the newborn in her arms. She set Brie down on the padded counter and cleaned her off, staring into those beautiful blue eyes all babies seemed to have. Once cleaned, she set the baby in Willow's outstretched arms. Tears ran down everyone's cheeks. Hannah washed herself off and walked out of the room to see her boys.

Mel was already there, relaying the news of the new addition, but Hannah only had eyes for her two men. Her men. She fell into their arms, holding them close, inhaling their scent. This was everything she'd never dreamed of. This was her perfection.

Chapter 24

Josh looked around the empty house and sighed. After training all day, his muscles ached to the point that even his hair hurt to move. It was like training in the SEALs all over again. Yeah, because of the damn demon bite, his strength had increased, but those werewolves could kick serious ass. All he wanted to do when he got home was have a good meal then hold his mates close. So what if he sounded like a pansy? Frankly, there was no way he could have sex tonight. He was just too fucking tired.

Okay, he could probably have sex tonight. *If* his mates provided the temptation.

He chuckled. Okay, whom was he kidding? His mates *always* provided the temptation.

But they weren't here to do that. Reed was out at the elders' cottage doing some painting work for their scrolls. Whatever that meant. Hannah had decided to stay at Willow's tonight and help with the baby since Jasper needed to go out with the youths for a hunt.

Josh smiled at the thought of Brie in his arms. Such a small bundle of warmth. She was like a little person, all wrapped up in a pink blanket.

He snorted.

Yeah, she was a little person. Just like Finn. He'd never thought he'd hold a baby, let alone be contemplating having one of his own. But they would. The look in Hannah's eyes when she held that baby was a clear sign she wanted that.

Fatherhood.

For some reason, that didn't scare him as much as it should.

A sharp pain ran up his arm, over his shoulder, through his neck and cheek, then pierced his temple. He grunted then almost puked at the smell of rotten eggs overloading his sinuses. He ran to the bathroom and washed his face. His hands tightened in a firm grip around the sink edge, and he looked at himself in the mirror.

What the hell was going on?

If he didn't know any better, he would have thought he was having a seizure. But he didn't think so. No, this was because of that damn bite.

He splashed water on his face again then dried it off with one of the towels Hannah had bought to brighten up the room.

Like she planned on living here forever.

Something he desperately wanted to do, but it didn't look like it would happen. Not with whatever clawed beneath the surface of his skin, something he didn't want to think about.

A knock on the door startled him.

"Josh? Is everything okay?" Reed asked.

He put the towel back and tried to regain some composure.

"Yeah, I'll be out in a minute."

"Are you sure? I smelled your fear from the front door."

Fucking werewolf noses.

"I'm fine, really."

Reed sighed through the door. "Okay, I'm going to go and work on the deck while we still have some light. Do you want a beer?"

"Sure."

Off and on for the past few weeks, they'd been building a wraparound deck to add on to the one in the back yard. Jasper or Kade, who owned their own contracting business, could have done it in a pinch. But Reed and Josh wanted to do it themselves, use their own hands to build their home.

Plus, he liked watching Reed without his shirt on. Even in the dead of winter, Reed would peel off his sweaty shirt and work. Werewolves were damn hot. In every sense of the word.

He should know. He'd had Reed in his arms, against his chest the night before. He shook his head. Who'd have thought he'd be in a committed relationship? Not only with a loving, curly haired, curvy woman, but with a sexy male werewolf with a sensitive side. Talk about odd. But he loved it. Loved them.

His ears rang as his headache roared back.

Okay, enough thinking about that.

He gave his reflection one last look in the mirror and tried not to think of the flash of red that illuminated the dark.

Josh walked out of the bathroom, through the house and stopped in his tracks. Reed stood shirtless, resting against a pillar. His throat worked as he swallowed his beer, his lips wrapped around the bottle opening.

Damn.

Josh broke out in a sweat and tried to think of something to say.

Reed smirked and quirked a brow.

Yep, the man could read his mind.

He passed Josh a beer and winked. Damn arrogant wolf. He could have been thinking about Hannah, and that's why his erection tented his jeans, straining at the material. Though now that Josh thought about her and those pouty lips, the teeth of his zipper dug into his dick. Fuck, that'd leave a mark. He adjusted himself, then let the cold brew go down his throat. Hopefully that'd take an edge off the heat coursing through his system. Sure.

"You ready?"

Hell yeah. An image of Reed on his knees, sucking him off as he thrust down the man's throat made him groan.

Wait. Ready for what?

Reed laughed and tossed him a hammer, which he barely managed to catch in his current state of arousal.

"I meant to finish the deck. But if you want to hammer something else, I'm game." He raised a brow.

"Oh." He cleared his throat. "We need to finish this before we get another storm, but I'll take you up on that offer later."

"I'm sure you will."

With that, they got to work, laying down planks and hammering nails until their work resembled the deck they were going for.

"Shit," Reed growled.

Josh broke out in a laugh. "I thought werewolves had amazing reflexes. How the hell did you hit your thumb?"

The other man scowled and shook his hand. "It's not my fault. I was distracted."

"Oh really?"

"Yeah, you were bent over in front of me, shaking that ass of yours as you worked that last piece of wood. What do you expect?"

He swallowed hard. "You're gonna blame me for that?"

Reed shrugged. "Pretty much."

"Okay then." Deliberately, Josh turned around and bent over again, inspecting his work.

His mate groaned and walked up behind him, resting his hands on Josh's thighs, rubbing the worn denim. He wiggled his butt, something out of character for him. He was usually the dominant one, not the playful one. But being with Reed in this position sent shivers down his spine and made him want to submit to him.

"You know we haven't actually done this since the night in the forest," Josh said. They'd slept with Hannah and touched a bit, but they hadn't shared sex between the two of them. A fact that bugged Josh. Didn't Reed want him?

His lover leaned over and kissed his cheek. "I know. I didn't want to come on too strong and jump you every day. Though the thought did cross my mind."

"Are we done here?" he grumbled. "Let's get inside. I know you don't have neighbors, but the idea of giving anyone a show might be too much for me."

Reed laughed. "Come on, big boy." He slapped his ass and walked into the house.

Slightly offended, he rubbed the sting as he followed him. "Big boy?"

"Well, it's the truth. Ask Hannah." Reed frowned.

"What do you mean by that?"

He shrugged. "Maybe I want to know what it feels like. What Hannah feels."

Josh gulped. "You mean…"

"Yeah." Reed shook his head. "But don't worry. I mean, it's just a thought."

He blinked then brought the other man in close for a hug. God, to think this man needed reassurance that he loved and wanted him, floored him. That meant Josh wasn't doing his job. Yeah, his own identity shit took up most of his thoughts these days, not to mention the changes in him. But that didn't mean he had to neglect Reed.

He took the other man's chin in a firm grip. "Never, *ever*, think I don't want you."

Reed exhaled a shaky breath. "I know that, Josh."

"Do you?"

He laughed a hollow laugh. "God, I'm such a middle child."

Josh chuckled and kissed his forehead. "No, you just aren't the beat-your-chest-and-drag-your-mate-back-to-the-cave by their hair type of guy your brothers are."

They both laughed until tears leaked from the corners of their eyes.

"Besides," he continued, "I can do enough of that for the both of us."

"True."

He ran a hand through Reed's sandy blond hair "I do want you. In every way."

His mate growled and pushed him down on the couch. They shed their clothes, nibbling and licking at each other's skin.

Josh could drown in that sandalwood scent. He twisted his body and crushed his mouth to his. The other man tasted of beer and that rich taste that was all Reed, so different from Hannah. But oh, when they both melded together in a medley of deliciousness, it was incredible.

Naked, he slid his hands up and down his lover's body, relishing the smooth contours of his body and the way the muscles on his stomach contracted and clenched when he trailed his calloused fingers up them. Reed lay beneath him, rubbing his hands down Josh's back and gripping his ass. Josh thrust in the same rhythm as Reed's rubbing, his cock sliding against his lover's. Thick tendrils of desire wrapped around his spine, and his balls grew heavy.

This was the first time it was only the two of them. No Hannah. He noticed the lack of her presence but had also wanted to know what it felt like to be with Reed alone.

"Damn," he grunted. "I want you."

"Then have me." Reed gripped his cock and pumped him.

Josh almost buckled of the couch and came. So different from Hannah. He loved her small hands on him, the way she twisted and worked him slowly. But with Reed, there wasn't any caution. Just pure passion and strength.

Jesus. He was one lucky man.

"You need to stop that," Josh choked. "I'm not like you; I don't have your kind of recovery time. I don't want to come until I'm inside you."

They both shivered at the thought.

"Then get inside me," Reed rasped.

"Oh, I will. But first I'm going to taste you."

"Fuck."

Josh knelt in front of Reed and took him in hand. He pumped his fist then slid slowly back down before rolling the other man's balls in his palm. Reed tilted his hips, and Josh licked the drop of pre-cum on the crown, letting the salty taste settle on his tongue before swallowing him whole.

They'd done this a few times before, but he still felt like he was learning how to please his lover and trying to find a rhythm both of them liked. That's what made this relationship feel real—the fact that they talked and tried to see what felt good. Josh relaxed his jaw and took him deeper, letting the other man's cock touch the back of his throat before he hollowed his cheeks and sucked. He lifted his head and released him then repeated the process until Reed panted with need, thrusting his hips.

"Shit, I'm gonna come."

Josh locked his hands around Reed's hips and swallowed that heady taste until he'd milked every last drop. He pulled back and let go of the man's still hard cock with a pop.

"I think I just died."

Josh licked his lips. "What a way to go."

Reed smiled then rolled over, putting his ass in Josh's face.

"Are you trying to tell me something?"

The other man laughed. "Well, I didn't mean to be that obvious. No, I was just reaching for the lube. Can you get it? It's in the drawer in the bottom of the side table. I'm too boneless."

Josh raised a brow and looked at the rock hard erection pressed between his lover and the couch.

"That's not what I meant."

"Oh, you aren't boneless at all, babe."

He laughed then dug around the drawer for the lube. His heart raced at the thought of what he was about to do. Such an unknown territory. Taboo to most. But, fuck, he wanted this.

"Uh, Reed, we may have to move the lube to a different room at some point. Not that I mind the fact that we are ready in every room in the house. But once Finn and Brie are big enough to walk around, that could get a little embarrassing."

Reed laughed. "Not to mention our children."

Josh smiled and ignored the headache forming then lowered his head to bite Reed's lip.

"Tell me what to do."

"Just rub me. Circle the rim with lube then put a finger in to stretch me out. Eventually you should be able to get three in. Okay?"

He took a deep breath and tried not to come just at the thought.

He dabbed his finger with the lube, then dribbled it on Reed's crease and his lover shuddered.

Nice.

He circled the rim, loving the way Reed clenched in response. Slowly, he entered a finger, and Reed clamped down.

"Shh, relax." Josh rubbed circles on his lover's back, and he calmed.

He played some more then added a second finger, finding that bundle of nerves that Reed played with on him then circled it.

"Yeah, right there, Josh."

He fucked him with his fingers, adding a third one when he was ready. Josh pulled out then stood behind him, positioning his cock at the entrance.

"Ready?"

"Always."

Josh pushed forward, the head of his cock disappearing into his lover's ass. Fuck. He'd never felt anything like it. So hot. So tight. So different from Hannah. But he wanted her too. Wanted them both. Fuck.

He pushed forward, pausing at intervals while Reed adjusted to him. Finally, his legs touched the back of his lover's. Josh paused, sinking into the feeling of the vise around his cock. Then he pulled back until just the head remained buried and slammed forward again.

"Josh."

"Reed."

He grunted then thrust over and over, panting, sweat dripping, until only the sounds of pounding flesh and groans filled the room. The couch shifted forward with each thrust, and Reed pushed backwards, wanting more contact.

Lightning shot up his back, tingling his arms and legs, ending in his balls, until he came with a shout, his body pumping his seed into his mate, Reed soon following. Josh collapsed on top of him, his cock still buried. They were both sweaty and he pulled out then rolled them to the floor, a tangle of limbs and heat.

"I love you," Reed whispered. "That was fucking amazing."

"I love you, too. And tell me about it."

Pain shot up his arm, and his head throbbed.

Reed got up on one elbow and ran his fingertips down Josh's temple. "What's wrong? Are you okay?"

"Never better," he answered through tight lips.

If only that were true.

Chapter 25

Josh scratched at the scab on his arm, frustrated the damn thing wouldn't heal fully. No matter what Hannah or North did, it still looked like a gaping wound. At least it didn't bleed anymore. But it was beyond annoying.

Pin-pricks of sensation danced along his skin, ending at his temples. Growling, he rubbed them. Why wouldn't this damn headache go away? It'd been acting up, getting progressively worse for the past week, since his interlude with Reed on the couch.

The three of them had made love every night, in various positions and couplings, and he felt closer to the both of them. Like they were a real family.

Blinding pain shot across his body, and he fought the urge to vomit. He let out a string of curses.

Hannah ran into the living room and held her hand out. "I felt your pain across the house. Let me help."

He stepped back, cradling his arm. "I'm fine," he bit out.

Her eyes widened, and Reed stepped into the room.

"What's going on?" he asked.

Josh shook his head. "I just have a headache and acted like an ass." He shifted closer to Hannah and kissed her softly. "I'm sorry, baby."

She smiled, but her eyes still look weary. "It's okay. Pain makes everyone nasty. But let me help." She held out her hands, and Josh shook his head.

"I'm fine, really." Something nagged at him, some reason not to let her touch him. He didn't know why, but she couldn't be allowed to Heal him.

She shrugged but still looked hurt. "Fine. But please let me know if something is wrong. I want to help. Okay?"

He didn't answer.

She brushed a lock of hair out of his eyes and reached up to place her lips on his. When the kissed ended, she walked back into the living room to look over a few of the Pack's medical books she'd brought over from North's clinic.

Josh looked over at Reed, who scowled at him.

"You're not fine," he growled.

"Back the fuck off. I just need a minute," Josh's voice raised with each word.

Why the hell was he yelling at him?

Reed growled again, this time his eyes glowing gold. "Watch it. Please."

"Reed, leave off," Hannah scolded. "Come and help me. Josh needs some space. I need your help placing names in this book with the faces I've seen."

"Always the mediator, our Hannah," Josh snarled.

What the fuck is going on?

"Josh, what's up your ass? Why are you acting like this?" Reed asked, both anger and sadness on his face.

I have no idea.

"What? I can't act like I want to? I can't speak my mind? I'm sorry if I don't want to act like the husband in this calamity of a relationship with the two of you. I'm not a sick fuck who needs this shit." His vision reddened. The fury of his lies and anger tasted metallic on his tongue, but urged him to stand tall.

Reed scowled, pain in his features.

Hannah paled, her breaths shallow. "Josh, why are you saying these things? What's wrong?"

"You're what's wrong. Everything about this. I don't want this. I just want to go back to what I had and not even think about the two of you and your fucking mind games."

"Josh." Reed lowered his voice to a guttural growl, his eyes shiny. "I love you. Hannah loves you. But you can't speak to us this way."

He screamed, his fury echoing off their walls. He stumbled forward and shoved everything off the counter. Hannah yelped, and Josh turned towards her.

Just like the dream. Her neck begged for his hands. Josh clenched his fists, his mouth salivating for the kill.

Reed jumped in front of Josh's prey, protecting her.

"I don't need this!" he screamed. "I don't need the two of you."

"Calm down, Josh," Reed soothed. "Let's just talk about this."

Hannah bit her lip, her eyes shiny. Why didn't his prey cry? Shouldn't she be sad? Her breaths grew shaky, her curly hair bouncing on her shoulders with each movement.

"Please, let us help," she whispered.

Josh screamed again, a red haze filling his vision. The room lit in an eerie red glow. Apparently it wasn't just his vision that was red, but his eyes as well. "I don't need your fucking witch and werewolf help. I was fine before I met you. And I don't need you now."

He picked up the clay sculpture of a curly-haired girl Reed had made for him and threw it into the wall. It shattered into a hundred pieces, and Josh reveled in it. He turned from them and ran out the house, destroying more as he went.

The cool air brushed his face as he left the porch.

Wait. Where was he going? Shit. Go Back. Find them. Apologize. Let Hannah Heal you. Anything to stop the pain. Not just his arm and head, but the bleeding in his heart.

A blinding pain came again, and he vomited in the bushes. Fuck. He needed to leave. Leave the Pack. Leave that sick filth behind him.

He didn't care where he ran; he just needed to go. A flash made him blink. Then he saw nothing.

****

Hannah let the tears fell from her eyes as the front door slammed. Her chest ached as she struggled to breathe.

Josh had left. He'd actually left. He'd just broken their things, said words he couldn't have meant, and walked out the door. Her heart quivered and she fought to remain standing. She'd thought everything was going well. The three of them were a family, and they'd been looking toward the future. They wanted babies.

She let out a sob.

"What was that, Reed?" she choked out.

"I don't know, baby."

She ran to his arms, sinking into his warmth. He sheltered her, holding her close and she inhaled that forest scent that came from his wolf.

"That wasn't him."

"I know. It was that damned fucking bite. We knew something was wrong but we pussy footed around about it. All we did was hope for the best and ask the elders. What the hell was that for, huh? I feel so useless. I'm a werewolf; I'm not supposed to be useless."

She took a steadying breath. "We can't just let him leave that that."

"I know, come on. He can't have gone far."

He held her hand and led her outside. He turned his face up to the wind and followed Josh's scent.

Oh, please let him be okay.

She didn't know what she'd do if she lost him. She loved Reed, but it was the three of them that made their bond work. Giving herself a mental slap, she shook her head. She couldn't think that way. They'd find him, restrain him however they could, and she'd Heal him. She'd use any power she could and find their Josh in the imposter that claimed him in fury.

Reed stopped and paled. Oh no.

"What?" she whispered. She bit her lip and looked around. She couldn't see their lost mate. Where had he gone?

"He's gone," he whispered.

"Gone?"

"He's gone. His trail ends here."

She looked around. Only trees and greenery surrounded her. Most of the trees had lost their leaves before she moved in. Now in the dead of winter, their leaves lay like corpses on the ground.

"But there's nothing here."

"I know. It's like he disappeared." Reed gripped her hand and looked into her eyes.

"But what could do that?"

A pained look crossed his face, and he shook his head.

"Only one thing can do that, Hannah."

"A demon," she whispered and he nodded.

What had that demon done to Josh?

Reed pulled out his phone. "I need to call my dad. We'll find him."

Hannah let another tear fall down her cheek. Thoughts of what Josh's new ability could mean warred with what she knew of demons. She felt sick. "But what if we can't? What if the Pack won't let him stay because he might be a demon?"

Reed moved the phone away from his ear as the person on the other end yelled. "Um, Dad heard that. Josh is Pack. We'll find him."

She wrapped her arms around her waist. They could only hope.

****

Josh couldn't hear anything around him and didn't know where he was. He blinked and quickly shut his eyes again. That damned light that brought about the darkness hurt like hell.

Where was he? How had he gotten here? Wherever here was.

"I see you've made it."

He looked up. The demon, Caym, smiled.

Oh sweet Jesus.

He shook his head. "I don't know what's going on but take me back. Now."

Caym threw his head back and laughed. "You don't have any room to negotiate. But I didn't bring you here. You did."

His heart beat in his ears. "You mean I teleported here or something?"

The demon smirked. "Or something. You did it all on your own. But you won't be able to do it again. So don't try and go back to the Redwoods. You aren't a full demon. When your powers came to fruition, you needed to find your maker. So you did." He shrugged, like telling a human he'd turned him into a partial demon was an everyday occurrence.

Maybe it was.

What the hell had happened? He needed to get back to Reed and Hannah. To apologize. To do something, anything, to get out of this new hell.

His head ached again at the thought of his mates, and he clenched his jaw.

Caym clucked his tongue. "Silly human. Stop thinking of them. That part of your life is over. You're not their mate, or whatever you thought you were, anymore. You're just like me.

Something glorious. Every time you think of them, it will hurt. So stop."

Josh let out a hollow sound. Like it could be that easy. Like he could drop everything he wanted—no, needed—because a demon told him to.

Wait. What was it he wanted? His vision blurred and his memories grew hazy, like he couldn't quite reach that thought of happiness.

He knelt on the grassy ground and stared into the abyss. The demon brushed his fingertip along Josh's forehead, and he gasped. Ice cold skin left a fiery trail. He closed his eyes and let the demon's deep words resonate over his body. A sense of eerie peace settled over his rage and he calmed. Blackness swept over him and he slept.

****

"Wake up," a voice whispered at Josh.

He blinked. Dark eyes set in a tanned face stared at him.

He shot up and jumped away from her with a growl.

Dark hair in a tangle surrounded her face. she looked like she had curves, but was dressed in such baggy clothing he couldn't tell.

Who was this woman?

Anger crawled up his body and raged within him. Should he kill her?

"Stop fighting," she scolded, her hands on her hips. "My name is Ellie. I'll get you out of here."

He scrunched his brows. "But I don't want to leave."

A pained look passed over her face. "It's too late then."

"I don't understand. What's too late? I'm healed. I'm reborn."

She shook her head. "I'm so sorry. I was happy when you came and rescued your mates. At least someone should have their fairy tale ending. I thought it'd be over and you'd all move on. But I should have known. It's never over. Not with my family."

"Your family?" Now he was really confused. Why was she rambling about mates? He didn't have a mate. He only had Caym.

"I'm the daughter of the Alpha." She shrugged.

This seemed like it should be important, but he couldn't tell why. Bored with her, he turned away. He stood up, patiently waiting for his master to come and tell him what to do. Yes, that would be a good thing. He acted like a good soldier.

He'd prove his worth.

He hoped his task would be to kill the dark-eyed girl in front of him. He didn't like what she spoke of, because he'd never saved two people without the master telling him to. He didn't have mates. No, he had only himself and the demon who was his master. Pure satisfaction rolled over him.

The metal door to the room creaked open, and a man walked through, his master following. Josh stood at attention and waited for his orders.

The other man clapped his hands and leered. "Oh, this is wonderful. I love it. You've done well, Caym."

His master nodded regally. "Thank you, Hector," he purred.

Hector looked past Josh and scowled. "Ellie? What are you doing here? Leave. Go see Corbin. He wanted you earlier. And if I hear you disobeyed me and didn't go to him directly, I'll let him have you for two days straight."

Josh turned his head and watched Ellie shudder.

"Ah," Hector said with a sneer. "I see you remember the last time. Don't disappoint me more than you already do, child."

She ran out of the room, but she held her head high.

A strong soul in such a weak body.

"Well, Josh," he said. "I'm your Alpha. You will obey me."

Confusion swept through him. He thought Caym was his master. What was an Alpha?

Hector smacked him across the face with the back of his hand. Blood trickled from his lip, but he didn't move.

"Ah, Hector," Caym drawled, "he's a partial demon. He thinks he only answers to a demon. But if you punish him hard enough, he'll listen to you. It's part of his training."

Hector growled. Behind the Alpha, Caym gave a small nod.

Ah, his master wanted him to follow the Alpha. Okay.

Josh nodded toward Hector and didn't shout when the man's fist connected with his face. Nor did he when the man punched him in the ribs, the stomach, or any other part of his body. He took it. It was his due because that's what his master wanted. And he always did what his master wanted. No matter what.

Chapter 26

Reed clenched his fists and scowled. He didn't want to be in this room, doing nothing but waiting. Josh had left. He'd walked out the door then vanished like a demon. Icy fear wrapped around his stomach and leveled him. Without a trail, they couldn't go after him. Couldn't find him. His mate, the other third of his heart. Gone. And turning into something Reed might not be strong enough to pull him out of.

Instead of running toward a goal that they didn't have a clear path to, he sat in his parents' home, talking about what they could do. Talk about futile. Hannah sat by his side, a broken expression on her face. She'd quit crying, almost like she'd given up. Utter failure washed through him. He'd let Josh walk away, now he let Hannah feel like there was no hope.

Reed glanced over at her and blinked. He was wrong. She sat like a stone, but not cold. Energy radiated off of her, like she was ready to pounce on any scrap of information that might lead to their mate.

He pulled her closer, her body melting into his. He'd mated a hidden warrior, a woman who'd find their mate by his side and kick ass while doing it. He couldn't ask for anything more. When Josh had spoken those venomous words, his heart had shattered. It took every ounce of strength not to hit back and demand the other man take them back, to pound on him until he was once again the man he'd fallen in love with. Not the monster lurking behind a red glow. But Reed had seen through the vicious words thrown at him to the man beneath struggling for control.

He sighed. He'd grown too complacent and fallen into a routine, practically sweeping their problems under the rug. The fault lay on his shoulders, a heavy burden if there ever was one.

"Hey." Hannah rubbed her palm on his knee, bringing him out of his thoughts. "Stop thinking that."

Reed lifted the side of his mouth. "How did you know what I was thinking?"

"It's all over your face." She frowned then bit her lip. "We did everything we could, but no one has seen this before. Josh is a first. There was nothing we could do. But that doesn't mean we can't do something now."

He nodded but didn't believe a word of it. There had to have been something he could have done to save him.

His arms tingled, adrenaline rising through him. He'd save Josh. There wasn't another option. He couldn't let his family lose another mate. Not like Anna.

The broken, dejected look on Adam's face filled his mind. The unfathomable anger his brother still carried after all this time had a tangible life of its own. Reed shuddered. He couldn't end up like that, and he refused to bring Hannah down too.

"We'll find him, son." His father gripped his shoulder, the familiar soothing of his Alpha's bond ebbed through him.

Reed shook it off. He didn't want to be fucking soothed.

"Really? And what then?" he shouted. "How can we save him? You didn't see him, Dad. You don't know. He's a fucking demon."

Reed panted and froze. Oh shit. Had he just yelled at his father? His Alpha? What the fuck was he thinking?

His father raised a brow. "You may be in pain, but I am your Alpha. You best remember that, son. But I'll let it slide this once."

He swallowed hard but didn't lower his gaze.

Hannah held on to his hand and squeezed. Calmness rippled through their bond, and he settled, finally showing proper respect.

His dad growled then shook his head. "I've never heard of what happened to Josh occurring before. But there may be a way to overcome it."

Alert, Reed slid to the edge of the couch. "What?"

Hannah tightened her grip.

His dad held up a hand, forcing Reed to calm. Dammit, he didn't want calm.

"Your bond," his father stated.

"What about our bond?" he gritted out. *Come on, speak faster. Josh might not have that much time.*

"The trinity bond is powerful."

"I remember you saying something about a trinity bond when we first mated, but I thought you meant because there were three of us in a bond."

His dad shook his head. "It's a powerful bond that has certain powers. The elders think it will bind a demon's power to this plane so he can't open another portal. Meaning that your bond can make the demon weaker and may give us an advantage in this war."

Reed stood up, anger pulsing in his veins. "Are you fucking kidding me? You've known about this the whole time? We could have done something before this. Why didn't you fucking tell us?"

"I didn't know until you called, Reed. I promise you that. The elders went into a deep trance and contacted the moon goddess."

"They can do that?"

"Apparently." His dad sighed. "It takes a lot of energy, but these are dark times."

"Okay, then let's use our bond to at least stop the demon."

"It's not that easy."

"Why?" His pulse pounded in his ears. The fact that they could bind the demon didn't help Josh, at least not directly. But it was something. Something worth moving toward and something that made him feel less helpless.

"We can't do it because I don't know if you actually have the bond."

"Huh? I don't get it. I thought you said we had the trinity bond." The vein on the side of his head began to beat harder. Reed rubbed it, trying not to attack his father for more information.

"Your bond whispers something different to me."

"What? I don't get it."

"It's not a normal bond. That's why I think it's the trinity bond. But it's not a full bond yet, so I don't know its truth or its strength." His father raised a brow and gave him a pointed look.

Reed cursed and paced around the room. "We aren't marked."

Fuck. Why did they wait? Oh yeah, because they didn't feel comfortable with the bite, because they wanted to wait until after the mating ceremony. They could've save Josh by marking each other. He was sure of it.

His body shook with rage and his arm shot out, his fist crashing through the plaster and dry wall. Pain ricocheted up his arm, but he welcomed it. It was a small price to pay for his stupidity.

"Reed!" His mother shouted. "That is not how you handle this. Go outside and punch something, fight your brothers, but do not attack our home. You don't know what marking would have done to Josh beforehand. He isn't a normal human anymore. We just didn't know. You took a risk either way, but at least this way you didn't potentially kill him. And it's not over. You can fix this. But not by breaking our home in the process."

Shamed, he pulled his hand out of the wall and stretched his bloody fingers. "I'm sorry, Mom."

Hannah grabbed his hand none too gently, and he winced. She clucked her tongue and didn't even look at him. "Stupid wolf," she muttered.

He brought his other hand up and brushed a wayward curl out of her eyes. "I'm sorry. I'm just frustrated that I was so stupid and reluctant."

She glared at him, a fire burning in her eyes, her curls swaying around her face. "You think you're the only one with the right to feel that way? Huh? I'm not marked either, Reed. Maybe that's why we've all been feeling on edge lately. Because we aren't truly mates with our supernatural halves—only our human halves. We've been denying it. And now its cost us Josh." Her voice broke at the last sentence, tears filled her eyes, but she shook it off.

They'd mated their human halves through their love making in the woods after the fire. He'd spilled his seed in both his mates, cementing the initial sparks of their bond. But without the marks on their shoulders, his wolf wasn't mated to them, something he needed to fix but had been too afraid.

He pulled her close, enveloping her in his arms. "I know we wanted to wait for our mating ceremony and for more information on Josh, but we can't wait any longer. As it is, we probably waited too long."

She nodded, her face pressing into his chest. "Now we need to find him."

"You might be able to through your bond, but it's tricky," his father said.

Reed's eyes widened. "I've never heard of that before."

"It's something that happens to some couples after a mating. Not all, but it's worth a shot."

"Then let's do it. Let's find him."

"We'll go with you," his father said. "But if he's where we think he is, we can't go through the boundaries protecting them. I can still feel Josh slightly through my Alpha bonds, but it feels oily—slick. I think, though, through your bond, you should be able to get through. The trinity bond should have enough power to do it."

"You think? All of this is just a guess?"

His father growled, but a sad look passed over his face. "It's the best you have."

Reed closed his eyes, praying for strength and whatever magic went into their bond. "Okay, let's go."

"Bring Jasper and North. We need to leave Kade and Maddox here to protect the Pack."

Reed nodded. No matter what, he'd bring Josh home. Demon or not.

****

Josh held his stomach and groaned. Another wave of pain smashed through him and he threw up on the floor. His kidneys felt like mutilated raisins. He was sure his face resembled a black and blue likeness of his normal self. Bruises covered every inch of his body.

He took another breath and tried not to hurl again. As he did, he could feel his skin knit together, healing in soft bursts of warmth that itched.

Was this what it meant to be a partial demon?

He could apparently heal. His strength increased with each passing hour. He raged out more often than not. And he had flashed from one place to another with just a thought—once. The emptiness inside him spread.

He missed two people, but he couldn't think of whom. Flashes of gray and green, interspersed with laughter and heat filled his mind, but he couldn't remember who they were. His head pounded at the thought, and he promptly forgot.

The door opened, and Caym walked in. Josh bit his lip and pulled himself off the floor.

He must please his master.

"I like your obedience." Caym sneered.

Josh lowered his eyes. He wasn't worthy of looking at him.

"You've proven yourself to Hector by submitting to him. You will listen to him and follow his orders until I say otherwise. Do you understand?"

Josh nodded. Anything for his master.

"Your next mission will be to take back what has been lost."

He raised his head, keeping his gaze low. "Yes, master."

"I need the two that walked out of here by your hands. They are very important to me. They must die."

Josh nodded.

"You will bring them here, and I will drain them of their powers. And then you will have the pleasure of killing them."

"Yes, anything."

"The witch and the wolf will die by your hand. Good. Now take off your shirt." Caym raised the whip in his hand and grinned. "It's time for your training in obedience."

Josh quickly took off his shirt, not giving it a moment's thought. When the first blow came, he bit his lip but didn't cry out. He needed the training to kill the witch and the wolf. Anything for his master.

Chapter 27

The Jeep hit a rut, and Hannah braced her hand against the door so she wouldn't hit her head. She gripped Reed's hand in a desperate attempt to keep her grounded. Her nerves frayed further as they moved closer to the Centrals' territory. She sat in the back seat huddled next to Reed, praying for the strength to get through this.

Because she had to. No other option remained Without Josh, they'd fracture and dissolve into the wind. He was their steady rock, the one that held them together, that melded Reed's outgoing personality to her hesitant and yet not-so-hesitant one, that took all of their strengths and weaknesses and made them better for it.

The car hit another bump, and Jasper cursed. "Sorry, guys, these back roads suck. But we're getting close." His knuckles whitened on the steering wheel, and another wash of sadness swept over her.

He'd left Willow and their new baby at home so he could be their backup for whatever danger lay ahead. North, in the passenger seat, rubbed his temples and looked just as stressed as Jasper.

The bond between her and Reed pulsed with each ragged breath. She could feel him in her soul. Not his pain, but his presence. That at least comforted her. But the bond between her and Josh felt like glass, like it could break at any moment, that any movement or breath would shatter it. She closed her eyes. Her teeth bit into her lip, and she concentrated.

Please, Josh. Be okay.

He had to be. She didn't know what she'd do without him. Or the man sitting next to her. But something from his conversation with his father churned her stomach.

"Reed?" Hannah asked. "Why didn't you mark me at your parents' house? Wouldn't it have been easier?"

North coughed up a laugh while Jasper snorted.

"What?" She looked at them both. "What did I say?"

Reed blushed. "Um, I wouldn't suggest that. The bite is an intimate thing."

"Oh, like it's personal? That makes sense."

North laughed again, and Reed kicked the back of his seat.

Okay, what's going on?

"No." Reed cleared his throat.

This could be bad.

Her mate smiled wanly. "Once I bite you, you'll orgasm."

"Oh." Her cheeks scalded, and she lowered her gaze from the brothers. *Talk about awkward.*

Jasper growled from the front of the Jeep, and Reed rubbed circles into her palm.

"What's wrong Jasper? Did I say something?" she asked.

North cracked up again. "I'm sorry. I'm not trying to be an ass. Really. Jasper gave Willow her mating mark in front of a bunch of us and most of the Centrals."

Oh geez. "So that means Willow…"

"Yes." Jasper growled louder this time.

Oh.

"Why would you do that Jasper?" Hannah had thought him a nice guy who cared for his mate with every breath he had. Why would he humiliate her like that?

"I didn't have a choice," he answered plainly, his grip on the steering wheel tighter. "They were going to kill her."

Damn Centrals. They messed everything up. Destroyed all of the precious moments.

Something else nagged at her.

"Reed," she said, "if we're going to mate Josh now, does that mean we'll have to... um...you know..."

Reed shifted in his seat. "I don't see a way around that."

"So Josh will, um...be really happy in front of everyone?"

He nodded in the fading light, but something flashed over his eyes.

"What?"

He took a deep breath and shook his head. "To make sure the bond actually clicks and we can use whatever power comes with it, I'll have to mark you too."

She felt a blush rise up her cheeks. "You're telling me I'm going to have to come in front of whoever is in the room?"

Oh dear goddess. Talk about awkward.

Jasper cleared his throat. "If it makes you feel any better, North and I won't be in the room. We can't cross the barrier. So you won't have to do that in front of the family—like Willow did."

She had a whole new amount of respect for her Beta's mate now.

She closed her eyes and bit her lip. "Josh and I don't have to bite each other or you, right?"

Reed shook his head. "No, I'm the only wolf. You two can mark each other, but it won't add to the bond other than the emotional aspects."

She exhaled the breath she held. "Okay, then why can't the two of us just mark each other now?"

North snorted. "Please, not in the back seat."

Jasper shook his head.

Reed pulled her close, his calloused painter's fingers trailing goose bumps down her arms. He lowered his head, his lips pressing against hers, and she melted. She pulled back and panted.

"Oh my. I didn't mean while we were all still in the car."

North threw a wad of paper at the two of them, laugher dancing in his eyes above the nervous tension radiating in all of them.

Reed trailed his fingers down her cheek. "I just wanted to kiss you. I love you, Hannah. But I need to mark Josh first. Just in case."

His face shut down, and she couldn't read him. Couldn't feel him through their bond other than the faint wisp of his presence.

Her heart sped up and she looked into his iced eyes. "Just in case of what?"

He lowered his gaze then took a deep breath before meeting it again. "Just in case we're wrong and I can only mark one."

Her vision blurred, and her body shook. "You mean you might not be able to mark me afterwards. That the feelings we have are wrong and ugly? Is that what you mean, Reed?" How could he say that? They'd completed part of the mating that night in the forest. The three of them had made love and sent the tendrils of their souls through each other, anchoring them for all time. How could that be wrong?

"That's not what I'm saying at all, baby. But with the demon bite and everything attacking us at all sides, we can't be too careful. We are mates. I know it in my heart."

He held his fist to his heart, and she knew he desperately believed that. But what if they were wrong? The inkling of doubt spread through her and threatened to choke her.

"I trust you, baby. This just sucks." *What an inadequate word.*

Reed let out a hollow laugh. "Yeah, it does. No matter what, you and Josh are my mates. Mate marking be dammed."

She sank into his arms as dread filled her belly. What if it didn't work? What if all the powers of her Healing and the Pack couldn't save Josh?

The car lurched to a stop, and Jasper cut off the engine. "We're about a mile outside the Centrals' wards. I don't want to risk going any farther."

Hannah closed her eyes and felt her bond to Josh. Sadness swept over her. A small part of her had hoped he hadn't gone to the Centrals, that he'd be just fine and in a cabin somewhere, waiting for them. But no. She felt their fragile bond going into the dark abyss of the Centrals' den.

"I wish there was a way I could tell you to say here with my brothers and be safe," Reed whispered and kissed her temple.

"We're a team. Always."

****

Josh tugged at his chains, and blood trickled down from the cuts created by the rivets from the handcuffs digging into his wrists. His muscles ached in their awkward position, but his legs barely had enough strength to lift himself off the floor so all his weight didn't pull on his arms and shoulders.

Where did the master go?

Shudders wracked his body, and his arm flared in pain. The bite mark had scabbed and scarred, though it now only ached for hours at a time with pain-free minutes in between. At least that was something.

Red light glowed in the darkness. According to his master, his transformation was almost complete, the rim around his irises almost completely red.

Good.

The metal door creaked open, and the daughter of the Alpha, Ellie, walked in. She held what must be his lunch in her hands but didn't look at him. Bruises covered her face, and her right eye was swollen shut. She walked with a limp, her left leg trailing behind her slightly, but she held her chin high.

"I have your lunch, Josh," she whispered.

He grunted. She wasn't the master. Why would he speak to her?

She shook her head. "Fine, don't say thank you."

He grunted again, and she put the tray on the floor before rigging the chains behind him so he could reach for his food but not reach for her. He grabbed his tray as soon as his chains loosened and shoved the roll and meat into his mouth. He barely chewed before he swallowed, then he slurped up the oatmeal in two gulps.

Ellie let out a disgusted snort but sighed. "Look at you. Look at what they've made you. An animal. Is this what you wanted to be? What you trained for?"

His vision reddened, and he swung his fist, connecting with Ellie's chest. She flew across the room with a whimper and crashed into the wall. A flash of pain and regret passed over him. What the hell was he doing?

"I..." He tried to talk, but nothing would come out.

She held up her hand and struggled to get up. He shoved the tray out of the way and tried to help her. Why was he trying to help her? She was just a girl. But when he tried to move forward, his chains held him back, just like the animal she compared him to.

"Don't bother." She whispered. "I shouldn't have antagonized you." She sighed and shook her head then winced. "I thought I saw something that clearly wasn't there."

What? He wasn't anything. Just the master's tool. Why would he be anything else? Maybe he should just kill...

A scent of honey and bitter apples mixed with sandalwood came to mind.

Home.

His body shuddered, and a fog cleared from his mind. Shit. Where was he? What did he do? Where were they? Hannah? Josh? Oh God, he'd hit her. How did he do that?

His thoughts jumbled together and his body convulsed as he took a deep breath.

"I'm sorry, Ellie," he whispered.

Her eyes widened, and she gave him a small smile.

"Fight it, Josh. I know it's not you who does these things. Fight it. Come back to them. We'll find them."

She took a step toward him, and the scents of home faded away.

"Find who?"

****

Reed took Hannah's hand and stepped lightly into the forest, on alert for any sign of the Centrals or their dark witch friends. An eerie silence enveloped him. But for their breathing, he couldn't hear a thing. Not even a bird or animal.

Not good.

Oily magic bore down on him, suffocating in its choke hold, as they continued toward the wards. Leaves brushed by his face and he flicked them away. His pulse beat in his ears, but he ignored the fast pace.

"We're getting there, Reed. We'll find him. We must. And we'll keep Hannah safe. Keep the faith."

Easy for his wolf to say. Reed shook his head. No, it wasn't. His wolf was hurting just as badly as he was. His wolf didn't have the mate mark and didn't feel the deep bond he so desperately desired. Reed had deprived his wolf half of that. More regrets piled on, adding to the ever-increasing pile of doubt and disgrace.

Reed growled. He needed to get out of his pity party. He could wallow later. Now he needed the strength to find his mate and keep his other mate safe. He was a fucking werewolf, dammit. A strong one at that. He could do this. Needed to do this.

He closed his eyes and lightly pulled at the thread that remained of their bond to Josh and followed its path to the barrier. When they finally reached it, they paused. Unlike the wards set at the Redwood den, the Centrals' didn't have the sense of peace surrounding it. That oily magic oozed through it and hazed its presence, shielding it completely from view. If it weren't for the bond, they wouldn't have been able to find it.

Hannah lifted to her toes and kissed his jaw. "Are you ready?"

"Ready to get him and get out. I love you, baby."

"Love you."

They closed their eyes and took a step through the barrier. Thousands of tiny pinpricks assaulted his skin. He fought the urge to scratch and howl, and he pulled Hannah closer to him until they found the edge. Immediately the sensation stopped and they gasped for fresh air. Reed looked around then pulled her toward a grouping of bushes and knelt behind them. He kissed the top of her head then shook his to clear it.

Though he wanted to stop and let Hannah take a break just to make sure she was all right, they couldn't. They were on Central ground now. For all he knew, the Centrals knew they were there. But they needed to find Josh. Now.

He looked down at his curly-haired mate and smiled. She absentmindedly waved her fingers in the air, the earth around them moving in small cascading waves, mimicking her movements.

"Nervous?" he asked.

She jolted, her fingers stopped moving, and the earth fell quietly to the ground. "Yes, but I'm also making sure my powers are still charged after that sticky ward."

Reed's mind wandered to the time when Josh and he had charged her magic on the kitchen table, her body writhing under him as she panted with need.

"I can always charge them for you." He grinned.

"Really, Reed?" she growled. "You're thinking about sex now?"

"I'm always thinking about sex. I'm a man." His smile fell, and he stood up straight. "But you're right. Let's get Josh out of here. Then we can have sex. That sounds like a plan."

She shook her head, her curls bouncing around her face. "Goddess. I don't understand the male species." She squared her shoulders and looked into his eyes, holding his hands "Let's go mark him and then you can mark me. Deal?"

God. The bravado in her voice broke his heart. He pulled her close and brushed his hand through her hair. "I love you, Hannah. This will work out. It has to."

She pulled back and bit her lip. "Sometimes I think you put a little too much in fate's hands."

He leaned down and kissed her softly, letting her honey and bitter apple taste dance on his tongue. "Fate brought me to you, didn't it?"

"And Josh."

"And Josh." The wind shifted, and he froze. "There. I think I can scent him. Dear Lord. It's him, but he smells different. I don't know how to explain it. But we need to find him. Be careful, baby."

Hannah nodded, hope flaring in her eyes. "I'm cloaking us somewhat. It's not the type of magic I'm strong in, but I'm trying. I don't know if the demon can see through it though."

He kissed her again, letting her know he had faith in her. "Then we'll see, shall we?"

****

Hannah followed Reed as he entered the stone building. It was a different one than the one where they'd met. Had it only been a few weeks ago that her life changed and she met her mates? Now their roles were reversed. Instead of Josh saving them, they had to save Josh. She only hoped she had the strength.

The earth pulsated around her, but it felt different here than it felt outside the wards. It was as if the earth was a prisoner as well, begging to be free of the chains the Centrals had placed on it. She needed to find her mate, but then she'd find a way to release the earth as well. It might not have been her initial duty, but her blood called for it. She needed it.

She looked around at the drab stone walls and sighed. She couldn't really feel where Josh was. He was here, but that was all she knew. Darn. If only she had a werewolf's nose. She couldn't scent anyone's trail, couldn't tell if anyone was around unless they walked on the soil. She only smelled the evil that possessed the pores of the compound.

Reed pulled her close, his heated skin warming her coolness. He tilted his head to the right then put a finger against his mouth.

Her heart sped up. They were getting close. Reed held her hand, and they crept down the hall, her body breaking out in goose bumps as they neared a metal door. Reed squeezed her hand, and the bond between them flared.

Josh was in there. Their mate.

Could she stand what she was about to see?

Did she have a choice?

Reed pushed against the door, and it creaked open, the sound echoing in the hall. Crap. Who'd heard that? Would they be coming for them? She didn't see any surveillance equipment like the one she was held in, but they could never be sure.

What she saw when she looked in the room made her blood freeze.

A bruised and bloodied woman ran from Josh as he growled and fought against chains. His muscles bulged, and his veins almost popped as he screamed in rage. He pulled at his bindings, and the metal broke.

The other woman stayed in the room, her wide eyes never leaving Josh.

Her shattered mate growled and bent to charge, and she did the first thing that came to mind. She threw herself in front of him, her palms raised and her gaze on his.

The rim around his irises were blood red, pulsating with a need that scared her. Tattoos of spiraled lines trailed up his arms and down his sides. His body lay thick with sweat, and his chest heaved with heavy breaths.

My goddess. What did they do to my Josh?

Josh growled and lifted his arm to swipe at her. Every ounce of love poured out of her through their bond, begging for something to hold. He didn't stop his violent movements, and she braced for impact.

A growl rumbled behind her, and Reed jumped and landed on Josh. Fists flew as Reed pushed Josh back, slamming both of their bodies against the wall with a crash. Josh screamed and clawed at Reed's arms, leaving layers of torn flesh, blood dripping from the wounds.

Hannah jumped when a small hand grabbed hers. The bruised woman squeezed and watched the door, presumably for anyone who could come in after hearing the loud noise of the fight between Hannah's two mates. She felt so useless. In the stark building, she was cut off from her magic. So she had nothing to pull on to separate the two loves of her life and protect them. She hated standing back. But without her magic, she'd be crushed like a bug between the two hulking strong masculine bodies.

The sounds of flesh slapping against flesh filled the room as the two men fought, and sweat poured from their bodies. Reed growled, his eyes glowing gold. Josh rasped out a curse, his glowing red. Blood seeped from cuts and gashes on both of them. Hannah instinctively reached for magic, but couldn't find any. Her soul ached, and dread filled her belly. She could lose them both.

Reed bent low and rammed Josh into the floor, pinning him. Hope started to make its uneasy pass through her. Could they beat Josh and save him? Josh struggled against Reed's strong hold and her wolf bent low, his fangs elongated on his still-human face, and bit into the fleshy part of Josh's shoulder where it met the neck. Josh screamed, and Hannah moved forward, a desperate need to protect them both from each other driving her, but the other woman shook her head and held her back. Hannah couldn't help. She could only sit back and watch and pray it worked. She hated being weak. Josh's body convulsed under Reed's powerful form. The bond rippled between the three of them, filling her womb with heat as energy pulsed in a rhythmic beat.

Tears fell down her cheeks, the salty taste burning her dry lips. Reed lifted his head, blood coating his lips, his eyes wet, and licked the wound shut. Josh heaved a breath and passed out. Reed held out a hand toward her, and she froze.

"Please. Now." A guttural growl.

The other woman released her hand. Hannah ran to them and knelt beside her two mates. She placed her hand over Josh's slow-moving chest. The heartbeat beneath her palm made her want to weep. Had they saved him? Reed brushed a bloody knuckle down her cheek then pulled her close, pressing his lips to hers. She could taste both men mixed with Josh's blood on her tongue. But it didn't gross her out; it was the only way to bring him back. With that taste, she could feel the hope of their bond growing and surviving. Reed pulled back, grabbed a fistful of her curls and leaned her head to the side, exposing her neck.

Please let this bond work. Don't let the mark be for nothing.

Reed bit into her shoulder, the piercing pain flashing through her and shocking her body. Was it supposed to feel like this? She thought it was supposed to bring her to pleasure. If it was this painful, did that mean she really wasn't their mate and she'd lose them?

And achy feeling of despair fought with the overwhelming pain in her shoulder, threatening to shatter her heart and soul. Just as she was about to give up hope, a viscous honey sensation slid through her body, coming to rest in her core. Her center thrummed, and she rocked against Reed, his erection brushing against her hip. He growled, the vibrations sending shivers down her body, and she came, shattering in her mate's arms.

Home.

Mates.

Trinity.

Forever.

Reed released her, and she slid down his body, resting her head on Josh's chest, his heartbeat steady against her cheek. Josh shifted, and she shot up. His eyes opened, a confused expression covering his face.

Her mind still foggy from the mate marking, she stared down at her clear eyed mate. His irises still had a rim of red but surrounded that clear, ocean-water blue she loved so much. Reed squeezed her shoulder and she fought the urge to throw herself on the two of them and cry.

"What did I do?" he rasped.

"Shh," she whispered. "It's okay."

Josh lifted his arm and held her face with his large, calloused hand before using his other to pull at Reed.

They'd done it. He was theirs. Thank the goddess.

A polite cough behind them pulled Hannah out of her thoughts.

The woman smiled. "I'm sorry. I know you guys are in the moment and everything, but we need to go."

She nodded and stood. No embarrassment filled her, though she'd just had an orgasm with an audience. She needed only to be with her men and get them the hell out of there.

Chapter 28

Josh stood between his mates, his mind freeing itself from the fog that had threatened their mating. He'd been lost for so long, since the bite, but now he felt free, like he'd seen through the darkness and had come out on the other side. Not unscathed, but alive. Hannah, with her dark curls and gray eyes, stared up at him, and he could feel her soul wrapped around his, trying to ease his hurts. Reed fisted his hands as he looked around the room and through the door to make sure they were safe. With his new heightened senses, Josh knew it was safe. He could hear nothing outside the room coming for them.

He was home.

Well, at least on his way.

Josh pulled Hannah to him and kissed her fully on the lips, letting her honey and bitter apple taste settle on his tongue. It wasn't the time for it, but he needed it. Craved it. He let go of her and kissed Reed, letting their tongues clash in a harsher tone before he pulled back and took a good look at the other woman in the room.

A daughter of the Pack that had attacked him and the ones he loved. The Alpha's daughter in fact.

She was also the one who saved his life by keeping him grounded. She'd brought him food and talked to him when he would have rather screamed and fought. He owed her his life and would do anything to make sure she got a chance to live outside this hellhole.

"Hannah, Josh, this is Ellie. She kept me alive."

Ellie bowed her head and seemed to shrink into herself. What atrocities had she endured? He was responsible for some but not all.

"Ellie Reyes?" Reed asked, his eyes narrowing.

Ellie raised her head and met his gaze, defiance in her eyes. "Yes. The daughter of the Alpha. I won't waste my time defending myself by saying I'm not like my brother and father. It's not worth it."

Reed tilted his head and nodded.

"We'll get you out with us," Hannah promised. "Thank you for helping him."

Ellie nodded, her eyes wet with tears, but she didn't let them fall.

Josh grabbed Hannah's hand and led the way out the door with Ellie following and Reed taking up the rear. Nobody was in the hall, and they quietly wound their way through the deserted hall before they made it outside the building. The hairs on the back of his neck stood up, and Josh cursed.

Hector stood in their path, a cruel snarl on his face. "You think you can just leave, pet? No. I made you what you are. I ordered it. You are mine. And you'll do what you're told and kill those two. Now."

A wave of compulsion washed over him but didn't stick. He wasn't Hector's or Caym's pawn anymore. They'd lost. And Josh would make sure Hector wouldn't forget it.

"No," Josh growled.

Hector's brows rose, and confusion marred his face.

Oh, poor little Alpha. He just doesn't get it.

But he will.

Josh let go of Hannah's hand and leaped, his fist connecting with Hector's jaw before the other man had time to blink or defend himself.

Stupid wolf shouldn't have given him the strength. He'd pay.

The howls of other wolves reached his ears, but Josh had only one goal. Destroy his tormenter. At least one of them. Caym and Corbin would be dealt with later. Corbin may not have touched him, but the wolf had hurt his mates. Josh punched the Alpha with all his strength again, the feel of bone breaking and the sound of crunching a sweet symphony to his ears.

Out of the corner of his eye, he saw Ellie fighting another enemy, her nails digging into the flank of the opposing wolf. On his other side, Reed did the same with two other wolves, his hands forming claws and killing quickly and efficiently. Hannah pulled the soil and roots around them and buried anything that stood in their path.

"You shouldn't have given me the strength, Hector," Josh growled.

"You're still nothing, pathetic human," Hector spat, the veins in his neck bulging. The other man forced his hands to shift—a talent only the Alpha and a select few possessed—and swung his claws at Josh.

Josh howled in pain as the other man's claws gauged his arm and reopened his bite mark. Hannah screamed as a wolf jumped on top of her, knocking her down, its teeth bared. Reed grabbed the wolf by the scruff of this neck and took his other hand to break it then he flung the dead wolf against the wall.

Rage filled Josh at the site of his pale Hannah covered in dirt and blood, her eyes wide. He screamed, ducked another fist, then grabbed the bastard's neck and twisted. Hector's eyes widened, and with an echoing crack of his spine, his evil glare deadened. The Alpha's corpse fell to the ground with a plop.

No sense of retribution filled Josh, no feeling at all but the desire to go home and be with his mates.

****

Reed exhaled at the sheer daunting strength of Josh's hold.

Dear God. What had the Centrals done to him? It didn't matter though. He was theirs and Reed wouldn't let Josh go again.

Leaves crunched under feet as Caym and Corbin walked toward them.

"I see my charge has learned a new trick," Caym drawled.

Reed went on alert, putting Hannah behind him, Josh doing the same with Ellie. Caym and Corbin stood on top of a hill about two hundred feet ahead of them. A grouping of wolves in human and animal form stood between them.

"You're a traitor, dear sister." Corbin sneered.

Ellie stepped out from behind Josh and raised her chin. "I'd rather die than stay here with you."

"Good," Corbin growled. "Because I'm going to kill you slowly. After I play with you some more, my pet."

Ellie shivered but didn't move nor did she lower her gaze. Good girl.

"Your father is dead," Reed snarled. "We won't hesitate to kill you as well."

Corbin threw back his head and laughed. "Are you kidding me? You did me a favor. That bastard deserved to die. He didn't have the vision I have. Now I'm Alpha. I should be thanking you. But I think I'll kill you instead."

Josh growled on the other side of Hannah and clenched his fists, Ellie joining in with a growl of her own.

Oh, he already liked her. She was nothing like her family.

Hannah lifted her head, quirked a smile, and waved her fingers. A wall of dirt and rocks slammed into the wolves in front of them. Whimpers and growls echoed and Reed let out a yell.

It was on.

Corbin and the other wolves fell to the ground, the dirt burying them, but Caym stood tall and raised a brow, the magic not harming him.

Bastard.

The other wolves dug their way out of their dirt grave and ran towards the four of them, teeth bared, eyes glaring. Hannah hit them with another round of soil, but some broke through. Ellie charged, picking up a wolf and slamming him into the ground, Josh following with the same. Reed rushed forward, grabbed a wolf, and dug his claws into its pelt. It whimpered, and he snapped its neck and threw it across the field. More wolves came at them all. They tore at his skin, but he was stronger. They did the same to Ellie and Josh, but they pushed farther. Hannah stayed behind and used the earth to protect herself and the others as she went on the offensive.

Sexy as hell.

Hannah ran to Reed, grabbing his arm, and he pulled her toward Caym. Even though they'd fought against the attack, they needed to get close to the demon to use their bond. That much he knew. They needed to bind the fucker, though he didn't know how to do it. But being near him would help. It had to. Josh followed them, protecting Hannah's other side. They reached halfway up the hill where the demon stood with a smirk on his face then were thrown back. Reed landed with a crunch on the ground, pain radiating up his back. Hannah lay on her side, her body close to his.

"Hannah," He reached for her, and she shook her head.

"I'm okay. Just knocked the breath out of me. Josh?"

"I'm fine," Josh growled "But that fucker can't get away with this. We need to *do* something."

Reed grabbed both of their hands, their bond pulsating between the three of them. Hannah held on to Josh, and they all looked at each other. Dirt covered their faces. Blood splatter and cuts dotted them like a mosaic of carnage.

This was it. Their only chance.

Reed closed his eyes and pulled deeply on their bond. Warmth and energy pooled and resonated through them. As a unit they used this mass of energy and power and pushed it toward Caym. Reed's body shook as the power flowed through him. Immense heat made his body break out into a sweat, but it didn't hurt. White light erupted all around them and Hannah screamed. Josh grunted and Caym's eyes widened.

This was the trinity bond.

Caym screamed in pain, his body convulsing as a bright light surrounded him. Reed held onto both his mates' hands, not letting go for the world. Whatever magic their bond held, he didn't want to sever the connection. The demon writhed on the floor, the light dispersing, and his screams faded into a hiccupped pant.

"What have you done?" Caym panted.

The three of them let go of each other and released the power of their bond. Josh started to run up the hill, Reed and Hannah on his heels. This might be the only chance. If they could kill the demon now, it would be better for them all.

Caym screamed, and fire trailed out of his fingertips, cascading in waves around him and flicking against the trees.

Demon fire.

"Hannah, Josh, stop!" Reed yelled and pulled Hannah close as a flame came at her.

Josh fell back and pulled Hannah's other arm until the three of them were away from the fire. But it wasn't enough. The flames came closer, licking and burning anything in their path. Red and orange flames danced along the tree line, burning an unforgiving trail. Josh covered Hannah with his body as the fire didn't seem to hurt him. The heat radiated off the flames, searing Reed's hair on his arms. Smoke filled his lungs and he coughed. The corpses of the dead wolves burned to ash, and Corbin now stood near Caym, bleeding but still alive.

"We need to go. Now!" Reed yelled over the roaring flames.

Josh nodded then turned and ran toward a body on the ground. Shit. Ellie. Josh bent and picked her up just as a tree fell directly where she had lain. He ran toward where Hannah and Reed stood. It didn't look good, but Reed could see at least the rise and fall of Ellie's chest.

Thank God.

The fire surrounded them but for a small gap, and Josh ran toward it, the fallen wolf in his arms. Reed held Hannah's hand and followed Josh into the forest. The leaves crunched beneath their feet as smoke filled their lungs.

Josh stopped and looked behind him. "I don't know where I'm going, guys."

Fuck. Reed wondered where his mind had been. "Follow me."

He ran forward, practically pulling a tired Hannah in his wake. The fire roared behind them, coming too close for comfort. Hannah tripped over a root. Reed cursed and picked her up, cradling her to his chest. Why hadn't he held her closer before? She was a witch, not a wolf or whatever Josh now was. She didn't have their endurance.

They ran farther away, the fire losing ground behind them. Reed didn't have time to think about what happened, including the fact Hector was dead, and Corbin, though hurt, was now the Alpha. He couldn't comprehend they'd actually bound a demon or the fact that he'd marked Hannah and Josh. Or that Josh wasn't the same as before, and they didn't know what the future held. Oh, and not to mention, they'd brought along the Centrals' princess, who looked like someone had thrown her into a wall then stomped on her.

No there wasn't time to think about any of that. He needed to get his new family and their new friend to safety. Then he could think about the consequences of their fight.

****

Blood raced through Josh's veins as he huffed a breath. But at least he didn't have the haze in his vision that meant he wasn't himself. Their bond settled in like home and felt like honey, comforting him.

They'd found him.

They'd saved him.

He didn't know what he was now, but all that mattered at this point was going home. With his mates. They crested a ridge, and the Jeep came into his vision.

Thank God.

Ellie stirred in his arms. He felt a connection to the female wolf. Not a mate bond or anything near to what he felt with Hannah and Reed, but like a sister. He was also thankful that she was stronger than him, and he owed Ellie so much. He'd care for her and make sure the Redwoods accepted her. From the looks on Reed's and Hannah's faces, he'd have help in this possibly immense endeavor.

Ellie stirred again, and Josh held her close. "Hey, it's okay. I'm going to get you in the Jeep and get you away from here. Okay?"

She nodded and passed out again. One of the wolves must have knocked her unconscious. Or maybe she'd just lost all of her energy. She'd been fighting the battle longer than any of them knew.

Jasper and North ran from the forest behind the Jeep yet had a cautious look on their faces. He didn't blame them. He'd gone demon. He didn't know if he'd trust himself in their place.

"What happened?" Jasper asked.

Reed opened his mouth and coughed up a lungful of smoke. "Caym set demon fire behind the boundaries. It hasn't breached it, but it's bad in there."

Josh looked down and grimaced. Their clothes had burn holes and smelled of ash and smoke. Nice. He hadn't even noticed; he'd been too focused on getting out of there.

North walked toward him tentatively, a concerned look on his face. "Who's this?"

There was no reason to lie. They'd find out soon enough. "Ellie. Corbin's sister."

North's eyes widened and Jasper took a step forward.

"Is she safe?" Jasper growled.

"She saved my life," Josh said simply. "The things Corbin did to her..." He couldn't continue. They were Ellie's secrets told to him during his darkest moments, and were not his to divulge.

North nodded and took her from Josh's arms. He placed her gently on the back seat of the Jeep. Hannah walked up from behind Josh and wrapped her arms around his waist, burying her face in his chest. He held her close, relief pouring through her. His body shook, and he fought back tears.

"We should go," he rasped.

Reed leaned in and kissed both of their temples, lingering for a moment. "Come on."

Jasper got in the front, and Reed sat in the passenger seat. It wasn't a large Jeep, so North held Ellie in his lap and Josh sat with Hannah on his. The sickly feeling that plagued him since he'd flashed to the Centrals and knelt before Caym slowly ebbed away to be replaced by the warmth from the little witch on his lap currently rubbing against his cock and the wolf in front of him who turned to stare into his eyes.

They were his salvation. Now he just needed to feel like he earned it.

Jasper drove like a bat out of hell until they finally reached the den. The wards surrounding it melted over him as they passed through, calling him home. Ellie sat up abruptly and whimpered.

"Shh..." North whispered. "We're at the Redwood den."

Her eyes widened, fear wafting off her.

"You'll be safe here." North held her hand and brushed a long brown lock of hair out of her face. "We know what you did for Josh. We'll get you fixed up. I promise."

"Corbin?" she rasped.

Hannah gently placed her hand on the woman's and Ellie flinched, snatching her hand back.

Oh geez.

"He's still alive," Hannah said. "But he's hurt. Caym is alive too, but we bound him to this plane."

Ellie scrunched her face, the bruises stark against the caramel of her skin. "What?"

Reed turned around in his seat to face her. "According to the elders, he can't leave this plane. Nor can he bring any more demons to Earth. He's weakened, but still strong."

Relief poured over her face. "Oh."

The Jeep came to a stop in front of North's clinic, and Maddox practically ripped the door off its hinges. Maddox growled, and his eyes widened. Ellie gasped and shrank into North.

North merely raised a brow, and Maddox stepped back, allowing North to get out the car with Ellie in his arms. "I'm going to take Ellie to the clinic. Hannah, get your boys Healed and don't forget about yourself. When you have the energy and your magic's replenished, come on over and help."

North walked away, Ellie still in his arms. Josh helped Hannah out of the car and stared at Maddox. A stormy look crossed over the man's face, but it was so full of longing it made Josh shift away.

What the hell?

Maddox turned to him, his face now carefully composed. "Good to see you back," he grunted, and punched Josh in the arm. "Don't leave again."

"I'm not planning on it," Josh said.

"You better not," Jasper added.

Maddox and Jasper walked away, leaving Josh with his mates. Reed pulled him into a tight hug and kissed him hard. His mate's taste burst on his tongue as their teeth clashed together and Josh was hungry for more. They broke apart, both panting heavily.

Hannah slipped in between them and pressed her lips to his. Her sweet taste mingled with Reed's, and he fell into bliss.

He pulled back and tucked a curl behind her ear. "Let's go home." His voice was a rough, needy whisper on the wind.

Home. His heaven.

Chapter 29

Hannah sighed as she stretched, her muscles aching from their fight. She couldn't heal herself, a drawback of her powers. But she'd heal eventually. She wasn't too bad. Her men were worse off. She pulled at her magic but felt depleted. Empty. Worn out. She looked in the mirror at her pale face, her brown curls framing the slight bruising, her gray eyes wide. She should go outside and lay on the soil to replenish, but she wanted to do it another way. A way she hadn't yet done before. A way the men in her life would appreciate. She grinned at her reflection.

When they got home, she'd Healed them then went back to North's clinic to check on Ellie. The other woman's bruises were already fading due to her werewolf powers, but Hannah had done more just in case. Just as she'd finished, Edward and Pat had walked in. A shiver had gone down her back at the look on the Alpha's face.

Pain at seeing his enemy's daughter? Or pain at the defeated look on her face that she couldn't quite cover up quick enough? Without thinking, Hannah had stood in front of Ellie, trying to protect her. But what good could she do? Ellie, however, moved out of the way and knelt on the floor in front of Edward, her throat bared.

Magic had pooled in the room, warm tingles tracing up her arms. Pack magic wrapped its way around her body and held her close. It felt like summer and smelled like forest, rain, sunshine, and wolf.

"You are Pack," Edward whispered.

Ellie had broken down in gut-wrenching sobs and fallen into Pat's awaiting arms. Hannah knew what if felt like to be enveloped by the Pack. But by the way Ellie reacted, Hannah had no idea how it felt to be part of a Pack that hated. Hannah had left them at the clinic and come home, heavy thoughts on her mind. Though she'd healed the beautiful, exotic wolf, there were some things she couldn't touch. Some things ran deeper than a cut or bruise.

Maybe Maddox could help...

Hannah shook her head and brought herself to the present. She put on a black and red lacy number she'd bought to surprise her men before all of this. With a secret smile on her face, she walked out of the bathroom and into the bedroom. The two froze.

She looked at her two men, and tingles spread like syrup over her body. Reed with his sandy blond hair that was getting too long and almost reached his shoulders begging her fingers to grab hold, stared at her with a heated look on his face. The locks framed his face and his forest green eyes. Josh with his short brown hair, spiking slightly on top, flexed his newly tattooed arms, fisted his hands and breathed deeply. His deep blue eyes stared back at her with their rim of red, reminding her how close they'd been to losing him.

Goddess. I love them.

"When did you get that?" Reed asked, his voice deep with need.

Hannah walked into the room toward them, cocked her head to the side, and swiveled her hips. "What? This old thing? Do you like it?" She turned on her heel slowly, the heat of their gazes warming her up to a molten flame.

Josh growled, the vibrations sending shivers up her spine. "Come here."

Butterflies danced in her stomach and she turned then prowled towards her men, both panting with need, their chests rising and falling in heavy breaths. Reed took her in his arms and lowered his lips to hers. His heady male taste weakened her knees, but Josh was there to catch her. Oh the joys of having two men.

Reed pulled her closer and kissed her, his fingers playing with her nipples and caressing the underside of her breasts. Josh knelt between her legs and dragged the lace up her body, exposing the fact she was not wearing underwear. Both men inhaled a deep breath and Josh rubbed his face on her mound. She rocked against him, edging him closer. He put both hands on her ass and used his knee to spread her legs before he licked her clit.

Oh goddess.

Reed kissed her, dividing her attention between the two men. But did she care? No. She was happy just where she was, sandwiched between the two of them. Josh sucked harder, humming against her, and she closed her eyes in bliss. She trailed her hand down Reed's bare chest until she could blindly unsnap his jeans and grab his cock. Reed moaned in her mouth and flicked her nipple, making her moan right back. She twisted her wrist and stroked Reed, who took a minute to disrobe completely. She opened her eyes to see Josh doing the same, then he raised his face and smiled, her juices on his lips.

Damn.

He stood and lifted the lace above her head, leaving her naked before her two naked men. Did it get any better than this? Her fist tightened on Reed, and he groaned. She worked him harder, and he trailed kisses down her neck, her breasts, her lips. Josh licked and sucked until she couldn't hold on anymore and shattered against his face, Reed following right behind. Her knees turned to jelly, and she fell into Josh's embrace. Josh sat on the floor with her in his lap and kissed her, and she could taste herself.

"Oh goddess. Was it ever this good?" She moaned.

"It's always been good, but this was better." Josh smiled and winked.

"Hell yeah," Reed agreed.

Hannah grinned and wiggled off Josh's lap and knelt in front of him before licking the engorged head of his penis. He groaned and lifted his hips.

Oh, her boy wanted more. Okay, then.

She opened her mouth and swallowed him whole, the tip hitting the back of her throat. He worked his way in and out. She looked up at his and batted her eyelashes.

"Oh God, I love you, baby." Josh groaned and stroked Reed's cock.

She loved that the three of them could touch each other always. She hollowed her cheeks and wrapped her fingers around the base until Josh's balls drew up and he came down her throat with a guttural scream.

Still hard, Reed stood up, his cock bouncing against his stomach, and laid on the bed. Josh lifted her from the floor and carried her to the bed, her head cradled to his chest. Josh set her down, and she moved to straddle Reed. With a grin on her face, she slowly lowered herself on him, and they both released a strangled groan.

"Bend over him, Hannah," Josh ordered, and she heard him mess with something in the nightstand drawer.

She looked down at Reed and stared into his green eyes.

"You feel so good around me, baby," Reed moaned.

Josh got on the bed, the movement making her clit rub against Reed.

Yes.

Josh moved behind her and rubbed something cool between her cheeks. "You said you wanted to do this earlier. Are you sure, baby?"

She loved the way they both cared for her, but she wanted them both in her. Now.

"I'm ready, Josh. Please," she moaned.

He worked a finger in to the knuckle, and she froze. They'd done finger play before to prepare her, but the anticipation of what was to come sent tingles down her spine.

"Shh, Hannah." Josh groaned. "I won't go any farther. Just relax. You're tight, baby. You're gonna feel fucking amazing around my cock."

Hannah rocked on top of Reed, and he flicked her clit while Josh entered a second then third finger. She stretched and burned, but it was the good kind. Reed rocked against her, and she reached the edge of her crest but fell back once Josh removed his fingers.

She whimpered at the loss.

"It's okay, baby. I'm here. Are you ready for me?"

She nodded, lowered her chest farther, pressing to Reed, then wiggled her butt. She was past ready. Needy and achy.

Josh pressed the tip of his cock to her back entrance, and she moaned. He pressed forward, and her body burned and stretched, letting him in. He paused as she adjusted to his size because he was far greater in girth than just fingers. Reed held still, his cock in her pussy, as Josh seated himself fully in her ass.

So. Full.

They worked in tandem, filling her, and she sank deep into her bliss, only hearing them breathe and groan at the contact. Finally she reached her crest and came in an explosion of tingles,

Josh and Reed following close behind. They all collapsed in a sweaty heap, limbs entangled and chests rising and falling.

Josh kissed her neck. "This may hurt." He pulled out, the burning increasing, but she felt too much like liquid honey to care.

"We need to do this more often." Josh laughed.

"I think you both killed me," Hannah said.

"Well," Reed added, "it is called the little death after all."

Josh grunted. "Who you calling little?"

They laughed and kissed, and Hannah snuggled in to their embrace.

Yeah, this was totally worth it.

****

A couple of weeks later, Reed leaned into Josh's side and watched North dance with their wife around the room, while she looked beautiful in her wedding dress. The strapless gown hugged her generous curves and flared out like a mermaid's fins. To him, she looked like a princess.

His princess.

Josh put an arm around his shoulders and hugged him closer. "She's pretty hot, isn't she?"

"We're two very lucky guys."

Josh sighed. "Tell me about it."

Reed took a deep breath. "I know we don't know everything that will happen, but the bond will hold us together. You're home."

Josh lifted his lips in a small smile. "Yeah, I know. And now that I'm an enforcer for your dad, I can actually do something with all this new-found strength."

"Well, I like your strength for other things too." Reed grinned.

Josh laughed and kissed his temple.

Ellie stormed past them, glaring, with Maddox trailing behind her.

"Maddox." Reed grabbed his brother's arm and stopped him. "What's going on?"

"Nothing. I just need to deal with something. Go on, enjoy your day." Maddox walked away, froze, shook his head, and turned in the opposite direction Ellie had gone.

Reed looked to Josh for a clue, but Josh just shook his head.

Whatever. This wasn't the time. This was their day. Well, Hannah's day. He and Josh were there to watch her. Nothing wrong with that.

The room quieted, and Reed stiffened at the newcomer to their reception. No one moved or dared to take a breath.

Adam.

His brother looked like hell. Dark circles smeared under his eyes, and he looked like he'd just come off a bender. Shit. What had happened?

"Adam?" his mother asked, taking a hesitant step toward him.

"Sorry it took me so long to come back," Adam grunted.

And yet for all the time he'd been gone, he looked even worse.

Hannah walked up to Reed and Josh, and they held her close. "Remember, we can't heal him if he doesn't want it, Reed. We'll just be here for him and wait."

He pulled her closer, and hugged Josh who leaned toward them both. Their trinity bond sparked between them, flaring with a heat that that would only extinguish in their bedroom. With their clothes off.

Though not all was bedroom activities.

The Centrals were out there watching. They'd lost their Alpha, but was that a good thing? Corbin's ruthless soul sunk into the depths of a dark morality. He might be an enemy far worse than the narcissistic Hector. They'd bound the demon to their world. According to the elders, Caym couldn't bring his friends into this world. And hopefully they could kill him now. But was that enough? The odds against them seemed insurmountable.

Josh leaned over and kissed him, bringing him out of his thoughts.

"Hey, stop thinking," Josh admonished. "It's our mating ceremony."

Hannah kissed his jaw. "Everything will still be here tomorrow. Let's just take a day that's all for us."

"I could do that." Reed grinned.

Across the room, baby Brie squealed, and Finn giggled. Hannah sighed in Reed's arms.

"So," he whispered in her ear, "you wanna go start making one of those?"

Josh coughed. "Smooth."

Hannah smiled. "Okay, let's go."

Reed's eyes widened. "Really?"

Hannah hiked up her dress to her knees. "Come on. Let's go. Let's not waste any more time." She scurried through the throngs of people, and Josh laughed.

"I love that woman." Reed sighed.

"Oh, I know. I love her too." Josh agreed.

Reed quirked a brow. "Race ya to her."

"You're on."

They followed their curly-haired beauty, pointedly ignoring the laughter of his knowing family. Yeah, it was good to be a Jamenson.

Epilogue

Dammit!

Corbin flung the glass against the wall. The shattered pieces splattered over the floor.

Caym walked up from behind him and caressed his cheek. "Why are you so upset?"

"Why do you think? We lost them, and they bound you."

"Hush, we didn't need them. They took care of your father anyway."

Caym leaned down and brushed his lips across Corbin's. Tingles shot down his spine.

"Plus," Caym added, "I don't need to open another portal. I think I have our answers right here."

"What?"

"Another of my kind."

"What? Why didn't you tell me?"

"It just came to my attention. But don't worry. I think this one will be of help to us. Nothing that's happened will foil our plans."

Corbin sneered. He'd lost his father and sister, but now he was Alpha. He'd make the Redwoods pay for what they'd done. And with Caym and the other demon by his side, nothing could stop them.

A Night Away

Redwood Pack book 3.5

A Night Away
Book 3.5 in the Redwood Pack Series

Kade Jamenson has been mated to Melanie for almost two years. They've been through mating circles, battles, loss, misunderstandings, and finally, the birth of their son, Finn. The world is in turmoil around them as the Redwoods engage in war with the Centrals. But for Kade and Melanie, the turmoil is also happening at home. The responsibility of a restless baby and their Pack has taken a toll and they need a break.

Not from each other. But from their Pack. Just for a night.

Kade takes Mel away for a romantic getaway and leaves Uncle Maddox alone with baby Finn. The Omega of the Redwood Pack may be adept at emotions but the idea of a baby may be beyond his immense capabilities.

Author's Note: This is a novella set between books 3 and 4 to give you a taste of Mel and Kade. It is best that you have already immersed yourselves in the Redwood Pack world, however even new readers will enjoy a glimpse of one of the Redwood's favorite couples.

Chapter 1

Kade Jamenson closed his eyes and prayed for resolution. A piercing shriek startled him, making him jump to his feet.

Finn.

Finn. His eleven-month-old son, who wouldn't stop screaming, no matter what they did. The kid always needed something, either to be fed, changed, held, burped, played with, or just stared at. It seemed never ending. Even now that he was older, he still screamed or babbled constantly.

Dear God. How the hell did humans do this? Kade had more endurance than any human, witch, and most werewolves out there. Yet a tiny fifteen-pound baby with big blue eyes took every ounce of strength he possessed. Not to mention sleep time.

Kade groaned and rolled his neck before he walked into his son's room. He and Melanie had painted the room in a soft green to match the Jameson eyes and added cream borders to break it up. Dark wood furniture filled the room along with cream linens covered with frog princes and bumblebees. Stuffed animals of every sort covered the tops of most pieces of furniture, gifts from his Pack and family, who cherished Finn like their own son. He took another step in and realized he hadn't been the first one to answer his son's call.

His mate, Mel, sat in the rocking chair, her blonde hair in a frazzled halo around her face. She cradled Finn to her chest and rocked back and forth. Her blouse was unbuttoned, and their son suckled on his mate's breast. Pure male satisfaction rolled through him at the thought of the love of his life feeding their young. He'd thought he'd been insatiable watching her waddle when she'd been round and heavy, but that was nothing compared to her now. He always wanted her, though the times of touching had been far and few between lately.

After the birth, she'd rounded a bit more than when he'd first met her. She'd always had delicious curves, but now she looked motherly, womanly, and his. Her head rested on the headrest, her body in auto mode while she fed their son.

Darkening circles lay heavily under her eyes, and Kade wanted to curse himself.

No matter how much Finn took from him, Mel dealt with the worst of it. Kade at least got a moments relief when he went to work or dealt with Pack business. But Mel didn't have that option. Even when she did her duties for the Pack and acted as the Heir's mate, she would hold Finn or wrap him around her in a sling.

Mel didn't get a break.

But she needed one.

Immediately Kade felt like shit. How could he blame that little bundle of everything that held parts of both him and Mel? It wasn't Finn's fault he was so small and helpless. He relied on his parents for everything and sometimes Kade felt like it wasn't enough.

"You are a good father, Kade. Doubt only spreads pain. Your son will grow strong and intelligent because of you and Mel."

If only Kade could agree with his wolf. Sometimes he felt so helpless. Not like the Heir of the Redwood Pack, the strongest Pack of werewolves on the continent.

He shook his head, clearing his thoughts, and walked towards his life. He knelt beside the rocking chair and grazed a knuckle along the sweet swell of his mate's breast. Finn scrunched his nose and continued to suckle. Kade ran a fingertip down his son's cheek, the soft feel of his skin like sweet cream.

"He's always hungry it seems," Mel whispered, her eyes still closed.

Kade lowered his head and kissed Finn on the top of his baby-soft hair. "I wish there were a way for me to help. I know we have bottles of breast milk, but it takes so long for you to pump, that I hate wasting it."

"It's okay. I like doing it, even though sometimes I feel like he's draining the life out of me. I like the connection."

He stood up and kissed his mate on the mouth. Her velvet soft lips parted, and his tongue darted inside for a quick taste. Kade pulled back, his eyes at half-mast. Mel's pale skin flushed, and her blue eyes clouded with lust, but that didn't hide the evidence of her exhaustion. Though she was a werewolf, little or no sleep took its toll.

"I love you," he whispered.

"I love you, too, my Kade."

His wolf growled and clawed at his skin. Mel and Kade had only made love a few times since Finn had been born. Having only a handful of memories to sate a need of such intensity kept him and his wolf on edge. And being on edge in the times of war was dangerous, though he couldn't use their war with the Centrals as an excuse. No, he wanted his wife. But between the Pack, Finn, work, exhaustion, and family...they'd grown apart.

He couldn't let that happen. They were mates, a connection far beyond the simplicity of a marriage. No, their souls were connected deeper than anything imaginable to a human. But though their souls and lives were connected, it took more than that to be happy. They needed to be together physically, and it was need so primal that his wolf wanted to take control and mount his mate any time they were together.

Kade missed being with his mate. He missed sitting on the porch and talking about their day. He missed lying next to her when she slept and tracing his fingers along her brow, her breasts, down her stomach, and then waking her up with a release that would make them both beg for more.

But they couldn't do that anymore.

"Kade? Will you burp Finn? I need to go clean up." Mel leaned forward, depositing the warm weight of their son in his arms, and Kade pulled back and stood up, his other arm outstretched.

Mel placed her small hand in his, and he pulled her close to his body. She sagged against him and sighed.

"I miss you," she rumbled into his chest, her warm breath tickling his chest hairs through the open collar on his shirt.

He let out a breath and held his life close. "I miss you, too."

Mel pulled back and smiled a tired smile. "I'll meet you in the kitchen. Willow left us some oatmeal-chocolate chip cookies."

His hunger for sugar couldn't compete against the hunger for his wife, but he still let her go clean up. Kade rubbed small circles into Finn's back before patting him. Finn released a loud belch and cooed.

"Yeah, that's my boy. A burp worthy of any Jameson male. And, well, Cailin too. I warn you now, don't mess with your auntie. She may be small, but she can take most of us on a good day. But don't tell her I said that." Kade paced around the room, willing Finn to sleep.

"You know I love you right? Because, Finn, I do. I know your momma and I seem tired when we're around, but that doesn't mean it's your fault. You're just an itty-bitty baby. You need us. So don't feel bad that we look so out of it when we're with you. We love you so much, Finn." Kade paused and took a calming breath. "You are our everything. Never forget that."

The dangers that lurked outside their Pack wards were of such a dark power it scared the hell out of him. With each battle, they gained a lead, a new way to fight back. But it still didn't seem good enough. And without resorting to inhuman and evil methods, Kade was afraid they'd never take the upper hand again and win. And what would happen then? What would happen to his mate and son?

Kade's body shook, but he tamped it down. He was the Heir of the Redwood Pack. The second-in-command, it was his job to set out his father's orders and to take care of his Pack. Yet sometimes he didn't feel good enough, even though it had been better recently. Before he had met Mel, he had drifted. Lost without a real cause or purpose. But then Jasper had made him go on a blind date with a lonely chemist...

"And the rest, as they say, is history," he murmured, gazing at his son.

At this point, though, he'd like the history to be a bit less exhausting. He needed a night away with his mate.

Kade smiled and put his sleeping son in his crib.

Yes. That's exactly what he and Mel needed. A night away from their home, the Pack, Finn, and their responsibilities. He wasn't naive enough to think it would solve everything, but he and Mel needed to reconnect and be with each other. And he needed to do it away from the Pack. Not just a night off with the babysitter. The demands of the Pack and the war were taking a toll on his mating, and without a solid connection, he and Mel wouldn't be able to lead in the future when his father stepped down as Alpha.

No, they needed a break. Not from each other, but from everyone else.

A sharp pain shot through his heart.

He looked down at his sleeping son and closed his eyes. A break. Yeah. Like that could happen. No matter how much he and Mel needed time for each other, he couldn't leave Finn. He didn't want to. He didn't want to miss a moment of his son's life. What if he grew or learned something new? Kade would never forgive himself if he and Mel missed a milestone in their son's life because he felt like he needed a break.

Did that make him a bad father? Failure seeped over him. God. What if he couldn't do it? What if he failed at raising his son, defending his Pack...everything?

Kade shook his head. No. That was not the right path to take. He was the Heir, damn it. He didn't have time for self-doubt. People relied on him.

He left Finn's room and walked to the kitchen where Mel stood in one of his old T-shirts and a pair of volley-ball shorts. She rocked from foot to foot, a cookie in hand, and her eyes closed, as she hummed a tune off-key.

Damn. His woman was sexy.

Kade prowled behind her, the gold glow of his eyes, evidence of his arousal, marking his path. He wrapped his calloused palms around her hips, and she swiveled. His erection dug into his zipper, and he growled.

"Eating something sweet, are you?" He bit her earlobe, and she shivered in his hold.

"Willow's cookies are manna."

"Uh huh. I think I want something a bit sweeter." He pressed his erection into the small of her back and ground against her.

She arched her back, a soft growl rumbling in her throat, and her honey-vanilla scent grew sharper as her arousal flared. His little wolf was just as turned on as he was. Good.

"We have ice cream in the freezer, I think." She gasped as he licked a trail from behind her ear to the back of her neck.

"Not sweet enough."

"I think I have an idea then."

"Do you?" He thrust his hips and pushed her against the counter-top. Her hands gripped the marble, and he trailed his palms down her sides and slapped her ass with one quick sting.

She gasped and wiggled her butt.

Kade smiled a feral smile, gripped the edge of her shorts, then slid them down to her ankles. Her bare bottom fit his hands perfectly, and he threw his head back and howled softly.

"You weren't wearing any panties, you little minx."

"Kade..."

He bent over, lifted the shirt she wore, and trailed kisses down her spine. He licked and caressed before biting down on one soft globe.

"More."

He bit harder then licked the sting. He parted her cheeks and lowered his face...

Finn cried out, and the smell of a dirty diaper filled the room, breaking the moment.

Kade rested his head on Mel's backside and sighed.

Mel moaned and bent farther to pull up her shorts. "I've got it. Will you start breakfast? We have a Pack circle this morning and Larissa said she'd watch Finn so I can go." Mel scurried away, and Kade groaned.

Could a wolf die of a hard-on?

Suddenly that vacation away from everything sounded not like a dream, but a necessity. Just one night away. He'd do whatever it took to make that happen because, if he didn't get time alone with his mate, he just might scream.

Chapter 2

The next morning, Melanie lifted Finn's little bottom and removed the dirty diaper. He looked up at her with too-wise eyes and babbled with his normal incoherence. With the efficiency of practice, she wiped, powdered, and clothed him a new diaper before he cried out again. They said werewolf babies didn't get colic, but Mel wasn't too sure of that. Her baby cried more than she'd ever thought possible. And for such a small thing, he had a voice that rivaled any of his uncles. And a temperament to match. He was a Jamenson through and through.

Sometimes that was a good thing. And yet, when Mel needed just one more moment of rest.... Yeah, she wanted to scream.

She looked down at her little bundle of joy and sighed. Yeah, the little monster was a handful of cute all right. Beware, ladies. Already, he had a full head of dark brown hair that matched his daddy's. Finn had her eyes though, and she liked that a little part of her was in their son as well. The Jamenson genes were so dominant she had been afraid she would be lost in Finn's genetics. But as a scientist, she should have known better. There was always a probability of mixed features. She shouldn't have been worried.

Mel picked Finn up and held him against her chest, and he wrapped his chubby arms around her neck. She sighed. How was it possible she could love something so small so deeply in such a short amount of time? She'd felt the connection to Finn when she'd been pregnant, but it was nothing compared to the feeling she had whenever she looked down in those blue eyes. It was like Finn had known who she was from the moment he took his first breath. Like he knew she'd be the one by his side and there to hold him when he needed her.

But that was just it. He seemed to need her every waking and sleeping moment. Even though he was on solid foods now, he still needed to be nursed at least a couple of times a day. Mel was beyond exhausted, and she knew Kade was too. Though he'd try to deny it, she knew he'd been disappointed that their interlude in the kitchen had been fruitless.

She shivered and rocked Finn. She missed the feel of her mate's work-worn hands on her soft skin. She missed the way he'd walk in a room with eyes for only her. Oh, he still looked at her like she was a center of his world, but she wasn't the only center anymore.

Oh God. She was a horrible mother. Who in their right mind would be so selfish to want to be the only one in their mate's eyes? It wasn't Finn's fault his family loved him.

Mel choked back a sob. What was wrong with her? She cried at the drop of a hat, and she was always so tired. But everything she did was for Finn or the Pack. She didn't have time to think about herself. And even letting her thoughts trail beyond that made her feel worthless and not worthy of being called the Heir's mate and Finn's mother.

Was it so bad that, if only for a moment, she missed being just Mel? Or even just the Mel part of Mel and Kade?

Sometimes she felt lost within herself and the people around her. And that wasn't the sign of a good future Alpha's mate. How could she expect the Pack to follow her if she didn't even know herself?

Finn nuzzled her breast and Mel let out another sigh. Dear Lord. All this kid seemed to do was poop, sleep, cry, and eat. A never-ending cycle that was quickly sucking the life out of her.

"Mel?" Willow called out from the living room. "Are you okay? Come out here with Finn."

Mel tugged Finn closer, grabbed a nursing cloth, and walked out to the living room. Hannah was plating up cookies and fruit with glasses of milk. Willow sat on the couch, her breast out, feeding baby Brie.

"You ever feel like a cow?" Willow asked, and Mel chuckled.

"All the time. It's like I'm just a factory for this kid." Mel sat back in the arm chair and deftly unbuttoned her blouse, unsnapped the cup of her nursing bra, and brought Finn closer. She tapped his chubby cheek, and he latched onto the nipple like a drunken sailor.

She laughed at the reference.

"What's so funny?" Hannah asked and nibbled on a sugar cookie.

"I think I just mentally compared my hungry son to a drunken sailor. There must be something wrong with me."

The three women broke out in laughter, and tears spilled onto their cheeks.

"Oh my God. That's a perfect description." Brie whimpered in Willow's arms. "Shh, Brie." She patted her daughter's bottom and guided her back to her nipple. Brie latched on again, greedily sucking. "I can actually see Finn and Brie in the little sailors' uniforms."

Hannah's face brightened. "Oh, me too."

Mel shook her head. "I think our men would strangle us."

Willow smiled. "All the more reason to do it. Come on, Mom and Cailin would join in."

Mel tilted her head. "I think I'd like to see that."

Hannah jumped up and down in her seat and rubbed her hands together. "Leave it to me."

"When did we become the type of mothers that dressed our kids in funny costumes?" Mel asked.

"You met me." Hannah shrugged, unrepentant.

"I would have thought it would have been Cailin's fault," Willow added.

"True." Mel nodded and lay back while Finn finished feeding.

"So, Hannah, how are your boys?"

Hannah blushed. She'd mated Reed, Mel's brother-in-law, and Josh a human-turned-partial-demon, and looked like she loved every bit of it. Mel could barely handle Kade and all the testosterone that came with him; she didn't know how Hannah dealt with twice the male flesh and intensity.

"They're good. Real good."

Hannah blushed again, and Mel and Willow laughed.

"That's always a good sign." Mel smiled, and Finn cooed. She shifted and put him on her shoulder, burped him, buttoned up, then relaxed against the backrest. Finn stared up at her with his big blue eyes and babbled that incoherent baby language that, even though no one understood it, she loved. Well, at least she did when he was being cute. When he was babbling and screaming, she thought she'd pull her hair out.

She looked up and felt Hannah's gaze on her. Mel frowned and tilted her head. "Is everything okay, hon?"

Hannah let out a sigh, and Willow gripped her hand. "Tell us," the other woman softly demanded.

"It's nothing really."

"If it's nothing, then you won't mind telling us," Mel said. "But it has to be something if it's bothering you."

"You're going to think it's stupid," Hannah said. "But Reed, Josh, and I have been trying to have a baby since the wedding.

Well, if you want to be serious, since the night of the fire when we stopped using condoms. But every time I get my period, I want to break down and weep. It's just so frustrating, you know?"

Mel's heart broke for her sister-in-law. "You're just getting started. Don't worry. It will happen for you."

Willow hugged Hannah closer, and Brie held out a chubby fist, seeming to know that Hannah needed all the comfort she could get. Hannah gave a small smile and trailed her finger along Brie's fist. The little girl opened her hand and then gripped Hannah's finger. Hannah gasped, and a tear fell down her cheek.

"I know it takes some people a long time. But I'm the Healer. I should be able to figure out a way for this to happen for my boys and me. I just want it to happen for us. I mean, I have two. You'd think that would increase the possibility."

The women laughed at that.

"But then I think, well, if I can't get pregnant with two men, maybe it's me." Hannah choked out a sob, and Willow kissed her brow.

Mel got up, Finn in her arms, and sat on the woman's other side and held her close. "Hannah, you can't think like that. You know that."

Hannah took a deep breath. "I know. I just can't help it. And then I watch the two of you and your precious babies, and I feel so jealous. And then I feel worse that I feel jealous over it."

"Oh, Hannah," Willow whispered. "You can't think that way. It will happen for you. I know it. It just takes time. And when it does happen, it will be because you and your boys are ready and willing. You won't be caught unaware like me and Mel."

Mel nodded. "True, we were both surprised by our babies."

Willow smiled. "But it was worth it. I wouldn't trade a minute. I can't wait for you to feel what we feel."

Mel looked away. Warm anger and resentment burned. It wasn't rational, but she couldn't help it. How did Willow do it? How was she so happy and healthy and how could she look so amazing? Was Willow a better mother than her?

"Mel?" Willow asked. "What's wrong? What did I say?"

"What?" Mel shook herself. She would not break down in front of these women. "I'm fine."

Hannah leaned into her. "You can't lie to the Healer when it comes to something being wrong. You're more tired than usual, Mel. What's going on?"

Mel held Finn closer and looked into his blue eyes. "Nothing. I'm fine."

"Melanie," Willow said, "you're not fine. Tell us."

Mel closed her eyes and choked back a sob. Could she tell these women that she felt like a failure? That she missed her husband and mate, though they slept next to each other every night?

"I'm just so tired," Mel finally let out.

Both women waited silently for her to continue.

"I haven't had a decent night's sleep since I was six months pregnant. They tell me that werewolves don't have colic, but I don't believe them. And yes, I know, Hannah. You said there was nothing wrong with him. He's a perfectly healthy baby. Yet, he cries all the time. And I can't ignore him. I know some people say to let them cry it out, so Kade and I tried that once. And it about killed us both. Finn cried and cried and called out for us. But we sat on the floor outside his room and had to listen to him scream for us. I felt like such a bad mother."

Hannah gripped her hand and squeezed.

"I feel like a bad mom all the time these days. I feel like nothing I do is right. Everything I do is for Finn or for the Pack, but I don't feel like it's doing any good. I feel like I'm failing my son. I never have any time for myself. I don't remember the last time I just sat on the porch with my Kindle and read a book. I don't remember the last time I watched TV without a baby attached to my boob. And I'm so tired all the time..."

"Mel, why didn't you say anything? And where was Kade?" Willow asked.

"Kade was right by my side. He does so much and picks up the slack when I feel useless. We do our duties and protect the Pack, but when we come home...it's like we're drowning." Mel hiccupped and wiped her eyes. She broke down in gut-wrenching sobs and Finn patted her chest.

Even her son was trying to comfort her. What was wrong with her?

"Your son loves you, Mel. You are just tired."

Mel closed her eyes at her wolf's words.

"Mel." Hannah took her face in her hands, and Mel stared into those dove gray eyes. "You are *not* a bad mother. You are amazing. You just need a moment or two to breathe."

"But..." Mel hiccupped again but shook her head. She needed to stop crying. She was stronger than that. "I miss Kade so much."

Willow scrunched her brows. "I thought he was by your side."

"He is, but I miss him and me. You know? We haven't..."

Willow nodded in understanding. "Brie is much quieter than Finn, so Jasper and I have time alone. But you know, with the amount of family you have, we can always take him for the night."

Mel shook her head. "But he'll scream the whole night. Mom and Dad tried to take him for the night, but he screamed all night for us. I just don't understand it. I miss my mate, girls. I miss myself. I just need a break or something." Mel looked down at her son, who stared back at her and babbled. "God, did I just say that? What is wrong with me?"

Willow smiled. "You sound like a tired mom. It's okay to want a break every now and then, Melanie. You aren't a bad person for voicing it."

"Then why do I feel like I don't deserve him?"

Hannah brushed a lock of hair out of Finn's face, tears in her eyes. "All babies are precious, and you deserve that baby in your arms. You do, Mel, and it's okay to ask for help."

Mel held Finn closer. Was it really that easy? No, of course not, nothing ever was these days. But maybe she and Kade could talk about it. She loved their time in the kitchen. She just wanted more. But did he?

Chapter 3

Kade struck the hammer against the nail head and relished the power of his strength and working with his hands. He missed this. With the demands of the Pack, he hadn't been able to do much with Jasper's and his contracting business. Though Jasper did most of the building and Kade handled the architectural aspects, he still loved working with his hands. He took the last nail from his mouth and hammered it into the stud and stood back. The frame of the new school house was coming along nicely.

After the attack that had killed so many and had taken Reed from them, if only for a few short days, the Pack had slowly begun to rebuild. They'd already built new homes for those that had lost theirs, though they couldn't replace the memories and everything else they'd lost. The school-house was the last big thing on their list. Pups were allowed to go to public school if their parents wanted, but it was easier to just have them go to school in the den. There was always something going on, and by the time they were old enough to be in school, they could change into a wolf. It was just too dangerous to have a small child, who was still learning control, in a classroom with other children who were human. Human and witch children who had werewolves in their families attended the den school as well. But if there was a control problem, there were adults who knew how to deal with it around. It was a one-room school with just one teacher and parents who helped. But it was high-tech with computers and online programming so they had a top-of-the-line education. It was more of a place to meet and be homeschooled. It worked better than most of the public schools that some of the pups went to and Kade was pretty sure Finn would be attending there. Mel was so smart it was actually a bit scary and he had no doubt his wide-eyed son would inherit at least a small fraction of that, if not more.

Kade leaned against the post and looked out onto the den. It was his home. He had always had the misguided notion it was safe. But that wasn't the case. They'd learn the hard way that, no matter the strength of their wolves and their wards, dark magic was stronger.

Kade shook his head, disgusted. It sickened him that his own species would resort to the level the Centrals had. And the Redwoods were losing.

Not a place he liked to be.

"Hey, Kade, get your head out of your ass and help," Jasper called. His brother looked just like him, except Jasper was a bit bigger, his hair a shade darker.

"Sorry, Jas."

Reed, his other brother, shook his sandy-blond hair and furrowed his brows. "Why are you apologizing? You just put up a whole wall by yourself. Jasper was being an ass. What's up?"

That damn sensitive brother of his was too attentive for his own good.

"Kade's a bit tired is all," Maddox chimed in.

Speaking of attentive brothers, Maddox was the Omega of the Pack, meaning his dark-blond-haired brother could feel the emotions of the entire Pack and Kade couldn't hide his current dilemma from him. The bastard.

Josh, Reed's male mate, walked up to him and looked him over. "Tired? Melanie keeping you up late?"

Kade groaned. "I wish. That's precisely the problem."

Oh shit. He hadn't meant to say that aloud. Kade quickly looked over his shoulder to see if anyone else was around, but they were alone, the rest of the Pack up in the residential area of the den.

Jasper set his tools down and walked over to him. "Something going on between you and Melanie? I thought you guys got past all of that before you mated."

Kade closed his eyes and fought back the anger at the memories of Mel's and his past. He'd had to fight for the right to mate her because of that jerk...and then she'd walked away. She'd been too overwhelmed by the prospect of the supernatural, and Kade hadn't given her time to think about it. And since she had such an analytical mind, she needed that time. Without it, she'd left, and Kade's world had fallen apart. Thank God Mel had come back.

"We're past that, Jasper. This is a different issue."

Josh pulled out the cooler and passed around beers. Kade popped off the top and let the cold brew wash down his throat. The beer wouldn't give him a buzz, but he still loved the taste, and he could at least pretend it did the trick. It took copious amounts of hard liquor for a werewolf to get intoxicated, too much for him to deal with. He lowered his head, his hair falling in front of his face.

"Just spit it out," Maddox growled. "We can't help you if you clam up."

Kade looked at his younger brother and raised a brow. Ironic that the most closely guarded Jamenson would say that.

"Fine," Kade spat. "Mel and I are beyond tired. We need a break."

Reed sputtered, his beer spraying everywhere. "What do you mean break?"

Jasper wiped the foam off his face and growled. "I don't think Kade meant *that*. But thanks for the shower, douchebag."

Josh threw a bottle cap at Jasper. "Watch whose mate you call a douchebag, *Grease*-lover."

Jasper's face colored, and Kade laughed. God, when was the last time he'd just sat back, shooting the shit with his brothers? He shook his head. Whenever it had been, it'd been too damn long ago. Not only did he and Mel need some time together, he needed some time with his family.

"Jasper is right, Reed. But thanks for being so appalled at the thought. But really, do you think I'd be sitting here right now if Mel and I were beyond repair?" A copper taste settled on his tongue, and bile rose in his throat at the thought. No, he couldn't even think that. "But we do need a break from *here*."

Josh sat forward. "You mean from the Pack?"

Maddox frowned. "You can't leave the Pack, Kade."

Jasper and Reed growled.

This wasn't going well.

Kade held up his hands. "No, that's not what I mean. For the love of God, let me finish a sentence before you all think the worst of me. Though I can't think of anything worse than what you guys were thinking."

The other men settled back, glares on their faces. But at least they were quiet.

"Finn won't sleep through the night, even now. I don't know what exactly is going on. North and Hannah have both looked at him, and they say he's just restless and growing up. I don't know. But whatever it is, it's killing Mel and me. We haven't had a moment to ourselves since she was pregnant."

Jasper's brows rose. "You mean..."

"We've made love a few times, but that was only because we were on a hunt and had a moment away. But it isn't enough."

"Damn right," Josh put in. "I'm not a werewolf, but I have similar energies when it comes to that. You need more release than what you're getting. No wonder you're on edge."

All of them nodded.

Kade ground the heels of his hands into his eyes. "I'm just so frustrated. And not because I'm not getting any. Well, not only because of that. But have you seen my mate? She's so tired and is constantly taking care of Finn. I'm there by her side, but there is only so much I can do since I don't have tits."

Maddox opened his mouth, but Jasper knocked him upside the head. "Not the time."

"Mel is so drawn and exhausted that I feel like I'm failing her. She's got bags under her eyes, and I can't fix it. I can't stand to see my mate in pain." Kade held his head in his hands and his body shuddered.

He hated to show weakness in front of others, but this was his family God dammit. He needed them to be strong for him for once.

"Well, what are you going to do about it?" Jasper asked, ever the Beta.

"I want to take her away just for a night."

"You mean outside of the den's boundaries?" Reed asked. "Is that safe?"

Kade shook his head. "Nothing is really truly safe anymore. But Mel and I need this. I want to take her away and pretend we're alone. I know it won't fix our problems. We need to figure out a way to manage what we have, but in order to do that, we need to recharge."

Josh nodded. "Okay, how can we help?"

Kade loved this new brother of his. As an ex-SEAL, he saw the objective and knew there needed to be a plan. Just what Kade needed.

"I need someone to stay at our house for the night and take Finn. He screamed so much when he stayed over at Mom's and Dad's. Hopefully, staying in his own room, it won't be so bad." Kade crossed his fingers.

"When do you want to do this?" Jasper asked.

"Tomorrow. The sooner the better. Plus, I have a plan, but the place won't be open after that."

Josh and Reed looked at each other and shook their heads.

"What?" Kade asked.

Reed cleared his throat. "We can't. I'm sorry, Kade. Hannah is, um..."

"Hannah is ovulating tomorrow, so we will be busy," Josh cut in.

An awkward silence settled over the group, and they each shifted in their chairs.

Jasper finally spoke up. "And I can't leave Willow at home with Brie. Brie's teething."

Kade closed his eyes and groaned at the memory of Finn's first tooth.

"And," Jasper continued, "I don't know if you want to ask Adam."

The group went silent again. Their brother Adam had come back from his trek to God knows-where a changed man. Though ever since he'd lost Anna and their baby to the Centrals he'd been dark and quiet, it was even worse now. They didn't know what had happened to him where he'd been, but it couldn't have been good.

"I agree," Kade said. "And I think North said he had plans with Ellie."

Maddox growled, and his beer bottle shattered in his hands.

What the hell?

Maddox wiped the blood on his pants. "I can take care of Finn."

Kade's brows rose. "Are you sure?" From what he could remember, Maddox had never really had an affinity toward Finn or Brie. Since his brother could feel every single emotion, maybe a small child with only brightness and thing to dull it within them would be too much for him.

Maddox nodded. "I don't mind. It's just for a night, right? Don't you trust me?" Maddox glared at Kade, a defiant look in his eyes.

"Of course I trust you, Mad," Kade assured him.

"Then it's settled. Jasper will take care of Brie, Reed and Josh will knock up Hannah, you'll have your way with Mel, and I'll take care of the rug rat. Problem solved."

The group merely blinked at him.

"Kade," Jasper said, "this won't solve all of your problems. You guys are going to have to figure out what to do with Finn. He can't keep running you ragged."

Kade sighed. "I know. We'll have to figure something out. But I need time away from here that's just for me and my mate."

"Then we'll help you," Josh put in. "That's what family's for."

Kade looked around at his brothers and gave a small smile. Yeah, thank God for them. And with their help, he'd get his Mel alone and naked. And preferably sweaty and glowing. Yeah, that sounded perfect.

He just had to get his mate to agree to leave their son at home with Maddox.

Sure, that would be simple. Right?

Chapter 4

Finn wiggled in Mel's arms, and she sat him down on the floor. He scooted on his bottom to his blocks and began to make a tower, just like his daddy. Though he could crawl and pull himself up when he gripped the table, he seemed in no hurry to walk. He babbled away, a smile on his face.

Mel groaned and stretched her arms over her head. Her body ached from carrying Finn around all the time. She couldn't wait for him to be able to walk, but then the thought of him walking and getting into more trouble than usual would enter her mind, and she'd dread it.

With Finn occupied with his blocks, she tidied the living room, picking up nursing cloths, stuffed animals, and other toys. Their home always looked like a tornado had blown through. Well, it had. The Finn tornado. She and Kade were constantly picking up after the little terror. But she loved the little guy. Even if he was sucking the life out of her.

The front door opened, and Kade walked in, a sensual smile on his face. Oh Lord, she loved that smile. She missed that smile. He prowled toward her, his eyes never leaving her face. She sighed and held the stuffed frog to her chest. Oh, how she loved this man.

He leaned over her and kissed her softly on the lips, lingering for a moment but not long enough for her. Kade pulled back.

"Hey, buddy." He leaned down and picked up Finn, who stood by his daddy's leg, pulling on the denim material.

Kade held Mel in one arm and Finn in the other. She leaned into him, and he kissed Finn's chubby cheek. It was times like these that she could almost forget the mess of the house, the lack of sleep, and the fact that she hadn't made love to her husband in months. Almost.

"Finn's a big boy, isn't he?" Kade asked.

And, yes, Finn was getting bigger every second it seemed.

"Just like his daddy," Mel agreed.

Kade gave her a smoldering look and raised a brow.

She swatted him with the stuffed frog. "Stop it. You know that's not what I meant. Keep your mind out of the gutter. You're holding Finn."

A sad expression passed over his face, but he quickly blanked it. "Come on, Finn, you wanna show me what you've been building?"

Finn smiled and wiggled down from Kade's arms. Her little boy stood on wobbly legs and then walked—walked—toward his tower of blocks.

Mel gripped Kade's arm. "Kade..."

"I see, Mel. Look at you go, buddy!" Kade beamed like a proud daddy and Mel's eyes filled with tears.

"Look at our baby boy."

Mel sniffed at her wolf's voice. Yes, he was truly their little boy, but he wasn't so little anymore. What was wrong with her? She'd just been thinking that she couldn't wait for Finn to grow up so she'd have a moment to think and now she couldn't bear the thought. Is this what all parents went through?

Finn waddled to his blocks and landed on his bottom with a thump before putting another block on his tower. He turned his head and smiled at his daddy, and Mel choked back a sob.

Kade held her close and kissed her temple. "Hey, are you okay, baby?"

He looked into her eyes, and she melted. She could just sit there for hours and gaze at his jade green eyes. His pupils dilated with lust, and a small rim of gold glowed around the iris. His brown hair fell around his face and brushed his shoulders. She used to love running her fingers through it when he slept and trailing her fingers down his smooth chest before reaching the crisp hair at the base of his sex.

God, she missed him.

"I'm okay. I just can't believe he's walking."

Kade lifted a corner of his lips and brushed a lock of hair behind her ear. "He was bound to do that eventually. Though now we may have a terror on our hands."

Mel groaned. "What do you mean? Now he's just more mobile."

Kade's gaze darkened. "Hey, I'm sorry, baby. I didn't mean to make you feel bad."

Mel shook her head. "No, I'm okay. Really. Just tired." Oh, so tired. Like every other day.

Kade kissed her forehead. "I know you are; I am too."

She leaned into his embrace and inhaled his clean wolf and man scent. He smelled like home, salvation, and future.

Finn let out a wail and scrunched his face. Mel sighed and then smiled at her baby boy. She sat next to him and brushed the hair from his face. He would need a haircut soon, but she couldn't take that step. Plus, Kade liked his little boy's hair long because it looked so much like his.

"What's wrong little man? Mommy and Daddy weren't ignoring you." *Much.*

Kade let out a hollow laugh and sat next to her. "No, we would never do that."

Mel frowned. "Hey, what's that laugh about?"

He shook his head. "Nothing, just thinking."

"About what."

"Let's put Finn down for a nap and we can talk about it."

Chills raced up her arms, and a lead weight settled in her stomach. Oh God. Was it too much for him? Was he leaving her and Finn? What if he didn't want them anymore? Her pulse raced, and she gripped the stuffed frog so she wouldn't hold on to Kade and never let him go.

Kade stroked her cheek. "Hey, none of that. Everything's fine. At least it will be."

She leaned into his touch but didn't calm down. What did he want to talk about?

"Hey, buddy, it's time for your nap," Kade said.

Finn scrunched his brows and frowned.

"Yep, it is, baby," Mel agreed.

"Come on, buddy." Kade settled Finn into his arms and stood before walking into Finn's room.

Mel let out a ragged sigh and leaned against the entertainment center. Too much had just happened. Her little boy had taken his first steps, and Kade was leaving her.

Well, he hadn't come out and said it, but what else could that cryptic comment mean? She knew she and Kade had been drifting apart since the baby was born. They'd just been too busy and too tired to do anything about it. And other than the casual touches recently, it hadn't felt like they were really mated. Her wolf whined and Mel shut her eyes. Even her wolf missed Kade's wolf. They didn't go out hunting anymore, really. She only shifted when she needed to, and Kade did a little more because he was training the adolescents and protecting the den. She just needed a night off where she could focus on their bond, and then, she'd be okay. They needed to talk about how to manage their son and their time, but if Kade wanted to leave, how would that work?

Mel set her shoulders. She wasn't a push-over. She was the Heir's mate, damn it. Kade couldn't leave. Not unless she wanted him to. And by God, she didn't.

"I can see the wheels turning in your head. Stop it, baby. It's not what you think," Kade said as he walked back in the room and sat on the floor across from her.

Mel raised her chin. "And just what am I thinking?"

"I'm not quite sure, but it doesn't look good."

"You can't leave us, Kade," Mel blurted out.

Oh God. She hadn't meant to say it like that. Her pulse raced, but her gaze never left his face.

Kade paled and gripped her upper arms. "Dear God. Is that what you thought? I would never, *ever*, leave you and Finn. What kind of man do you think I am?" He let her go, stood, and paced around the room.

Mel held back a sob. She wouldn't cry. Not now. "I don't know, Kade. I just feel so cut off from you that I don't know what to think anymore."

He ran a hand over his face and let out a soft growl. "See? This is our problem. We don't talk anymore. I'm so sorry that you'd even thought about that. It makes me wonder what I've done to make you even think I didn't want to be in this mating anymore."

He looked so broken that Mel stood and ran into his arms. She inhaled his scent and let her heartbeat sync with his.

"I'm sorry. I just miss you."

"I miss you too, baby. But I have an idea."

She looked up at him and sniffed. "What idea?"

"Let's go away tomorrow."

"Away? You know we can't do that." But hope spread through her.

"Yes, we can. Just for a night." Kade kissed her forehead. "We need it, Mel. Even more than I thought if you were thinking that I'd leave you."

Mel kissed under his chin. "I'm sorry, I didn't really think it. It was just sort of a worst case scenario kind of thing. But you know we can't leave, Kade. We have Finn and other responsibilities."

Kade let out a frustrated breath. "Those responsibilities are exactly why we need to leave. Just for a night. It's too much, Mel. We haven't had a decent conversation that didn't revolve around the Pack or Finn in months. And we haven't made love in that time either." He groaned, and she leaned into him.

"I know, Kade. I miss it too. But we can't."

"We can. And we will. Just for a night."

"Okay, let's for a second pretend we do this. What about Finn?"

"That's where I come in," Maddox said from the doorway.

Kade and Mel turned around. How had they not heard him? She swore that wolf had special stealth powers she didn't know about.

"What?" she asked.

"Maddox has agreed to watch Finn tomorrow night," Kade said.

Maddox walked into the house and closed the door.

Mel frowned. "Are you sure, Maddox?"

He scowled. "Of course I'm sure. I wouldn't have volunteered if I weren't."

Volunteered? Just what had Kade said to the wolf for that to happen?

"Okay." Mel let out a breath. "But what about the dangers and the Pack?"

Kade kissed her nose and smiled. "The Pack can handle a night without us. And as for the dangers..." His eyes darkened. "It's dangerous anywhere, but we can take that risk. I'll protect you, no matter what."

Mel kissed his jaw. "I know you will."

"As touching as this is, what is your answer, Mel?" Maddox asked.

Mel looked into Kade's green eyes and focused. She needed time with this man. Just the fact that she'd thought for a moment he'd leave her meant she did. And Kade cemented the fact that she was scared. Yes, she could admit that at least to herself. She was scared to death. She was floundering as a mother, as a mate, and a Pack leader. She needed a moment to escape. To sit back and remember why she loved doing all these things. To remember that she loved her mate and needed him more than the air she breathed.

She placed her palm on his face, his unshaved cheek scraping against her skin and she shivered at the thought of where else his five-o'-clock shadow could scrape her. His tanned skin looked like caramel against her pallor. She wanted to see where else they'd contrast when they lay naked in a sweaty pile.

She needed a break. If only for a night.

"Okay," she finally whispered. "That sounds wonderful."

Maddox released a sigh, and Kade smiled. "Good."

"Where are we going?"

"It's a surprise." Kade gave a smoldering look and Mel melted into a puddle.

"And that's my cue to leave," Maddox grunted. "I'll be here in the morning to take care of the rug rat. Bye, folks."

Maddox closed the door, and Mel sank into Kade. "Can we leave now?" she whispered into his ear.

He leaned down and bit her earlobe. "Tomorrow, my love." His voice rumbled against her skin, and she shivered.

Maybe they could start their vacation early...

The phone rang, halting her sweet thoughts. *Darn it. Pack duty calls.* But at least now she had something to look forward to.

Chapter 5

Kade inhaled the crisp scent of ocean and closed his eyes. The sounds of waves crashing against the surf and seagulls flying overhead sent a sensation of peace through him. He and Mel had been parked outside their rented beach house for only five minutes and he already felt loads more relaxed.

Maybe he needed only that moment away to feel better.

Mel walked up beside him, and he wrapped his arms around her and drew her to stand in front of him. Her little bottom rubbed against his erection, and he groaned. Okay, he needed a bit more. But now that he was alone with his mate, there was no doubt he'd take her in every fashion possible. His body was strung tight, primed.

He needed her more than anything. Now.

It had been a chore leaving the house a few hours before. They'd had to make sure the Pack was taken care of and his brother Adam had said he'd manage everything. Even though he knew his brother was going through some things, Kade could always trust Adam. Then they had to make sure they were safe when they got here, so Hannah had made a few herb bags that could act as mobile wards. They weren't as efficient as sentries or the actual den wards, but it would keep them cloaked to most seeing eyes and would alert them to intruders faster than his keen senses.

However, even though all of that had taken time, it didn't compare to leaving Finn alone. He and Mel had almost called it off before they even started. Finn screamed for them, and Maddox, the man who rarely revealed any hints of emotion, looked overwhelmed. But his brother had shaken his head and told them to leave, that he and his nephew needed some time alone to get to know one another.

And frankly, Mel and Kade needed to make sure their lives weren't controlled by their son. Yes, Finn was the center of their world, but he couldn't have every aspect of it and get everything he wanted. It didn't work that way.

They'd kissed their son and walked out the door stiffly. Finn's cries came through the door, but they got in the car anyway. He and Mel held hands on the drive but stayed silent. They hadn't talked like he had wanted, but the silence was something they hadn't had in months. It was soothing and mind-clearing. Needed.

Kade leaned down and kissed the top of his mate's head. She rolled her neck, and he trailed kisses down her skin, her honey-vanilla taste settling on his tongue. He nibbled her neck and ran his hand up her stomach under her shirt and cupped her breast. She arched against him and moaned.

"Kade."

"I've wanted this for months."

"Just be careful, I'll leak."

Kade let the heavy mounds lay firm in his hold, and he squeezed just a little, not hard enough to let the milk come out.

"I'll be careful, but it may get messy."

Mel pressed her breast into his palm, her nipple pebbling through her bra. "Anything, Kade. Anything you want."

Kade leaned back and released her with a groan. She whimpered and he fought the urge to bend her over the SUV and take her right there.

"I want to spend the whole night with you, and I plan on it. But let's at least unload the SUV first so we don't have to get out of bed unless we want to." He bit her earlobe, and she shivered.

She turned in his arms, bit his chin, and hurried to the car to get her bag. Kade chuckled and watched her ass move in her tight jeans. She should have worn a skirt. He wanted to flip it over and fuck her senseless. But he'd settle with peeling her out of those skinny jeans and licking trails to her pussy. His body shook, and he grabbed his bag. Yeah, that sounded fucking delicious.

He followed his mate as she ran to the beach cottage and unlocked the door; as soon as she set her bag down, he dropped the ice chest and gripped her hips.

"Kade!"

"Shh." He walked her backwards until she stood on the porch looking over the ocean with him.

The cool Oregon breeze wove through their hair as the salty ocean scent surrounded them. He turned her so she faced him, and he stood there transfixed.

This was his mate.

His Melanie.

God, how he'd missed her.

She gave a small smile and exhaled slowly. "It's beautiful here, Kade. Thank you."

"Not as beautiful as you."

"That is such a line, but I love you anyway."

Kade raised a brow. "Really?"

She nodded. "Uh huh. Let me show you how much." She gripped his hips and slowly lowered to her knees.

Shocked, he looked down. "Mel, baby, you don't need to do that. This is supposed to be about you."

"No, this is supposed to be about us. We're secluded, no one around for miles, and with the wards set on the house, no one can see. Let me taste you, Kade."

He groaned and stroked her cheek. "Far be it from me to hold you back."

She smiled and unsnapped his cargo shorts. He sucked in a breath and brushed a hand through her hair.

Mel nuzzled his dick through his boxer briefs, and he gripped her hair. She lowered his shorts and pants so they lay around his ankles. Tendrils of pleasure shot up his spine as she kissed his thighs and around the base of his cock. Unconsciously, he let his head fall back and thrust against her mouth.

She licked up the vein on the bottom of his dick, and he moaned and opened his eyes to look down at her. Her blue eyes were wide and dark with passion. Gazes locked, she wrapped her warm mouth around the head of his cock and swirled her tongue.

"Hell." She was going to kill him.

She lowered her head slowly, his dick disappearing in her mouth, her lips enveloping his shaft.

This was perfection.

She hollowed her cheeks and sucked him whole. Kade tightened his grip on her hair and thrust between her lips. He hit the back of her throat but didn't pause. She looked up at him, her blue eyes deep with lust and love. He thrust in and out as she worked him. Her left hand scraped his thigh as her right one fondled his balls.

"Mel, baby, I'm gonna..."

His gaze locked with hers, and he came. He shot down her throat and she swallowed every bit of him. He caressed her cheek and groaned.

"I think you almost killed me."

"Oh really? So you only had one good hit in you?" his mate teased.

"Oh really? Is that all you think I have?" Kade growled and tore her clothes from her body then removed the rest of his.

She gasped and froze. He smiled a feral smile, gripped her hips, and set her bottom on the porch railing.

"Kade, I loved those jeans."

"I'll buy you more."

He spread her legs and lowered his head. He sucked on her clit, and she bucked against his face. He held her hips down and licked along her seam before trusting his tongue in and out.

"Kade."

She tangled her fingers in his hair, and he bit down on her clit. Her honey-vanilla taste spread on his tongue, and she came against his face. Her juices spread over his lips, and he drank greedily.

He kissed her pussy then trailed his lips up her stomach and her breasts. Laving her nipple, he bit then suckled. Milk gushed, and he sucked.

"Kade, that's unsanitary."

He raised his face and let go with a pop. "You were going to pump anyway. I'm just helping the process along."

He nuzzled her other breast and repeated the process. She wiggled against him, her wet core teasing his cock.

"Kade, please. I need you. I'm on birth control from Hannah."

"Thank God."

He positioned himself at her core and thrust home. They both froze, and tears leaked from her eyes.

"Oh God, did I hurt you, baby?" He tried to move back, but she wrapped her legs around his hips and locked him in.

"Don't you dare leave me. I just missed you so much. I can really feel you, Kade. You're in me."

He looked into her big blue eyes then lowered his head so his lips brushed hers. "I love you."

"I love you too, my wolf. Now take me. Please."

Kade drew out of her, oh so slowly, and she whimpered. "Shh, I'll never leave you." He thrust to the hilt, hard.

Her body rocked against his, and she raked her fingernails down his back, the sweet coppery scent of blood filled the air from where she broke the skin. He rocked back and thrust over again, their moans, grunts, and pants the only sounds they made. She threw her head back in a ragged gasp, and he sucked on her neck. She came against him but he didn't stop there. He pounded into her and moved to suck her nipple again. Her breasts were empty of milk, but he bit down on the nipple anyway, relishing in her honey-vanilla scent. He thrust against, hitting her G-spot. His balls drew tight, and he came, his seed filling her womb, making her come again.

She fell limp against him and fought for breath. He brushed her sweaty hair from her face and kissed her soft lips.

"Now I think you killed me for sure," he rumbled.

"I don't think I can move."

"Evidence of a job well done."

She swatted at him half-heartedly and chuckled. "I think my butt may have a splinter."

"Want me to check?" He grinned.

She smiled and bit his chin. "Take me inside, oh He-Man."

"Gladly."

****

Mel rested against Kade's chest, listening to his heartbeat while he carried her into their cottage. Her body felt heavy yet weightless at the same time. Her mate had rocked her world, and she just wanted to curl up and never let go.

The threats of responsibility homed in on her, but she brushed them away. She just needed one night. Yes, she missed Finn like a lost limb, but she had to trust in her family and the fact that they'd take care of him and call if they needed help. Maddox may have looked out of his depth, but he loved Finn and would do what was best.

So right now she had to think about only her Kade, every wicked thing he did to her, and every other wicked thing she wanted him to do to her. She shuddered in his hold and he laughed.

"Dirty thoughts, baby?"

"Of course, we're both naked and you're walking to the bedroom. What else could I be thinking about?" She batted her eye lashes, and he threw back his head and laughed.

They reached the bed, a white-washed wood frame and cream and navy blue sheets pulled back on a corner. The nautical room looked so different than anything else she'd lived in; it was a nice place to visit. To escape. Something they desperately needed. Kade lowered her on the bed, and she sighed.

"Did we leave our clothes out there?" she asked, not really caring.

Kade shrugged. "I'll get them later. I'm busy." He grinned, knelt between her legs, and licked her hip.

Tingles shot through her, and she lifted herself off the bed.

"Stay there, Mel. Don't move. Let me pleasure you."

She closed her eyes and let her husband kiss, nibble, and lick her hips and thighs. He licked her nether lips, and she writhed and pushed her core closer, but he tsked and passed her clit.

Damn wolf.

He nibbled and stroked his fingers around her pussy, but he didn't let any dip inside her.

"Kade," she moaned.

"What is it, baby? What do you want?" He traced a finger around her clit but didn't stop.

"You know."

"You have to tell me." He bit her inner thigh.

"Kade, I want you in me. Please." She squirmed and bit her lip. Damn man was so frustrating. But all hers for the night.

"What do you want in you?"

She groaned. "Your fingers, your tongue, your dick. I don't care. Anything."

He gave a husky chuckle, and his eyes glowed gold. "I like the way your mind works, love. I think I can do that."

He kissed her inner thigh again and finally—finally—brushed his tongue across her clit. She almost came on the spot, but he pulled back and traced another finger around her opening. She was about to moan again, but then he shoved three fingers in her at once, curling them and hitting her G-spot. She came against his hand, her body convulsing on the bed as all rational thoughts fled. Kade lowered and bit her clit, prolonging her orgasm.

The man was diabolical.

And all hers.

"I love the way your body blushes when you come."

She mumbled something, but even she couldn't tell what it was.

He laughed a laugh full of pure male satisfaction and flipped her over onto her stomach.

"Hold on to the slat on the headboard, Mel."

Shivers of anticipation ran through her as the gripped the whitewashed slats. Kade lifted her hips and settled a pillow under them so her bottom was raised.

"What are you doing?" she asked breathlessly.

"Having my way with you."

"I thought we were supposed to rest on this trip." Not that she was complaining.

"Oh, we will. But I missed the sweet taste of your skin. The way your tight pussy clenches my cock when you come. The way your eyes glow gold when you're so aroused you can't even breathe. I missed all of that."

She almost came at his words alone.

He lowered his head and kissed both of her cheeks then massaged them with his calloused hands. He rubbed every inch of her body...slowly. She thrummed with anticipation and arousal. He kissed and licked where he massaged until she was so relaxed she thought she could melt right there on the blue sheets.

She closed her eyes and let his fingers say what they couldn't say for so long. She relished her time with him. Oh, how she had missed him.

He lowered his body over hers and gripped her forearms.

"I love you," he whispered.

"I love you, too."

He bit her earlobe and entered her from behind, inch by agonizing inch. He thrust slowly and methodically until they gradually reached their peak and fell down in climax together. They panted in unison, and Kade rolled to the side, pulling her with him, so they lay spooned.

"That was..."

"Yeah."

"Did that remind you of our first time?" She closed her eyes and remembered their blind date that had led to so much more.

"Yes and no." He kissed her temple. "Yes, because I always think about our first time and how we went after each other like rabbits. But, no, because this time I knew your body but still wanted to learn every inch again."

"You are so sweet you actually scare me, baby."

"I am the sweetest of the bunch."

"Don't I know it."

She settled into his arms and rested her eyes. Her body sank into his, and he pulled the sheet over them. She didn't even move when he shifted to turn off the light, and they both fell asleep, content and together.

Chapter 6

It was official. Maddox would never be a father. There was no way he could do it. Though he'd offered to watch Finn for Kade and Melanie because Kade had actually asked, it wasn't until now he truly understood only a fraction of what parents went through on a day-to-day basis.

The little bundle of terror, also known as Finn Jamenson, made Maddox want to go out and ensure he'd never have kids. Ever.

Well, it wasn't as bad as that. But it was close. He still loved the little guy. After all, he was family. He had Kade's dark brown hair, but Mel's blue eyes. It was nice to look at something other than green anyway. Finn was actually a pretty good kid, just full of energy. Maddox didn't mind watching and playing with him. But he was fucking exhausted.

And Mel and Kade had only been gone for six hours. He still had about twenty-four to go.

Dear. God.

Finn waddled past him on two chubby legs, his gaze intent on the bookshelf and the books that weren't meant for his grubby little hands.

Oh yeah, that was another thing. He hadn't known the little guy could walk when he agreed to this. Didn't it seem prudent to mention that to potential babysitters? Yeah, Mel had mentioned it had just happened the night before. But really? Coincidence? Maddox didn't believe in those. No, the little tyke must have had a gut feeling it was Uncle Maddox's turn to take care of him and wanted to get every ounce of enjoyment he could out of the deal.

Damn kid.

Maddox took two giant steps and lifted Finn above his head. His nephew squealed and pumped his legs in the air, as if he were still running. Finn wiggled and twisted until his face was in front of Maddox's. The little guy smiled and patted sticky fingers against Maddox's cheeks. He shuddered at the thought of where those hands had been and what would now be on his skin.

Wait. He'd just cleaned him up. Where the hell had he found something sticky?

Oh. My. God.

What was on him? And how the hell did kids always manage to be sticky? It was like they had secret radar for gooey things and made sure they spread it around. Like all over the couch, the floor, and Maddox.

Finn wiggled his butt and let out a scream before pumping his legs again, his intent evident. Oh yes, he wanted to made Uncle Maddox's life hell.

Damn it.

Maddox didn't want to think about the amount of energy this kid would have once he got his wolf. How on earth had his own parents done this seven times?

Six little baby-boy wolves in less than a decade. Thank God Cailin was so much younger. If she had been the same age as the rest of them, his parents might have turned tail and run.

And Maddox didn't think he'd have blamed them.

Finn squirmed, and Maddox lowered him to the floor before he fell out of his arms. The tyke ran—well as much as an almost-one-year-old could run—across the room and dove head first into a pile of stuffed animals. Maddox winced when Finn let out a piercing cry and then shook it off.

Was that progress?

Maddox watched as Finn put all of his stuffed animals back where they were before going to his blocks and organizing them.

Huh. Maddox ran a hand through his hair. So the kid made messes but cleaned them up? Except for the endless crying, the kid was actually pretty good. Maybe he just needed to start talking. Like now. Maddox didn't feel any pain or sadness from whenever Finn cried. It was as if that was the only way Finn knew how to communicate, something that would have to change. Soon.

Finn accidentally knocked down his tower and screamed.

Maddox winced. "How about we have quiet time?"

Dear God, Uncle Maddox needed it. The exuberant emotions flooding him from this kid just about weighed him down to the floor. Usually he could block most of the emotions surrounding him so it was just a dull hum, but not with children. They were too good, too full of everything sweet and pure and didn't have a way to funnel that. They showed all their emotions with each facial expression, each cry, each grin. Every emotion wound its way around Maddox and threatened to suffocate him. He didn't want those. He needed to breathe.

Hence the reason why he usually stayed away from them until they learned to control themselves a bit more. So at least until after the teenage years.

Oh God, Finn as a teenager. Maddox closed his eyes and groaned. He might have to be far, far away for that part of his nephew's life.

Finn tilted his head and looked at him with blue eyes too full of knowledge. What did babies think of? He could feel them, but he couldn't sense thoughts. He wasn't aware of any wolves that could for that matter.

His nephew squirmed then smiled widely. A pungent order hit Maddox's nose, and he gagged.

Oh. God.

"Finn. You suck. I'm just saying that now. Wipe that grin off your face."

Finn just smiled and then froze before he broke out into gut-wrenching sobs.

"Hey now, stop it." Maddox panicked and carried Finn to his room to change him. "You need to stop crying like the world is caving in every time you don't get your way. You will be Alpha one day. And despite popular belief, you won't get what you want. Just the opposite in fact." Maddox peeled the offending diaper off and put it in the Diaper Genie that Mel promised would keep the smell at bay before it went to the disposal area.

"You're going to have to learn to control your emotions better, buddy." He wiped Finns bottom, powdered him, and somehow got the sticky straps on the diaper to work. He'd changed Cailin's diaper when she was a baby, but that had been a couple of decades before and he was out of practice.

Finn looked up at him, contentment at getting what he wanted flowing from him and into Maddox.

"Now, don't do that. You didn't get what you wanted because you screamed. You stank and it would have been unsanitary had I left you in that. But you are the Heir's first son. You need to learn some responsibility and let your parents be individuals as well as parents. They can't do that if you keep acting like a butt."

Finn's lower lip wobbled, but he didn't cry.

That seemed to be progress.

"Yelling at babies now, are you?" Ellie asked from the doorway.

He'd known she and North had walked into the house; he had just chosen to ignore them. Well, at least as much as he could ignore his twin and...her.

"Finn and I are just having a talk, right?" He looked down at Finn, and Maddox could have sworn the little guy winked.

"At eleven months, he can understand you, Maddox," North chimed in, the ever-helpful doctor.

"I would hope so," Maddox grunted. "But the reason I'm here is because, between the Pack and this little guy, Mel and Kade can't breathe. So I thought I'd try and talk a little sense into him. Whatever it takes."

A shadow passed over Ellie's face and raw pain washed into the room. Maddox inwardly cursed. Her brother had used a different method of *talking* sense into her. Damn it. But he wouldn't say anything. That wouldn't do either of them any good.

North cleared his throat, a scowl on his face. "Ellie and I were just stopping by on our way from dinner to see if you needed anything."

Anger swept through Maddox. He tried to gauge North's emotions, but his twin had always been the best at shielding him.

"We're great. Nothing to worry about."

Ellie raised a brow and took Finn from Maddox's arms. Their skin brushed, and he held back a growl.

Her face didn't betray her reaction, and she bent to inhale Finn's baby scent.

Maddox clenched his jaw and stepped toward her, his arms outstretched. "Go back to your date." He bit out the last word. "I can handle Finn. Go."

Ellie frowned but gave Finn back. His nephew rested his head on Maddox's shoulder, seeming to know that Maddox needed a hug. Though he wouldn't have admitted that to anyone. Not even to himself.

North led Ellie out of the room by placing his hand in the small of her back, and Maddox's wolf growled. His wolf didn't speak much. If ever. Maddox guessed it was just another way he was fucked up.

He let out a breath and bounced Finn up and down in his arms.

"Okay, we're going to go get something to eat. Your job is to make sure it doesn't land on me. Got it? I don't care if you're going to be my Alpha in the distant future; I'm the Omega. I win right now."

Finn gave him an amused expression, and Maddox scowled. Damn kid.

He carried Finn into the kitchen and set him up in his highchair. Maddox fed him and ended up coated in strained peas and carrots. Apparently Finn didn't like veggies too much. Well, he was a werewolf after all.

He gave Finn a bath, ended up wet to the skin himself, then re-diapered him. Finally, he got a bottle of breast milk ready for Finn and fed him while sitting in the arm chair. Maddox looked down at the blue-eyed kid noisily sucking on the bottle.

"How on earth do your parents do this every day?"

Finn didn't answer, and Maddox shook his head.

"I can see why they needed a break."

Finn let go of the nipple and looked like he was about ready to cry again.

"That's not what I mean, Finn. You know they love you. I was just saying they needed some Mommy and Daddy time."

Finn reached up and traced the long, jagged scar on Maddox's cheek. He froze. No one had touched it before. They were all too afraid. They'd deny it, but they couldn't hide their emotions from him.

Finn looked into his eyes and patted his cheek before blinking and letting his hand fall. He latched onto the bottle again and closed his eyes.

What was that about?

His body relaxed marginally, and Maddox patted Finn's bottom and rocked him. Finn's mouth went lax, and the nipple fell from his mouth, a little dribble of milk running down his chin. Maddox quickly cleaned him up, burped him, and held him close, liking the heavy weight in his arms.

When Finn slept, his emotions were muted, sort of like in a dreamy haze. Maddox relished it. He could feel the whole Pack as it was. The frustration running through his father's veins at the thought of the Centrals, the lust and love running through Reed's body during Hannah's...um...time, the contentment running through Kade, the happiness running through Jasper.

The quiet despair and desperation running through Adam. The fragile strength running through Ellie.

Everyone but North.

But the little bundle of Kade and Mel in his arms calmed him. Something that hadn't happened in...well...ever.

Hmm...

Maddox closed his eyes and sank into the dark, lush armchair. Only twenty-one hours to go, and then they'd be back. Thank God.

Chapter 7

Kade woke up with a soft bottom pressed against his erection, and he closed his eyes again, sinking into his bliss. They'd made love two more times in the night. He felt sated, content, and oddly rested.

Though they hadn't slept too much, it was as if the idea of peace made him peaceful. What a novel concept.

Mel moaned in her sleep and shifted so his cock lay nestled in the crease of her ass. His hips flexed, and she pushed back.

His little wolf wanted more.

Kade smiled and beneath the sheet, ran his hand up her naked thigh, over her soft belly, and cupped her heavy breast. She arched into him and turned her head so he could reach her lips, though her eyes were still closed. He lowered his head and kissed her, his tongue darting into her mouth, tangling with hers.

Her sweet honey-vanilla taste burst on his tongue, making his already hard erection even harder. He ground against her and tweaked her nipple. She moved back and swiveled her hips, teasing.

Without saying a word, he lowered his hand and lifted her leg. She shifted, and he entered her from behind, oh so slowly. They gasped together, their heartbeats and breaths synchronized. When his thighs lay flush against hers, his cock surrounded by her warmth, he stayed there for a moment, letting peace and their mating bond wash over him. One hand wrapped around Mel, cupping her breast, and the other one lay between her legs, circling her clit. He pulled back and then entered her again and then again. They rocked together slowly, leisurely, restfully. Kade closed his eyes and rested his head against the back of hers and came when she did, their bodies sweaty and loose-limbed.

"Good morning," he whispered.

Mel laughed softly and turned in his arms. "I'd say."

He kissed her lips and jaw, nibbling along his way. "I think this is my favorite way to wake up."

She sighed and snuggled closer. "I wish we could do this every morning. But then I think about waking up and watching Finn wake. You know?"

Kade squeezed her. "I know what you mean. We called Maddox yesterday—three times. Everything was going fine."

Mel chuckled. "Poor Maddox. He sounded so frazzled."

"True. How about while I make you breakfast, you can go outside where we get better service and call Maddox. We'll shower, and then we can head home early."

"Are you sure? I mean, I know we aren't supposed to head back until later tonight but…"

"I want to see him too. I think this helped."

Mel smiled and bit his jaw. "I know it did. I feel energized and ready to start again." Despite her words, a shadow passed over her eyes and Kade kissed her brow.

"Let's eat and plan. I have a few ideas on what to do for when we get back. Okay?"

"Okay, I trust you."

"Good."

They got out of bed, and he threw on his jeans, sans boxer briefs. He liked the way Mel's eyes darkened every time he went shirtless, so he thought he'd use that for a bit. Mel pulled on a sweater dress and wore nothing underneath it. He groaned and she winked over her shoulder.

Damn.

They needed food and to talk before they could leave. Okay, maybe they could make love first.

Yep. That sounded like a plan.

Kade shuffled to the kitchen and pulled out the food they'd put in there the night before. Willow had quickly packed an ice chest for their journey and had included her mouthwatering cinnamon rolls. His brother, Jasper, had found a perfect mate in her. Yeah, he and Mel could cook, but they were no Willow.

He pulled them out and set the oven to warm. He started some coffee, then he pulled out some oranges and bananas. He peeled them and set them on a plate while the coffee brewed. When the oven buzzed, he set the buns inside and kept the door slightly ajar so they didn't get too hot and burn. The smell of freshly brewed coffee teased his nostrils, and he groaned.

God, that smelled delicious.

The front screen opened and Mel walked in, a smile on her face, and a tear running down her cheek.

He quickly put everything down and ran to her, his heart racing.

"What? What's going on? Why are you crying? Tell me." He held her upper arms in his hands and looked down at her face.

"Everything's fine, Kade." She lifted to her toes and kissed his jaw. "Finn and Maddox are fine. I just heard our little boy's voice when he babbled into the phone, and I got all emotional."

He relaxed and pulled her to his chest. "I miss him too. We'll be home later."

She sighed and wrapped her arms around his waist. "And then it will start all over again."

Kade patted her bottom and nipped her ear. "Then let's do something about it."

"I hate relying on others though."

Kade kissed her temple before releasing her and went to the oven to pull out the rolls. He turned and found Mel holding two steaming cups of coffee in her hands as she sat at the table. He took a mug and sipped the hot brew, the spicy roast tantalizing on his tongue.

Mel took a bite of the roll, a smear of frosting glistening on her lips. Kade fought the urge to lick it off. He had to talk about their plans for the future. They could make love again soon. Just not now.

"Finn is growing up," Kade said, and Mel nodded before licking her lips to get rid of the frosting.

Must. Not. Bend. Her. Over. Table.

"So," Kade cleared his throat and continued, "he will still rely on us but for different things. I think it may be time we wean him completely from you."

He held his breath and waited for her response. He knew her feeding Finn was a tremendous connection with their son, but it was killing her.

She closed her eyes, and Kade wanted to crawl under a rock and die. So much for being an Alpha. As soon as he'd hurt his mate he wanted to run away.

"I was thinking the same thing."

Relief spread through him, and he placed his hand on top of hers on the table. "And then I was thinking of employing Cailin."

"What?" She tilted her head, utter confusion in her blue eyes.

"Well, you've been putting your whole life into Finn and the Pack, but no one has been there to give it back to you."

"Kade, I love being a mom. And acting as the Heir's mate is truly rewarding and worthwhile. I don't want to change that."

"I know. But I think it's time that others know it's okay to help you."

She stiffened.

"And me. Honestly, I've been used to relying on myself and helping others. But maybe we can ask for help too."

"So how does Cailin fit into this?"

"I was thinking maybe she could be our nanny."

Mel burst out laughing and almost spilled her coffee. "Kade. Your sister? Cailin?"

"Hey, she's great with Finn."

"I know; she's amazing. But would she want to be a nanny?"

"She wouldn't have to live with us, or do much more than babysit daily. But it would give you time to do what you need and for us to be alone more."

She smiled softly and got up. What was she thinking? Would she feel like he was trying to take over?

Mel pulled his chair back and straddled his lap. His cock perked up and slowly filled.

"I think it's a perfect idea. I know your family has been trying to help, but we've both been resistant."

"I know. I think we just wanted to prove we could do it all because we're the Heirs."

"And yet, everyone else relied on us."

"Exactly." He leaned forward and kissed her lips while gripping her ass in his palms.

She shifted and rubbed against his now painfully-hard cock. "So," she purred, "does Cailin know she's been volunteered?"

"Actually, it was her idea."

"Really?"

"Really. She wanted to help out, and frankly, with the danger going on outside the den, she's bored. She offered a few months back, and now I want to take her up on it. "

"Okay. So Cailin will help out with Finn, I can work with the Pack and not have to be three places at once, and you can actually start drawing again."

He widened his eyes. "How did you know I hadn't been doing that?"

She kissed him. "I know you, my mate. We've been neglecting a few things in the past months."

"Speaking of neglecting things..." he growled in her ear, loving the way her body shivered at his touch.

With a quick look at the oven to make sure he'd turned it off, he stood up, his delectable mate in his arms. She licked and suckled his neck and tendrils of heat shot through him. He walked faster to the bedroom.

So close. Do not drop your mate.

He chanted that mantra to himself as they made it to the bedroom, Mel writhing in his arms. He laid her down and spread her legs.

"You look magnificent."

She laughed and shook her head. "I look like the only time I've slept in the past year is last night."

"Beautiful."

"Okay, oh mighty Heir, tell me what you're going to do to me."

He loved it when his Mel was like this. And he loved when she shivered and moaned when he talked dirty.

"Well, first I'm going to strip you out of this dress. Inch by inch." He ran his hands up her legs, the soft skin cool on his warm palms, and gripped the edge of her dress. He slowly pulled the dress up and off as she lifted her bottom and then her torso.

Kade stood at the end of the bed and looked down at his naked mate. He took in her lean legs, her widened hips since the birth of their son, her soft belly, her breasts that could spill over his palms when he held their heavy weight in his hands. He licked his lips and imagined them on her rosy nipples that had become hard points, on her elongated neck, her jaw, her soft lips.

God. He loved his woman.

"And she's our mate."

He growled in agreement with his wolf. Yes, she was their mate.

Mel sat up and gripped his hips. He raised a brow. "Yes?"

"You didn't finish telling me what you were going to do." She unsnapped his jeans and pulled them down. He stepped out of his pants, and she gripped his cock.

"Mel," he groaned.

She stood and led him to the bathroom by his cock.

"You said we needed to shower. I thought I'd help you out with this." She let him go and bent over to turn on the shower.

Taking advantage, he knelt behind her and bit one of the globes of her ass.

"Kade!"

He slapped her ass, leaving a red mark, then kissed away the sting. "You liked it."

"You bit me!"

"I'm a wolf, darling. I like biting." He bit her other cheek, and she moaned. "See? You like it."

"You're bad."

"And yours."

"Oh yes, definitely mine."

He ran his palms up her legs, past her belly, and cupped her breasts. She gasped in his hold, her nipples pressing into his palms.

The water from the shower pulsated, and steam filled the room. He stood up and pulled them both inside. Droplets ran down Mel's body and wet her hair. He turned her around and licked a stream of water, lapping at her nipples. He closed his eyes and pulled her away from the stream so it wouldn't get in her face. She pulled at him and moaned as he bit her nipple hard.

"Kade!"

He pulled back and smiled. "I love you."

"I love you, too. But please."

Kade maneuvered her until her bottom rested on the ledge so he was sure she couldn't fall. He knelt in front of her and spread her legs. Her core glistened from arousal and the water from the shower. He trailed a finger around her outer lips, and she gasped. He lowered his head and kissed her, his tongue darting in and out and circling her clit.

She rocked softly against his face, and he picked up the motion before she came. While she was still writhing, he stood and entered her in two quick movements. Her body fit around him like a tight glove, and they both gasped.

Water beat down on them, and he pistoned his hips, loving he way her breasts bounced with each thrust. His balls tightened, and he came as she did. The water grew cool around them, and he laughed.

"I guess we won't be getting clean," he whispered.

"We may need to take a cold shower because I want you again."

"True."

They quickly washed in the cold water and got out. Kade dried his mate and kissed her skin.

"Kade, stop. I can't focus when you do that."

"I'm just checking to make sure you're clean. It's my duty as your mate."

She threw back her head and laughed. "Well, then, continue."

He licked her skin, loving her honey-vanilla taste, before he groaned and pulled back.

"Okay, I need to stop. Let's go get everything packed away and then head home."

"And see our Finn."

Images of his smiling little boy filled his mind. "Yes, that sounds perfect."

Chapter 8

The SUV pulled through the wards surrounding the Redwood den, and a wave of peace settled over Mel from the pull of the Pack. This was her home. Yes, before she'd met Kade, she'd had a place where she lived, but it hadn't been a home. The Redwoods and her family were everything to her. Though it had taken a night away for her to realize they were everything, she needed to be someone else as well.

Someone just for her and Kade.

Someone just for her.

Kade reached out and stroked her hand before wrapping his palm around hers, tangling their fingers.

"Ready to enter the wolf's den?" he teased.

"Har har."

"I know. Jasper's the funny one."

"It's true."

"I'm wounded, baby. Wounded. However, I'm getting anxious to see Finn."

She bounced in her seat and smiled. "We're such dorky parents. I mean, we run away for the night and yet have to run home faster. What is wrong with us?"

"We love our life, even though we need time to breathe every once in a while."

Their home came into view, and Mel smiled.

"We're here," Kade said softly and squeezed her hand.

Mel unbuckled her seatbelt the moment the car stopped and threw open the door. She glanced over her shoulder and winked.

"Last one there gets to clean up Maddox's mess," she taunted.

Kade growled and smirked before jumping out of the car. But she had a head start and beat him by mere moments to the door.

"I win!"

"Damn it." Kade shook his head. "I'm afraid to see what they've done."

Mel laughed and opened the door, taking a step inside.

"I resent that remark, dear brother," Maddox said from the living room.

Mel stopped in her tracks and held back tears.

Her home was spotless. Absolutely and utterly spotless. Every toy was put away. Every piece of clothing gone. The room was dusted, vacuumed, and there were freshly cut flowers in wooden vases around the house.

Kade nudged her farther in the room and shut the door behind them.

"Maddox," she whispered, "what did you do?"

He shrugged and lowered his scarred face, clearly embarrassed. An unusual emotion from the usually closed off wolf.

A soft cry made Mel turn around. Her brown-haired baby boy ran on chubby legs toward them. She knelt and opened her arms. He jumped and settled his weight against her, kissing her cheeks.

"Oh, Finn. Did you have fun with Uncle Maddox?"

He grinned and she kissed his lips, his cheeks, and his brow. She pulled back to look him over.

"Did you grow?" Oh no. He couldn't have grown in a day right?

Kade reached over and pulled Finn into his arms. "You're a big boy, aren't you? Did you miss us?"

Finn squealed and hugged his daddy. Mel teared up and stood to fall into Kade's outstretched arm. God, she loved these men.

No matter what was going on in her life and how many directions they pulled her in, these two would forever be her everything.

A discreet cough pulled her from her thoughts, and she looked over at Maddox. He looked uncomfortable and shifted from side to side.

Darn it. She'd forgotten how he felt with so many emotions swirling around him. She usually tried to limit her exuberance about certain things around him out of respect, but she couldn't help it this time.

"I cleaned up a bit for you," Maddox grumbled. "I couldn't sleep anyway." He shrugged and tried to look like it didn't matter.

But it did matter. One day Maddox would make some woman very lucky. Mel just hoped it was soon because God knew the man needed someone in his life to share his burden.

Mel wiggled out of Kade's arms and Finn's reach and went to hug Maddox. He stiffened for only a moment and then held her close, his body shuddering with emotions. After about thirty seconds he pulled back and shook off his expression.

Mel smiled and kissed his unscarred cheek.

"Thank you for cleaning. You are an incredible man, Maddox."

"It was nothing. And Mom brought the flowers."

If Mel hadn't known any better, she would have sworn the wolf blushed under her scrutiny.

"So, how did Finn do?" Kade asked. "I see you have all of your limbs. Any bruising?"

Maddox gave a hollow laugh. "You know I love your son, Brie too, but I don't think I'll ever have kids."

Kade laughed, and Mel pulled Finn into her arms, wanting to feel him again.

"What? A little baby is too much for you?" her mate teased.

Maddox held up his hands in mock surrender. "I give up. I don't know how you do it, man."

Kade turned and looked into her eyes. "I don't know how we do it either, but it's worth it."

Maddox smiled and shook his head. "I see you two, uh, reconnected."

Kade punched his brother in the arm and scowled. "Enough of that."

"What? You two are back pretty early. Did things not live *up* to expectations?"

Mel blushed and shook her head.

"Okay, brother, it's time to go." Kade pulled the Omega through the living room toward the door. "Thank you very much for watching Finn. We'll repay you, I promise."

Maddox scowled. "You don't need to repay me. We're family."

Mel smiled. "Thank you anyway. And when you have your babies, I'll help you watch them."

Her brother-in-law visibly shuddered and waved them off before leaving.

Kade laughed and walked toward her and Finn.

"Should I call Cailin?" he asked.

"In a moment. We can get everything ready later. Let's just enjoy this time now."

"Sounds like a plan. What do you say, Finn?"

"Dada."

Mel and Kade froze. A lump rose in her throat.

Kade's eyes filled and he coughed. "Finn?" he said, his voice rough with emotion.

"Dada." He waved his arms and smiled like he knew he'd done something momentous.

"Did you hear that, Mel? Our big boy just said his first word."

Mel nodded.

"And you said my name. You are your daddy's son, aren't you?"

"Mama."

Mel laughed and kissed Finn's cheek. "That's right, you know us both, don't you? You are such a big boy, Finn."

Finn patted his chubby hand on her cheek, then Kade's.

Kade wrapped an arm around her and kissed her softly.

"I love you, my mate."

"I love you too, Kade."

Mel kissed Finn's brow and sighed, feeling rejuvenated. She felt like she was ready to take on the Pack, the Centrals, her baby boy...just about everything. Apparently, she'd only needed a breath and a night away.

Kade leaned down and whispered into her ear, "We'll have to take another night for ourselves again."

Mel shivered and turned her head to kiss him. "Soon."

The End

ABOUT THE AUTHOR

Carrie Ann Ryan is a bestselling paranormal and contemporary romance author. After spending too much time behind a lab bench, she decided to dive into the romance world and find her werewolf mate - even if it's just in her books. Happy endings are always near - even if you have to get over the challenges of falling in love first.

Her first book, *An Alpha's Path,* is the first in her Redwood Pack series. She's also an avid reader and lover of romance and fiction novels. She loves meeting new authors and new worlds. Any recommendations you have are appreciated. Carrie Ann lives in New England with her husband and two kittens.

www.carrieannryan.com